Blue Nightmares

WOL-VRIEY

Burning Bulb
PUBLISHING

Other Books By Wol-vriey:

The Bizarro Story of I

Meat Suitcase

Chainsaw Cop Corpse

Vegan Zombie Apocalypse

Boston Posh (Bud Malone #1)

Vegan Vampire Vaginas

Vagina Mundi

Melanie Nemesis Catchpole

Bizarro 101: A Basic Primer

Boston Corpse (Bud Malone #2)

Dr. Orgasm

Boston Lust (Bud Malone #3)

Pussy Transmission

Hell Dancer

Girls Are Not Smiling

Brainchew

Brainchew 2: Out of Their Heads

Novellas and Short Stories By Wol-vriey

Big Trouble in Little Ass

Forever Ago Sunshine

Blue Nightmares

WOL-VRIEY

Burning Bulb
PUBLISHING

Blue Nightmares
By **Wol-vriey**

Burning Bulb Publishing
P.O. Box 4721
Bridgeport, WV 26330-4721
United States of America
www.BurningBulbPublishing.com

Cover artwork by Anton Rosovsky.
Author Photo: Lolade Akinsowon © 2014.

First Edition.

Paperback Edition ISBN: 978-0997773088

Printed in the United States of America

MONDAY NIGHT

CHAPTER 1

The Dream . . .

She smelt decaying bodies. Like she was in a house built of rotting meat.

Everywhere around her was a clear blue. Blue like the sky. Blue like she was underwater in a swimming pool. She couldn't see a thing in the blue—it filled her eyes—but she could smell as well as a bloodhound. The terrible corpse-smell assailed her like an army of rotting soldiers. The stink was so bad that she wished she had no nose.

Like water streaming from a tap into a jar, a huge nausea filled her from toes to nose. She tried to vomit, but seemed to have no mouth. She felt the bile-ridden backflow of food pack itself behind her non-existent teeth and lips, felt it flowing up over her disgusted tongue. But it had no outlet. It was trapped inside her. She tried to snort the puke out through her nostrils, but it wouldn't rise. All it did was stink, stink, stink, stink, stink, stink.

She began to feel like she was made of vomit. The blueness around her was bile and nausea, and she was puke. Her universe was a sewer filled with the floating bloated bodies of dead rats.

She couldn't hear either—her whole body appeared to be a smell organ. Ugh! The smell, the smell, the disgusting smell!

And then, just like that, she sensed movement around her. A movement of large impossible shapes. Now, her eyes adjusted to the pale blue everywhere and she could see. See in a sense. What she saw looked like lines scrawled on the sky, like needle-thin storm clouds. The lines were animated; the gray, black, and dark brown stripes flailed in constant motion.

She realized that these moving lines were the outlines—the peripheral skin surfaces—of living creatures built on models totally alien to the human mind.

The lines flailed towards her in infernal welcome, bringing the reek of opened graves and melted flesh with them, swimming like fish and octopi in the impossible stench of their own bodies. She was unsure which she found more revolting: the smell, or the humongous monsters making it.

Tentacles . . . The creatures reached her through the stink, and wrapped themselves about her. Thick unseen tentacles, like the trunks of immense trees formed of meat, slapped themselves around her body, caressing her like a snakeskin jacket turned inside out. Their surfaces were rough, and in their constant motion they chafed her, making her skin bleed. But even though she had a concept of herself as an adult female human, she seemed to be bleeding not through her skin, but through her nose—the perpetual reek of death and murder made any other impressions impossible.

She could hear now. Crystalline voices rang out all around her. "Welcome, welcome, welcome, welcome!" they sang. The voices echoed through her body, permeating her as completely as the giant creatures' putrescent smell did. The voices—cold, impersonal, nonhuman, hellish, and of different pitches—were pleased to meet her.

"Welcome, welcome, welcome, welcome!" The single word rang endlessly through her soul, like she was a bell these creatures were tolling with their tentacles.

She remained there, in the midst of the flailing maelstrom of stink, caressed by limbs many times the size of the world's largest snakes. The tentacles seemed to pass through each other in their desire to touch her flesh.

Now she understood that the monsters meant her no harm. They had something to tell her. They were speaking to her, but she had no idea what they were saying. No idea at all. Maybe her unrelenting urge to throw up, the unsurmountable nausea, was blocking off her intelligence too, not just her mouth. All that made sense as the creatures swirled around her in their dark linear existence was that single word: "Welcome."

For a long time the universe was a stalemate. She felt filled to bursting with puke, with more bloating her by the moment, while the creatures wrapped her in their unseen bodies and smelt all over her, and spoke a musical cascade of ringing words that promised to elevate her to Heaven.

4

The conflict of complete degradation and exaltation was too complete. She saw her end clearly. She would die. And soon. The resolution to this impasse would be her body exploding into a mass of corrupted female meat. More decay in the blue.

But the creatures knew this too, and, just when she thought her end had surely come, they began receding from her, unwrapping their tentacles from around her body and falling backward into the paleness from which they'd appeared.

The creatures left, their dancing dark outlines fading into the blue nothing that surrounded her.

The one thing the creatures didn't take away with them was their stink. As they left her—oddly, with regret, she sensed—their smell of decomposing meat—of worm-riddled unburied carcasses—thickened around her like a gaseous tomb.

But they'd also left her the blessing of being able to throw up. She had a mouth again, and the pressure packed behind it—the need to purge herself—erupted from it.

She opened her mouth, but to her surprise and dismay, it wasn't endless gallons of vomit that streamed out between her lips, but rather a mass of tentacles. The tentacles—unseen in the blue, but felt all the same—burst forth from her mouth in such profusion that they filled it up completely. She quickly understood that the tentacles weren't something she could rid herself of. The tentacles came from inside her; they were a part of her.

And worst of all, she now discovered that the stink of death she'd been desperately trying to escape from was coming from inside her own body. It smelt like she was rotting at the core, like she was dissolving into a puddle of her own decaying flesh.

Her tentacles streamed down from her mouth and wrapped themselves around her body, quickly sealing her in a cocoon, a self-generated enclosure that now flickered in the same colors as the outlines of the departed monsters: black, gray, and brown. Enclosed in herself, she flickered amidst the endless blue . . .

TUESDAY

CHAPTER 2

Jessica

. . . Blue, blue, blue, blue, blue . . .

Jessica Schreiber jerked awake with the smell of rotting meat still in her nostrils. Too groggy to immediately relive her night horrors, she opened her eyes a crack and peeked out of her head at the morning.

The sun was already high in the sky. Through a gap between the windows a breeze was rustling her white bedroom drapes.

She shut her eyes again. She was on vacation, the day could wait.

Now she remembered her nightmare and winced. What the hell was that all about? Monsters and decaying corpses? *Did I pop pills with Lucy and Reby last night? Did we watch a horror movie?*

For a brief moment, she felt the unimaginably monstrous coils of the unseen dream creatures' tentacles caressing her again, again experiencing their rank smell permeating her like water in wet cloth. She gagged. The nausea was so intense she felt like she'd black out.

After a while her nausea subsided. The word 'Welcome,' faded from her mind. She felt emptied as she lay in her pajamas under the blanket, like she'd vomited out all her horror in her nightmare.

Grave-stink, tentacles, dark chalky outlines? She gripped her blanket even tighter than her shut eyelids. *Ugh—what an utterly disgusting way to wake up.*

Jessica forced the dream from her mind and tried to get back to sleep, aiming to awaken properly from a nicer tour of surreal shores. She tried hard to sleep some more, but it wasn't happening. Her brain seemed intent on getting her out of bed, which after a while she grudgingly agreed was sound subconscious protection—what if she dreamt the same nightmare again?

Finally conceding defeat in the sleep wars, Jessica opened her eyes again. She opened them slowly, like a child unwrapping a Christmas present little by little so as to keep the anticipation going for as long as possible. Once her eyes were wide open, she rubbed them to get the sleep out. Then she once more peeked out of the window. Oh, it was a lovely morning, the best weather so far this summer. The leaves on the old oak across the driveway looked extra green as they rippled in the slight breeze.

She smiled, sat up in bed, and prepared to meet the day.

It was while yawning and stretching that Jessica realized something was wrong. Not wrong with this gorgeous summer morning, but wrong with *her*.

For a while, however, she was unable to determine what the problem with herself was. Was it just her bad dream refusing to let go of her, harassing her with an afterglow of horror?

No, she quickly concluded, this wasn't just the dream. What was bothering her now was something tangible, something out here in the real world.

While trying to work out what was wrong, she kept yawning and stretching, turning herself left and right to flush as much sleep as possible from her body before she took those irreversible morning steps out of bed.

The problem? She truly had no idea. She felt great. A little groggy perhaps, but that would be the brandy she'd had last night. Thankfully not enough to cause her a real hangover though.

But—she tried remembering—*did I really have that much to drink? I honestly don't think I did.*

(Last night after dinner, Jessica and her two housemates Reby and Lucy had gotten out a bottle of Butchertown and begun drinking. While tipsy they'd spent a long time arguing about men. Most of their argument had centered on which were the best types of man to date and marry. They'd also tried to specify signs that warned a woman that a man she'd just met might prove to be an asshole down the line. Their discussion had finally turned to whether or not swallowing semen after performing fellatio on a man showed a woman's class. It had been a hung jury on that one. "The 'spit or swallow' debate," Lucy had drunkenly dubbed it. "To be continued in a bedroom near you.")

No, Jessica concluded finally, *this odd feeling I've got isn't the damn brandy at work. I didn't have that much to drink. If I had, my brain would be banging a gong now. So why the hell do I feel so damn weird now? And no—it isn't that stupid dream making me feel this way.*

Then an understanding came to her and she corrected herself. *No, it isn't that I feel weird. I feel good—lethargic, but nonetheless strong and refreshed. It's rather that I've noticed something strange, something unusual, and I've overlooked it, but my mind hasn't yet forgotten what it was and it's trying to remind me. Or alert me.*

She tried to figure out what it could possibly have been that she'd seen and forgotten in the short period of time since she'd first opened her eyes. She couldn't.

She then decided to get out of bed and have a look around the bedroom. Maybe she had a mouse co-tenant?

The moment she put her hands down on the blanket again to push it back, she understood what the problem was.

Her fingernails were blue. She gasped as she stared at them. Last night when she'd gotten into bed, her nails had been plain. She'd wiped their previous pink covering off yesterday afternoon and had been too busy later to redo them. That was supposed to be this afternoon's business after she'd been into town with Lucy to buy groceries.

So how come she had blue fingernails now?

Forgetting her desire to get out of bed, she instead scooted back till she was sitting against the headboard, then tried to figure out the puzzle.

How the heck did I get blue fingernails?

Jessica's first suspicion was that Lucy and Reby had decided to play a practical joke on her. Lucy Polk and Reby Butterfield were definitely mischievous enough to do that.

But . . . The 'but' was that Jessica's hands looked professionally manicured. There was no paint smearing onto her fingers, and also (and this was the real nail in the coffin of her suspicions of a practical joke), last night she'd left both Reby and Lucy close to inebriated in the living room. She pondered: *To color my nails blue they'd need to hold my hands in place till the paint dried. But they'd both likely be too drunk by the time they decided on such a prank to even walk straight, talk less of remembering the finer points of nail care. And there's no mess on the bed sheets or my pajamas . . .*

On a sudden suspicion, Jessica kicked the blanket off her feet.

She had blue toenails too.

That stumped her. Okay, while most unlikely, it *was* vaguely conceivable that her two friends could had painted her fingernails. But her toenails also? And with no resulting mess whatsoever? No, it couldn't have been them.

She regarded her nails very carefully now. They were a pale, light-blue—she looked up briefly—the exact shade of the sky outside.

And . . . but . . . was this blue stuff on her fingertips actually nail polish? On closer examination, the coloring looked *stained* into her nails. Yes, now that she was properly awake and her mind was working better, Jessica suddenly realized that her nails all looked *artificial*, like plastic strips growing out from her hands and feet.

This realization was the point at which her mild bemusement garbed itself in a cloak of fear. Such oddity brought with it the suggestion of illness, of something being wrong with her. Jessica utterly hated illness.

But she still had one test to perform. Dreading the outcome, she scratched the surface of her left thumbnail with the tip of her right one. The result was exactly what she'd thought it would be: the 'paint' didn't come off. Oh yes, whatever had colored her nails blue was *stained* into them.

And she couldn't help but think that the coloring agent had come from her own body. And if that was the case, it meant that she was ill.

After realizing this, Jessica couldn't bring herself to get out of bed anymore. She drew her knees up to her chest and gripped her legs tight. She stared out of the window. While fighting off her rising panic she pondered what was going on. First that crappy waking dream, and now *this?*

And worryingly, she was beginning to have a headache too—hopefully not a migraine. She was used to stress headaches anyway.

Stress—the kind caused by overwork—was the primary reason Jessica Schreiber was currently in Raynham.

CHAPTER 3

Jessica, mostly

Jessica Schreiber was in Raynham to relax and unwind. She needed to recharge her personal batteries. After spending the past seven years working in a high-powered managerial job at Argus, one of Boston's premier advertising agencies, her nerves were worse than shot.

Jessica was thirty-four. She was a brunette of average height, slightly skinny because she never ate enough. She was attractive in an average kind of way.

Up until a month ago, Jessica's primary passion in life had been work. A compulsive workaholic, she'd ascended the corporate ladder faster than most of her colleagues, faster even than some of her superiors.

Her relentless hard work ethic had paid off—she was both respected and highly regarded in advertising circles. But that payoff had come at a high personal cost; Jessica had finally paid the price for her overachieving. Living for her profession at full steam had destroyed her two marriages (thankfully without any children), evaporated most of her friendships and family relationships, and left her completely burnt out, energy-sapped, and enervated.

It wasn't that Jessica had been overly selfish with either her husbands or relationships, it was just that she'd indiscriminately *always* put her job first, before even her own need for love and companionship. It was the deepest of ironies: Jessica worked compulsively to get ahead in life so she could have everything she wanted and be happy, and then, when that same extreme work ethic separated her from her real desires, she took refuge in it again to cope with her heartbreaks. She simply couldn't stop herself.

Her second marriage had ended a year ago. Since then, Jessica had had only one date. The date had led nowhere. Though Jessica had really liked the guy, she'd forgotten all about him the next morning, at the exact moment she was handed the brief for the latest ad campaign, for Rabbitfield condoms ('So sheer, you'll forget it's there. Rabbitfield—your sexual shield!'). In the twelve months since her divorce she'd not slept with anyone. (Though she'd invited her last date upstairs to her apartment for a nightcap, she'd fallen asleep fully clothed in the living room before they could get down to lovemaking; and he'd been too much of a gentleman to take advantage of her.) In addition, during the entire twelve months of her second 'divorceehood' Jessica had masturbated only twice: both times on her birthday, when she'd not been in the office. She once remarked to her older sister that her vibrators felt 'neglected and lonely through gross underuse.'

And so, with neither platonic nor romantic relationships to distract her, Jessica Schreiber worked on and on and on, powered by endless cups of coffee, and eating donuts and takeouts by the basketful. She lost weight without exercising, but was never anorexic, simply because she realized her body needed fuel so she could work even harder.

Despite her primary focus on her job, however, Jessica was neither scruffy nor slovenly. She was always perfectly groomed. She always looked her very best. She looked after her appearance because her job required her to look good. Each week she made one or two trips to a beauty salon to keep herself beautiful.

Finally though, the end had come for Jessica. A month ago, Jessica had collapsed while showing a roomful of Argus executives the finished ads for Rabbitfield Deluxe condoms. Her collapse wasn't just an excited faint (as her male colleagues thought), or overly-heavy-period fallout (as some of her female colleagues imagined). No, Jessica was out for the count. She was rushed to hospital, where it was discovered that she'd suffered an 'almost complete nervous collapse, triggered by a severe overload of work and work-related stress.'

Sure, Jessica had often felt dog-tired on those endless nights when she'd sat reviewing copy and videos and risqué condom marketing strategies—*Do we dare show one on an actual dick? We could pixelate it like they do in Japan!*—late into the dawn hours after all her bosses, colleagues, and subordinates had gone home. Jessica had no one waiting for her at home. Not even a cat anymore. Tony, her second ex, had taken the family pet with him when he'd left, lest she starve the poor thing to death. So Jessica figured there was no point in making the twenty minute drive out to Roslindale, just to have to drive back again in the morning. So much could be achieved in those forty minutes she'd be wasting, *so much*—it was better to just pass the night in her office.

So yes, she'd often felt very enervated and out of it, but it was nothing a little more coffee wouldn't fix. Visine in the eyes before meetings, and always remember to eat well too—lots of chocolate (candy bars were easy to carry around and store). And lots of Red Bull and 5-hour Energy shots—more caffeine. She had to keep those energy levels up. And maybe she had to make another trip to the salon, get another power tan, keep herself looking perky and sharp, maybe even get a new sexy hairdo to turn a few male (and lez) heads. God knew she never had the energy to fuck nowadays—when was her last orgasm? what did orgasms feel like even?—but triggering a few office boners would likely energize her male subordinates and make them work that much harder just to please her. Staff motivation. The end justified the means. The work must be done at all costs. The work, the work, the work . . .

Not this time though, apparently.

Dr. Lopez had held up his right hand in front of Jessica, his thumb and forefinger separated by less than an eight of an inch. "You're this close to frying your nerves for good, Ms. Schreiber," he informed her. "You were lucky this time—your body's inbuilt early warning system short-circuited you before you could irreparably damage yourself." The doctor, a thin man in his mid-fifties, smiled somewhat grimly. "Now, Ms. Schreiber, at this point in your life you've only two options. You either take a break from your hectic work schedule and simply go on vacation somewhere for the next six months—"

Jessica instantly protested. "Six months!? Doc, you can't be serious! I *can't* go on vacation." She was lying in her hospital bed with an intravenous drip in her arm because she was still too tired to eat or drink anything. "Dammit, doc, I've got all this work to get through. The condom ads! And it's that time of the year when . . ."

Dr. Lopez fixed Jessica with a hard stare. "Well, that's *one* option you've got."

"What's the other one?" Jessica was impatient to get out of her hospital bed and back to the office. It was imperative that she explained to Argus and Rabbitfield the fine details of how they were going promote those goddam rubbers. But, oh God, she felt so damn tired. She couldn't even sit up unaided.

"Or you keep going," the doctor replied. "You keep on working non-stop, do yourself in both physically and mentally, and say a year from now, you wind up in a padded cell somewhere for the next five or six years." He smiled genially, then added, "In which case, of course, once you get out of the asylum, you'll be unemployable."

Unemployable. For Jessica, 'Unemployable' was the most horrible word in the dictionary—it meant not being able to labor.

The world 'Unemployable' single-handedly defeated Jessica.

"And absolutely no caffeine, Ms. Schreiber. And you can't take up smoking as a pastime either. Nicotine is equally bad for you."

She nodded. However, she still had one reservation:

"Doc, if I take that long off from work, they'll fire me."

Dr. Lopez shook his head. "Not true. They *won't* fire you. To your credit, you seem to be rather valuable to them. Almost indispensable in fact. I can understand why—you seem to have been accomplishing the workload of four people all by yourself."

Jessica discovered the doctor had told her the truth. Argus were happy to give her six months off work. (The ad agency actually offered her a year off, but she thought that would be too much: given too much free time, she might grow lazy.) And they'd even *pay her* to go. In truth, Jessica was due eight years' worth of accumulated leave, which she'd never taken, always finding an excuse to remain in the office and keep powering through ad campaigns.

Jessica conceded defeat, but felt like she'd won a huge victory. *Yes, I'll go on vacation. I'll go! And I'll come back to work rejuvenated. The ad world won't know what hit 'em. I'll show them what it means to work . . . work and work and work . . .*

But where to go for her vacation? That was the question.

***

During the past three or four years, most of Jessica's contacts with people outside her office had been via Facebook. Like clockwork, she logged into Facebook every lunch break, checked what everyone was up to, and logged out thirty minutes later.

Outside of faithfully 'liking' her older sister Olivia's endless photo updates of her latest son (*Oh see, Donny's walking now! Wow!*), Jessica never 'liked' anything that wasn't work-related. She never initiated conversations with anyone either. If she had a message, usually from one of her ex-husbands, she replied it as brusquely as she could, so that he'd not reply and keep her chatting. Lunch break only lasted so long each day, and she had to eat and perk herself up with some coffee.

Now, however, once out of hospital and banned from returning to the office to die by means of her own making, Jessica Schreiber found herself with lots of time on her hands to dedicate to the world's favorite social network.

One person Jessica knew on Facebook was Lucy Polk. Lucy was an old friend of hers, one of the few Jessica still chatted with. Lucy Polk now lived in Springfield. She'd originally been a friend of Olivia's, but Jessica had 'inherited' her when Olivia got married and moved south to Atlanta. Then they'd started hanging out together, before Lucy finally moved to Springfield to work in her brother's restaurant. (This was, of course, all in the 'young and carefree' days before Jessica had discovered the overwhelming satisfaction of full-blown workaholism.)

Lucy Polk did a hell of a lot of drugs. Until they'd met in person, Jessica would never have believed anyone—and a woman for that matter—could smoke that much pot and swallow that many pills and not melt their minds for good. Lucy always looked freaky, with spiky hair (though she wasn't even remotely a punk) and trashy, fringe-fashion clothes. Her makeup was always hit or miss.

Jessica had kept in touch with Lucy. With the straight-laced personality's attraction to the outré, she felt herself magnetized by the waif-like woman with the orange or green or blue hair and big earrings and fuck-the-devil attitude. (Lucy was even skinnier than Jessica, in addition to which she was only five feet tall.)

When stoned, Lucy wrote Jessica hilarious Facebook messages that Jessica replied with LOLs and smileys.

Two days after starting her enforced leave, Jessica read a post of Lucy's: *Hey! Moving back east to Raynham for three summer months. Doing a house share with Karen and Reby.*

Under the post was a picture of Lucy, Reby, and Karen. Jessica didn't know either of the other two women. Reby was slim, with long black hair; she seemed to project sex into the camera. Karen was a more subdued type: a plump bespectacled redhead. The three women were laughing and making 'V' peace signs with their fingers. Lucy, however, also looked a bit cross-eyed. Hey, was that a joint she was holding? Jessica was perplexed by Lucy's boldness. Could you even show stuff like that on Facebook? Wouldn't the DEA be after your butt?

Jessica 'liked' the post, wrote a *Wow! Welcome home and have fun! Might drive down to see you!* comment and let it go.

She was busy herself with trying to work out where to go on vacation. She didn't want to stray too far from Boston. She had the nervy suspicion that if she dared take a single step out of Massachusetts, the advertising industry would instantly forget all about her. In actuality, her fear was worse that this: More than once Jessica had daydreamed of returning to the States after vacationing in Europe to discover that not only did she no longer have a job, but that there'd never been such a place as the office where she worked—that she'd made up the Argus ad agency, and made up most of her adult life as well.

She recognized she was being silly to think this could possibly happen, but it nonetheless didn't quell her fears of 'something going wrong' if she so much as crossed the Massachusetts state line during her quest for relaxation.

But how did you go on vacation in the state you lived in?

In the meantime Lucy kept updating her Facebook timeline with her vacation preparations: *So, I'm leaving Smokey* (her dog) *with Robert and Dean* (her brother and brother's boyfriend), *along with two 40lb boxes of Performance Dog. My damn mutt sure does eats a lot.* This info was accompanied by a zoomed-in photo of a grinning Lucy holding Smokey—a massive St. Bernard—in a loving chokehold, her arms and hands all but invisible in the ruff of hair about Smokey's neck.

Jessica commented: *Wow, Lucy, your dog's even bigger than you are!* She refrained from adding (like she suspected most other respondents to Lucy's post did) that Smokey looked stoned out of his canine head. Did they smoke pot together? Or was the dog simply under consistent 'passive smoke' victimization?

The next day Lucy wrote: *Smokey gone* ☺ *Getting packed. Impatient to be back. I remember the sunrise looks different out east!!!*

To her relief, Jessica was discovering that being on leave wasn't as hard or scary as she'd imagined it would be. True, she did have those moments—in the first few days of her layoff, they'd come every five or so minutes—when she felt a deep panic about her not working her fingers to the bone. At those times she felt like she'd shortly lose her mind if she didn't have some challenging task to apply it to.

After her first week at home though, burning time watching TV and taking walks, she realized she'd survive.

Twice during that first week, she drove regretfully past the Argus offices at 75 Central Street, imagining all the labor and intense productivity happening there, all the great satisfaction she was missing out on. On both occasions, to soften her disappointment, she reminded herself of *the plan:* that this time of inactivity was an investment in her future—she wasn't working now so that later she could work harder than ever before.

So she ate (though not enough to put on weight—she still looked thinner than a mother with ten brawling sons), slept, and watched endless reruns of *America's Got Talent* and *American Idol.*

That took care of Week One. She still hadn't resolved what to do for the next five months and three weeks. She decided to take it one week at a time. That was easier than stressing out over how not to stress out.

Then, eight days into her leave, Jessica awoke to find this message on Lucy's Facebook timeline: *Aw, bummer.* ☹ *Karen pulled out of our vacation arrangement. Sudden family commitment. So it's just Reby and I taking some time off now.*

Jessica hadn't hesitated. She'd instantly messaged Lucy: *Hey, girl! Got to get away from the city for a while myself—doctor's orders. Can I take up Karen's space? Cost is no object, happy to share the rent. I can send you the money now or we do it when I arrive.*

(It had been a spur of the-moment decision for Jessica. Raynham, Lucy's destination, was a small east-Massachusetts town 37 miles south of Boston. It's advantage to Jessica was that its nearness to Boston (a mere forty minutes drive) would prevent her from feeling too far away from the center of things. This would be like having one's cake and eating it. Even with the best of intentions at heart, old habits did die hard, she'd conceded giggling.)

Ten minutes later, Lucy replied: *Great idea! Yippee! Love to see you, girl. Oops, I forgot, I need to clear it with Reby too. Gimme an hour. She's a health freak—lives from bedroom to gym—she's likely working out now.*

O.K., Jessica typed back. *Keeping fingers crossed here. Tell her I'm quiet and without accompanying vices.*

Thirty minutes later, Lucy replied: *Reby says it's cool you joining us, so long as you ain't either an alky, a dyke, or a Jesus Freak. She don't want anyone either stealing her booze, feeling her up, or preaching to her.*

Jessica grinned. People and their idiosyncrasies. Reby clearly didn't have a problem with drug addicts though, or she'd never have agreed to houseshare with Lucy.

She typed back: *Great, I'm in then. Let me know your schedule and when you two plan on arriving. And, what's it costing me?*

Lucy replied: *I'll send you the figures for the rental later. We've already paid, so you'll just be refunding Karen's share to her. Reby and I will be over there tomorrow.*

They ended the conversation. An hour later, Lucy updated her timeline with: *Yippee! We're 3 again! FUN FUN FUN FUN FUN.* The accompanying picture was a composite one: herself and Reby spliced to a copy of Jessica's Facebook profile photo.

Jessica winced on seeing the old picture. She now regretted always being too busy to regularly update her profile like everyone else did. Staring at the picture, there was no denying that behind her bright executive smile she looked very tired. For the first time she felt she understood the old adage 'all work and no play makes Jill a dull babe . . . or an old maid.'

Jessica Schreiber instantly began packing. The next day saw her arriving in Raynham town to meet with Lucy Polk and Reby Butterfield.

***

On reaching Raynham, Jessica was instantly struck with a deep sense that she'd done the right thing. This little town had just the right ambience to it—Raynham was one of those places that seemed to have more trees as residents than it did people. The endless swathes of greenery were a refreshing change from Boston's concrete-and-glass towers of commerce.

She met Lucy and Reby on the corner of Carver Street and Broadway. A short distance away a tall sign marked the entrance to the Sunflower Motel.

They got out of their cars, Jessica from her red Nissan Sentra, Lucy and Reby from Reby's silver BMW convertible.

Her two housemates were a refreshing break from the people she knew. (The ad industry was full of pretentious types, with everyone needing to be smarter than everyone else.) Lucy was as laid back as ever, with purple hair, black sunglasses, and half a joint in her hand. Clothes-wise, she was a color riot: Big blue boots, knee-length red coat with shiny gold buttons, white top and blue leather skirt, and dangling 'solar system' earrings—concentric rings with a single planetary bead on each. Jessica whimsically imagined that Lucy's clothes weighed more than she did.

"Hi, biatch," Lucy said, waving a hand. Her 'hi' sounded more like 'high,' as if she was informing Jessica that she was stoned, rather than saying hello.

Reby Butterfield was a surprise. She was tall and athletic, and wore a green sleeveless blouse (no bra, nipples visible) and tight brown shorts. In person, she was strikingly attractive—with that long standout black hair Jessica had already noticed in Lucy's Facebook posts, gray eyes, and nice breasts that were likely implants considering how muscular she was (Jessica knew that if you worked out too much you looked odd without implants). She came across as a warm, delightful person, rather than the stuck-up bitch Jessica had expected.

The first thing Reby said to Jessica on meeting her was: "I'm sure you're wondering about that 'no alkies, lesbians, or Jesus Freaks' comment. Ha ha ha. No, I'm not bigoted, not even against religious folks—but I hate being told what's right and wrong. I'm an adult; like, I can make my own decisions? And alky chicks just keep on throwing up all over the place. One girl once puked in the drawer where I kept my panties." She nodded emphatically at Jessica's look of disbelief. "Yeah, yeah, it really did happen. I had to buy myself an entire frigging new set of underwear. And lezzies? I'm totally into guys, see? I don't need a set of boobs stuck in my face—I've got a set of my own. And every gay chick I ever shared an apartment with has tried to fuck me. No exception—it's like I've got a sign on my head that reads 'Dyke Diner.' It's crazy how the lezzie girls never go for my other flatmates, just me. And when I say like, *no?* Then we have all this crazy woman-drama happening in the house, see? It just ain't worth it. I'm fine with us being 'no kiss' girlfriends, but there's no 'kiss and don't tell' playtime happening here."

She had a guileless, earnest way of talking. Jessica decided anyone who could be that straightforward on first meeting was someone she could like. She didn't say it, but she honestly couldn't blame or fault the gay girls for hitting on Reby.

Neither apparently did Lucy, who sat on the BMW's hood puffing on her joint while watching for squad cars. "Baby, with your athletic build you give off mixed signals," she said between inhalations of pot, "Maybe you need bigger boobs?"

Reby rolled her eyes.

Jessica agreed with Lucy. *In the right clothes, Reby definitely will give off androgynous signals.* If she'd been that way inclined, she'd likely have hit on her too. Reby exuded a powerful sexual magnetism. Jessica wondered what kind of animal effect she had on men. It had to be *deadly*, like shooting a rabbit with an elephant gun.

"Alright, ladies," Reby said finally, seeming to grow bored of standing looking cool as ice and hot as hell in the same place for so long, "let's roll."

They'd gotten back into their respective cars and driven over to Red Oak Crescent to settle in.

***

Red Oak Crescent was located off Raynham's North Main Street, in the midst of a thick intra-town forest that also bordered the Blue Star Memorial Highway (aka I-495).

Driving up the crescent that first time, following behind Reby's BMW, Jessica felt her pleasure at her decision to come to Raynham intensify. The town's soothing ambience felt concentrated here. The trees overhanging the sidewalks—old oaks, elms, maples, and willows—provided a lovely amount of shade from the sun's rays.

The further up the road she drove, the less worried about leaving work behind she became. She found that perception slightly odd too: *Why the hell this sudden feeling that I'm 'leaving things behind?' Boston and the office are less than an hour's drive away.*

There were only six houses on Red Oak Crescent. She, Lucy, and Reby were in No. 4, or Roe Cottage. A weird name for sure, with its suggestion of fish eggs, but the building itself was a delight. It was large and salmon-colored (which possibly explained its name). It had four spacious bedrooms, each with an en suite bathroom (their plan was to use the fourth as a guest room), a large living room and kitchen and pantry, and just about everything else one could possibly want in a vacation house. It was completely furnished too. Outside, on its right, the cottage had a parking shelter for three cars. Both the front and rear yards were large and well-manicured. A series of beautifully cultured flowerbeds ran from each side of the front porch around the house to the back door. An extensive woodland bordered the backyard.

Jessica was impressed. She asked Lucy how she'd come on this place. Lucy said she'd found the rental online, but she'd been stoned at the time and didn't remember on what search engine.

Jessica decided it was just good fortune. After some good-natured arguing and a 'Welcome to Raynham' pillow fight, she got her wish of the left front bedroom and moved her things in. Lucy and Reby moved into the two rearmost bedrooms; Reby on the left, Lucy on the right.

That first day, Jessica fell asleep the moment her back touched her bed, with her luggage lying half-unpacked around her, while out in the living room Lucy argued with Reby over whether or not she could put her Acapulco Gold, Afghan Kush, and NYC Diesel in the fridge's crisper drawer, something Reby was vociferously against, as she didn't want the smell of marijuana getting on her carrots and tomatoes.

When, an hour later, Jessica woke up feeling much refreshed, she took that as a clear sign that she was vacationing in the right place. Yes, all she wanted to do now—all she *needed* to do—was relax.

And she had been relaxing quite well indeed until this morning when she'd woken up with her fingernails and toenails all turned a brilliant sky-blue.

CHAPTER 4

Reby

The neighborhood streamed past Reby in a pleasant collage of green shades. Light green, mid-green, dark green. Grass, trees, summer blooms from flowerbeds. The black road vanished under her white running shoes. The blood thudded in her ears. Sweat wet her clothes. Her heart pumped her full of fitness.

Reby was in the full bloom of youthful health and wellbeing. She was however very disgruntled.

Her main problem since arriving in Raynham was a lack of male companionship.

She'd enjoyed just one sexual encounter since getting here, at a gym she'd gone to check out. She hadn't liked the place, but one of the trainers there had been hunky and they'd slipped away to a rear storeroom for quick bump of crotches. He'd also (she'd afterwards deduced from the angry stares she'd gotten from the blonde manning the front desk) been the receptionist's boyfriend. So that was over before it had even begun. Since then (last Wednesday) she'd not met anyone else she'd like to exchange body fluids with.

In Roe Cottage, everyone's got their own shit happening already, she thought as she ran herself into shape. *Everyone except me! Jessica has her relaxation therapies. Lucy has seemingly all the pills in the world, along with her pot. I wonder why the broad even bothered coming east at all when all she ever does is trip out on drugs. The universe has to look exactly the same wherever you are once viewed through an acid lens.*

Reby ran past Cottages 5 and 6. She reached the end of the curved road. She jogged in place for a few seconds before reversing direction. "I need a man," she said aloud with some violence. "I need a man to make love to." She scowled up at the blue sky and its cotton candy clouds. "Hey, You, if You're really up there—I want me a man. Find me one right now! Ya hear me!? Right now!"

Figuring God had better things to do than help her get laid, Reby laughed and resumed her jog back towards the North Main Street end of Red Oak Crescent.

It was on this lap of her run that the man emerged from Cottage No. 2. She slowed to see him better. *Hmmm, not bad. Oh, not bad at all, though he looks married.* Even from a distance, he had that domesticated vibe about him that married people tended to get, a calmness that spoke of a part of life's desperate struggle being over.

She waved, he waved back. When she saw a flicker of interest in his eyes and realized that he was walking quickly towards the foot of the drive, towards her, she decided she was done with jogging for the day.

She quit her running and walked a short distance into his driveway.

"Well, hello there," he said, with a grin brimming full of seductive charm, "My name's Larry . . . Larry Townsend. You're one of the ladies in No. 4, I guess."

"Yeah, that's us." She shook his extended hand. "I'm Reby Butterfield." She was amused. She'd guessed right: he *was* married. In addition to the gold band on his left ring finger, he *did* have that 'I gotta be responsible, I got a wife' expression. It was a funny look on a man's face—one of satisfaction and harassment and delight and torment all at the same time. Most of all, it screamed 'Yippee!—the search is over!'

Ha ha! All he's missing is a 'Hen-Pecked & Lovin' It' T-Shirt.

Larry was tall and dark and very handsome and middle aged. Very nice in Reby's books, except for the wife attachment.

For a moment, Reby recalled her joking prayer at the end of the crescent. Had God actually . . . ? But a married man?

Guiltily, she glanced skyward. The heavens darkened at that moment, going from the bright blue she'd been running under to a deep, deep blue, a blue so intense it seemed solid and about to fall on them both and crush them beneath its weight. Even the clouds seemed to vanish, like the blue had eaten them.

Then the strange effect reversed itself, and overhead was a normal summer morning again.

Reby had a really weird feeling then. She felt it was *the blue*, not God, who'd just answered her prayer. She also had the impression that it would be in her best interests not to accept this gift.

She had no idea what to make of it all. *Oh, whatever.* She looked quickly down at her neighbor again and resumed smiling seductively at him.

"So, how've you ladies been finding this neighborhood?" he asked.

"Oh, it's nice, if a little dull," she replied. "I'm glad to finally meet someone new—a man, I mean."

"No men, huh?" She felt a thrill. He was clearly flirting with her.

"Oh boy, you've no idea what it's like living in an all-woman house. It's like being at Uni all over again . . . Estrogen City . . ."

CHAPTER 5

Jessica

Jessica realized she needed to get out of bed. She'd already begun feeling like an invalid. Jessica utterly detested illness, since it meant she couldn't work.

She swung her feet down to the floor and stood up. She stretched twice more, then walked into her bedroom's en suite bathroom.

In the bathroom, she stared in the mirror for a long time. The more she looked at herself the more upset she felt. Her reflection distressed her. *No, I don't look ill,* she conceded to herself. She looked, however, as if illness was swimming under her skin, preparing to burst forth at any moment. Because of the color of her nails, she found herself visualizing this hidden malady as a large blue blob.

She suddenly felt woozy and shook her head to clear it. She sat on the toilet, both to take the weight off her feet till her dizziness cleared and to pee.

While her exhaust waters gently trickled from her, Jessica thought back through the previous days. She tried to remember if she'd had any warning signs, any foreshadowings of what had happened to her today.

The one thing she could put a finger on, that might be connected to her nails turning blue, was the bout of sudden nausea she'd felt two days ago.

The incident had happened at around noon. She and Reby had been looking through the bushes bordering the woods at the back of the house. Reby insisted she had seen a large tabby cat over there. Jessica, who liked cats, had gone along with her to look for the beast.

They'd been pushing aside the ferns to see better and prodding through the undergrowth with sticks, when all of a sudden, out of nowhere, Jessica had had a blinding headache and had completely blacked out. She'd come back to herself to discover that she'd thrown up. Like a regurgitated picnic treat, most of her breakfast—toast, apple jam, and scrambled eggs—was spread out over the grass in front of her. Beyond the mess, Reby's denim-clad butt was visible through the bushes as she poked around, calling, "Kitty, pretty kitty, where are you kitty?"

Staring at the mess she'd made, Jessica had felt very embarrassed, particularly since now that it was all over, she felt fine again. The nausea she'd felt on regaining her senses had completely passed. The headache too was vanished, gone like it had never been. She'd quickly wiped her mouth clean, pulled a dead branch over her regurgitated breakfast, then hurried after Reby into the trees.

They'd not found the cat. Jessica had since forgotten all about her nausea. As it hadn't repeated itself, she'd not mentioned it to either Reby or Lucy. She'd simply assumed that something out back—maybe the scent of a herb or a flower she was unused to—had triggered an allergic reaction in her.

Now, sitting in her bathroom, Jessica pondered that headache/nausea incident more closely. One detail about it struck her mental gong, ringing her alarm bells—a vivid blue flash. Either while entering or exiting her blackout, everything around her had turned sky-blue for a moment.

Blue . . . blue . . . blue . . . At the time it had happened, with the noonday sky vivid and clear overhead, the sudden overwhelming blue experience had merely seemed a moment of spatial dislocation linked to her entering or leaving unconsciousness.

But now . . . She stared down at her feet pressed on the thick maroon bathroom carpeting, her gaze riveted on her plastic-like blue toenails. Her expression turned glum. *THAT was definitely connected to THIS*, she decided. *It wasn't just some random incident.*

And last night's nightmare? That also had prominently featured the color blue. In her dream the universe had been blue, blue and reeking of decaying meat. The memory of the stench filled her afresh with disgust.

Jessica reconsidered her day. She'd originally planned to drive into town with Lucy and stock up on groceries. With almost nothing on its shelves, the cottage pantry looked forsaken. But now, with this new development, she wasn't certain she'd do that anymore. She needed to see a doctor first. She felt well enough to go shopping, but . . . *But*

I also felt fine two days ago just before I threw up. And I felt just as fine afterwards too.

Jessica realized she'd finished urinating a while ago. She wiped, then flushed. Then she wondered why she'd bothered wiping, since she was about bathing. Giggling, she got under the shower.

Sixteen minutes later, wrapped in a soft pink bathrobe, Jessica relaxed on a sofa out in the living room. She felt invigorated by her shower. Blue nails or not, she felt much better; more able to face the day.

On her cellphone, she opened up the Facebook app. It was a guilty pleasure now. Having been stingy with herself about social media for so long, she was splurging now, feeding herself fat with the thrills, chills, and emotions of other people's lives, until that wonderful moment when she once more returned to her Boston office and her own life. But still . . . She had a moment's twinge of conscience. It might be wiser to remain incommunicado, or . . . What Jessica really worried about was becoming addicted to Facebook and Instagram and YouTube and Twitter and Snapchat—everyone living their private lives in the public eye.

The way Jessica saw it, the world was now way beyond Andy Warhol's 'fifteen minutes of fame.' This was the age of the Me-List celebrity, where Mr./Mrs./Ms. Ordinary were stars in their own right. All you needed to do was be interesting, or a bit nutty. Like the girl (ugh! gross!) who'd posted a Facebook video of herself sucking on one of her own bloody tampons.

But . . . Jessica grinned. Facebook *was* the modern addiction; a woman simply couldn't help herself. One had to be part of the flow of the moment, no matter how surreal it was. She was better than Lucy anyhow. High, Lucy would sit in front of her laptop for literally hours 'liking' posts and writing witty comments.

And, where was Lucy anyway?

"Lucy!" Jessica called. The words echoed through the house, then bounced back at her.

"Lucy!" she howled again, then gave up. Lucy might be stoned, or still sleeping off last night's joint drunk.

For a moment, she wondered why she suddenly felt so blasé. True, it was just seven-thirty (much too early to rush to an outpatient's with anything less than a life threatening emergency), but the way she felt now was weirdly similar to her earlier feelings, both on waking up and later in the bathroom. Both of those times she'd been alarmed, but then her alarm had suddenly eroded away into a well-rounded sense of wellbeing. Eroded away like—she couldn't avoid the simile—like nails being filed smooth by a manicurist.

Jessica *knew* she shouldn't feel so relaxed about what was happening to her body. She recalled the impression of 'illness beneath wellness' she'd gotten while studying her face in the bathroom mirror. She felt she should actually be panicking. She was worried that she was unable to panic.

Then that didn't seem to matter either. Plastic nails or not, she felt good. Good enough to go shopping once Lucy got out of bed.

"Lucy!" she called one more time. She felt too lazy—like a well-fed puppy—to walk twenty feet and open Lucy's bedroom door and watch her sleeping (usually in just panties and with her socks and sleeping mask on).

She gave up on Lucy.

Reby, her other housemate, was certain to be out jogging, keeping herself in shape for the men in town. Jessica had quickly worked out that she was housesharing with *two* addicts: Reby's drug was sex—it was all she ever talked about, and apparently all she lived for. "Sex is my life," she'd once admitted. "The only time I'll never have room for a man between my legs is when they're pressed tight together in my coffin."

Reby styled herself as a female Casanova. 'Screw and kiss goodbye,' was one of her mottos. The other was 'Take every penis prisoner.' Somewhere, someday, *some guy* (Jessica had no idea whether to consider that man 'lucky' or 'unlucky'), would breach the barricades around Reby's unyielding heart. However, from the looks of Reby's current sexual rampaging, it wasn't going to happen anytime soon.

Jessica returned her thoughts to herself. So, here she was. On vacation. By herself. No, not exactly; she had friends with her. But she was 'by herself' in a way: she was apart from all the people she knew who could easily stress her the way she enjoyed being stressed, away from the job she wished to do until it killed her.

She viewed dealing with Lucy and Reby's quirky personalities as part of her rejuvenation process. Relaxation therapy.

Her two housemates were entertainment. Her personal 'In Cottage' reality show. She could (and did) laugh at Lucy's antics while she was high (which was most of the time). Reby's man-mindedness was even

30

funnier. Reby stalked her next fuck like she had a sexual quota to fulfill. When she and Jessica were out, she stared at men's buttocks like she wanted to bite into them. Jessica found that hilarious.

All of a sudden, Jessica gave up on checking Facebook. Just like that, she lost interest in finding out what everyone she knew was currently up to. She had fifteen notifications of posts and two friend invites, but she realized that for the last ten or so minutes, she'd been staring at the screen with her thoughts elsewhere.

She signed out of the app, dropped the phone, and got up.

She considered her nails again. Vivid sky-blue, as if she'd taken extraordinary care while painting them. They looked creepy. They seemed to pull her eyes towards them.

And then they tingled. Both her fingernails and toenails all tingled at once. Twenty tingles at the tips of her hands and feet.

The mass tingling smashed the illusion of wellness soothing her. What would happen next? Would her nails start falling out? The tingling convinced Jessica of what course of action was in her best interests. She shuddered, arms wrapped around herself. Oh no, she wasn't doing any shopping before she'd seen a doctor.

The tingling ceased in her fingers and toes. Her bother carried on. She fed her worry with scraps of memory, refusing to let it subside. Even when (as she'd suspected would happen) she began feeling calm again, she shook the tranquility off.

I am going to see a doctor and that is that!

To firm her resolve, she got to her feet and headed to her bedroom to start getting dressed.

Thankfully, the question of which hospital to visit and which doctor to see was already taken care of:

When Jessica had informed her Boston physician Dr. Lopez that she was moving to Raynham for a while, he'd given her the number of an old medical school colleague of his, a Dr. Frank Whitfield, who now ran the Raynham Outlook Clinic.

"It's my opinion that all you need is a long layoff from work," Dr. Lopez had told her. "However, if you start feeling odd again, go and see Frank. I'll call him up beforehand and let him know you'll be over. Meeting Frank will be good for you in a social sense too—his wife Adria throws fantastic parties."

Jessica was searching through her handbag for the card with Dr. Whitfield's number when Lucy walked into her bedroom.

"Morning, biatch," Lucy said. "You cool?"

Jessica straightened up from her card-search. She hugged Lucy and forced a smile. "Morning."

As was usual this early in the day, Lucy looked completely disheveled. Her purple hair dangled over half her face like she was the vengeful ghost in some Japanese horror flick. She still had her sleeping mask on, now tangled up in her hair like a sweatband. Her white panties looked wet at the crotch, like she'd peed herself, or been masturbating in her sleep. Jessica doubted it was the latter—all the drugs Lucy did meant she had zero sex-drive.

Lucy sat on the dresser stool. She grabbed her head in both hands and winced. "Damn, is my brain playing me a concert this morning or what. I didn't sleep well. I had all kinds of crappy dreams filled with monsters and shit."

Jessica let that one pass. Lucy always dreamt of monsters. She shook out her handbag on the bed and finally found the card for the Raynham Outlook Clinic. Yes, Dr. Frank Whitfield. A neat blue script on the rear of the card informed her that the clinic also conducted research into 'holistic medicine and alternate therapies for pain and stress relief.'

"You know, I really don't feel up to going shopping this morning," Lucy piped up. "Maybe later in the day?"

"Yeah, sure," Jessica agreed, turning to look at her. She felt better now that she'd found the card for the clinic, like it was a weapon in a war, even if she was uncertain what the battle was. "I want to go see the doc my doc recommended for me."

Lucy gave her a sly grin. "What's the matter? You preggers?"

"I wish." Now she had the card, Jessica could joke. "At the moment my biological clock is running on overdrive. My womb's so desperate for semen now, it'll soon start placing donor ads in the newspapers behind my back."

Lucy laughed then pouted and made smacking sounds with her lips. "Ooh, poor pussy. No love milk for poor pussy, eh? Whatever will Jesse's poor pussy ever do to get some milkie?"

Jessica laughed. "You see Reby?"

"Nah. Out jogging for sure."

"She normally doesn't take this long."

"Maybe she met a guy she likes. She really should keep it in her panties."

"Like we do, huh? At least she's pro-active about sex. We ain't getting younger and we ain't getting laid either."

"The first is unavoidable, the second both unacceptable and unforgivable."

"Yeah, you're right. Neither me or you have had a fuck in like forever. Me because I was too busy and you because you're too lazy."

Lucy laughed, then stopped and grabbed her head again. "Damn this goddam hangover. My poor little brain feels like the Rolling Stones on a Farewell Tour. I'm feeling really nauseated all of a sudden."

Jessica stiffened. She waited for Lucy to mention an accompanying splitting headache. Or even a blue flash. Lucy didn't, so she relaxed. It was just drunken nausea then.

"Wow, that's just fantastic," Lucy exclaimed suddenly, her eyes brightening.

"What is?"

Lucy pointed. "Your nails. "Damn, biatch, they look so friggin' good!" She took hold of both of Jessica's hands. "This is just a fucking fantastic manicure," she enthused, turning the hands over and then dropping her gaze to Jessica's feet also and bending to study her toenails as well. "They're so blue, so light-blue and pretty. And how you've done 'em—you'd think the color's actually a part of your body. Wow, and they don't look glued on either. No, they ain't glued on. Wow, Jessica, you're gonna have to show me how you achieved this look. It's so hot."

Jessica didn't reply Lucy's gushing words of praise. She began desperately looking around for her cellphone. She was calling Dr. Whitfield at the Raynham Outlook Clinic right now.

CHAPTER 6

Colleen

Her heart boiling with anger, Colleen Townsend watched her husband through their bedroom window. Larry was down at the foot of their driveway, chatting with that woman—their neighbor from Cottage No. 4. Colleen Townsend's heart ticked over with frustration and rage. The bedroom drapes were only half open; Larry didn't know she was watching him. He always rose earlier than she did, and yesterday he'd said he wanted to clean their white Chevrolet Tahoe SUV before she drove it into town. He was thoughtful like that.

Even from her vantage point almost forty yards away, Colleen could read the other woman's body language as she stood there in her running clothes—tight red shorts, sleeveless yellow T-shirt, and white sneakers and socks; her long black hair pegged back in a ponytail by a red scrunchie. Her body language said 'ready to go,' as in 'go to bed with you.' She was posed like a hooker, hand on hip like she'd been playing tennis, her hips in turn cocked slightly to the rear like she was aching to thrust them forward at a male organ. Colleen couldn't see the woman's face, but she could imagine its expression: all flirty, eye-teasing Larry with sultry 'come hither' glances.

And her Larry? Larry (in brown slacks and gray shirt and black flip flops) was looking at the thin bitch like he was gonna eat her up. Okay, so it wasn't really the girl's fault if she was attracted to Colleen's husband—Colleen agreed that Larry was a good-looking man: dark, handsome, and well-built; the sort most women went for—but couldn't the stupid bitch see the gold wedding band on his left hand?

For an intense, heart-pounding moment Colleen felt like running downstairs, grabbing a knife from the kitchen, and running outside and stabbing the pair of them dead. Fuck the police! She had a satisfying vision of herself gouging out her pretty neighbor's eyes with a pair of scissors and rolling the bloody little orbs out into the road like meat-marbles for the bitch's friends to drive their car over, and then she'd . . .

With a sudden start, Colleen came back to herself. She felt sick, like she'd throw up. Then, for the briefest of moments, everything around her turned a bright vivid blue.

After a final nauseous glance downstairs—her husband and her neighbor were still chatting blithely away—Colleen staggered over to the bed and fell flat on her belly on it.

She lay there looking somewhat like a jellyfish in her diaphanous nightie, her pale fat body trembling, curlers falling from her blonde hair, her slippers falling from her feet, her long red fingernails and toenails giving the illusion of her hands and feet dripping blood onto the bedcovers and the blue rug.

Her turquoise eyes were squeezed shut against the nausea and the blue flash she'd seen. She didn't want to see *that* again—it was too scary. At that instant it had seemed like an ocean was being poured into her eyes.

She waited for her nausea to pass. *What is wrong with me?* she wondered in horror. *Thinking of stabbing Larry and that girl to death? Me? That's totally unlike me!*

Usually such violent thoughts *were* totally unlike Colleen.

***

Colleen and Larry Townsend had been married for fifteen years now. Colleen was forty, Larry was forty-three. Larry was a successful New York stockbroker, now trying to write a book on Wall Street's greatest scandals. Colleen considered Larry to be her job. She often jokingly referred to herself as a 'traveling housewife'—"Wherever he goes, I go."

The couple had no children together, but Colleen had a son, Randy, from her first marriage back when she was eighteen. Randy was currently over in Iraq, in a US Military bomb disposal unit. (Colleen's endless prayer was that he wouldn't get blown sky-high by some device either Saddam or the Kurds had left behind.)

Colleen Townsend was a quiet, passive woman who avoided trouble. It was why her marriage had survived so long: she kept the peace. She would rather suffer hurt that make a noise. Even in the current situation—her suspicion that her pussy-hound husband was about to have an affair with the bimbo next door; yet another in his long line of infidelities—she'd have kept quiet and waited for it to burn out. The affairs always did; they ended and Larry never went back to the woman. Once over his latest lady love he'd run home to Colleen and be *very* nice to her for a while.

Until next time, of course. Colleen knew she could count on Larry always coming back to her—all she needed to do was turn a blind eye and she had nothing to worry about. She had that magic 'motherly pussy' men couldn't resist. As far as she could tell, overweight women gave men a greater feeling of comfort in bed that skinny ones did. There was something immensely satisfying about being enfolded in all that flesh, having pneumatic natural breasts pressing against one's chest, having thick, fleshy thighs and calves wrapping around the male body. Few men could resist the feeling. They might say they liked the model types, but boy, did they keep screwing the large ones. Oh, once you went fat, you never went back.

Disease? Colleen knew she didn't have to worry about those. Larry was scared shitless of STDs. He'd once said that if he ever caught AIDS—even from a blood transfusion—he'd blow his brains out with their shotgun.

Yes, Colleen was definitely insecure about her weight and looks, but Larry had his own insecurities too: about work, about losing his hair, worries that his dick wasn't long enough. That last one confused Colleen a bit. *We've been married for fifteen years and I've never ONCE complained and he's still worried about his size? Oh, men are so weird!*

And, Larry had also realized that Colleen never judged him like his mistresses did. So once he'd had some fun, back home to her he'd run.

Larry had been straying for the past three years. At first Colleen had wept, then she'd decided she could live with her situation. Was she happy about her husband's infidelity? No, she most definitely wasn't. However, she wasn't willing to divorce Larry—she felt too old and too fat to start over. (For someone as passive as Colleen it was hard work just remaining in the same place.) She'd figured that the best she could do was what she was doing now—travel everywhere with him and keep her eyes peeled for the sexy young things with their hot bodies that turned up with clockwork regularity like there was a nymphomaniac factory nearby. It was harder to philander when your wife was with you. Usually, the best you could hope for then was a threesome.

But Colleen wasn't fooling herself: Errant genitalia always found a way. It was a sexual law: once you had a will to cheat on your spouse, biology arranged the rest for you. Adultery was the game adults weren't supposed to play, but played anyway.

***

So, no, passive Colleen Townsend wasn't normally the type of woman to have violent, bloody thoughts. But ever since she and Larry had come to Raynham a fortnight ago so he could have peace and quiet to finish his book, she'd been having crazy flashes of herself carrying out increasingly violent behavior. All tinged with that vivid blue glow. She was frightened of seeing that blue glow now.

The blue flashes had started three days after they'd arrived here. She'd had just one on that first day. The next one had occurred two days later. Since then, though, they'd steadily gotten more and more frequent. Colleen had them two or three times a day now.

She had pills for her condition from a reputable clinic in town, along with the doctor's firm assurance that the blue flashes were certain to cease in two weeks maximum. Colleen hoped they would. Her sudden violent impulses the doctor attributed to the 'random surfacing of long-repressed anger.' He'd told her that if her rages didn't abate along with the blue flashes, he'd refer her to a good psychiatrist. Colleen felt the doctor's diagnosis was correct: during her consultation she'd not told him anything about her strained relationship with Larry.

But now, as she dragged herself off the bed and struggled back to the bedroom window and stared out again, she wasn't sure. *Yes, I do worry every time a pretty young woman walks by my husband, but I don't want to kill him! I love him! I just want the son-of-a-bitch all to myself.*

Downstairs, her sexy young neighbor had vanished. Larry had the door of their Chevrolet SUV open and was bent over with his head inside the vehicle. She saw him straighten out, and could clearly hear him whistling to himself. He sounded like a robin happy with the morning. Very pleased with himself. Colleen's heart fell. *Shit, it's started again. And just when things have been going so well between us. Now, I'll just have to endure the next few weeks, look the other way at the right times, and pretend not to notice when he smells of the damn girl's perfume, and . . .*

Larry looked up from their car then, saw her there at the window, and blew her a kiss. His gesture of affection made her feel even worse. *Oh God, can't this stupid man see what he's doing to me? How much he's hurting me? Why can't he just be faithful and make me happy?*

Still, she waved back, from long practice her face automatically taking on a pleased expression.

But, as she smiled at him, the rage overtook her again. She saw herself stabbing him in the belly with a rusty pitchfork, ramming it all the way through him so the bloody tines jutted from his back, then dropping the handle of the pitchfork so Larry fell forward on it and remained propped up like that, blood spurting from both his front and back wounds as his body slid further down the metal prongs.

The vision cut out in another blue flash. The dizziness and nausea returned. Not bothering to check if Larry had noticed anything amiss with her or not, Colleen backed away from the window to the bed and collapsed on it again, this time dropping flat on her back, her fat legs sticking out over the bed's edge.

My God, this has got to stop! she groaned as the headache that generally followed the nausea began. Eyes closed, Colleen felt desperately about for her nightstand and her pills.

CHAPTER 7

Jessica

Jessica reversed her Nissan Sentra along the driveway. She stared up over the woods behind the cottage, at the mid-morning sky. The sky was a barren, warm blue. She dropped her eyes from heaven to earth to consider her nails. They were still that same inexplicable blue.

Lips pressed tight together, her eyes grim, Jessica slid the red car out into the road and pointed it towards the start of the street.

The street. The crescent. The new-moon curve she currently lived on.

Jessica drove off slowly. She was focused on her objective: getting into town and seeing Dr. Whitfield at the Raynham Outlook Clinic. She was making an effort to remain alarmed. She was succeeding in this by centering her thoughts on the danger of the unnatural calm she'd felt since waking up.

She looked right as she passed No. 3 Red Oak Crescent. (The houses were staggered, with each driveway facing either a lawn or a wall of trees.)

No. 3 was empty, but without a 'For Rent' sign outside it. Empty also were No. 5 and No. 6, the pair at the end of the crescent, both similarly with no signs announcing that they'd welcome tenants. Houses 1, 2, and 4 were occupied. Jessica had not yet seen the occupants of Cottage No. 1, but twice while driving past, she'd noticed a blue Volvo sedan parked in front of it. All the houses were newish, built probably within the last three years.

When they'd moved in, Jessica had at first found it strange that a road as long as Red Oak Crescent—half a mile long at least—had only six residences, the first of those built almost a hundred yards inside it, and with all of the houses spaced well apart. Though all of different shapes and sizes, the houses on the crescent all bore the mark of a single mental process. So, most likely the same architectural firm had designed them. Considering the great landscaping and profusion of trees along the entire street—Lucy had told her there was even a large pond about three hundred yards out back of their cottage (you couldn't see it from the house because of the woods in the way)—Jessica thought the developers had initially intended to build a resort or spa or summer camp here in the middle of Raynham, but had run out of financing, and had instead just built the six houses they could afford to complete.

But if that's so, why aren't they all rented out?

She let it go. It was a mystery for another day. She continued navigating the residential curve. She shortly reached No. 2, a green/white two-story house on her left. Outside it, a dark, middle-aged man had the hood of his white SUV up and was peering inquisitively into its engine.

He looked up as Jessica drove past and waved.

She waved back; no time to socialize now—she had to remain upset till she saw the doctor. Reby had said the man's name was Larry Townsend. Reby had said he lived here with his wife. Reby had also come home with one of Mr. Townsend's business cards. Business cards meant cellphone numbers. Cellphone numbers meant hooking up. Jessica didn't approve of Reby and Mr. Townsend's future intentions towards each other.

She reached and passed No. 1, another two-floored building, this one with a split level to its rear. She laughed. *It looks like me and the girls got the only rentable cottage.*

She reached the end of the street, made a right turn, and on a sudden impulse looked back the way she'd come.

She had no explanation for what happened next:

First, she had the impression of a blue veil being stripped away from her eyes. Next, she found that instead of viewing placid Red Oak Crescent behind her, she was staring down a tunnel into Hell.

Where she was seeing clearly wasn't any place on earth. She was looking into a blue-tinted limitless tunnel of decay, their curved road straightened out into an underpass to a netherworld. (The 'tunnel' was aboveground, formed by the overhanging trees and the road, and yet it gave the impression of being a thousand miles deep inside the earth.)

She had crystal-clear knowledge that this tunnel led to the lair of the Evil Ones, to the House of Death, where abomination reigned supreme and corruption was the only law. Charnel-smelling turbulent winds blew out from beneath the trees, their relentless stench as bad as if the entire route was paved with roadkill.

The trees were evil pillars propping up the evil sky. They were covered with disgusting fungi, mold, and lichen. From their black branches creepers thick as pythons dangled onto the road, which was itself ridged and broken up and covered with foul-smelling goop that reeked like the pus from a burst abscess.

Like ships with skeleton crews sailing a sea of vomit, impressions of terrifying atrocities flooded at her from the transformed street. The evil tide weakened her like a raging fever would.

The world was tinted blue. The BLUE was an incurable sickness infecting the universe.

All these impressions of a ruined and decaying vista lasted the briefest of instants while Jessica glanced back. Then the blue veil flashed across her face again and the departing street once more looked perfectly normal.

Jessica was left disoriented and confused by what had just happened. She felt sapped by the evil she'd sensed radiating from the place. The memory of what she'd seen lingered in her brain. She knew it couldn't have been real. She had to have imagined it. Nowhere could be that desolate and horrible. And she'd only seen the highway, not the destination it led to.

She slowed the Nissan to a crawl to collect her thoughts. She felt dizzy, like she'd just stared down from the roof of the world. Dizzy and a little nauseated.

Not dizzy enough to put off her trip to the clinic though. This new experience utterly convinced Jessica that she needed medical help.

She stepped on the gas. The road downtown looked clear for the most part. She figured she'd better hurry; the nausea hadn't completely left her. If she was going to be sick, it would be best that it happened with a doctor around.

CHAPTER 8

Larry

About to step back into his house and assure his wife that no, he'd not been flirting with the beautiful woman next door, Larry Townsend froze and blinked.

"What the . . . ?" His jaw dropped and he gaped. All of a sudden, the front entrance to No. 2—a lovely set of French doors—had vanished. Actually, the entire house had vanished. Facing Larry now, and extending seemingly to infinity both left and right of him, was a pinkish wall beneath a cloudless blue sky. The blue was everywhere else, like the sun had exploded and become an ocean.

Directly in front of Larry, a pair of massive pink columns framed an archway leading into more of the blueness. Then, veins twitched in the pink masonry and Larry had a horrified realization that these columns facing him were both made of flesh. Living flesh. Organs and sinew and muscle. A few glances confirmed that the entire endless wall in front of him was also made of living flesh. Flesh that throbbed to the motion of heart-accelerated blood.

This dreadful knowledge entered Larry like air: it was essential for him to know. He needed to know it to survive. It terrified him, but there were no alternatives to this awful perception.

Like it filled the sky and the world around him, the blueness filled the archway too. The blue seemed a tangible thing, like a jelly. It was impossible to see inside the archway between the meat pillars. Still, Larry could see in there. He saw moving colored lines—black and brown and dark gray. He instinctively recognized the lines for what they were: the wavy crayon-outlines of monsters that, even unseen, offended his human conception of body design.

A horrible fetid odor poured from the blue archway, like the impenetrable color hid a mountain of dead fish that had been rotting for weeks. The smell was unbelievable, absolutely hideous. The smell—of decaying fish and of other rotten things, each more terrible than the last—puffed out from the archway like gusts of steam.

The stink surrounded Larry. It seemed to settle on him. Larry gagged, but found he couldn't throw up. Somewhere distant—it sounded like they were all around him—voices were booming. The voices cascaded over each other like musical waterfalls. Beyond the voices, Larry thought he heard people screaming for mercy. But the musical voices drowned out the screams. No one needed to tell Larry that what lay concealed behind the blue barrier, the unseen landscape behind the wall of throbbing and pulsating flesh, was a realm of the most absolute horror and wickedness imaginable.

Larry stepped back. He could see something shooting towards him inside the blue beyond the meat archway. The thing coming was huge and horrible and hungry. It had a thousand mouths and teeth. Its outline was as red as freshly-spilled blood and its thousands of tentacles flailed and reached out for him.

"No!" he whimpered. He flung up his hands to ward it off, crossing his forearms in front of his face in an effort to shield himself from certain death.

The monster broke through the blueness. Larry saw it in its full disgusting form, its horrible eyes bulging, torn human flesh spilling from its endless mouths.

"No . . . .!"

The vision cut out. The blue archway again became the French doors leading into Larry's living room. Suddenly there was no obscene monster flying at him, no gut-wrenching smell of decaying fish flesh everywhere. Nothing but a bug crawling right-to-left across the left half of the glass door.

Larry stood there staring, unable to move. He was scared that if he took a step forward, reality would instantly fade again and he'd be right back with the monster (yuck!—how could anything look that gross?), and this time he'd not escape being its meal.

He stood there with his heart beating fast, marking time's passage by the bug's slow plodding across the glass. He was trembling. He was certain he was losing his mind.

Then, inside the house, he saw Colleen walking towards him. She looked upset. As Colleen reached the French doors and slid them open, Larry tried to read his wife's face. He checked the layout of her eyes and lips to see if they had that 'disgusted' look to them. Such a look would mean she'd noticed him chatting up Reby Butterfield from next door.

He couldn't tell. She might have been upset with him, but beyond that, she looked exhausted, like sleeping all night was hard work.

"Darling, what are you doing standing out there?"

Larry slowly unstuck his feet from the front porch. His heart was still decelerating, but he had more control over himself now. The world made sense again. There was no monster, there never had been one. Most likely he'd subconsciously noticed Colleen approaching, and comparing her large body to Reby's trim and toned one had put 'monster' idea into his head. Then his overworked mind had done the rest. (Larry knew his thoughts were unreasonable, not to mention nasty to his wife, but his subconscious was clutching at straws here—looking for anything that would serve as a rock of sanity in the presence of the inexplicable.)

"Darling . . . ?"

"I just had a new idea for the book," he lied, "another mess from the Shocking Seventies that I just remembered."

"But you looked horrified," Colleen said. (As she said this, Larry noted that she looked horrified herself.) "Like you'd found a corpse in our yard."

Her voice was tired as she said this. Larry forced a smile. If she hadn't noticed he and Reby chatting, he didn't want to either anger or alarm her. Larry figured he was lucky: Colleen never made a fuss about his sexual shenanigans like other women would. Most other women would have divorced his ass two years ago and sued him for everything he had. Not Colleen. Nice, sweet, comfortable Colleen. He stared at her round face and wondered why the hell she wasn't enough for him anymore. She'd been just fine up until he'd turned forty. (Though he'd violently deny it if queried, Larry had a subconscious fear that he was getting old. All those young women he tasted were like tonics renewing his fast-departing youth.)

"Breakfast is ready," Colleen said wearily, standing back from the doors so he could come in.

"Thanks, honey," he said and stepped inside. He kissed her cheek and she didn't push him away. He followed her through their living room to the dining room. He was pleased. Colleen didn't suspect a thing. That meant she'd not find some excuse to hang around during the day and mess up his rendezvous with Ms. Hot Butt next door.

As he sat down to breakfast, Larry Townsend realized that during the short walk across his living room he'd somehow lost the terror of his strange vision. He thought back on that blue reeking archway for a moment, but now it didn't seem so frightening or unusual anymore.

And why the hell should it scare me anyway? The damn thing was so damn ridiculous, so damn silly. A temple built from meat? A living temple? And that damn monster that was all mouths and tentacles and was chewing bloody human flesh? He laughed at himself: *Ha ha ha ha ha! Dammit, Larry Townsend, you sure have thought up a good one this time! Ha ha ha!*

He grinned the vision off, then washed it down (along with a mouthful of scrambled eggs on buttered toast) with some strong black coffee. He felt good all of a sudden, largely because of the afternoon's planned tryst.

He smiled sweetly at Colleen. "Pass the butter, please, darling."

She did so without speaking. Larry noted that she looked upset about something. Her fat hands—with those two-inch-long red fingernails she always stabbed him in the back with when they fucked—were trembling. He looked up at her face. Her large lips—breadcrumbs dotted on them like glitter—were trembling too.

Larry shrugged that off as well. Maybe she was worrying about their kid Randy getting blown up over in Iraq again.

CHAPTER 9

Lucy

By 10 a.m., Lucy was on her third joint of the day. Like an alcoholic did with booze, she tended to start early. "I gotta make the most of the hours available," she'd explain if queried.

Lucy lay in bed, sort-of watching the sky through her window. Her purple hair was draped forward over her face and she could only see in strips, which was fine by her.

She was still wearing just her white panties. Her pale little body looked insignificant in the big bed.

She'd had some bad dreams last night. She'd been feeling a bit uneasy since waking up, but she knew that would pass. Pot and pills always helped even the world out. There were simply too many things out there to get one all riled up.

She reached out a skinny hand and selected a blue Quaalude from a saucer full of pills on the bed. (No ashtrays in the house!) She popped the Quaalude in her mouth, chewed it a little, and swallowed. She sipped some water to help it get properly started on its way to calming her down further.

Then she lay back again, enjoying the blend of colors outside. Right now, the sky looked just like Jessica's nails had this morning—that pale, bright, female blue that Lucy found oh so pretty. She wanted a manicure like that. She raised the hand holding her joint to her face and studied her own orange and green nails. Nah, Jessica's were way better. She'd get Jessica to do hers too.

She stuck the joint between the strands of hair lying on her mouth. Several strands found their way in as well and she spat them out. She took a long drag of the marijuana, then, without looking, fished about in the saucer for another pill. Any one would do to help the mood. At the moment, her senses felt enhanced. She imagined she could hear

46

Reby out in their kitchen, opening up the fridge and pulling out one of her goddam protein shakes—couldn't the biatch just eat normal food like everyone else? What was with all the veggies and low-fat and low-carb everything? Lucy grinned. *Oh, Reby, oh, Reby darlin'. You're scared of gettin' fat? Oh, oh, lemme show you the way, baby—all ya need to lose weight is heroin. Two shots of smack a day for a week or two till you're hooked good. Then you won't wanna eat at all and you'll be more skinny than a starving wolf.*

She grinned broadly, her mouth spreading like a wound splitting open her elfin face. Yeah, today was looking better now than when she'd woken up. *Stupid dreams. Dumb dreams. Can't they wait till I'm no longer on vacation?*

***

Lucy Polk was thirty-two now. She'd been doing drugs of one kind or the other since she was twelve. Lucy had essentially spent the last twenty years of her life stoned to varying degrees.

Lucy had grown up in the village of Dresden, Ohio. She'd neither had bad parents nor been raised on the wrong side of the tracks. She'd simply had older and 'bad' friends. Vince Collins, the father of one of those friends, was actually involved in the marijuana trade. Tommy Collins would sneak joints into school, and after class was over for the day, he, Lucy, and a few others would sit by the Wakatomika Creek and get high.

It was a wonder they never got caught.

When Lucy was fifteen, she and Tommy (who was seventeen then) started dating. This meant she was often over at his house. Tommy had been telling her for ages that his father's friends dealt in other drugs too; but he'd been scared to steal any of the pills and powders because he'd seen what they'd done to a guy named Ferret Morris, who'd snorted up some coke without permission—they'd cut his nose off and Ferret had had to have his nose stitched back on again. (This cautionary tale was to have a lasting effect on young Lucy Polk: it was the primary reason why she never developed an addiction to cocaine. In later life, just seeing a line of that powerful white powder filled Lucy with subconscious dread.)

Fear of losing their teenaged smelling organs notwithstanding, both Lucy and Tommy had sampled some of the 'goods' lying around

47

the place. Indeed, once they'd gotten brave enough to really search the Collins' house, they'd discovered a veritable treasure trove of narcotics, including several stashes that Tommy's dad Vince had apparently forgotten existed.

So they'd smoked and pill-popped away the next few years, both of them consistently getting atrociously low grades in their schoolwork.

Once out of high school, Tommy joined the family business, which just gave them both more drugs to mess around with.

Lucy's parents utterly hated what she was into. Her father was particularly upset. James Polk now felt like a total failure. His only son, Lucy's older brother Robert, had recently come out as gay and had left Dresden for Springfield, MA, to be with his rich painter boyfriend Dean Weaver. And now, their other child, who they'd dreamed would end up presenting on TV because of her sparky looks and witty speech, seemed destined to wind up mopping floors at McDonald's.

As for Lucy in her pill-haven, she put the tension at home down to the 'generation gap' and just managed to graduate high school. She wasn't interested in looking for a real job anyway. She'd already asked Vince Collins if he'd employ a girl.

"What about your folks?" he'd asked. "We don't want trouble."

"My folks are squares, they don't count," Lucy replied. "Just gimme a damn job."

Vince had agreed. Lucy knew her parents wouldn't be trouble. Her father was a timid chap; the sort of man who ran from rats and snakes. James Polk was breaking his back to pay off the twenty-year mortgage on their house and wasn't about either talking tough to Vince Collins or ratting him out to the cops either; he had no intention of winding up in hospital for six months and having the mortgage company foreclose on him with just nine payments left to make.

As for her mother? Norma Polk knew Vince from back when they were both kids. She was terrified of him. "He's a damn rapist and white slaver," she kept telling Lucy with tears in her eyes. "Stay away from him and his damn son. For heaven's sake, darling, scratch the teen itch in your panties somewhere else."

Prudence paid off. Lucy's parents finished paying off the twenty-year mortgage on the house. Without that drain on their finances, both were happier. They began planning a long vacation somewhere together, maybe even a cruise to Jamaica or The Bahamas.

Meanwhile, Lucy went to work for Vince, helping bag pot and pills for his dealers. Whenever the protests at home became too loud, she packed up her stuff and moved in with Tommy for a while.

Life went on. Lucy was stoned half the time and happy with her life. The future? The future was something that happened to adults, not delinquent teens. Besides, Lucy figured, what else did the future hold anyway? Except having a man of one's own (she already had one), kids (she wasn't sure she was ready for the noise yet), making money (she was getting paid, wasn't she?), and entertainment (she had more pot than she could smoke and at rock-bottom price too)? So she was happy enough.

Then it happened:

Her aunt Gertrude (her mother's older sister) died up north in Chicago, and Lucy's parent's traveled there for the funeral. Lucy, who was living at home at the time while resolving a lover's tiff with Tommy, was left in charge of the house.

The next night Lucy burnt the house down, every 20-years-mortgage-just-paid-off inch of it.

The forensic scientists at the Ohio Fire Marshall's Arson Laboratory later determined that Lucy had been smoking in three different beds at once and had left burning cigarettes in all three, plus two on the living room sofa. Their explanation for the fire sounded implausible to everyone, but Lucy did remember walking through the entire house that night while tripping out on Datura (a new hallucinogen she was test driving for Vince), and admiring all the great furniture. It was the first time she'd ever appreciated what a beautiful building she lived in. Every now and then she'd be unable to find the stick of marijuana she'd been smoking and, imagining she'd finished it off, would light another one, which she'd in turn forget someplace else.

Then she'd lie down for a bit to contemplate life. Beautiful as the house was, it was making her dizzy. The walls kept moving, approaching and receding from her so she had no idea how big each room was. And she felt it was really important that she worked that out tonight. So she'd lie down, ponder a bit why the ceiling seemed lower (then suddenly higher) than she remembered and why there were little green people swinging from it—in pretty purple clothes though—then she'd get up and move on along corridors and stairs that wobbled and shook as she traversed them. In addition, the stairs turned each step she took into a chatter of alarmed crickets. It was all so distracting, and all she really wanted to do was 'understand' the house. She felt no one empathized with the poor building.

"No one understands me like you do, housie," she'd exclaim from time to time with deep feeling. "Damn that Tommy. He's just a dick; all he ever thinks of is porking me. He ain't a pal like you, house. Us? We're good friends. We'll be lifelong buddies."

The house caught fire at 2:07 a.m., when the neighborhood was all asleep. Lucy herself only escaped death because feeling unnaturally hot, she went outside for some fresh air. Then, noticing that the house was on fire, she sat on the front lawn and admired the blaze, enjoying how the dancing pretty flames mingled with those from the hallucinogens in her head.

The house was mostly old wood; it stood no chance at all of survival.

By the time the smell of smoke woke the neighborhood and someone called the fire department, it was too late. There was nothing left to save, except Lucy, who feeling too hot again at her vantage point, had migrated to the sidewalk to continue watching the house burn, and had finally passed out there.

Her parents were incensed, mostly because the insurance didn't cover their daughter burning down their own home. Twenty years of back-breaking payments all gone up in smoke.

Lucy's father instantly had a stroke that left his left side permanently paralyzed. Lucy's mother Norma left his bedside in the hospital and went and found his old Civil War revolver. Then she went looking for Lucy. She told more than one friend that she'd "murder the little bitch on sight."

Lucy accepted that she'd just disowned herself.

She successfully eluded her enraged mother and slipped out of Dresden, hitching a ride east to New York with Tommy, who was making a coke purchase there for his father.

The Big Apple was sour. The Bronx coke dealers pulled a double cross, stealing their $200,000 and leaving Tommy in a ditch with his intestines hanging out of his belly.

Tommy didn't die though; Lucy got him to a hospital and called Vince. Then she skipped New York before she got blown up in the anticipated gang war Vince was sure to bring with him to NYC. Vince Collins wasn't a wimp like her dad; there were going to be corpses lying everywhere until he both found the guys who'd almost killed his son and got his money back. Lucy had no intention of getting caught in the crossfire.

Lucy had caught a Greyhound bus up to Boston, where she'd begun working as a waitress while dealing pot on the side. It was here that she'd met Olivia Schreiber and her workaholic younger sister Jessica.

In Boston, Lucy's life had normalized for a while: Work, drugs, food, more drugs, sex (once a month or so), a lot more drugs.

Then one night, a guy she'd just fucked and was getting stoned with had suggested that they both move out west to Springfield, where the grass (referring to cannabis) was greener, and the cops were less of a hassle. After dragging deep on her joint, Lucy replied, "Why not—I'll give it a shot."

Her friend knew a gay couple over in Springfield who were recruiting staff for their new restaurant. In a roundabout homecoming twist, that pair turned out to be Lucy's brother Robert and his boyfriend Dean.

Two phone calls later, Lucy handed in her notice at the diner where she worked, loaded her things into the trunk of her car, and headed west.

She'd wanted a job in the restaurant kitchen, but her brother had been scared that she might burn the place down. (And yes, he'd confirmed, their mother *was* still howling for her blood.)

That was ten years ago. Lucy been waitressing (and getting high as a kite) in Springfield ever since. She was, of course, forbidden from smoking anywhere on the restaurant premises.

And then she'd come back for this short vacation.

***

Now, a sharp noise cut through Lucy's pleasant daze.

She stirred slightly. What was that she'd just heard? It sounded like rain.

No, no, no, wetness, she pleaded in her thoughts, *don't ruin this day for me.*

The sound continued. Lucy tracked it, looking down from the fingernail-colored sky and the stony clouds to the right side of the windowsill.

Her hair was still draped over her face. Through those purple face-curtains and the haze of smoke from her latest reefer she made out a face at her window. And a tapping hand.

She felt too calm to be bothered. She shut her eyes and the tapping stopped.

Ah, I just imagined it then.

The tapping started again.

"Go round the front door," Lucy mumbled.

The tapping persisted. Lucy pushed herself up on her elbows. Then she brushed her hair off her face.

Then she felt alarmed. It was hard to accomplish this feeling when one was high, but Lucy managed it.

There was a policeman standing outside her window and peeking in at her.

Shit, I'm fucked, she thought.

The cop was uniformed, but without a hat. He had a hard cold face like he ate drug users like Lucy Polk for breakfast, lunch, and dinner and shat them out afterwards. He had long and thick red hair, small eyes, and a large jaw. His thick lips were creased in a sadistic smile.

Seeing he now had Lucy's attention, he rapped on the window glass again.

The bedroom window was open anyway. Lucy wondered why he didn't just climb in and get it over with. Seeing the cop gave her really odd feelings. It felt like mixing uppers and downers all at once. She was troubled but unable to panic appropriately. She felt surges of nervous energy, but they had no focus. All she could think was: *He's gonna find my stash in the fridge and . . . and I'm too tired to run or anything. . . . I'll be busted and next stop . . . Soberville.*

(Unlike a straight male convict's fear of dropping the soap in the prison showers, Lucy's dread of jail had nothing to do with being sexually victimized. Her fear of incarceration revolved entirely around her not being able to get high once locked away. Her intense desire to not have this happen to her meant Lucy Polk was one of the most law-abiding users of illicit drugs on American soil. Possibly in US history even.)

Then Lucy noticed that she'd been mistaken in one detail concerning the policeman: he didn't have long red hair, he had red tentacles on his head. Like shiny crimson snakes, the tentacles fell past his large ears, coiled over his broad shoulders, and writhed uneasily across his equally broad chest.

Tentacle hair? This detail confused Lucy. Still, she took it neatly in her stride: nowadays anything was possible. She waved nicely at the cop, then on the off chance that he was crooked and she might be able to bribe him, asked, "Hey, man, you like a smoke?"

He didn't reply, just kept smiling. He had purple eyes. First time she'd ever seen anyone with eyes like that.

Lucy was distracted for a moment and looked towards her bathroom door. When she looked back at the window, the strange policeman was gone.

Just to confirm this, she looked all around the window, starting at the top corners, and working her vision all around the frame, just to ensure that he wasn't hiding anywhere.

But no, he wasn't there.

Then she heard a sound outside, like the rustling noises Jessica and Reby had made amongst the bushes while searching for that cat two days ago. It was a nice sound that fit in nicely with her high. She'd have lain back down and enjoyed it, but she was still alarmed enough from seeing that policeman (even if she'd only imagined him and his crazy hair) to let it go like that.

She got groggily out of bed. Carrying her joint as stylishly as a female aristocrat with a cigarette holder, she staggered over to her window to peek out at the backyard.

The policeman was still out there. He was bent down amongst the bushes near the woods, searching for something. As he searched, the red tentacles on his head writhed madly about.

He finally stood up and waved to Lucy. She felt she should wave back and did so; he seemed friendly enough. She saw that he was holding a cat—a large brown and white tabby.

Lucy puffed her joint and watched. It was really sad though: the damn cat looked dead. It lay limp in the cop's huge hand, with its eyes closed and a thin thread of blood dribbling from its open mouth.

Then the policeman raised the cat to his mouth and took a bite out of it. In the moment before his teeth bit into the creature, Lucy noticed that they seemed to have been filed to sharp points. Then the teeth were in the cat and out of the cat again, and the policeman had a mouthful of meat and bloody fur, and there was a massive hole in the cat's back from which more blood was seeping.

Yeah, the cat's dead, Lucy decided. *Else it'd be howling like mad now.*

Bemused by what was going on, Lucy took another hit of her joint. The marijuana was helping her keep everything in proper perspective. There wasn't anything really odd happening here. This cop had to really hungry though; he hadn't even washed the cat first.

The policeman swallowed and took another bite out of the dead cat. He was walking towards Lucy again, but seemed more concerned about his feline breakfast than he was about her. She was relieved. He wasn't after her stash. She didn't want to deal with law enforcement hassle today. She just wanted to enjoy her vacation.

The policeman took another bite of tabby cat. The hole in the animal's back was now almost a complete 'U.' Lucy figured the policeman had eaten out its spine. The front of his blue uniform was covered with blood and draped with cat entrails that had spilled from its back. (To Lucy's mind, the man's tentacles seemed satisfied with his meal: they weren't flailing wildly about anymore.) The red tentacles lay slack about his face and neck, flecked with clotting drops of blood. They glittered like reptile scales in the sunlight. And yes, there was absolutely no doubt about it now—this cop's teeth definitely had been filed to sharp points.

Then the cop, still eating away, waved at Lucy again, turned, and walked off out of sight, heading left towards No. 6 on their street.

Lucy stood staring out at the morning for a while. She finished her joint and flicked the roach out into the flowerbed. She still had that disoriented feeling of being both 'up' and 'down' at the same time. To normalize herself, she turned and picked out three pills from the saucer on the bed. She wasn't sure which pill would have the right effect, but they were all different pretty colors, so one of them had to work.

She swallowed the pills, then left her bedroom and walked down the short hallway to Reby's room.

Reby was lying in bed, propped up on her elbows facing her laptop.

Lucy propped herself up in the doorway. After noting that Reby had pretty black lingerie on, she said, "Reby, I just saw a policeman eating a cat."

Reby didn't even look up from her laptop. "Yeah? And the Pope ain't a Catholic anymore."

Lucy persisted. "Reby, I'm dead serious. This cop, he had long red tentacles instead of hair; they were big like garter snakes. He *did* eat the cat—he bit it almost into two halves. I think it's the same cat you and Jessica were looking for that time."

Reby still didn't look her way. "Stop bugging me with your damn hallucinations, you pillhead."

"But, Reby . . ."

Now Reby did look up, her face dark and unsmiling. "Listen, beyotch, I'm composing my weekly sex blog, and you're interrupting my flow of sensual words. Please go away." She winced in disgust. "Damn medusa-cop eating a cat. Next thing you'll be seeing damn giant earthworms eating the tires off my damn BMW."

Lucy shrugged and left. She returned to her room and lit another joint.

Yeah, maybe I did imagine it all, she reasoned as she settled back into bed. *Who the hell knows what sort of shit Massachusetts dealers are mixing with pot nowadays.*

To calm herself, she grabbed a few more pills. She thought the white ones would do the trick and calm her down before Jessica got back from the doctor's.

CHAPTER 10

Jessica

The Raynham Outlook Center was situated at the corner of Broadway and Lincoln Avenue. It was a large complex of white buildings. Ultramodern gloss and glass.

Jessica stated her appointment at the front gate and a black security guard directed her toward one of the rear parking lots. Her mind brooding, she drove alongside the gleaming wall of an all-glass tower that seemed transplanted from the pages of a futurist magazine.

Now that she was out in the town, Jessica was properly worried. She no longer felt that weird calm she had back at the cottage.

The interior of the Outlook Center was sparsely furnished and as clean as a nun's mind. Cream walls with the occasional painting; a black-and-silver checkered floor; a long reception desk with a seemingly airbrushed receptionist; gray doors and long corridors; the subliminal hum of expensive air conditioning. It looked like Jessica expected it to.

What she'd not expected, however, was for it to be so empty of people. When she arrived, Jessica found she was the only person there.

She mentioned her surprise at this to the receptionist, a tall blonde who introduced herself as McKenzie.

McKenzie nodded. "Yes, it does seem surprising, but these are Dr. Whitfield's personal offices, where he attends to special patients." (She emphasized the word 'special.') "Had you been directed to the other side of our complex you'd see how busy we really are."

"You're not government-funded?" Jessica asked as McKenzie led the way to Dr. Whitfield's office.

"No, we're privately financed. You might have heard that we also provide holistic, alternative cures." She laughed and Jessica warmed to her. "We're too risky to assign the taxpayer's hard earned income to fund—too many chances of a messy lawsuit that would harm some politician's career."

Jessica nodded. They paused outside a gray door before a small brass plaque that read: *F. Whitfield, M.D.*

McKenzie knocked on the door. "You know," she said coolly, "were it not that you're not sure what's responsible for them changing color like this, your blue nails look absolutely fabulous."

So as to quickly make her point in the doctor's office, Jessica was wearing sandals, meaning her toenails were on display too. She grimaced at the receptionist's comment, then replied in a flat voice, "You're the second person today to say that. It almost makes me feel guilty to want them back to normal."

"Oh, I don't mean any offence by saying so. They just do look pretty. Really hot, you know."

A voice sounded from inside the room.

"That's the doctor," McKenzie said. "Please go in. See you later."

Jessica nodded and pushed the door open.

***

Dr. Frank Whitfield was a large man in his mid-fifties. He had a long face, thick brown hair that was balding on top, and a large nose that he scratched meditatively from time to time. He had brown eyes and bushy eyebrows. He wore a pin-striped gray suit over a rose-colored shirt and dark tie, and an expensive gold wristwatch.

Dr. Whitfield stood to welcome Jessica warmly. He sat her in the chair across from him. He listened without interruption while she explained how her nails had suddenly turned blue. He nodded understandingly while she told him about her bouts of nausea and the accompanying splitting headache she'd felt the first time it had happened to her.

When she'd finished speaking, he smiled.

"Fortunately," he said, "there isn't too much wrong with you."

Jessica gaped at him. "You're joking, right?" She lifted her hands, held them with their backs facing him. "Doc, my nails . . . ?"

He laughed. "Oh, what I mean is, there isn't anything wrong with you that we can't fix."

They can fix it, Jessica thought with relief. *They can fix it.* "Will you need to carry out some tests on me?" she asked nervously.

"No, no, no," Dr. Whitfield said. "I already know what's wrong with you."

"Huh? You've seen this before?"

He nodded, then pushed a green folder across the desk at her. "See for yourself."

Jessica opened up the folder. It contained two glossy printed sheets: 'Before' and 'After' pictures of hands. All the 'Before' images had blue fingernails. The 'After' pictures were all normal.

"Why, they're exactly like mine!" Jessica exclaimed in surprise. "I mean, the blue ones are."

"You've merely got Bobbet's allergy," Dr. Whitfield explained as she returned the folder to him. "It's rare, but a common enough affliction that we've a cure for it. A simple course of pills will have you back to normal in no time at all." He smiled grimly. "You're very fortunate, Ms. Schreiber, that my friend Dr. Lopez referred you to me—to us here at Raynham Outlook. Elsewhere, you'd have found yourself subjected to a barrage of tests by confused physicians."

"But what caused it?" Jessica asked. "How in the world did I get it?"

Dr. Whitfield replied her while writing out her prescription. "We're not entirely sure what causes Bobbet's allergy. Like I said, it's very rare, one of those conditions you never realize exists on the planet until you catch it." He leaned forward, smiling, and handed Jessica the prescription. "Here. Hand this to Miss Clark at reception. She'll get it filled for you."

Jessica assumed 'Miss Clark' meant McKenzie. "Thanks, doctor. But what about the headaches and vomiting?"

"They're also part of Bobbet's. I've prescribed you something for the nausea also."

Jessica remembered then. "Are my nightmares also part of Bobbet's syndrome?"

On her asking this, Dr. Whitfield's eyebrows squeezed together and deep furrows appeared in his forehead. His calm demeanor instantly vanished. He looked agitated.

"What nightmares?" he asked in a voice that sounded like he had a bad case of asthma.

Oh shit! Jessica thought. *Just look at how alarmed he is. Or is the damn diagnosis wrong?*

Dr. Whitfield seemed to compose himself. "What nightmares?" he asked in a more stable voice.

Jessica still thought he was faking his calmness. For one thing, he'd begun relentlessly scratching his large nose. She told him about her dream, and then remembering, told him also about the weird hallucination she'd had on turning her car off Red Oak Crescent half an hour ago.

"So, doc, I'm really worried," she concluded. "For that split second it really looked like . . . I mean, I was absolutely convinced that I was staring down the road to Hell. It was so damn real!"

Dr. Whitfield heaved a loud sigh. Next, to Jessica's surprise, he pulled a roseate handkerchief from his breast pocket and dabbed sweat from his brow.

"Are you okay, doctor?" Jessica asked anxiously, unsure what the matter was with him.

"Please excuse me," Dr. Whitfield apologized with a smile. "Your mention of nightmares threw me off."

"I noticed that, doc. But why?"

"For a moment there," he said, confirming her suspicions, "I thought I'd misdiagnosed you and given you the wrong pills. There's a type of Bobbet's allergy for which one of these medicines I wrote down could prove dangerous, even fatal. But we're still good."

He pointed to the prescription she was holding, then crooked his index finger, indicating that she give it back to him.

She did so and he penned another line of medication on it, afterwards explaining: "I've added another sedative for you—take one each night before going to bed. You can also take one of them if you feel pressurized during the day; but never more than three a day under any circumstances. The Bobbet's—all the blueness and vomiting—should clear up in three days at most. The nightmares may last a day or two longer. The hallucinations you mentioned are likely the result of the mental exhaustion you're currently recovering from."

At this point Jessica had the strong feeling that Dr. Whitfield was hiding something from her. (He'd begun scratching his nose again, and was still forming beads of sweat on his forehead.) Yes, she had been mentally exhausted before coming to Raynham, but no, she'd not had any similar hallucinations in Boston, nor had she in the week since arriving here. But then, her nails hadn't turned blue back in Boston either.

"But . . ." she began protesting, then ran out of words to say. The confused look was back in the doctor's brown eyes again.

"But . . ." he continued as if finishing her train of thought for her, "I *might* be wrong, and we may be dealing here with a mutation of Bobbet's virus." He smiled (she was certain the smile was forced). "To be on the safe side, I'll need you to leave us a urine sample. I'll call Miss Clark, she'll take care of that for you. The lab results will determine our next course of action." He smiled again (this smile also seemed forced) and handed the finalized prescription back to Jessica. "For the moment, however, we'll continue with this treatment. I'll give you another appointment for four days from now, by which time the medication should have shown results."

She nodded.

"But," the doctor added, "please call me if you get worse instead of better. I'll arrange for you to come in immediately. And, Ms. Schreiber, try not to worry. I do think we'll be able to end this without you needing to visit a psychiatrist."

Jessica now forced a smile of her own. He'd just stated her biggest worry: that she might be descending into mania, and once thus diagnosed, would be *unemployable*—the most horrible fate in the world.

Still smiling, Dr. Whitfield rose to shake hands with her. Jessica left his office and walked back to see McKenzie Clark. She couldn't immediately shake off her fear that she might be going nuts. The benign cream corridors leading to the lobby unpleasantly reminded her of the walls of a padded cell.

***

When Jessica got back from providing her urine sample, a young couple were just leaving the front desk to exit the building. She watched them push open the glass double door and step out into the sunshine. Something about the pair bothered her; she wasn't certain what.

"So, here you are." McKenzie handed Jessica her medicine. "Oh, and there's one more thing: Dr. Whitfield said not to charge you this time. You'll only get a bill from us if the lab analysis of your urine indicates you need more treatment." She shrugged in a non-committal way. "That might cost a lot."

Jessica nodded. "Thanks. I'll thank Dr. Whitfield personally the next time I'm here."

"You look bothered," McKenzie said. "But really, you shouldn't be. I already knew we could cure you when I commented on how fab your nails looked. We've had three similar cases already this year, each of them a successful cure."

"It's not that," Jessica said. She felt uncertain how much she could and should confide in the blonde receptionist. "It's just that Dr. Whitfield seemed very bothered about something, which he wouldn't say."

McKenzie smiled coolly. "Oh, the doctor is always like that. He worries too much about everyone's health. Everyone except himself, that is. He was most likely scared he'd misdiagnosed your condition, which"—she lowered her voice to a whisper, and pointed at Jessica's hands—"is silly if you ask me. What you've got is so glaringly obvious."

"I guess you're right," Jessica agreed. "I'll be leaving now." McKenzie was most likely correct: she only found Dr. Whitfield's behavior odd because she was meeting him for the first time.

However, she'd just realized that this environment—this ultramodern ultra-clean building with its atmosphere of cold digital efficiency—was depressing her. It felt more to Jessica like an office than a hospital, which made her feel lazy. This was a place of work, and she . . . she . . . wasn't working. She was slacking—she was being inefficient and unproductive.

"Hey—are you okay?"

She broke out of her nervy reverie to see McKenzie peering concernedly at her. The blonde had pretty hazel eyes.

"Huh?" she asked.

"You look distracted," McKenzie said. "Don't you feel well? Do you need to sit down? Can I get you a glass of water?"

Jessica tucked her plastic envelopes of pills away into her handbag. "No, no, I'm fine," she replied. Inside she felt weak and oppressed, like her rights had been stripped from her. Just looking at McKenzie upset her. The receptionist was young (in her mid-to-late-twenties), pretty (though her nose and chin were both rather pointy so she looked like a snotty socialite—inbred old money—fallen on hard times), and well groomed (white long-sleeved blouse with slightly ruffled neckline over gray skirt, dark pantyhose, gray shoes). Above all, McKenzie Clark reeked efficiency. She stank of being good at her job. That was what Jessica suddenly found so disturbing and distracting about this woman who was still staring at her with a look of great concern on her face. *She's busy, busy working. She's doing something to advance herself, working to get ahead in life, certain to soon get a raise . . . while me, I'm just . . . I'm just . . .* She felt like crying. Indeed, the hot tears began forming in her eyes. *Oh, God, why me? It's just so goddam unfair . . . !*

McKenzie began shaking Jessica's shoulder. "Ms. Schreiber, are you okay? Ms. Schreiber, answer me please."

Jessica snapped out of it, and got a grip on herself. *God help me!* she thought in horror, realizing what had just happened. *I'm freaking losing it.*

"I'm sorry, so sorry," she told McKenzie. Then she turned and dashed out of the clinic. She could feel McKenzie Clark staring after her in confusion.

***

Out in the parking lot, Jessica felt the weight on her slowly lift. She crossed to her car. She now felt embarrassed. *Oh my gosh! I was almost having a nervous meltdown in there! Am I that addicted to work? Like a junkie craving a fix? I see a neat office and go all gaga?* For the first time, Jessica began thinking she might have gone overboard in her dedication to service. *Yes, working is a good thing, but there's such a thing as too much of a good thing; and too much of a good thing is a bad thing.*

She felt through her handbag for her car keys. She now had a fresh worry: McKenzie reporting her odd behavior in the clinic's lobby to Dr. Whitfield. Jessica conceded it was most likely the receptionist would tell, if only because of her concern over Jessica's state of mental health. And Dr. Whitfield would most certainly conclude that she'd been having another of those hallucinations that had so alarmed him.

Jessica sighed, slipped her car key in its slot, and turned it.

"Good morning, sister, can you spare us a few minutes of your time?" a pleasant male voice said behind her.

"We'd like to discuss Alternity with you," an equally pleasant female voice added.

They were behind her. Two of them. Jessica could see them reflected in the glass of the car door. *Aw no, not religious fundamentalists. Not now.*

She turned to ask the Jesus Freaks to please let her be. She was in too much of a hurry this morning to waste her precious time arguing the relative merits and demerits of gods. Then she stopped: it was the young couple she'd seen leaving McKenzie's desk on her return from the sample lab.

The girl was a redhead, the boy a blonde. Both were in their late teens/early twenties. Both had warm, friendly faces, despite which she found them both creepy. Instinctively, she found herself glancing left, towards the security post at the front gate, in case they assaulted her. The black security guard was looking away from her, waving at a car just coming into the complex.

She looked back at the young pair. She felt vulnerable alone here with them. Their guileless eyes seemed to hide horrible secrets, their smiling lips seemed about to utter blasphemies. Both kids looked very clean, almost sterile in fact. They had short hair. The girl wore pale pink lipstick, and light blue shading on her upper eyelids. She had on little round blue earrings.

Blue. That was really what had frozen Jessica's retort, had prevented her from giving the Christian couple a brusque brush-off. Blue. The pair both had on light-blue suits (in the girl's case a skirt suit) which looked distressingly familiar. Then it hit Jessica: the couple's clothes were the exact same color as her fingernails. Sky-blue. But how . . . ?

Her bemusement continued. They made her uneasy by not doing anything, but she found herself unable to depart. As if they'd hypnotized her with their creepy smiles. Her forming frown evened out into a thin nervous line of quivering lips that expressed neither welcome nor rejection.

"I can only spare you a minute or two," she said as bravely as she could. She nodded towards the clinic door. "I'm not really feeling good today. I need to drive home and get some rest. Doctor's orders."

"Ice or cynic," the girl said, out of the blue.

"A cynical sky," the boy added.

"Huh?" Jessica asked.

The young couple both smiled again. Their smiles made Jessica uneasy. They seemed condescending in a way, as though the pair felt

63

they were party to some special knowledge she didn't have. She began thinking she'd made a grave mistake by granting them audience.

"What we both said is a chant to bless you with positive energy," the boy explained.

"It's meant to bring you healing," the girl added.

Jessica nodded. She didn't want to be rude to the pair, but she wanted to be gone. "So, what did you want to talk to me about?"

The redhead girl smiled. "Oh, we're from the Realms of Consciousness Temple. It's over on South Street East. We'd like to invite you to attend one of our services."

"I don't go to church," Jessica replied. "I like Jesus, but you his followers just confuse me. At times you seem to preach as much hatred as love. So, I'm sorry but I really must turn you down."

The blond boy in the sky-blue suit looked about to say something. She waited to hear what he would say. She pumped herself up for the argument, readied her throat muscles for the verbal wrestling match. After her recent bouts of anxiety, she suddenly felt better. She felt as calm as she had this morning, like her worries didn't matter. It was the blue, she knew, this delicious sky-blue. The young couple's clothes were eerily mesmerizing.

"It's fine if you don't go to church, sister," the boy said. "We don't recommend it either. Church drains you of yourself."

"Huh?" Jessica asked.

"We're not a church," the girl said. "We accept people of all faiths. Or lack of faith."

"Interdenominational?" Jessica queried.

"No. The Realms of Consciousness order is a humanist organization founded to advance the human spirit."

The girl looked at the boy. He nodded and they both said together, "To bring out the God in all of us. We offer more than Christianity or Islam or any other system of belief does. We don't seek to connect you to God, but to connect you to the unknown God that you are and can and should be."

After reciting this obviously rehearsed litany, the pair smiled their creepy smiles again.

Jessica now felt like the pair were crowding in on her, even though the boy had actually stepped back while speaking. Their blue suits gave her the disorienting impression that she was up in the air floating. She felt panicked. She wondered how she'd misread them. These two weren't from a church, but from some kind of kooky New Age cult. They were clearly dangerous.

The boy read her confusion and fear. He reached into a pocket and produced a card. It was white, with red lettering. He handed the card to Jessica. Weirdly, his smile as he did so didn't seem forced. (In retrospect, even some of McKenzie's empathy now seemed artificial.)

"Well, like you said, sister," the boy said, "you're not feeling too good at the moment, so we shan't press you. But maybe you'll change your mind. Folks sometimes do—they tire of believing in Jesus or not believing in him, and then . . . If you do too, please don't hesitate to attend one of our temple services. The temple address is on the card. In addition to the Sunday morning meeting, we've evening services every day; except on Wednesdays and Saturdays because of the music rehearsals."

Jessica took the card. "I can't promise anything. I really don't—"

"Wow, I just *love* your manicure!" the girl interrupted, gaping open-mouthed at Jessica's hand as it gripped the card. "It's so pretty." The girl's own nails were done in the same sedate pink as her lips.

"It's a disease," Jessica replied nonchalantly. "If you like I can ask how you can catch it."

The girl's face turned a bit sour, then she smiled. And again, this was a *genuine* smile, creepy with its nutty beliefs, but honest and open. The girl had somehow dispersed with her forming anger.

Jessica didn't get that. *I just was nasty to you and you shrugged it off?*

"So long, sister," the blond boy in the blue suit said. "We sure hope you make it to a temple service sometime."

"Goodbye," Jessica replied. Though scared of them, she felt disappointed that they were leaving her.

"Ice or cynic," the redhead girl said once again in a flash of pink tongue and even white teeth.

"A cynical sky," the boy finished.

Jessica nodded at the strange statement. "Yeah, cynics to you too."

They double-grinned at her comment, then turned and left. She nervously stared at the pair as they walked (stalked?) over to accost a just-arrived elderly couple parked a few cars away from her.

Jessica got into her car. For half a minute she sat quietly behind the wheel of the Nissan calming herself, staring at the white and red card the boy and girl had given her:

The Realms of Consciousness Temple.
No. 380, S Street E, Raynham, MA.
Founder/Host: Brother Crowley.
Special music by TSM.

There were two contact phone numbers on the front of the card. She turned it over. Printed on its rear was a list of times of services. And then, below that list of meeting times, right at the bottom of the card, Jessica noticed a cryptic line of text:

I saw Sinis, a Sinis was I

With a start, Jessica realized that this was what the young pair had been quoting to her, in two parts: 'I saw Sinis, a Sinis was I,' not 'Ice or cynic, a cynical sky.' Solving that, however, only created a fresh riddle for her to ponder on. I saw Sinis, a Sinis was I? What the heck did that mean?

She gazed right, through her front passenger window, over to where the blonde boy and redhead girl in blue were engaging the old couple in an animated talk. There was visibly a lot of emotion involved in their discussion. Jessica, however, couldn't tell if the older pair were opponents or allies of the religious affiliation being proselytized by the younger one.

Her eyes fell again to the white card. I saw Sinis, a Sinis was I? The kids had said it was a chant to bless her with positive energy and bring her healing.

Oh, she didn't know about that. To Jessica's mind, this Realms of Consciousness order had all the signs of being a dangerous cult. Jim Jones and David Koresh all over again. She made up her mind on the spot to keep as far away as possible from their temple. And next time she met any of their disciples, she wasn't going to grant them audience. She'd just ignore them.

Jessica looked right, out of the window again. She imagined that a few cars away, she saw two young wolves in blue suits lying to two old sheep ready for butchering. Or to two old cows just ripe for a good financial milking. The thought chilled her. She looked away again, put her car in 'Drive' and left the Raynham Outlook Clinic, heading for home. She was glad to see the last of the preaching pair.

On the way she considered throwing the 'Realms of Consciousness' card out of her car window, but instead decided to hold on to it. She was suddenly entranced by the riddle it posed. That 'I saw Sinis, a Sinis was I' line might prove something to occupy her mind with if she ever found herself bored. She wondered what on earth its real meaning was, if it wasn't just something the organization's leader—Brother Crowley—had thought up to enrich himself.

CHAPTER 11

Colleen & Larry

Colleen Townsend reversed the white Chevrolet SUV out of the driveway and straightened it out on the blacktop. For a moment, frozen like a statue behind the black leather-bound steering wheel, she stared wistfully inward at her house. Larry was in there somewhere, getting ready to break her heart again.

Her lips puckered up in unease. She felt about to cry. Her fat hands squeezed the wheel. Larry might even sleep with that horrible woman *today*, in their house, in their bed. In her bed. Giving the slut what was rightfully hers.

Colleen finally accepted that she was merely torturing herself. Besides, it was already 1 p.m. She was late for her appointment at the Luxury Nails and Spa salon on upper Broadway.

Colleen was almost neurotic about the state of her nails. To her, manicures and pedicures were one of the few areas of her general appearance which she had complete control over. She might be overweight, but her hands and feet could still look great.

And at the moment her hands didn't. They were a mess. That was completely unacceptable.

After a last pissed-off look back at the house, Colleen drove off.

***

From the upstairs bedroom, Larry watched the white SUV vanish from sight. Once it was gone, he heaved a sigh of relief. Colleen had been behaving so odd all morning that he'd expected her to cancel her nail appointment.

Colleen had somehow broken two fingernails while loading the dishwasher after breakfast. How she'd managed? Larry didn't know, he figured accidents did happen.

He'd however found the incident disturbing. For two reasons:

Firstly, because his wife was always incredibly careful where her nails were concerned; breaking one was almost like losing a child. (Larry appreciated Colleen's long nails; he just wished she'd stop stabbing him in the back with them each time they made love. He had enough of a guilty conscience over his treatment of her to suspect that at a subconscious level Colleen was mentally stabbing him to death by drawing blood from his body during her passion.)

The second, and more bothering thing, was that he'd found Colleen standing in a trance beside the dishwasher. She'd been holding a plate but her eyes were glazed. She'd been staring at the wall and muttering about 'The Big Blue.'

"Colleen," he'd called. "Colleen, are you okay?"

She'd not replied, so he'd walked over and touched her arm.

She'd come to herself then, all abrupt-like, giving him a chilling 'lost and miserable' look. Then she'd seemed to realize who he was and where she was, and resumed her task of loading the dishwasher. She'd not even realized that her nails were broken till later. Ordinarily, she'd have instantly thrown a fit.

Larry had been confused. He'd left the kitchen to think. He'd gone upstairs to his study and sat to ponder.

Larry had picked that particular back room to work in because it looked out over the forest at the rear of the house. The house stood on a rise, with the land dropping away towards the north, and at the end of the greenery he could see a large pond. Normally the view relaxed him, but this morning the wide expanse of blue-gray water mirroring the overhead clouds had done nothing for his state of mind. He'd sat in his chair, stared at his laptop screen, and tried to make sense of things.

She was muttering about 'The Big Blue.' Now what the damn hell was that about?

For certain, Larry didn't know. *The Big Blue*. The phrase did, however, remind Larry of his own morning vision of that massive archway made of meat with the sky-blue space beyond, and the terrible monster coming at him from it with a half-eaten human leg in one of its mouths. Suddenly, even though he'd successfully downplayed it all through breakfast, the vision had seemed a big deal again. He'd shuddered. *How the hell did I ever imagine that crap? And no, it's nothing to do with me being creative—it ain't that for sure. I'm writing book about friggin' Wall Street, not some horror movie script!*

He'd stared glumly at his laptop, at the screen loaded with a blank Word document. *I'd better get to the day's work.*

But he hadn't. For some reason, he hadn't been getting any work done of late. He'd not told Colleen about this, of course. She'd only worry, and her honest concern would then pressurize him to get something written, which would only make his writer's block worse.

He had no idea what the problem with him was. He had all his research done (and Wikipedia for what he hadn't). Most of what his book required now was for him to collate and arrange his findings in a way that would entertain and amuse the reader. And that hadn't proved hard at all. Larry had been getting the book together at the rate of about a chapter a week. He was halfway through it now (Chapter 9) and expected to finish his first draft in another two months. Then he'd do a rewrite or two before sending it to the editor (Random House were publishing it). The book had been coming along just fine until . . . until three or four days ago—he put his dry spell as beginning on Saturday, or was it Friday?—when, just like that, the creative well had suddenly run dry. Since then, he'd sit staring at the laptop screen for hours and . . . nothing. Nothing except a weird floating feeling that occasionally came over him for a few seconds, a few seconds during which his study would take on a blue hue. Blue like the desktop background of his laptop, but transparent, like he was only imagining it was there.

To Larry's surprise, he apparently no longer had any desire to write his book about Wall Street's greatest scandals.

Earlier, hearing Colleen having her bath, he'd left the laptop to go talk to her. While she'd dressed for her trip to town, he'd asked her what she'd meant by 'The Big Blue.' Colleen hadn't known what he was talking about. (She'd by now noticed her damaged manicure and was growing frantic about that.) Larry hadn't pressed her. He'd recalled her trance state and figured she'd honestly forgotten what she'd said.

But he couldn't forget how she'd looked—completely lost. And there was more. There had been something really nasty in Colleen's gaze. Larry had seen that look on TV before . . . in the mug shot of serial killer Aileen Wuoronos. Yes, her stare had seemed demonic to him. And now that he dared admit it, it had frightened the bejesus out of him at the time.

***

Now that his wife had left the house though, Larry stopped worrying. If he wasn't going to work, at least he could play. And fortuitously, today had lined up a new playmate for him. And dammit, if Miss Reby Butterfield couldn't have stepped right out of an 80's Playboy magazine.

There was one problem, however. The jogging beauty with the hot body was supposed to call him, not the other way around. He'd not taken his phone downstairs with him in the morning, so he'd not stored her number. Instead, he'd given her his business card and asked her to call 'sometime after noon.'

Well it was 'after noon' now. Larry hoped she'd call. She'd had nice breasts and a firm, tight ass (joggers always did, didn't they?) that he wanted to cup in his palms and squeeze hard like those buttocks were stress balls.

Then his phone rang. Larry dashed over to the bed and picked it up. *It's her! It's Reby!*

He clamped the phone to his ear and breathlessly listened to her on the other end asking him if he was free to chat 'up close and personal' at the moment:

"There's so much I'd *love* for us to talk about if you're able to meet up," she said in that sweet husky voice that instantly gave him a hard-on.

"Oh yes I am," Larry agreed, his mouth suddenly dry. "I'm as free as a damn honeybee, baby."

"Okay, I'll see you soon. Expect me at your back door."

She hung up.

Larry dropped his phone on the bed again. He licked his lips and rubbed his palms together with glee. *Yes, yes, she's coming over. Ha ha!*

Larry forgot all about Colleen and their strange domestic occurrences for the moment. Colleen—normally so prominent in his thoughts—receded away hastily, vanishing like a shoreline did behind an ocean-bound liner. He dashed into his bathroom for a quick shower. He used a lot of soap. One didn't stink up a first date. Not with a woman this smoking hot.

CHAPTER 12

Reby

Reby Butterfield walked with a happy spring in her step through the woods separating No. 2 and No. 4 Red Oak Crescent. The smell of flowers filled her nostrils. The sun was right overhead. As she walked, the noise of a car alerted her to Jessica's return from town. She called and waved, but Jessica didn't hear her. Jessica had seemed really preoccupied this morning anyhow.

That woman really needs to learn how to chill out, Reby thought. From what Lucy had told her, Jessica worked as if God was going to tally up everyone's office hours on Judgment Day and use that as His criteria to determine if you deserved eternal residence in Heaven or Hell.

She laughed. *Maybe Jessica should start doing drugs with Lucy. That'll mellow her down for certain.*

Reby made her way through a tall patch of unmown grass, running her fingers over the tops of the highest stalks. She could see the Townsend's house fifty yards ahead. She'd told Larry she'd visit by the back door. She wondered if he'd caught the anal metaphor in her parting remark on the phone.

She laughed some more. The warmth of the sun mirrored the warmth in her crotch.

***

If work was Jessica Schreiber's addiction, and drugs were Lucy Polk's, sex was what Rebecca Butterfield found it impossible to go without.

Reby had two main interests in life: men, and sleeping with them. She simply adored male bodies. She couldn't get enough of them—of their size, of their shape and hairiness, of their masculine smells.

She considered herself a sexual predator, but in a positive sense: she fed on the male of the species, taking what they gave her, and feeding them intense pleasure in return.

Reby was thirty years old. She was from Billings, Montana. Her parents were RICH—her father owned a chain of supermarkets extending all the way down the west coast, and the money just kept pouring in.

There had been nothing remarkable whatsoever about Reby's childhood: she'd just done all the usual things rich young girls did.

Once out of high school, she'd attended Crump College in Bozeman, a place designed specifically to provided degrees to the sons and daughters of the extremely rich. There, she'd studied Interior Decoration, a favorite Rich Girl course, most Rich Girl's of Reby's level of wealth having no other future employment than buying furniture and fittings for their three-story mansions and making lots of children to sit on the furniture. (When you had as much dough as, for instance, the Butterfields did, you never thought of work/career opportunities. What was important after school was to find an even richer husband than yourself and continue the dynasty.) Other favorite Rich Girl courses? English (so one understood what the occasional long word in the bestseller novels meant), Cosmetology (one needed to look one's best at all times), and Journalism (so you could meet—and date—rock stars and A-list movie actors.)

At Crump, Reby Butterfield had pledged the Kappa Kappa Gamma sorority, the Decadent Rich Girl sorority. While she'd been there, fully half of her sorority sisters had lamented the fact that their college didn't offer courses in Husband Management and BDSM. They'd even tried to start a Divorce and Alimony Studies department, but their wealthy fathers and mothers had refused to fund the required grant.

So, maintaining Rich Girl standards and aspirations was Reby's entire college experience.

Once unleashed on the world after graduation, however, young Rebecca Butterfield declared that her intention in life was to, "Have as many men as I can, for as long as I can."

Her parents couldn't be bothered what she did with herself. Her father was too busy making money and her mother was trying to become Mayor of their city.

The one provision that had been explained very clearly to Reby by her mother when she'd embarked on her stated path of hedonism, was: "Don't you dare create any scandals, darling, or we'll cut your allowance off."

Reby promised to be a good 'bad' girl. She understood what momma meant. The wealthy throve on bad behavior; it was *exposure* of their bad behavior that was taboo.

(Cutting off her funds would be like cutting off her head. Or worse. Reby had an allowance of $30,000 a month. This in addition to an expense account for stuff like all the gas her car used and her hotel bills or apartment rent [whichever she preferred]. She also got a new sports car every two years. In her own amused words: "I work for my dad—as the Invisible Daughter Executive. My job is staying out of trouble.")

Reby had kept to her word too. To be as far away from home as possible, she'd moved east to Boston.

She knew she wouldn't be missed. She had an identical twin sister, Leah, and their parents *still* got them both mixed up. (Her mother Hannah was Jewish, her father Kevin Butterfield one of those mongrel associations which had resulted from the Pocahontas-style mingling of English and Native American blood, further diluted by a large helping of German and Spanish ancestry.)

Leah Butterfield had married extremely well, hooking Carl Kingston of the Kingston clan, major shareholders in the Stillwater Mining Company. Leah was busy making grandchildren by the wombful and momma was delighted.

So all Rebecca Butterfield did as her life's work was have bedroom fun with as many men as she could.

Oddly, for one so obsessed with the male sex, Reby had been a slow starter. She'd not lost her virginity till she was nineteen. However, once she'd discovered the pleasures of the body, she'd plunged into them with abandon.

She had her limits, of course. And her sexual idiosyncrasies. For one thing, she was strictly monogamous, as in she only dated/fucked one man at a time. She'd had one threesome (with two men), hated it, and sworn off them for life.

Similarly, she didn't fuck girls. Reby had had exactly two lesbian experiences. Both with high school friends. She'd found both experiences shallow. Yes, an orgasm was an orgasm, but she could get those from playing with herself. She simply found no satisfaction in another woman's body.

What Reby Butterfield craved in sex was a *male* body pressed against hers and thrusting into hers. The ageless, winless war of Testosterone versus Estrogen. It was a big thrill to Reby each time she spread her legs and accepted a throbbing piece of male meat into her nether mouth.

There was something else that Reby got out of sex with men, something she'd never told anyone: intense ego gratification.

This was another reason lesbianism hadn't worked for her. Two women in bed considered themselves as equals. They knew each other as the same; there could be no other interpretation of their roles. Between a man and a woman, however, the dynamic was entirely different. Most men considered themselves superior to women. It was the erection of course, that prong that stood erect and boasted to the woman, "Ha ha—you don't have one of these!" It didn't matter the size of it—what counted was its arrogant prominence in the man's crotch. Even the most prominent of clitorises was no competition. But of course, the penile arrogance never lasted. It was just macho bluster. The cock entered the cunt and came. After which, the same man who'd been a lion suddenly became a lamb, tamed by the lady's loins. Reby got intense pleasure from taming men this way. She got an immense kick on feeling them go all weak on her body, like she'd just killed them.

This guy, Larry, whom she'd just met this morning? He was okay. So far for her, it had been slim pickings since she'd been here in Raynham. Just that one gym fuck. She needed a stable guy, a 'booty call' as it were. She'd sized Larry Townsend up on their first meeting, noted how his eyes appraised her breasts, and decided he'd do. His living next door was great; his wife wasn't. But everything could be worked out. In a way, for a woman of Reby's occupation (she could technically be called a professional bimbo) married men were better partners than single ones. The ones she chose just wanted some quick no-frills fun. With their wives (and kids and careers) lurking in the background, they understood that it was over once she said it was. They didn't stalk, either.

So, with Larry now on sex-call a mere five minutes walk away, Reby felt she was set here in Raynham.

How she'd gotten to Raynham? Reby had first met Lucy three years ago, when she'd been trying to get Lucy's brother Robert into bed. Robert had seemed strangely uninterested in her. Reby couldn't understand that. She knew she was extra-hot. She kept in shape for a reason (for the men, duh!?), and so for a man to not be entranced by her super sexy body was insulting to her.

Lucy finally took the pissed-off Reby aside, offered her a drag of her joint, and explained to her that her older brother was 'as queer as an eighty-dollar bill.'

Reby and Lucy had remained friends since then. And then, circumstances had placed Reby in Springfield just when Lucy had had her 'summer vacation idea.' Once Lucy found the cottage in Raynham, Reby had decided to come along too for some fun.

***

Reby stepped on a dry branch and it snapped. Twenty or so yards ahead the rear eaves of the Townsend's place peeked through a wall of elm leaves.

She smiled and licked her lips. The sun warmed her face. Her anticipation of sex burnt her loins. She was wet down there. She was certain to orgasm immediately he penetrated her.

She trampled another dry branch. It snapped like a gunshot. She looked left, then right. Behind her, she thought she heard Jessica parking then leaving her car. Then . . .

Then, just like that, Reby's vision went all blue and blurry. For a moment, she felt as if the sky had fallen to the ground around her, and that it was seeping away into the forest floor. Her head spun. Dizzy and with the grass out of focus, she stretched out a hand for the nearest tree trunk to steady herself.

She stood leaning against the tree for five or six seconds, not quite herself—uncertain of who or where she was—then the world normalized again. The sky was overhead once more, not everywhere around her. The blue cleared from her vision and she felt alright enough to straighten up. She pulled her hand back to herself, then recoiled from it in shock. In that state of shock she staggered backwards till another tree trunk stopped her reverse motion.

What . . . ? Her entire right arm now seemed to be composed of writhing snakes. The serpents were bruise-purple in color and plaited together like a rope, the loose ends of which formed her fingers. Fingers with hissing mouths and fangs dripping pale venom.

Reby was too confused to be scared. She gaped at her hand in disbelief. Then she blinked, and just like that, the odd hallucination was over. Her arm was just her arm again. She was herself, like the forest was itself, like the sky was itself.

However, a horrible smell lingered. It smelt like the body of a run-over dog was rotting somewhere nearby.

Then the decaying smell vanished too and all that tickled Reby's nostrils were the luscious smells of summer, the scents of leaves and flowers.

She had no idea what had just happened. She didn't know what to think. Instead of pondering on it all, she hurried the remaining few steps to Larry's back door.

***

Their greeting was brief. Then the fires of passion took over. Reby wanted something to take her mind off her weird experience on her way over; Larry was equally desperate to not think about his day so far. Their eyes conversed, in seconds establishing what their lips might need an hour to spell out clearly. There was also something in the air; something that ignited the simmering physical attraction between them into a blaze.

There was that awkward "Hi! Hi!" moment, and then Reby was in Larry's arms and they were kissing. After that, nature took its course. The back door was just off the way from the kitchen. Larry rushed her in there, hastily lifted her up onto the kitchen counter, and pulled off her shorts.

She wasn't wearing any panties. That was good—neither was he. He dropped his shorts and faced her, his stiffness telling her of his want for her in that physical way words could never express.

She was soaking wet, her lubrication shimmering on her thighs. That was good too. His violent erotic need of her had no time for the niceties of foreplay. He slid himself into her wetness. She grunted at the penetration, then threw her arms around his neck and locked her legs about his waist. Her mouth hungrily sought his and sucked his tongue and saliva.

She'd been right. She had her first orgasm almost immediately he entered her. And after that her climaxes continued in an almost unbroken sequence for the next five or so minutes while he thrust into her, grunting each time as if her vagina was a burden his penis was carrying up a hill.

Their bodies sang together, till finally he thrust as deep as he could into her and froze stiff. She trembled around him as he filled her. Then he sagged against her, gasping out God's name like he was praying.

She held him tight. She'd won again. Another lion tamed, another penis schooled in love's ultimate lesson. It had been as great as always. The orgasm was as important to her as the chase. What use was it being a slut if you didn't enjoy the payoff?

"Shit!" he said afterwards, looking sheepish. "I forgot to use a rubber."

"Don't worry," she comforted him, "I'll take a morning-after pill." Then she leaned close and kissed him coquettishly. "How was it for you? Did you enjoy it?"

He gasped. "Baby, you're so hot, I'm amazed you didn't burn my dick to ashes."

He lifted her down off the counter. Their legs weak, they walked the short distance into the living room. There they sank together onto the sofa and breathed together.

Then they fucked again. Twice more before his wife was due back.

CHAPTER 13

Jessica

She was in a wide and domed space, with shiny walls of roseate brick. She was seated in the midst of many people, neatly dressed people with serious faces, all sitting on padded pews and facing a man up ahead on a raised dais.

A man with a booming voice.

Ah, she understood it now: she was in worship service. Around her were the congregation. The man—tall and powerful like a football player and with a shaven head and black goatee—was the minister.

She somehow knew that she was in the Realms of Consciousness temple, and that the speaker on the pulpit was Brother Crowley.

Brother Crowley was talking loudly, but she couldn't hear what he was saying. Or rather, she could hear, but didn't understand. He wasn't speaking English, but some religious gobbledygook. It didn't sound like Latin either. He spoke, and the congregation chanted replies. They weren't speaking English either.

She tried to see beyond Brother Crowley and the people, but couldn't. She was aware of a mist, such as might form over the sea, blurring the edges of the temple building. This mist was a spectral blue, its color ripped from the center of a rainbow. In its presence, the previously stark rose walls had dimmed into purple haze.

She felt cold. She realized that the infilling blue haze was alive. It was a living creature, with its own thoughts and desires, and its own plans for the worshippers in this temple.

And . . . she gasped with understanding . . . its plans were EVIL. Absolutely EVIL.

Then she *smelt* the blue mist. It stank, stank more foully than a mix of excrement, rotting fish, and the maggot-tunneled contents of a mass grave. It smelt worse than a lake filled with half the sewer content of New York City. It smelt like boiled Death.

The evil smell felt solid in her nostrils, like a plug blocking them. She yielded to it—yielded to the Evil Mist—because it was supreme in here. It ruled over all.

Then her attention was caught by something else altogether:

Up on the dais, Brother Crowley was finally saying something she could understand. No, she didn't *understand* it, but it was familiar. She'd heard it somewhere before.

"I saw Sinis!" he yelled. "A Sinis was I!"

At once, the entire congregation around her began screaming the same: "I saw Sinis, a Sinis was I! I saw Sinis, a Sinis was I!!" The noise in the mist-obscured hall was loud, defiant, and celebratory. Above all, it was reverent.

Then Brother Crowley shouted, "And now, brothers and sisters, we must show ourselves as we really are, as we shall in future be, in Alternity!!"

He shed his jacket and shirt. Next, grabbing hold of his nipples like they were handles, he pulled his chest open.

She gasped. A mass of tentacles spilled out of Brother Crowley's muscular chest. Fat red tentacles, like giant eyeless pythons, flopped out of his body and waved in the air before him.

And so too, with the rest of the faithful. All of them—women, men, young and old—were shedding their clothes and then their skins, revealing the insides of their bodies to be full of big red tentacles.

She looked up. The Evil Mist had a face in it. A face formed of billows and spaces. A cold, approving face.

She looked down again, and discovered that she was naked. How her clothes had vanished and where they'd gone, she had no idea. She couldn't even remember clearly if she'd had any on when she'd arrived here.

And now her own skin was opening up down the middle. Painlessly, and with a delicious sensation like sexual ecstasy, the front of her body between her neck and crotch was separating as if unzipped, her breasts falling left and right as . . .

Like bloody guts spilled by gang violence, a pile of huge red tentacles uncurled from her torso. She laughed as they floated and waved in front of her, their roots tingling inside her. They were part of her and she was part of them and she was part of everyone here, and . . . and she was Evil as SIN. She was living evil.

She was an integral part of the reek of putrescence that filled the temple from end to end. She and the congregation were sewers packed with unending filth. They and she and the Evil Mist were one and the same.

She looked up at the platform. "I saw Sinis, a Sinis was I!" Brother Crowley was shouting. While shouting, he was peeling off his skin. Beneath his muscular human exterior, his entire body was formed of the red tentacles.

She looked down at herself. Her own white skin was also peeling away. Tentacles emerged from the spaces between her wet muscles like red saplings from bloodstained earth.

"I saw Sinis, a Sinis was I!" yelled the Realms of Consciousness faithful, while all the while their skins similarly dropped off, revealing the horrific writhing shapelessness beneath. Leathery wings also unfolded out of some of them. Others were covered with innumerable eyes, implanted like white gems around the bases of their tentacles. Others had mouths all over their bodies. The awful smell in the temple—the reek of death and decay and other unnamable, but much worse, things—increased till it seemed alive, the infernal heartbeat of the worshipping monsters.

She looked up. The face in the Evil Mist smiled. It smiled at her. It approved of her. She smiled back and began yelling too:

"I saw Sinis, a Sinis was I! I saw Sinis, a Sinis was I!" She screamed with not one, but a hundred voices. She had a hundred mouths between her hundred tentacles and all of them were desperate to proclaim her dedication to the cause of the Evil Mist.

The Evil Mist fell as smelly rain over the faithful monsters worshipping it.

The Evil Mist was delighted. It was ecstatic.

***

Jessica woke up and flicked on her bedside light. It was 3 a.m.

Shit, she thought, as the dream faded into something manageable. *What the fuck?*

Her heart was racing. At first her thoughts were disheveled, but she finally got sufficient of a hold on herself so as not to panic. Yes, this *was* the second time she'd seen herself full of tentacles, but now she had a good explanation as to why the nightmare had recurred. The "I saw Sinis" chant was the key: it helped her trace her dream's origin back to yesterday's encounter with that spooky young couple outside the clinic.

She exhaled in relief. *At least I'm not getting worse.*

She examined her nails. They didn't seem any better; were exactly as blue as before. But then again, they didn't look any worse either. Well, she was taking her medicine. *Hey, these pills had better do what they're supposed to*—she stifled a sudden yawn—*or else Dr. Whitfield will be hearing from me.*

She sank back down on the pillows and fell asleep again.

CHAPTER 14

Lucy

It was a warm night. Since falling asleep, Lucy had kept dreaming of weird stuff. In one of her dreams, she'd been smoking weed from a mountain-sized hookah. Then someone—it had looked like Jessica—had thrown a pack of condoms at the hookah, and it had shattered to bits and rained all the marijuana down on Lucy. Lucy had tried to push the marijuana off of herself and get up, but then she'd discovered that she too had become a marijuana leaf. And next thing, someone (again the person had looked like Jessica—a brunette executive talking prissily into a cellphone) had swept Lucy-marijuana up and rolled her up into a joint and was smoking her to relieve her work stress. So yes, it was Jessica.

Lucy had woken up from that dream and gone to pee.

Her next dream had been the really weird one. In this dream, she'd been in her bedroom, on her bed. The only way she knew she was dreaming was because the walls of the room were the walls of a blue cave and there were lots of dead people nailed to the walls of the cave. More dead people hung from the ceiling, dangling from nooses about their necks. Their necks were all stretched out like giraffe necks because their neck vertebrae had snapped. The corpses all smelt of death. A smelly wind blew through the room and the corpses swayed left and right to it.

But that was overhead. Down in her bed, Lucy heard a voice and opened her eyes. Yes, she was dreaming, but she was awake in the dream. A stoned kind of awake. Because she saw the same policeman who'd been eating the cat just that morning—the tentacle-haired one with the filed-to-sharp-points teeth—inside her bedroom.

This time the cop was eating a human hand. She watched him expertly use his teeth to strip the meat off the hand's fingers. He placed one finger at a time in his mouth, bit deep into the swollen skin just in front of the third knuckle, then slowly pulled the digit out between his teeth. Each finger came out as bare white bones, having left all its meat on his tongue.

The cop was holding a cellphone. Her cellphone. "Hey, that's mine!" she growled at him.

He turned and looked at her. "Lucy, you're frigging dreaming. It's both our phones. It'll be yours again when you wake up."

She wanted to protest, to warn him not to delete any of her text messages, but then she saw a big black creature walk into the cave. The creature looked like a huge skinless bear. It had no face and its skin was rotting. It stank like a volcanic eruption of boiling shit. In its hands the monster carried a laptop. Lucy recognized the laptop as hers. The tentacled cop accepted the laptop from the monster and replaced it on the table. He put her cellphone back down beside the laptop.

Lucy grinned. "Thanks," she said.

The black rotting and stinking bear-thing looked in her direction. Rather, since it had no face, it turned its head in her direction. It nodded at her. It had two sores where its eyes should have been, and another in place of its mouth.

"You're welcome," it replied her from somewhere in its body.

"You got any more meat?" the cop asked it.

"Yeah, sure." The monster ripped off a chunk of its right thigh and handed it to the policeman, who began eating the raw meat greedily.

Lucy smiled at the monster. It was such a nice, self-sacrificing monster; clear proof that looks weren't everything in life.

Then she felt herself floating upward. She levitated higher and higher till she was right at the top of the cave. Suddenly she was face-to-face with the dead people dangling from the roof of the massive chamber. She looked from one to the next. Their expressions were all the same: all blank-eyed, slack-mouthed, swollen-tongued; all with their necks broken by the drop that had strangled them; all already half rotted away. All stinking of death.

Lucy grinned at them. "Ha, ha, ya'll look so dead! You're all de-e-ed, de-e-ed, de-e-ed!" She kept grinning while a rope—it looked like a snake—slithered down from the ceiling and wound itself around her neck.

Lucy was still grinning as invisible hands hauled her up close to the ceiling of the cave. Lucy was grateful for the change. Up here the stink was way less. She lit a joint and took a deep drag of the pot, a good long hit. The rope around her neck didn't hurt at all.

Then the hands let go of the rope and Lucy fell. She plummeted past the dangling dead people, and fell and fell and fell and fell . . .

. . . And woke up again.

She lay in bed staring at the ceiling, which had a weird blue flicker to it. Then that vanished and the ceiling looked normal.

She looked down, at her bedroom door. Something seemed to lurk in the shadows there, something hulking and bear-shaped, but without a face . . .

Worried now, she squinted. The shadow thing seemed to be shrinking. As she watched it, it got smaller and smaller like it was being vacuumed up.

Then it was all gone and her bedroom door looked ordinary again.

Lucy relaxed. She was used to hallucinations. She'd long ago accepted them as a fact of life. Once you'd been getting stoned awhile, you understood that drug phantasms couldn't hurt you and you didn't freak out anymore.

In cases like this, 'If you get high, then don't ask why,' was the maxim she tended to follow. Why? Because weird shit happened.

Lucy was very relieved that the tentacle-haired cop wasn't in her bedroom. She didn't like him one bit. Harmless or not, some illusions were just mind-fucks. And why did this one keep recurring anyway?

She had no answers. She wasn't sleepy anymore either. She was used to nights like this. She got out of bed and lit another joint. She took a few drags, then powered up her laptop. Thankfully, the dream hadn't damaged it.

Time to pay a predawn visit to cyberspace. First stop: Facebook. Her friends in Europe should be awake by now.

WEDNESDAY

CHAPTER 15

Jessica

On waking on Wednesday morning, Jessica felt strangely nervous and oddly hungover. The room was nice and warm with the summer, but the heat sat in her head like her brain was evaporating.

"Ooooh," she yawned, then sat up. Then her brain opened the floodgates of memory and reloaded yesterday for her.

She examined her nails and felt a moment of pure undiluted delight. "Yes!"

There was definite, visible, improvement at the tips of her hands and feet. Already, the scary plastic look had faded from both her fingernails and toenails. In addition, strips of several nails were 'transparent' again; she could see the finger flesh beneath them.

The medicine worked, she thought. *It worked.* She almost broke down and cried tears of relief there and then.

Next, she did a post mortem on her nightmare. She'd not dreamed again after falling asleep, and now, in the warmth of a nice summer morning—the late-July heat and happiness were practically pouring in through the windows—she once again dismissed as much of the dream as she could remember. It was simply mind-stew as a result of being hassled by those two creepy kids.

Now, though she was properly awake, her brain still felt like scrambled eggs. She tried to clear it. She got out of bed, walked over to the windows, and flung them wide open.

The day flooded in and with it came a flood of anxiety.

I should be at work! she thought in a sudden burst of desperation. *Oh my God, oh my God, I'm late again! I'm gonna get fired! It's eight, it's eight, I'm fucking late!* Then she remembered that there was no work to go to— she was on enforced vacation. Besides, even if she had been late to

89

the office, she'd been way above the 'fire on impulse' employee bracket for years now.

She felt silly. *However did I forget that?*

She still felt nervous, however, staring at the world outside her window, outside where all the Big Things were happening. She felt guilty, like she used to feel all the time up in Boston if she wasn't slaving away at some backbreaking task.

In the distance she saw Reby in her running garb, sweating herself into man-bait shape. She smirked. Last night Reby had looked all smug, very pleased with herself. ("You did him, didn't you?" "Nah, we just discussed human biology." "What?" "Ah, you know, animal gestures and body language, communication and reproduction in the wild." "Aha! So you *did* do him!" "Ha ha ha! I ain't telling ya!")

Reby vanished beyond a patch of trees.

Triggered by her reflections on Reby's sex life, Jessica now remembered Rabbitfield Condoms. ('Don't be scared, now you're prepared'; 'It's there; you just can't feel it'; and 'You get in—it doesn't get in the way.') She was proud of the work she'd done on that ad campaign, and now . . . she winced . . . someone else (most likely that slacker Neil Corden, with his massive beer belly) was going to take all the credit for it.

Jessica suddenly felt right on the edge of losing it. She quickly got a grip of herself. *Alright, this is weird. I've not felt this worried about work since arriving in Raynham. What's up this morning?*

She left her bedroom window, with its view of luscious summer grass and trees, and walked into the bathroom. She headed straight for the medicine chest over the washbasin. Before opening the chest, she checked her reflection in its mirror doors. *Cripes, I look like Lucy this morning.* In particular, her chestnut-brown hair was a glorious mess. She was overdue for a styling. But that was part of the freedom of being on vacation, wasn't it? *Oh, I'm letting my hair down in more than one sense. By now, my hair must feel utterly let down by me.*

Until she cared enough about her appearance to visit a salon though, her hairbrush would be working overtime. She smirked at the thought. *At least something around here's gonna be working.*

She opened the white cabinet, then stood staring suspiciously at the four packets of pills Dr. Whitfield had prescribed for her. One of them had to be responsible for her sudden relapse into agitation. But which?

She figured she could reliably put her still wooly state of mind down to the sedatives. She knew those were in the plastic envelope on the left. But the others? Two were white circular pills with crosses on them, while the third was a blue lozenge. She guessed the blue lozenge was for her nails. Which left the other two.

She tried to work out which of the white medicines was stressing her out, then decided 'fuck it.'

She picked up the sedative pack, got out one of its soft red pills, and swallowed it with some water from the sink. She dried her hands on her pajama top, then remembered she was supposed to take the other three pills twice a day. *Best I just take 'em all now,* she decided. She stared dubiously at one of the white circular ones. The instruction on the envelope read 'Twice daily after meals.' Jessica wasn't hungry, and she really didn't want to wait till either Reby or Lucy felt like cooking breakfast either. She grimaced. *No, no please—not Reby, or we'll be on a health food regime again.* All Lucy ever cooked was 'fry stuff' and burgers but at least she didn't calorie-count everything.

Jessica decided to take the white pill anyway. A late breakfast shouldn't make that much difference.

Working envelope by envelope, she dropped a small hill of tablets into her palm. She was also taking some vitamin pills and her stress medication from her Boston physician, Dr. Lopez. For a moment, the amount of medication scared her. *All this for just li'l me?* Then she steeled herself, flung her mouth open, flung the pills in, tried to swallow them all without chewing on any, almost succeeded, then finally bent over the faucet and filled her mouth with water. After swallowing, she gargled with more water to wash the residual pill taste out of her mouth.

Done, she thought with relief as she straightened up.

She dried her hands on her pajamas again, shut the medicine chest and once more stared at her face. *I still look tired.* She decided that was normal, since she'd just woken up. *Okay, I'll just go make some coffee. Aw shucks—I'm not allowed to have any caffeine!*

Her face crinkled up with displeasure. Coffee had been one of the joys of her working life. And no caffeine meant no Coke or Pepsi or Dr. Pepper or Mountain Dew or any such like either. It sucked. It really did. Without caffeine, what was one supposed to do to pick oneself up on a morning like this?

The way Jessica saw it, she had two choices. She could either go and rouse Lucy and ask her for some uppers, or she could endure her current state of mind, and hope she'd feel better in a little while.

Oh, she really did feel like seeking Lucy's help to perk herself up.

Finally, however, she decided she wasn't suicidal: there was no telling what one of those pills of Lucy's might do to her if combined with all the arcane medication already swimming around her body.

She brushed her teeth, then returned to her bedroom to wait for the day to get better. If the improved state of her nails was anything to go by, it would.

CHAPTER 16

Colleen

Colleen was sitting downstairs in her living room watching TV. The program was a religious one, broadcast from somewhere called the Realms of Consciousness Temple, which was apparently located here in Raynham. She wasn't really paying attention to the service, but the preacher was well-built and striking-looking, shaven-headed and with a dark goatee. He also had a seductive baritone voice.

"I saw Sinis, a Sinis was I!" he proclaimed, which made no sense to her.

Colleen had arrived at this program by accident. While trying to tune to the Food Network, she'd somehow pressed two wrong numbers on the remote and . . .

She didn't even wonder at her error. Since waking this morning, she'd felt heavily distracted. Almost sedated. She absentmindedly examined her manicure. She found nothing to upset her—her fingernails were once again perfect. Long and red and gleaming. (She took her time with growing her nails, nurturing them like they were plants. And for two of them to break like they had yesterday? To her, that was like losing one's life's savings, or being jilted by a lover. It was like having one's favorite child turn out a juvenile delinquent. Oh, it just so fucking hurt. But that was fixed now, the damage all repaired.)

"I saw Sinis, a Sinis was I!" the TV preacher proclaimed again. His congregation echoed him loudly.

Colleen wasn't religious. And though he was good-looking, this preacher wasn't making any sense anyway. She turned the sound off. She dully regarded the flickering TV image, too preoccupied with her thoughts to bother with switching to the Food Network instead.

***

Colleen had woken up this morning feeling inexplicably trapped. As she'd opened her eyes to the dawn, a desperate feeling had poured in through them and into her soul, filling her with the intense sense of being chained and held captive in a marital jail.

She'd turned and stared at Larry. He'd been lying on his belly in just his boxers. For a moment, Colleen had hated him, hated him with such passion that she'd felt like grabbing something and bashing in his head. She'd looked around for something heavy to kill him with.

Then, as suddenly as it had arrived in her heart, her rage had abruptly vanished, and she'd felt perplexed as to why it had come at all.

She'd stared at Larry some more, with her attention finally focusing on his buttocks. She was surprised to find herself aroused.

A moment ago I wanted to murder him, and now . . .

She was still glum over Larry's planned philandering on her, but her sex organ apparently didn't care. Her vagina wanted Larry and it wanted him right away.

She did something then she hadn't done before. Something she'd always thought was dirty, really dirty.

While Larry slept on, Colleen had pulled down his gray boxers and stuck her tongue between his buttocks. Carefully, she'd spread his buttocks and licked his anus. The tight opening had both smelt and tasted dirty, but instead of revolting her, this had excited her. Her vagina had filled with juice and her large legs trembled with desire for him. After a while of tonguing him, she'd begun tickling his hole with a fingernail. Her other hand had reached lower and grabbed his balls and tugged gently on them. Then she'd gone back to licking his anus again while squeezing his balls.

Larry's erection had woken him up. Or, maybe he'd been awake for a while, enjoying what she was doing? Colleen didn't know. Either way, the result had been the same. He'd rolled her over onto her back, spat on his penis and slid it into her. He'd not even bothered to wait for her to remove her nightie first. She'd half-struggled out of the nightdress while he thrust into her, but it had gotten tangled up around her neck, so she'd left it alone lest she choke herself. Instead, she'd grabbed a firm hold of Larry with her arms and legs and concentrated on reaching orgasm. And when she came, she'd dug her nails into his back and clawed and scratched him, while he'd grimaced and spurted into her.

She'd again marked him as her own.

Afterwards, she'd lain gasping, staring at the ceiling. The sex had been great, the best in quite a while. Larry must have felt it too. He'd kissed her tenderly, then rolled over on his back and fallen asleep again.

For a moment she'd tried to quantify the amount of semen running out of her: was it as much as usual, or had he already begun giving her entitlement to that other woman?

Colleen loved being ejaculated into. After the initial thrill of being opened up deliciously at the moment of penetration, it was her favorite part of the sexual act—that moment when she received Larry's liquid love into herself. His semen was something she'd extracted from his body for her own use. Colleen utterly adored sperm. Sperm was a love message sent from Larry's body to hers.

It really angered her to imagine another woman sharing in their physical conversation.

She'd fallen asleep and dreamt of being in a blue room. In the blue room, someone forcefully took away a full glass of milk meant for her and poured most of it into shot glasses that he then placed in front of an endless sequence of faceless women, till finally there was almost nothing left in the glass for she, Colleen, to drink. In the dream the faceless women were mocking her, calling her 'fattie' and 'unloved,' while she cried and cried and cried.

When she'd woken, the disquiet of the dream had haunted her. Larry had still been asleep and Colleen had sat up and stared at him. She'd felt wounded deep in her heart. Oh, he was killing her with his behavior—sharing his love with other women—and she had to do something about it.

Her previous rage had returned then, and she'd considered dashing downstairs to their kitchen, fetching a knife, and slicing his balls off. That would teach him not to fuck around on her.

The horrifying vision of herself pulling Larry's scrotum taut and slicing it away as close to the body as she could, while he bled and screamed in pain, had been so vivid and compelling (wrapped in a filter of blue like a scene from a spy thriller) that Colleen had actually started out of bed to go get the knife and come castrate Larry.

But then, as her feet touched the rug, the rage had vanished again. The sudden change in her emotions had left Colleen exhausted and confused. Most of all, it left her very scared.

I don't want to kill Larry! Colleen had moaned silently to herself as she'd lain back down in bed. *I love him. I love him. I love him. I just want him to treat me better. I want him to do right by me. Then I'll be happy. I DON'T WANT TO MURDER HIM!*

***

Now, seated watching the muted temple service on the TV, Colleen struggled to get a handle on her emotions.

It was proving much harder than she'd have imagined. One thing in particular was becoming abundantly clear to her since yesterday: *I'm in a goddam abusive relationship with Larry. I can't deceive myself about that anymore. I should get out and get away from him. Sue for divorce, take half of whatever we've got, and run as far away from him as I can get!*

It was a comforting thought for a few seconds, but then her self-doubt returned: *But I'm so damn old, and I'm not pretty and I'm overweight. Who'll ever want me? At least Larry never complains about how fat I am . . .*

She ran her mind through her fears of divorcing Larry: Being a lonely, bitter, middle-aged wealthy woman, reduced to hiring an escort whenever she wanted a fuck. Knowing that the young, handsome and muscular men she hired despised her. (But who cared what hookers thought anyway, right?) What scared Colleen most of all was the thought of all those lonely years stretching ahead of her into old age, of being alone all the time, except when Randy came home on leave.

And Randy was still single now. What happened when he got married and his wife didn't want his 'nosy, interfering obese mother' anywhere around their house?

These were all old arguments, and they'd served Colleen well over the past three years since Larry had begun straying from her side. But not now though. Now, for some reason, doing something about her situation seemed imperative to Colleen.

At that moment Larry walked into the living room carrying a cup of coffee. "Hey, baby, what'cha watchin'?"

She looked at him, handsome and smug—*Yes, he would be smug, wouldn't he? He's got two of us silly women to fuck!*—and she hated him even more than before. So much that she couldn't even reply him.

He'd been smiling at her, but the smile drooped on seeing how cold to him she was. He now watched her nervously. She was certain he felt guilty. He'd been happy because she'd made love to him earlier, but now he wasn't sure what she was thinking. Or suspecting.

He settled into the armchair beside the sofa she sat on, then reached forward and picked up the TV remote and dialed up Info.

He winced. "'We can be Gods? Service at the Realms of Consciousness Temple with Brother Crowley?' Dammit, Colleen, what is this shit? Scientology? Tom Cruise, Kirstie Alley, and John Travolta? Aw, c'mon, babe, you're not planning on becoming a Scientologist now, are ya?"

"I'm not watching it," she replied him hotly, then wondered why she was bothering to reply. It felt like she was apologizing for watching TV. If that wasn't evidence of being abused, then what was? "And . . . supposing I do want to watch the damn program, what about it?"

Larry rolled his eyes, then pointed the remote at the TV to change the channel. "Look, I wanna see the stock market news on CNN."

"Don't you dare change it!" Colleen shrieked at him, almost launching herself off the sofa in her anger. "I'm watching that!"

Larry stared at her confused. "But you just said you weren't."

"I just changed my mind. It looks interesting." She reached over and grabbed the remote from him. "Gimme that!" She settled back on the sofa and now unmuted the TV sound.

"I saw Sinis," Brother Crowley was saying, "a Sinis was I."

"What the hell did he just say?" Larry asked, a perplexed look on his face.

Colleen waved a dismissive hand back at him. "Oh, I dunno. Listen, darling, you're bothering me. How am I gonna know what he's talking about if you keep interrupting? If you wanna jerk off to Richard Quest, go do it on your laptop."

Larry sat staring at her. "Alright, alright, the TV's yours. Say, how about some breakfast, baby? I'm so hungry . . . I feel like I've been working out in my sleep."

She knew he was trying to be conciliatory to her, but she didn't care. "Make yourself a sandwich," she said flatly without turning to look at him. "I've got a headache."

She could feel him staring at her. Then he got up and walked off, his footsteps slowly growing more distant. She heard him in the kitchen opening the fridge door.

She relaxed back on the sofa. *Why did I just behave like that to him? I was really nasty just now.* She muted the TV again. *And over what? I don't even like this goddam program! Sinis bullcrap and some David Berg wannabe!*

And, right then, Colleen felt like a voice whispered to her: *Kill the abusive son-of-a-bitch. Kill Larry. He's been taking advantage of you. You know he's already screwing that slut next door.*

So why don't I just kill the slut then? Colleen queried her mental adviser.

Because there's an endless supply of sluts in the world, her mind replied her. *You kill one and he'll simply replace her with another. If you kill Larry, however . . . Look, it's easy—just use the shotgun upstairs. Put it in his mouth and blow him away. Don't worry about the trial; the asshole has made you suffer for years until now you couldn't take anymore; you just snapped all of a sudden. The jury will let you go for certain.*

Colleen didn't have time to think up a reply to this, because at that moment, the scene on the TV switched from showing the crowd in the Realms of Consciousness Temple to showing Colleen and Larry.

Colleen gaped. On the TV screen, she had Larry tied down on a table. He was naked and there were bleeding wounds on his body as if he'd been tortured. Colleen wore a pale blue dress, blue lipstick, and blue eyeshadow. She had on blue high heels too. She was smiling at Larry, a sadistic smile that left the viewer in no doubt that she'd been the one torturing him.

"And now . . ." the onscreen version of herself said (Colleen didn't then realize how odd that was, seeing as she'd just muted the TV), "and now, let's ensure that you never look at another woman again."

"I won't, I won't, I won't!" onscreen-Larry pleaded.

"Oh, I'm gonna make certain of it," Colleen's onscreen version said. Then without further ado, she bent over him and dug her long blue fingernails into his face, deep into his eye sockets. Larry screamed and screamed. Blood spurted from his face, jetting out between her nails like a flock of red birds fleeing their blue cage.

When the onscreen Colleen straightened up again, she was holding both of Larry's eyes in her hands, freshly plucked-out and dripping with blood. On the table, her husband stared sightlessly at the future, both his eye sockets bloody pools. He was howling pitifully.

The onscreen Colleen bent over Larry's head and began lapping up the blood from his eye sockets like a thirsty animal . . .

In a flash of blinding blue light, the vision cut out. The TV image reverted back to Brother Crowley, and was once again silent.

Colleen became aware of a horrible smell around her. She discovered that she'd vomited on herself where she sat. Despite which, she remained seated for a while. Her head was ringing cathedral bells. It was all she could do not to puke again. The nausea felt centered in the middle of her throat, both making and blocking itself. She couldn't puke, but she also couldn't stop feeling like she must either throw up or explode.

She was close to panic. *What the fuck did I just see? I was doing what to Larry?*

She considered calling for him, but thought better of it. *He's likely very angry with me for just now.*

Finally, Colleen felt strong enough to get up. The nausea had receded a little and her headache had subsided. All she could think of now was simply climbing up the stairs and flopping down in bed.

She made her slow way past the dining room and past Larry, who was seated at the dining table reading Forbes magazine and eating a sandwich. Larry was making a point of not looking at her.

She found the steps and began climbing them.

As she reached the top of the stairs, she remembered she'd not yet taken her medication today, the pills the kindly doctor had given her. Maybe that was why she'd seen that mad stuff on the television? Wincing, Colleen pulled herself up onto the landing. The doctor had said it might take a while for the medicine to produce results. The hell with that! No matter what he'd said, she couldn't go on living like this. If she didn't feel noticeably improved by tomorrow, she was going back to the clinic to see him again.

Colleen trudged into the bedroom. Her eyes strayed to the shotgun standing over in the corner between the wardrobe and the front window. She groaned, then suddenly, out of nowhere, she laughed.

The laughter remained as she walked into the bathroom to clean herself off. Just like that, she felt much better.

After a while Colleen's mirth became quite manic. And with good reason: as she stood under the shower and soaped herself, Colleen Townsend was pondering what it would be like to actually use that shotgun on her husband. She now found herself belatedly agreeing with *herself* (that evil version of herself which had downstairs been urging her to kill him): ridding herself of Larry just might be the right thing to do. The asshole *was* cheating on her after all. Oh yes, if Larry didn't stop fucking with her, she really might murder him.

Giggling like a maniac, she lifted her right hand and studied her two-inch-long red fingernails, all freshly polished and glossy. And then—just like her TV-version had—she'd pluck Larry's eyes out of his face.

She spent the rest of her bath wondering what she'd do with Larry's eyes after plucking them out. Preserve them? Throw them away? Feed them to a pet?

While toweling herself off, Colleen also pondered what sort of a mood she'd need to be in to actually go through with it. Murdering Larry, that was.

She walked out of the bathroom and stood staring at the shotgun. It beckoned to her like a lover, seducing her to come make use of it for its preordained deadly purpose. As she stared at it, she felt a rekindling of her old anger. All of a sudden Larry was *really* pissing her off again.

"No, not now," she said aloud to calm herself. "Not, not now. Worth it or not, I still love the piece-of-shit. But he'd better take care from now on. Oh, that's for hell sure—Larry had better watch himself. I'm not the pushover he married any more. Larry, you'd better watch it. Or else, I'll . . ."

Leaving her threat unfinished, Colleen headed for her nightstand to find her medicine. She still had traces of her headache, and didn't want the nausea to return.

CHAPTER 17

Reby, with Jessica & Lucy

It was early afternoon. After shopping for over two hours, the three of them were sitting having lunch in the McDonald's down on the New State Highway. They had a table near the front window, trays of burgers, fries, and drinks in front of them, and for the most part, all felt okay.

They'd driven downtown in Reby's silver BMW convertible, chosen over Jessica's Nissan because with the top down, they could bask in the sunlight.

As a last stop after making all their purchases, they'd also checked out Body Revolution, a gym located about three miles farther down the New State Highway. Reby had liked the place. She intended to start working out there tomorrow. She had some serious catching up to do on her fitness routine. Finding the gym had been a major relief to Reby. Even with all the running she'd been doing every morning, she still couldn't shake off the neurotic feeling that she was getting fat.

Fat. Reby regarded her burger with distrust and suspicion. She didn't normally do fast food. She was too conscious of her health and figure. Fried stuff had all that fat in it. Polyunsaturated or not, 'good' cholesterol or not, fat was still fat. Soft drinks were just as bad. Some soft drinks had more cubes of sugar in them that three cups of coffee. And besides, all you were eating/drinking was carbs, carbs, and more carbs anyway. Better to stay safe, and stay slim. But once in a while with friends, Reby figured it couldn't do too much harm. She'd just cut down on what she had for dinner. She wasn't having any soft drinks though, it was too much work burning off all those calories afterward. She had a bottle of water; that was fine. Taste didn't matter, having a sexy body did. Sodas were for slobs.

At the moment, Reby was trying to figure out a title for this week's blog post. Posting as 'Becky Butterfly' she updated her eponymous blog once or twice a week. 'Becky Butterfly' was an X-rated blog. Its primary content was detailed posts about Reby's own sexual escapades, but she also answered sex questions, both about her own life and about other people's problems. She tried to be as accessible as possible to her fans. She found blogging quite fulfilling, something to do when in actuality you had nothing to do.

For this week's post she was writing about herself and Larry Townsend. Under an assumed name for Larry, of course. Reby was nothing if not discreet; she'd never 'kiss and tell' on anyone. She'd enjoyed fucking Larry and planned on fucking him some more. But online she was going to present him as a single guy. She'd already decided to simply call him Mr. L. If she let on that he was married, she was certain to get a lot of angry feedback from married women who disapproved of her behavior.

She bit into her burger then shrugged. *Sometimes I disapprove of my behavior too, ladies. That doesn't stop it being fun though.*

Still, she needed a title. *How about 'Mr. L's long . . .'? No, no, no.*

She slipped out of her thoughts for a moment. Jessica's hands. Before they'd left home, Jessica had borrowed blue nail polish from Lucy to touch up her fingernails. Reby had seen her nails before she'd done them over: they'd looked all patchy, like she'd tried to wipe their previous blue coating off but had run out of nail polish remover. She'd asked what was up with Jessica's hands. Jessica had replied that it was a medical thing, something she was taking pills for. It didn't hurt or anything, and wasn't contagious, but if they were going to town together, she'd be embarrassed if her hands looked funny.

Reby understood and sympathized. In public, a woman must always, always look her very best. She lifted her eyes from Jessica's hands to her face and smiled at her. Jessica met her eyes and smiled back around her mouthful of hamburger. Reby forked some fries into her mouth and turned towards Lucy.

Lucy was staring down at her lunch in intense concentration, as if her hamburger was telepathic and she was mentally speaking to it; or maybe it was pleading with her not to eat it. She didn't look overly spaced out, but Reby wasn't fooled. Lucy had an abnormally high tolerance for narcotics.

"You know," Lucy said after finally taking a bite of her meal, "the cheese in this burger tastes off." She didn't wait for their reply, but took another bite, said, "Yeah, I'm right—the cheese *is* off," and continued to eat it voraciously till it was all gone. Then she began to fork her fries into her mouth as fast as she could, not bothering to ketchup them first. When everything was gone, she burped loudly then got to her feet.

"Hey, guys, I'll be right back. I need to use the ladies'."

She dashed off across McDonald's, navigating haphazardly between people carrying trays to their tables.

Reby turned from staring after her to look at Jessica again.

"What I don't get," Jessica said seriously, putting down her half-empty cup of Fanta, "is how all the pills she takes haven't run her mad yet. If I was her, I'd be hallucinating all the time."

Reby laughed. "Oh, she is hallucinating. Yesterday she told me she saw a policeman eating a cat . . . in our backyard."

Jessica stared at her. Then she almost choked on her fries with laughter. "What? She said *that?*"

Reby nodded. "The beyotch was totally convinced of it too. I was gonna . . . Wow! Now *that's* what I call a tight ass."

***

Jessica was at first shocked by the sudden change of topic. *Huh? What's she talking about?*

Then she understood and grinned. Reby was staring out of the window at two men who were walking from the McDonald's entrance to their parked car.

"Wow," Reby said, totally unaware she was thinking aloud. "I wanna grab me some of those."

Jessica said nothing. By now she was used to it: Reby apparently couldn't help herself. She ogled men the way men ogled women. Personally, Jessica thought it odd that a woman would be like that. She was certain though that it had to be an exciting way to live, leaping from bed to bed with no future plans except locating the next penis in line so you could stiffen then soften it. How did Reby keep count of her men? Via her blog? Would she one day in the far-off future tally up all her blog posts to number her conquests?

The two men hopped into their ride and drove off. Reby looked back inside to see Jessica laughing at her.

Reby wasn't offended. "They both had nice firm buttocks, I'm telling you. I've seen enough of them to know." Then she grinned. "C'mon, if it's okay for guys to look, then I can look too."

"I'm not judging you," Jessica said. "I just think it's funny." She laughed some more. "You need to have seen the look on your face. You were staring at those two like you're starving and their dicks are hot-dogs."

Reby giggled demurely. "Jessica, darling, penises are absolutely delicious—*that's why* they're called wieners; a woman most likely first named them that. And . . . you don't even need mustard sauce to eat them." She picked up a paper napkin and flung it at Jessica. "Hey, look, stop laughing at me, it's not funny."

Jessica laughed even harder. Reby's face now took on an expression of hurt, almost choirgirl 'innocence.' Jessica liked that about her: how simple and open and honest she was about her pleasures. But, Jessica felt, there was such a thing as *too much* honesty. Jessica definitely didn't approve of Reby's 'and-other-women's-husbands-too-because-they're-safer' policy.

***

"Look at what? Eat what? Who's got hot dogs?" Lucy asked, plumping herself back down in her seat. She looked as pretty and impish as ever and twice as wasted. Her overly-bright eyes told a telltale.

"C'mon, Lucy, don't tell us you went to get high in the toilet at McDonald's."

"I had to. That burger was making me nauseous. So what were you both talking 'bout? Was it the 'spit or swallow' argument again?"

"Shush, lower your voice. There's kids nearby."

Lucy looked around the room, her gaze skipping from table to table like she was noticing for the first time that there were others in the eatery besides them.

"Yeah, there are," she finally agreed. "Where'd they all come from?"

Reby looked at Jessica, who shrugged back. She figured they were thinking the same thing: Lucy was harmless enough and good fun to be around. One just had to keep an eye on her at all times so she didn't accidentally kill herself. Reby wondered how Lucy's brother Robert coped with her back in Springfield.

But then, a confusing thought struck Reby: *I've known Lucy for three years now. Sure, she's a pillhead freak, but in all that time I've never seen her this perpetually wasted. Yes, she smokes chimneys of pot, but . . . there's been something abnormal about her addiction since we got to this town. She's suddenly like, completely over-the-top. Now her drug usage seems out of control, self-destructive, like she's questing for some ultimate high and will happily destroy herself to experience it.*

Perplexed and worried, she stared at Lucy. Lucy grinned back, then began licking her Coke straw like it was a penis.

Then . . .

Everything changed. Just like yesterday, when she'd been on her way over to Larry's house, Reby suddenly noticed that her arms looked different. Once again, her smooth, toned limbs had become a mass of plaited snakes. No, this was different: her arms looked normal, but she could see through her skin into them, and the coiling mass of reptiles was inside her. Black and fluid and glistening like oiled machine gears. There were no bones in her arms, just that disgusting, writhing mass. And there was an awful odor coming from her body, like she was dead and her flesh was rotting.

Reby started back in her chair so it scraped across the tiles. She gaped. She was horrified. She looked down at her legs. Thankfully, she couldn't see through her black pants. If her legs had looked the same—empty of bones but filled with writhing ophidians—she'd had screamed.

She looked at the others. Couldn't they see what had happened to her? Couldn't they smell her?

Apparently not. Jessica, meanwhile, was staring through the window at a pregnant woman who stood on the sidewalk across the road from the McDonald's, in front of the Chalet Jewelers shop. Lucy had now stopped fellating her Coca-Cola and was drinking it instead.

Reby looked desperately around at the other diners in the McDonald's. No one was even looking her way. Not even at the next table to theirs, where a tired-looking woman was sternly warning her son not to play with his food. Reby found this incredible—that the woman couldn't smell her—because she really *reeked*. She smelt like the gas escaping from a bloated corpse as it is punctured by the beaks of impatient vultures. She was choking on herself.

And then it was over. Just like that, the gangrenous stink vanished. Reby found that her arms and hands were normal again. But had they ever changed? If Jessica and Lucy hadn't noticed, they hadn't, had they?

Reby was shaken. She was almost trembling. She desperately needed something to calm herself. Something with an anchor of normalcy. Anything, no matter how absurd. Usually when upset, she anchored herself with sex. Either a guy or a toy, either would do. She couldn't masturbate in public though. Talking about fucking would have to substitute.

She quickly said, "Hey, two nights ago we never agreed on whether swallowing semen makes you cool or a fool." She placed her palms flat on either side of her lunch tray, daring their opinions. "Alright, out with it, guys, which is it?"

"Aw please, not now, Reby," Jessica pleaded. "Not while we're eating. It's such an yucky topic."

"Ha ha," Lucy said, a childish gleam entering her eyes. "I knew it, I just knew it! I knew you guys were having the 'spit or swallow' debate again."

"So," Reby continued, desperate for the conversation to take off but hiding it well, "you beyotches are the jury here. Tell me—and keep your damn voices down 'cos of the little kids everywhere—does swallowing a guy's come made a woman look classy or slutty? As for me, I say it shows total class. It also shows that you're the kind of woman who finishes what she starts, i.e. the committing type. Plus, it's the easiest way to get a guy to call you back after a one night stand."

"Or run him off," Lucy countered, "'cos he thinks you're a trollop who humps everyone she meets on every first date."

"He humped me, didn't he?"

"Oh, sure, and he'll boast about it to his friends, telling them how many positions of the Kama Sutra you two did together. It's the male double-standard, see—I can slut, you cannot. Unfortunately, like it or not, in the end it's us girls who always get screwed." Her expression turned sad. "Not me though—I ain't been laid since God knows when."

"Yeah," Reby nodded, looking just as sad. "Pussy is priceless until you give away to a guy; then it's worthless. Look, whatever you say—

I still insist that swallowing is the mark of a strong independent woman."

Jessica pushed her empty tray away. She leaned forward and whispered, "I disagree too, but for a different reason. Me, I just dislike men ejaculating in my mouth. Look, you two, I ain't a prude. I mean, I like sucking dick as much as the next woman, but . . . but the semen . . . argh! Come has a thick obnoxious taste to it that my taste buds just can't deal with."

"But that's the best thing about it," Reby protested. "I like how slimy and icky semen tastes. It make me feel so dirty and I just love it!"

"Not I," Jessica said. "Maybe it depends on the guy, but that taste just ruins sex for me." She looked to Lucy for support.

Lucy giggled. "Oh, come's an acquired taste for sure. It took me two years before I didn't feel like puking each time a guy fed me his love milk."

"That's a whole lot of yoghurt to drink," Jessica said. "I'd have thrown up to death by then. I wonder how you survived the ordeal."

Lucy giggled. "Most of 'em wore rubbers."

Jessica nodded. "Now there's a good solution for you, Reby—no come without a condom on. Then you don't have to either spit or swallow. Besides, if it's a one night stand, you really don't want some medically untested semen in your mouth anyway. That's just playing Russian roulette."

Reby said, "You're cheating. Okay, forget one night stands. Assume you're in a loving relationship. Husbands and boyfriends? Do they think less or more of you if you spit out the juice of their loins after sucking them to orgasm?"

Jessica laughed. "Now *you're* playing unfair. I *never* swallow and I'm twice divorced. Maybe that's why?"

Lucy said, "And so once again, biatches, in our debate on the appropriate female response to male ejaculation during fellatio, we've a hung jury."

"Not hung like a horse, I hope," Jessica said and they all laughed.

Reby felt marginally better now. Semen was reality. Seeing yourself as full of snakes when you knew you were a perfectly normal woman wasn't reality. Neither was smelling like a mass grave when you were wearing a $1,000-an-ounce Caron *Poivre* perfume. That was the stuff of nightmares.

Reby gazed out of the window. The pregnant woman Jessica had been watching was now crossing the road to the McDonald's side.

***

Lucy watched the pregnant woman cross the road with mixed feelings. Seeing the woman, all swollen with new life on the way, made her smile. But it was a sad smile. The approaching woman brought memories to Lucy. Bittersweet memories.

For most of her twenties, Lucy had been almost nun-like in her chemically induced abstinence. She'd not say no if a guy hit on her, but the drugs had leeched her of all interest in romance. Indeed, Lucy herself admitted that fully half of the sex she'd had in her adult life consisted of men taking advantage of her while she was passed out from alcohol or something stronger. She'd just wake up with her private parts sore and semen on her lips or thighs and accept that she'd been fucked again, and hope they'd not gotten her pregnant or given her an STD. And it was always her own doing too: to her knowledge no one had yet slipped Rohypnol into any of her drinks.

Of course, sooner or later, getting fucked while comatose and without the guys using rubbers had to pay biological dividends.

Lucy had thrice gotten pregnant this way and had had three abortions. She didn't regret the abortions. She felt that only an idiot would want a drug dealer's baby.

Bulging belly leading the way, the pregnant woman was just stepping into the McDonald's driveway. Lucy surfaced from her thoughts and got a good look at her for the first time. Her eyes brightened with recognition. "Damn, I don't believe it—it's Megan!"

Laughing, she leapt up and dashed off out of McDonald's.

***

Reby watched Lucy go. The pregnant woman was now walking towards a black SUV in the McDonald's parking lot. She was tall and plump, with long brown hair. She was carrying a blue shopping bag. Reby figured that she'd had lunch here in McDonald's, then afterwards crossed the road to buy something in the shops opposite.

Lucy was meanwhile running across the parking lot towards the pregnant woman and waving her hands. The woman paused from opening her car door and turned. Even from this distance, Reby could make out the sudden smile of recognition on her face when she saw Lucy. Then the pair were hugging each other, and hopping around in delight, and holding each other out at arm's length.

Reby discovered that she couldn't take her attention off the pregnant woman's belly. Her eyes felt glued there. *What's it like to be knocked up and expecting?* It was a question she'd often asked herself, but one she was scared to let her body answer. Of course pregnancy was wonderful. As a woman, Reby knew that instinctively. Besides, most of the planet's women went through it, and hardly any of them seemed to regret it afterwards, at least not until the child was grown and became a pain in the ass.

So, yes, being preggers was wonderful. But so was sex. Actually, sex was even more wonderful than kids.

Most women had . . . how many kids? Between two and four. And then menopause set in and they were pooped, just completely used up. You looked at them and it seemed like they'd ejected all the vitality from their bodies along with the babies.

But sex? You could screw till the cows came home! And it just got better and better! Ye-haa!

Besides which, children tied one down and Reby wanted to travel.

Her twin sister Leah, for instance, was more-or-less now a prisoner of her own wonderful fertility: five kids so far with Carl Kingston and counting. Leah couldn't leave town or do anything. Leah seemed to enjoy being pregnant though, and why not? The Kingston clan had almost as much money as the Butterfields did. So Leah kept spreading her legs for Carl to squirt the babies in, and nine months later, she'd spread her legs again to squirt them out.

Reby grimaced, her eyes still on Lucy and her friend—Megan—who'd now both gotten over the hysterics of reunion and were seated inside Megan's car chatting. No, married life and babies weren't for her. She wasn't ready to be tied down yet. Maybe she'd never be ready.

She realized with relief that she was now completely over her shock from that horrid snake hallucination.

She smiled at Jessica, who was just turning back from staring out at Lucy and her friend, and asked, "Do you like babies too?"

***

Jessica gaped at Reby's question. "Huh?" The abruptness of the query had startled her. She actually *had* been thinking about how much she liked children.

She nodded. "Yes, I do. I really do. I'd love to have one or two or three of my own."

"Why'd you never have any then? You're wildly successful and you're older than me."

Jessica grimaced. "Oh, I'm scared I'll never have the time to be a good mom to my children. And that's just unforgiveable, right?"

She wasn't lying or making up an excuse. When she'd been married, even the cat had been neglected. Indeed, her refusal to get pregnant had been mostly responsible for ending her first marriage.

Dave, her first ex, couldn't for the life of him understand why she couldn't just put her career on hold for 'a year or so' like some of her female colleagues in the office did. But Jessica had stood her ground.

Dave had hidden her birth control pills. He'd also sabotaged his condoms with pin pricks before usage. Before she'd worked out what was going on, Jessica had wondered how Dave's rubbers always seemed to break when she was in her fertile period of the month.

Once she'd discovered what he was doing, however, she'd had an IUD inserted. She'd not told him about the IUD.

Things had carried on like before. Dave had kept sabotaging his condoms and she'd kept welcoming him inside herself with open arms and legs.

This had gone on until one morning, Jessica had suddenly developed intense abdominal pains.

Imagining she was pregnant and possibly about to miscarry, Dave rushed her to the doctor. The doctor carried out an examination and told Dave (Jessica being sedated at the time) that his wife's IUD had somehow pierced the wall of her uterus and would have to be removed immediately.

Dave filed for divorce the next day. Jessica had begged him with tears to stay, but he'd left anyway. He was now married again, to a woman who seemed as baby-mad as he was. They already had four children together, and the last that Jessica had heard, Helen was pregnant again, this time with twins.

Uh uh, not me, she thought. *Babies can visit me when I'm safe and sound at the top of the corporate ladder.*

After the 'Dave Disaster' (as she thought of her first marriage) Jessica had simply had a Nexplanon implant put in her arm. That way she didn't need to worry about fertile periods or other such nonsense for the next three years.

Her second husband Tony had understood her feelings on the subject of babies. She'd made certain that Tony understood. Jessica had actually discussed a 'no kids' pre-nup contract with her lawyer. She'd abandoned the idea only when he told her it would make her look silly.

That marriage had lasted longer, only ending when Jessica stopped coming home from work for days on end.

Jessica smiled. Maybe she just wasn't cut out for marriage and kids. Not everyone was. A child wasn't a cat or dog. Kids had rights, both legal and emotional. They had expectations too. They expected their parents to be like their playmates' parents—there at home with them, taking them to school and bringing them back, helping them with their homework, taking them to the park and the zoo, and to the candy store and PG movies and to other kid's birthday parties, reading them bedtime stories and . . . and . . .

Jessica conceded defeat. She couldn't do all that. She'd never be able to cope. With her career preoccupations, she'd never make a good mom. She'd want to, but . . . How did the other women in the office manage anyway? Lots of them had children and somehow managed to make it work. That baffled Jessica for a moment or two, before she remembered that none of those mothers 'worked' as hard as she did. *She* was always here, there, and everywhere, on each and every floor in the Argus building, doing things, putting in endless hours of overtime to ensure that the company was top in the ad business; going well beyond the call of duty; seeing to it that each client's project was handled the way it should be. And *they*—the mothers? Uh uh. The mothers all clocked-off at 5 p.m. sharp and drove home to husbands and kids.

She sighed and finished off her Fanta. She realized that Reby hadn't said anything else since she'd gone off on her mental wandering. She wondered why. Reby was staring out at the parking lot again. Lucy was waving after her pregnant friend, who was just driving away in her black SUV.

Out there alone on the concrete, Lucy looked sad and abandoned, a purple-haired orphan who'd grown up too fast and had no one in the world to look after her. She turned away from the departing car and began walking towards the restaurant again.

Reby touched Jessica's arm. "We'd best just go outside and join her. We've been sitting in here long enough."

Jessica agreed. They rose, picked up Lucy's purse, and walked over to meet her outside the door.

***

"Wow, people really do change!" Lucy remarked as Reby backed the silver BMW out of their parking space.

"You mean your friend?" Jessica asked, leaning forward. She was sitting in the back, Lucy was in front beside Reby. "She seemed normal enough to me. Nice and homely even."

Reby eased the car out of the McDonald's lot and onto the road. "Where d'you guys know each other from? You both go way back?"

Lucy grinned. "Oh, way, way back. That's why I'm so damn surprised. See, she used to be a complete, total, drug freak." She paused for effect. "And now she's a Jesus Freak."

Reby rolled her eyes. "What's so special about that? Both are just forms of addiction, aren't they?"

Lucy giggled with mirth. "Oh, oh, not in this case. See, you really need to have known Megan back then. She was a complete mess. She was a heroin addict, a real junkie—used to whore herself out for fixes all the time. It's lucky she found religion: She used to OD all the time too—each and every week we thought she was gonna die on us. Megan spent more time in an oxygen tent than Obama did as President. She's got AIDS from sharing needles, but now she's got Jesus too, you know—which I think is pretty cool—and she claims God talks to her sometimes. And she's married and happy and everything. And has a baby on the way."

Lucy fell silent. She popped a pill, sat back, and grinned at the houses and people they were passing.

Reby said nothing. She still maintained her 'religion is mass delusion' point of view, but, coming from the kind of lifestyle Lucy had just recounted, getting 'saved' had to be a step up, right? Even if all it did was enslave your mind, not your body this time around.

To be accurate and fair, Reby Butterfield didn't really dislike religion. She was fine with God, per se, His being up there and being a good father who loved everyone. (As for the old argument that, 'if God's so good, why's there so much evil everywhere?', Reby figured that was just folks trying to pass the buck for their own bad behavior onto the Almighty.)

Reby's real beef with religion was the constraints the faiths all placed on one's bedroom behavior. Particularly the 'Thou shalt not commit fornication and adultery' part of pious doctrine. ("Oh, sex is wonderful—it's God's gift to men and woman—but get married first," the religions all said.) If those parts hadn't been in the Torah, Reby would most likely be a preacher's wife (he'd have to be a Rabbi though, because of her mother). It was crazy, she thought, just about every religion she knew had strict sexual conduct rules, along with anti-gay theology. Reby occasionally imagined she'd become religious herself . . . once she'd had enough sex. The problem was, she didn't see herself as ever having enough sex. And being faithful to one man forever? *Forever* was just *too* long. She didn't mind being faithful to a guy for a month or two, until the thrill died. In fact, she'd never, ever, cheated on any of her boyfriends (though they might have been cheating on their wives to be with her). And besides, Reby considered, why tie herself down at all? Why do that when she could have all the men she wanted, and all over the world too? She was young, beautiful, and rich. All she had to do was keep in motion, and keep fit and sexy. And not catch any STDs.

Jessica too was thinking about Megan. It was a lot to process—that that nice-looking pregnant lady who'd driven off in the black car had once been a junkie hooker and had gotten AIDS from her addiction. That was a major lifelong paycheck to cash.

Damn, she thought, *it really is impossible to read the past in people's faces.*

"Ha ha," Lucy piped up suddenly, "Megan even invited me to her church! Imagine *Megan* in church—oh, that's just fuckin' priceless!" After that she couldn't stop giggling till they got home.

CHAPTER 18

Larry

The laptop screen was as blank as before. Just a white MS Word page with a line of tabs at the top. No matter what Larry Townsend tried, Chapter 10 of Wall Street's Greatest Scandals refused to be written.

Larry finished his fifth or sixth cup of coffee today, and got up in disgust. He tried to work out what the trouble was, to understand why the sentences simply wouldn't flow from his fingers into Word. Was it what he'd at first thought, that he'd just lost interest? If so, that wouldn't make sense. Larry had been wanting to do this book for years; no way could he just up and lose the drive to write it now.

Or maybe, he was just tired and needed a rest? That made no sense either. Most days before his writer's block had come calling, he'd had to pull himself away from the keyboard to go sleep at night; he'd been that fascinated with the subject matter. And he'd always woken up raring to go, impatiently waiting till breakfast was over to get into his study and start typing away.

So no, neither of those explanations held water.

There *was* a third explanation that had occurred to Larry as to why his writing had suddenly slammed into a brick wall. He'd been avoiding considering it because it seemed insane. But now, he had little choice:

Oops, it's not that I've lost interest in finishing the book—a feeling of alarm fell on him as he realized this—*I've not lost interest. There's SOMETHING preventing me from writing it.* His next conclusion really scared him with its lack of logic: *Something that wants to use my mind for something else instead.*

Disturbed by his thoughts, Larry began pacing around his study. Back and forth, back and forth, like a pendulum. Every now and then he'd stop and stare out back, at the pond. He was sure the dark specks he saw moving on the far-off water were ducks or geese.

He could hear Colleen puttering about downstairs. He didn't understand women. He figured he never would. This morning's sex with Colleen had been the best they'd had in ages, and then two hours later she was being all snarky with him again. He didn't get it.

It ain't like she knows I've been stepping out on her. Or does she?

He mused on that for a moment, then quashed it. *She can't know. I've been discreet.* He grinned to himself with the philanderer's satisfaction at not being caught. *Yeah, that Reby chick sure is dynamite. I can't wait for our date tomorrow.*

Colleen stopped moving stuff downstairs and Larry forgot about her. He wasn't taking her for granted by forgetting about her; it was a normal marital thing. You felt a comfort from not being alone at home, but you didn't remember your spouse was actually also in the house until you remembered they were. They made a noise and flashed into existence for a second or two, then were gone again. It was kind of a way of preserving a sense of personal space where none actually existed.

"So, alright then," Larry thought aloud with a short, skeptical laugh, "so I'm receiving messages from spirits, or aliens who want to colonize the earth, is it? Only"—he corrected himself—"so far they've not told me anything."

He was walking back towards his laptop when he said this. He stood by his work desk, stared at the blank onscreen page, and wondered.

"Look, I'm being dumb here," he told himself. "There's no damn spooks or little green men trying to talk to me. Look, I'll convince myself—I'll sit down and type something off-hand."

Larry sat down. Convinced nothing was going to happen—he hadn't written a line for four days now—he let his fingers rove over the keys:

Man can evolve to be Gods. I saw Sinis, a Sinis was I . . . I saw Sinis, a Sinis was I . . . I saw Sinis . . . Gods are not ghosts, ghosts are not Gods. Man is simply meat, but can evolve into spirit. Alternity Alternity Alternity . . . I saw Sinis, a Sinis was I . . . a Sinis was I, a Sinis was I . . . A SINIS WAS I!

Larry stopped typing. As he did so, a haze seemed to leave him, only he hadn't been dopey while writing. He was certain of one thing though: he hadn't just been typing at random just now—he'd written what he'd *thought*. Only, what he'd apparently thought made no sense at all to him.

He made another attempt:

Soul can become meat, blood evaporate into spirit, spirit condense to bone. Soul-meat is the ultimate aim. I saw Sinis, a Sinis was I. Evolution is dissolution and reconstitution. I saw Sinis . . . SINIS SINIS SINIS SINIS SINIS SINIS SINIS SINIS.

Larry jerked his fingers away from the laptop like the keyboard had teeth. He stared at the screen in horror. *No, this ain't any kinda accident. I just thought this! But how the hell?*

For a moment his study vanished and he sat in a blue space with massive black tentacles flailing all about him. The smell of rotten meat in here was thicker than six smearings of rancid butter on both sides of a slice of moldy bread.

He gagged, and was instantly back in his study again. A single word floated in his head: *SINIS*.

Larry sat like a deflated balloon in his chair. He had no idea what to think.

Larry Townsend didn't believe in God, or angels, or ghosts, or any other supernatural phenomena. He utterly refused to accept the existence of anything that didn't show up in the picture when you took a digital photograph of it. Shit, Larry Townsend was a *skeptic*. Like he was fond of telling Colleen, he didn't believe in No-God, god of the atheists, either.

He figured he just might be about to start believing in the Devil and demons though. Just before his vision cut out, he'd seen a face in the blueness. A face that seemed sculpted out of the revolting smell of decay everywhere, like goddam farts that had developed a life. The face had been distorted. All he'd really been able to make out of its features was that it had a hell of a lot of teeth. Sharp bloody teeth.

The one good thing about the experience was that the face hadn't been trying to bite him. It had been talking to him, in loud musical words, but all he'd heard clearly was 'Sinis.'

The study door opened then and Colleen walked in. Larry jerked up in his chair as if he'd been shot. He swung around and glared at her.

"Colleen, goddam knock before you come in, wilya? You almost just gave me a damn coronary!"

Her face, which had been smiling, crumpled into upsetness. "I did, Larry. I did knock."

He realized she'd come to smooth things over with him for her earlier behavior, and calmed down. "Sorry, sweetheart, I'm just feeling so uptight this morning."

Colleen's smile reappeared in suspicious stages. "And no wonder; it's all the damn coffee you've been drinking. That's the eight cup you've had today."

Larry didn't reply. Eight? He'd thought it was just five or six.

Colleen moved into the room. Her large body seemed to take up half of its space. Larry felt inexplicably smothered, as if his wife was squashing the air against him. Then she came and pressed her softness against him. "Oh, I just came to see how you were doing, darling. To check if maybe you needed anything."

Yes, Larry thought, *I'll never understand women. First she loves me, then she hates me, now she loves me again. What's next, she's gonna kill me before dinner?* Still, having her there with him felt comforting. There was something very nice about having Colleen's bulk beside him. He reached out a hand and traced the contours of her large ass. As he felt her up, his concerns about his weird visions drained away. Fuck faces from strange places. Colleen was solid; solidity was what mattered, not abstract shit with demonic overtones.

Colleen leaned towards the laptop. "Hey—what's this you're typing?"

Larry moved to delete it.

"No, don't," Colleen said, pulling his hand away from the touchpad.

He thought she was about doing something unreasonable again, till she said: "See, that's what the bald guy on TV was saying."

"What bald guy?"

"You know, the crazy religious one. When we had the fight over CNN and the remote?"

"Yeah?"

"Yeah. He was saying 'I saw Sinis, a Sinis was I.' Kept repeating it like a mantra."

Larry suddenly felt relieved. He wasn't going crazy. No he wasn't. He had a good clear explanation now for his seeming burst of automatic writing. He'd heard that guy on TV say this stuff, and he'd stored it in his memory and later typed it out.

Elated, he grabbed hold of his wife's plump arms and pulled her down to him and kissed her wetly on the lips. She smelt oh so nice, sweet and fresh like a flower garden. "Oh, I love you, baby!"

She smiled at him, pleased. So pleased, she clearly forgot to enquire why he'd been typing the funny mantra anyway. He held her tight, taking refuge in her soft, plush body.

Then a measure of sanity reasserted itself in Larry's mind. *Hey—hold on a minute. Whoa, cowboy, pull up the reins! What's going on here? Okay, so I might have heard part of this stuff on TV*—he peeked around Colleen to see what he'd typed—*but there's no way I'd ever remember all of that. And alright, even assuming I did remember it—what about the crazy vision? The demon face that was speaking to me? Was that just imagination too? Just the fevered working of an overtaxed mind?*

Yes, it was, a voice he didn't hear convinced him. *There's nothing to worry about.*

Larry got up, carefully so he didn't knock Colleen over. "You know what, honey?" he told her. "Let's just go lie in bed together for a little while. I don't know why, but I really don't feel like writing anything more today. I just wanna be with you."

To emphasize his meaning, he grabbed hold of both her nipples through her top and tweaked them gently.

Colleen grinned back. "Remember how when I came in I said I came to see if you wanted anything? Well, pussy's what I had in mind."

Larry felt a sudden surge of triumph. He was the Great Hunter on sexual safari, off to slay his elephantine wife, she of the huge body and long blonde mane, and long red claws. She would fight him in bed, savaging his back, but he would shoot his sperm deep into her core and overcome her. He was the archetypal hero. No, he was even greater than those ancient guys—he had *two* women lusting after him.

Well, I might not be writing shit at the moment, Larry thought happily, *but I'm sure as hell getting laid!*

"Come on, sweetheart," he said, taking Colleen's hand and pulling her towards the study door, "Let's go do what men and women in love do."

Colleen padded meekly after him, already wet between the legs.

CHAPTER 19

Jessica, with Lucy and Reby

Lucy was first out of the car. She staggered halfway towards their front door, then seemed to remember that they'd all been out shopping and turned back towards the silver BMW.

Reby was already waving a bag of groceries at her. "Give us a hand with carrying them inside?"

Lucy walked back to help unload the car.

Jessica watched her approach them. The way Lucy's eyes were glazed over, it looked like she'd mixed up pills again. She shook her head at Reby, then threw Lucy the house keys. "Don't worry, just let yourself in—you look like you need to lie down."

Miraculously, Lucy caught the keys in midair. She turned and staggered off again.

"Let her go," Jessica told Reby. "Else she'll just spill the veggies everywhere and we'll be searching under the car for your tomatoes and carrots."

Reby nodded and they got to work offloading. In addition to Reby's organic foods, eggs, and drinks, they also had a bag of frozen Asian food in microwave packs. Those were Jessica's, a carryover from her 'nose to the grindstone' days, when cooking had seemed a total waste of time. (Working women were the reason God invented microwave ovens!) In fact, she'd spent so little time in the kitchen, that Tony, her second husband, had been shocked the day she'd scrambled eggs for their breakfast. Jessica also had a bag of chocolate bars and energy bars. Lucy's food purchases consisted of lots of burger patties and burger buns, hotdogs and hotdog buns, cheese and pickles and lettuce. There were two full shopping bags of these. Lucy didn't eat regularly, but when she did, she ate A LOT. Then there were five 6-packs of beer, five bottles of wine, three bottles of brandy, and four 12-packs of canned soft drinks. All the excess was going into the pantry. Aside from their food purchases, Jessica had bought tampons and a copy of a book on increasing one's personal productivity; Reby had bought lipstick, KY jelly, and condoms (Jessica had insisted she buy Rabbitfield Deluxe); and Lucy had bought several bottles of nail polish, several packs of Swisher Sweets cigarillos, four or five T-shirts, and some 'Blue King Size' Rizla rolling papers (to help bring out the real flavor of her marijuana).

It was while returning from their second trip to the kitchen that Jessica noticed the footprint. It was large but indistinct, as if there hadn't been enough dislodged sand to properly form it. The footprint was at the edge of the front porch, to the right of the top step as one descended. It was pointed outward, as if . . .

Jessica peered down over the porch. At the edge of the left flowerbed, where it met the gravel in front of the house, was another footprint.

Jessica had a sudden blue 'flash,' an impression of a tall, tentacled shadow seeking access into Roe Cottage. The impression passed. She blinked and calmed herself. *There's no one else out here, no one except me. Still, I'll take a sedative once I'm back inside.*

Visions aside however, there remained the matter of these two clearly male (the gender was simply a matter of size) footprints to address.

Reby was just stepping out of the house. Jessica pulled her aside. "I think we've been intruded," she said.

"Oh shit," Reby said on seeing the footprints herself. "I thought this place was supposed to be safe."

"I thought so too," Jessica agreed. "But I haven't seen any guards about since we arrived. We only ever see the landscaping guys when they're mowing the lawns."

Reby winced. "I assumed the guards were watching on CCTV somewhere. Those look like bootprints too—like a man's been in the house."

"Let's get Lucy."

They forgot about offloading the car for a while. They got Lucy out of bed, waited till she'd found some uppers to pep herself up with, then each checked through their stuff to see if anything was missing.

"Everything's exactly where I left it," Lucy announced to the other two when she was done. Reby and Jessica were in Jessica's room, sitting on her bed. "Nothing's missing. I don't think anyone got in."

"Same thing in my room," Reby said. "But Jessica says something's been moved in here."

"Moved?" Lucy walked in and sat on the dresser seat. "To where?"

"I don't know—that's the problem." Jessica gestured around the room with both hands. "I just have the sense that something's different in here, but I can't say what."

Lucy nodded. "You know, I had a similar feeling myself. As if someone came in, just looked around, then left."

"But why would anyone do that?" Reby asked. "Guys, I'm getting scared. Maybe we should call the police."

Jessica looked unconvinced. "Yeah, but what do we say happened?"

"We've those two bootprints as evidence," Reby replied. "They weren't there before. The cops will have to listen to us. I for one am suddenly terrified."

"Hell no, we're not calling the fuzz," Lucy said.

Jessica and Reby turned to look at her. "But why?" Jessica asked.

Lucy stared at them angrily, tugging on her purple hair as if doing so helped her make her point. "For the obvious reason: detectives. We've got drugs on the premises. If the cops can't find the intruder, they'll bring in their damn sniffer dogs to smell that goddam footprint. Only, the stupid dogs'll suddenly pick up the smell of my stash in the fridge instead and get us all arrested."

Jessica considered that Lucy might have a point. There were quite a lot of narcotics in the house. So much drugs in fact that the police might slap a 'possession with intent to distribute' rap on them all.

"Be reasonable!" Reby snapped. "I came to Raynham to have sex, but not if it's against my will. I don't plan on being raped just because you misinterpret the First Amendment as giving you the freedom to get high!"

Lucy shook her head. "Forget it. Don't you two dare call the police."

Reby looked at Lucy's adamant face, her eyes chiseled from angry flint, then turned to Jessica for support. "Back me up?"

Jessica looked from one of them to the other. "I don't know what to say. You're both right, but—"

"Forget it—no cops!" Lucy snarled.

They both stared at her in surprise. She'd sounded like an enraged tigress just now, the first hint of possible violent behavior Jessica had ever known in her.

"Yeah, yeah, sure," Jessica agreed. "Have it your way. No police." She looked pleading at Reby, a look that begged, *Just agree with her too, for chrissakes.*

"Yeah, yeah, no problem, Lucy," Reby said sourly. "We're both fine with being sexually molested by hoodlums just so you can escape reality forever."

With that, Reby got up. "I'm going to finish bringing in the groceries." She left the bedroom, her body language conveying her frustrated anger back to the other two.

Lucy watched her go. Afterwards, she turned to Jessica. "That chick needs to mellow out big time. Seriously. If she don't, she'll crack up someday." Lucy got to her feet and waved to Jessica. "See ya later, biatch. I gotta go roll myself a joint to calm me."

Lucy left too.

After two minutes of sitting in bemusement, Jessica got up. She quickly squelched a thought of going to help Reby offload the car. Reby might be mad that she'd not backed her up by insisting they call the police. Jessica wasn't in the mood for any arguments or heavy drama. She had enough weird vibes going on as it was. She sighed, wishing now that she'd not mentioned the footprints outside the house to Reby.

She fetched her bottle of nail polish remover from her vanity, then began wiping the 'borrowed blue' off her fingernails, so she could see what sort of recovery progress her nails were making.

Once she had three left hand fingernails clean, she was delighted. Dr. Whitfield's pills were working wonders. Fully two-thirds of the surface of her nails had normalized. This morning it had only been a third. She felt so good about the cure. *All I have to do now is wait. The nightmares and hallucinations will soon clear up too. And then—*

Her thoughts were interrupted by a loud rapping on her window. It was Reby. She walked over and opened the window.

"Come outside," Reby said in a scared voice. "Use the kitchen door. Don't fucking ask why. Just come."

Jessica left her room. She went outside through the kitchen door. Reby was waiting for her there.

Reby pointed down. "Have a look."

Jessica looked. There were another two large footprints in the earth by the kitchen door. The imprints were clearly from male boots.

"We definitely were intruded," Reby said. "There's similar bootprints outside Lucy's window too."

Jessica didn't know what to think. She just wanted this nonsense to go away. She looked at Reby. Reby stared back. Reby wasn't quite white-faced with panic yet, but she was definitely unsettled. Jessica understood: this wasn't the sort of stuff anyone wanted to deal with during their vacation. Calling the cops was the sensible thing to do in this situation.

But . . . she remembered Lucy's reaction to their suggestion to call the police: she'd looked primal, animalistic, like an enraged she-bear bent on protecting her cubs. After seeing Lucy like that, Jessica figured she'd never look at a stick of marijuana or a handful of pills exactly the same way again. Drugs certainly were powerful.

Reby, meanwhile, was waiting for her to say something.

"Maybe it's Lucy's cat-famished policeman," Jessica said finally, "come back to check if we had a puppy he could snack on too." Then, seeing a dark look enter Reby's eyes, she added, "Oh, alright, that isn't funny. Listen, girl, I totally agree with you that some man came around here. But, please, fucking pleaaaassseee, let's just go along with Lucy on this, huh? Let's just humor her. We've already agreed not to call the police. So we won't, not until we've further proof."

"She's gonna get us three raped in our beds," Reby said nervously. "I'm serious. Maybe even a lot worse. We might wind up with our throats slit."

Weirdly, Jessica had the knowledge that that wouldn't happen. Just as she suddenly 'knew' for certain that Reby had already started having sex with Mr. Townsend next door, and that after this 'intruder' incident, she was going to be spending as much time as possible over there, out of fear as well as lust. Without Mrs. Townsend's knowledge, of course.

"Don't worry about it," she told Reby, taking her hand and leading her back around to the front of the house. "None of us'll be raped. We three are going to be just fine."

They went to finish offloading the groceries from the BMW.

CHAPTER 20

Reby

Reby was about to give birth. She lay on the delivery bed with her legs raised and her crotch exposed.

She hated getting so fat during pregnancy. From a trim 125 pounds, she now weighed almost 230. Her cheeks bulged like they were little pregnancies glued to her face. Her arms, legs, nose, feet . . . everywhere was swollen. For the third trimester of her pregnancy she'd felt like an overinflated tire, soon to burst, soon to burst, soon to burst . . .

But she hadn't burst, had she? Women were designed not to. They were fated to want dick stuck in them, to react with semen, and to grow super-fat for nine months. Each time she'd looked in the mirror, she'd felt like crying, felt like running off to a lipo clinic and having them suck all the fat away. Then, like all good, well-behaved, expectant mommies did, she'd go to the kitchen and resume eating for two. Health foods and protein shakes had become obsolete in her fourth month. Chocolate and cookies tasted much better.

Reby had kept jogging up till the sixth month, then decided 'What the hell?' and taken a three-month break from exercising. She was fat anyway, her baby had seen to that. Better to sit it out (literally), accept her prenatal defeat graciously, and take walks in the park to the admiring (and occasionally jealous) looks of her fellow females.

And so her pregnancy had run its course. The one thing she'd not quit on was sex. Hell no. She'd been balling Larry (who was, of course, the father of her kid) up till yesterday evening, when she'd had her first contractions. Right at the end he'd complained that she was too loose for him to feel anything. She'd told him to shut up and put it in her ass when he wanted to come, but to get her off first. She had to keep having orgasms right up till D-Day. Delivery Day, that was. That was crucial. Orgasms were essential to her. They also kept her feeling sexy when she was all bloated. Larry should know that. Once a pregnant wife complained that she felt swollen and unattractive, the best cure was a quick round of sensual lovemaking. A woman's ego occasionally needed boosting too.

Larry was here now with her in the delivery room, dressed in a long green surgical gown, a surgical mask, and an orange bandanna sort of hat. She turned towards him, happy for his support. He gripped her hand. He looked nervous—her first-time baby daddy. She was nervous too, but then she had the consolation of knowing she wasn't the first woman to give birth. Not by a long shot, she wasn't—before her, billions of chicks had split their equally grossly swollen thighs and had ejected the current US and Russian presidents, amongst others, from their grossly distended bellies.

So she had good precedents. All she had to do now was hold in there and 'push' when told to do so.

The doctor came into view. He was a large balding man who reminded her of a bear. He was dressed exactly like Larry was. Or maybe (seeing as he was the physician here), Larry was dressed like he was. He had a jovial manner to him. He also scratched his big nose a lot. "Alright, Miss Butterfield, I think we're ready to get started, don't you?" He peeked down between her legs. "I daresay Junior's in a hurry to leave the comfort of your body."

"Yes!" she groaned back. "Pleeease, doc, let's get on with it." She was hurting now. All at once she'd had an intense contraction that felt like she was about to squirt her guts out. Shit!—her earlier contractions hadn't hurt like this.

She screamed as another massive contraction squeezed her middle in iron tongs. Her belly felt like it had been flattened. She looked down at it. Her belly was still there. It was now throbbing. Milk was dribbling from her nipples.

She turned to Larry. He looked helpless; as limp as his penis looked after he'd come on her breasts. He was sweating bullets—like *he* was the one suffering. She laughed at that: him looking like he was the one in pain. *Ouch, ouch, ouch, ouch, ouch! Eve, you silly bitch, why the hell did you ever eat that goddam apple!? OUCH!* Her love for Larry now inverted into primal hatred. She HATED the prick. He was a stupid, sadistic, misogynistic asshole. A total BDSM wanker. *He* was the one torturing her like this.

Reby screamed again.

"This is a quite difficult delivery," the doctor said, scratching his big nose. "I do think we should give her something for the pain. I suggest a shot of lidocaine."

"No, doctor," a female voice said. "We might harm the baby."

Pregnant Reby looked right, to see who'd spoken. The speaker was completely naked, a slim woman with big breasts. She was totally blue in color, except for her hair, which was all red. Then Reby saw that the blue-skinned woman's hair was actually tentacles: fat, red, eyeless snakes that hung halfway down her back.

Another contraction squeezed Reby. She screamed again. Her eyes gaped open in her agony.

"I really do suggest we give Miss Butterfield a little something to settle her, Mistress Jezebub," the doctor said. His voice conveyed nervousness. "Otherwise, she might not survive the delivery. I mean, you've already forbidden me from performing a cesarean section on her."

The blue woman—Jezebub—laughed. It was a very sadistic laugh, and one that revealed her sharp, filed teeth. She looked frightening with her mouth open like that, not the least because the inside of her mouth (including her tongue) was completely blue as well.

"No, doctor," she replied. "You must not assist her delivery in any way. Her pain is important, it is an invaluable asset. She is a mother, representative of all mothers worldwide. Her agony announces the true child."

Reby's birth waters broke then. She was surprised; she'd thought they'd broken earlier. Now, instead of just running feebly away under her buttocks to spill over the bed's edge, the water jetted out from her sex in a fierce gush that splattered both the doctor and Mistress Jezebub. The doctor was drenched from head to waist. His thick eyebrows seemed to knit together in his displeasure.

Jezebub, however, cupped her hands into the gush of fetal waters pouring from Reby's yawning sex, then she bent and dipped her mouth in the flow so that the squirting liquid filled it. She swallowed and swallowed, rubbing her hands over her blue breasts and belly, bathing in the water that kept pouring from the clenching vagina before her.

The gush of water finally abated. Reby was proud of herself: there had been quite a lot of it. Looking over the edge of the bed, she could see that the floor was flooded. Both Larry and the doctor stood in water up to their ankles. Their hospital clogs looked like miserable blue fish from a Disney cartoon. Their socks and the bottoms of their trousers were soaked.

Jezebub, however, stood *on* the water. She'd stepped back now from Reby and was writhing and caressing herself like she was having an orgasm.

Then Jezebub walked on the water towards Reby. She bent her head between Reby's legs and peered closely into the split.

"Hmm," she said in an 'interested' voice, "I think she's about ready now."

Reby felt something thick inserted inside her. "Yes, I'm right," Jezebub went on. "My whole fist is inside her and I suspect I could insert the other one too if I wanted."

"Please don't," the doctor pleaded, scratching his nose.

"Well at least she won't need an episiotomy. Vaginas nowadays aren't what they once were; they've lost much of their stoic character." Reby felt the blue woman's fist inserted deep inside her, then a ticking sensation. "Yes, I've three fingers inside her cervix. She's ready, for sure. Ooh, one of the little darlings just bit me!"

With a sucking sound, she pulled her hand out of Reby's sex. She knelt to wash her arm clean of mucus in the birth water that filled the room, then straightened up to stare Reby in the face. Her red tentacles throbbed around her blue head. She kissed Reby on the cheek, then smiled at her. "Time for you to do what you were born for, my dear."

Jezebub stepped back and turned to the doctor. "Alright, go on."

"Now push, Miss Butterfield," the kindly bear-like doctor instructed.

Reby PUSHED. Oh, she PUSHED. She'd been biding her time, keeping her mouth shut while they'd been discussing her, focusing all her energies on being ready to PUSH for all she was worth. She'd surfed over the intervening painful contractions (less painful since her waters broke for the second time) by thinking of the end of her labor shortly to come.

She PUUUUUUSSHHEEDD!

It wasn't easy. In those thirty seconds when she concentrated every muscle in her body to eject the contents of her belly from between her legs, it felt as though every horror story she'd ever heard about childbirth was coming true. The fucking PAIN. *Oh, my fucking God, where art thou now when I need thee most?!"*

She gaped left at Larry, her eyes bulging. She wanted to shriek at him, to let him how much she was hurting, but the pain had rendered her mute. He took her hand but she didn't even feel the contact. All that mattered was the pain of the baby sliding out. *Wait a moment: did Jezebub just say 'darlings,' implying that there's TWO of them? That can't be right. There's only one child inside me! I know it—I saw the damn ultrasound!*

And then, finally, she felt the child's head squirt out between her legs, and her agonized squirming everywhere ended. The pain reduced once the head escaped her.

The doctor was bent over, peering between her spread and raised thighs. All she could see of him over the hump of her belly was the green rear of his clothes. She felt him poking around at the mouth of her. She looked aside, at Jezebub. The blue-skinned nude was watching intently, licking her blue lips with her blue tongue, playing with her red tentacles like they were real hair.

It was during this period of calm that she noticed that Jezebub had neither nipples nor a navel. *Now that's really odd,* she thought.

She looked sideways at Larry. He'd not fainted like husbands were sometimes wont to do, but he looked alarmed, like he couldn't believe what he was seeing. She wondered what their baby looked like. She felt triumphant: she'd achieved what a woman was born a woman for, and now her son (unfortunately not a daughter to follow in her fertile footsteps) would worship her as Mother.

Then Reby felt a strange squirming between her legs and looked forward. She'd felt the squirming before, but she'd thought it was the doctor's fingers. Now she realized that it wasn't.

As if he'd sensed her watching him, the doctor raised his head from between her thighs. He beamed at Reby, then looked sideways at Jezebub and nodded.

"I can see them," Jezebub said, striding forward over the birth water again, her feet sending ripples across the water surface to smack against the sky-blue walls of the delivery room. "They're nice and shiny. But are they healthy?"

What are they talking about? Reby wondered. "My baby, doctor," she moaned. "Please let me see my little Lawrence!" She'd decided to name him after his father.

The doctor nodded at her, then bent between her legs again. She could feel the kid squirming furiously down there, as if resisting being picked up. Larry junior was thrashing around against her thighs. And why was her baby bulge still not deflated? In fact, she felt like there was another kid inside there. No, that was wrong. How she felt was like she was packed full of boisterous children, all impatient to burst forth from her.

The doctor straightened up again. "Here's your babies, Miss Butterfield. Aren't they really pretty?"

He wasn't holding Larry Jnr. He was holding up a pile of snakes.

Reby screamed. Beside her, Larry, who'd been holding her left hand, finally fainted. She never even heard the loud splash as he hit the water. She was too busy yelling at the doctor: "What the fucking hell is that!!?? WHAT!!?? WHAT!!??"

The doctor walked out from between her legs and around the side of the bed. In his arms he bore a bright yellow viper, a diamond-patterned rattler, a gold-and-green python, and a black mamba, all hissing and flailing angrily.

Reby began weeping. Jezebub walked quickly to her side and stroked her cheek. "Now, now, don't be like that, dear," she cooed into Reby's ear. "Oh, I know they're all a bit small, but that's normal when you have more than one baby in you—there's only so much space in a womb for each to occupy. But look on the positive side: they're all healthy, and really bright and shiny. Just see how nicely the light reflects off their scales. So pretty, so—"

The end of Jezebub's sentence vanished into the doctor's screams. All at once, and all as one, the serpents he carried had turned on him. They swarmed all over him and covered him and bit him to death. Reby caught sight of one terrified brown eye peeking out through a parting in the snakes' coils, and then the doctor was crumpling to the floor and kicking and splashing wildly as the snakes destroyed him. There was a squirting up of blood that splashed all over Reby, then silence from the watery floor.

"Oh shit!" Jezebub said. "You're not another one of *those*, are you? And I really thought you'd be different."

"Huh?" Reby turned on the bed to gape at her. The blue woman had sounded really worried. And she looked worried too. Her face was squeezed up like that of a Kansas homeowner who'd just heard that a tornado would flatten her house in two minutes.

She turned to look down at the floor. In a bloody pile, the snakes—her children? (the thought made her weep)—were still thrashing all over the doctor's half-submerged body.

Reby couldn't dwell long on either Jezebub's discomfiture or the doctor's passing. She had new problems of her own:

Her labor contractions had returned. And this time they were twice as painful. Once again, she was unable to scream. All she could do was PUSH and gasp.

Something *was* emerging from her sex. And this time, whatever was coming out of her made no pretense of being a baby, or even of being human.

Then the first part of it was out. She heard loud splashing in the water as whatever it was slid forward off the delivery bed.

Jezebub hurried forward, her bare feet making no sound on the water surface, not even leaving ripples now. She took up the doctor's former position between Reby's legs and peeked down. Then, delighted, she raised her gaze to meet Reby's, her sadistic smile firmly back in place. "Oh goody," she gushed, "I was completely wrong about you, darling. You're a *real* one."

She bent once more between Reby's legs. When she raised her head again, she had a pale blue snake between her teeth. She was eating it. The snake flailed; Jezebub bit the snake's head off and swallowed it. She flung the rest of the snake away, then grabbed up a handful of them. She crammed the blue serpents into her mouth and bit down hard on them. Their blood and guts squirted out between her lips.

Reby was disgusted. She was outraged. She was also exhausted. She'd been all this while locked in an endless contraction of childbirth, one that was seemingly pushing the world's longest infant out of her tortured and sore loins. And it wasn't over yet, the damn kid was still coming.

She raised herself on her elbows, then sat upright, bracing herself on straight arms so she could see below the obstruction of her belly.

God no! She was giving birth to an endless river of snakes, a literal flood of them. The snakes were multicolored and multi-sized. There were pythons, boa constrictors, black and white mambas, grass snakes, cobras, anacondas, vipers, horned snakes, rattlers and puff-adders. There were also many other species of legless reptile that she didn't recognize. They streamed out of her vagina mingled with blood and mucus.

The snakes writhed and gushed out of her and fell off the birth bed. They began piling up in the delivery room, spreading across its water-covered floor in a colored mass that slowly filled up everywhere.

Reby gaped in horror at her 'children.' They squirmed around the bed. With each passing second their level in the room rose higher.

She looked at Jezebub. Jezebub stood buried up to her waist in the snakes. From being worried five minutes ago, she now didn't seem in the least bit bothered by what was happening. She was eating more of the blue snakes. She saw Reby staring at her and winked saucily. She bit several of the snakes in two, chewed and swallowed the parts she wanted, cast the rest away over her shoulders, then giggled.

"These blue ones are low-fat," she said, wiping a splatter of snake guts off her nippleless breasts. "You should try them sometimes."

Reby nodded. She still couldn't speak; her seemingly endless 'snakebirth' was too agonizing for words. On her left, the snake-level was so high that the reptiles had lifted Larry off the floor like they were a bed.

No, no, don't attack daddy, Reby thought. *Daddy loves you all.*

She caught one final glance of Jezebub, her pointy teeth buried deep in the head of an anaconda with a body thicker than her thighs, then the level of the snakes rose above her, and she was lying in a pit with them as its living walls. She was alone in there. There was no sign of Jezebub, or of Larry (who must by now have been crushed against the ceiling by the press of his own reptilian offspring).

And still her belly bulged and her vagina squirted the reptiles out.

Then, suddenly, the snake-walls around her gave way. The entire reptile mass forming the sides of her pit fell inward and covered her. And buried her. She could see nothing. There was no light. She was trapped in there, wrapped in the scaly rustle of serpents. Big and small, they wove themselves around her body like living clothing.

And still, impossibly, Reby was giving birth to yet more and more snakes.

***

Reby snapped awake like she'd been struck by lightning. Her pulse was racing and she was trembling. Once she understood that she'd merely been dreaming, she sat up in bed with the covers pulled up over her breasts, and stared wide-eyed at the opposite wall.

She was so scared, she felt like fleeing the house screaming.

It was ages before she calmed down enough to go back to sleep.

This second time, she dreamt of floating peacefully through a blue nothing. And then of dissolving and becoming nothing.

THURSDAY

CHAPTER 21

Lucy

Lucy waved at the onscreen dog. "Hey, Smokey, how you doin'?"

The massive St. Bernard leapt and wagged his tail at her. "Woof, woof!" he barked.

"Woof, woof!" Lucy barked back. "Alright, Smokey, now sit, I wanna talk to ya."

"Woof! Woof!"

"Hey, I said *sit*, boy, or it's no more hash brownies for you once I'm home again."

The threat worked. The dog sat obediently and stared at the screen. He loved hash brownies. They made him feel . . . 'undoglike.' Hash brownies made Smokey feel 'enhanced,' like his canine intellect was expanding to become human.

"Good, good, boy," Lucy cooed. "That's a nice big doggie. Now listen to mommy."

"Woof, woof!"

Lucy Polk had woken up this Thursday morning with a burning desire to talk to someone. After considering her two housemates for a while as possible conversation partners, she'd settled instead on her dog, mainly because her housemates were part of what she wanted to talk about.

That decided, she'd phoned her brother Robert and asked him to set up a webcam chat with her dog.

Robert had leashed the St. Bernard in the kitchen, put a laptop on a chair far away enough from Smokey so the dog couldn't either scratch or lick its screen, put down a plate of dog food, and left for the restaurant.

Currently, Lucy lay facing her own laptop, joint in hand, saucerful of pills within arm's reach.

"So, Smokey," she explained through puffs of pot smoke, "That's the situation here, boy. I don't get it myself, you know. You know how I'm always in the groove of things? But since getting to this place—I feel like I'm an astronaut who's just touched down on a cavegirl planet, baby. Miss Future in the Stoned Age. I really do."

"Woof! Woof!"

"Yeah, I knew you'd understand. Listen, Smokey boy, I mean, I'm seeing things now. Yesterday, I saw a man eat a cat. It was sick, ya know—he was crunching it like it was delicious. Thank heavens the cat was dead. I mean, I imagined it, you know. I know what you're thinking: how sick is she, right? Imagining something as horrible as that? . . . Ah, shit, doggie, and you know what else happened? Someone's stalking us. There's footprints, footprints outside! Oh, God, help us!" Lucy stopped talking to wipe tears from her eyes. "And we can't even call the cops to save us. And you know why?"

On her laptop screen the St. Bernard did his best to look intelligent; he cocked an ear.

"Shit, it's 'cos of all the drugs, Smokey. Just imagine what'd happen if some policeman found all my lovely Acapulco strain in the fridge. And you know . . . anyway, so we're likely to be raped any day now. That's okay, I guess. I'm used to that kind of thing now, so long as I don't wind up preggered again or get AIDS from it. But we might get killed too—so I just wanna say goodbye now before it all ends for me, alright? Okay, so you be a good dog now and don't bite mom or dad at my funeral. Oh shit—they won't come, I'm still disowned. Anyhow, that's my farewell, I'll leave you all my pot so Rob can make you some brownies . . . you know, Smokey, I'm getting confused here. Yeah, go on, I'll wait."

She waited, puffing away, while Smokey took several bites of chunky dog food and chewed them thoughtfully. To keep her mind focused, she grabbed a handful of pills and chewed them, trying to match her chewing with her dog's.

When she had the dog's attention again, she continued:

"Yeah, okay, so it's about Jessica. I like her, but she's creeping me out. She's always looking around like she's seeing shit that ain't there. You know, like in those psychopath movies. Yeah, it's scary as hell. I dunno, but maybe she'll slit our throats before the stalker does. Oh, I'm gonna die, Smokey—I just know it, baby." She pressed her hands to her face and began weeping profusely.

"Woof! Woof!" Smokey barked.

Lucy wiped her tears away. "Thanks, Smokey, you're a real canine friend. Soooooo, see, Jessica's like insane like that, right, and also . . . also . . ." Lucy tried hard to remember what she was going to say, "yeah, I remember . . . yeah, her fingernails keep changing color. First they were all blue, and then yesterday, they were patchy-like, and today they're normal again. How'd you like that? Just imagine it—like she's mutating. Oh, it's just so crazy!"

"Woof!"

"Okay, yes, I'll calm down. Okay, I'm calm now." Lucy leapt down from the bed and began pacing agitatedly back and forth. Half the state away, her dog similarly leapt up and began pacing nervously about in front of his own laptop.

After walking for a while, Lucy sat on the edge of her bed and placed her laptop on her knees. "Alright, now you need to calm down, Smokey. Hey—sit down, mutt, I'm talking to you! Oh, I'm sorry, I'm sorry, I'm sorry I shouted. No, don't look so sad, baby, baby, baby. Brighten up and I'll let you have some downers too when I'm home. Okay, so where was I? . . . Yeah, so Jessica is clearly thinking of killing me and Reby . . . while Reby . . . yeah, you remember Aunt Reby don't'cha? The skinny one with muscles everywhere and breasts like oranges. The one that pushed you out of bed that time when you licked her ankles? Yeah, it's her I mean. Okay, now, she's here too, and she's screwing around as usual, and this time the guy is married."

"Woof! Woof! Woof! Woof! Woof!"

"Yeah, Smokey, I think it's horrible too. I really do. Believe me, I'm not supporting Reby; I'm just letting you know what she's up to. And the man's wife is such a nice woman too. I met her yesterday. I was walking out the street and she was walking in, and she was such a sweet lady. She's really fat though, but pretty with it too. You remember Dean's sister Gracie? . . . Yes? . . . Okay, she's that big. She's blonde and she's got a big nose and greenish-blue eyes like seawater, and quite large ears, and she looks a bit like Bette Midler, but not that much. Wow, her arms are huge and I was praying she wouldn't hug me with them, 'cos they'd have squashed me, broken all my poor ribs. No shit, Smokey. But, honestly, she's really nice, and she's got fantastic dress sense. She had on these long black trousers and a white-and-black striped top which I think made her look thinner . . . I *think*, 'cos I could still tell that she was a fat woman. Her thighs were just ginormous. Plus-sized for real. Her name's Colleen, Colleen Townsend, and her husband's cheating on her with Reby. That's so sad, isn't it? Just imagine that. Okay, so Mrs. Colleen Townsend . . . yeah, I was describing her clothes, wasn't I? . . . Yeah? . . . So, black and white striped top with gold buttons, black trousers. She's got a humongous ass though, it's real *big*. You know, like there's pillows in the back of her pants. Or giant marshmallows. Imagine toasting *her* over a campfire; but you're not a wolf, are you? You're just a dog, Smokey. Aw well. Still, her butt is big enough for you to explore and get lost in, believe me. She might even have foxes to hunt in there. And she had on a nice black Dior belt with gold buckles. Yeah, she's rich and classy, that one, for sure. And she speaks nicely too; she's not uppity and posh like all those rich biatches on TV. No, she's quiet, almost nervous-like, like she's scared to say the wrong thing. But you know what? Wow!—she had a blackhead on her chin. I was just staring at it. I kept staring at it. I was gonna say, 'Hey, lady, I'm gonna pop you now'—like we were gonna fuck—and pop her blackhead, but I decided not to, 'cos she might faint and the cops might come here and arrest me, and then my pot would . . . 'cos I popped . . . but she was really chic, she needed a Chihuahua, a pink Chihuahua . . . and she had this black-and-silver purse, I think it was Dior too. Man, I was so fucking jealous, huh . . . but then I noticed her blackhead again and I could hear it speaking to me, begging me to pop it, saying, 'PLEASE POP ME RIGHT NOW!' But I couldn't, 'cos she . . . okay, so she's really pretty and classy and has big thighs and . . . yes, expensive open sandals, black too, though her toenails were all red. Red and long. Her fingernails too—really, really long and red like she'd been dipping them in blood. They scared me shitless. I asked her about them, she says they're one hundred percent natural, no plastic involved, though two of them had to be silk-wrapped 'cos they broke. She says she grows her red nails like they're roses, pampers them like they're her pets. Scary that, right? Then she had on several rings. Expensive ones with diamonds—they're both quite rich. Oh, but her husband's fucking Reby with her skinny little ass. I think my ass is tighter than Reby's—it's less muscular. Colleen's either got natural boobs or really small implants. Oh, I hope she sues her cheating husband to a heart attack and takes all his money. I really do. I'm so, so, so rooting for her in divorce court! Soooo, she had on great fucking wonderful rings, and a great necklace too and her hands and feet were all very pampered, and so was her face. Her teeth were just fantastic, so even and white; she must share Angelina Jolie's dentist. Her lipstick was purple, and her eyelids were shaded blue. Hey—you know, they were blue just like Jessica's nails turned! And Mrs. Towns— . . . Colleen's blonde hair was nicely styled, just great, beautifully curled and really glossy; she must spend lots on looking so classy. Not like me, ha ha ha. And she had on really nice earrings. I think they were blue too. Everything's blue around here, Smokey darling. Me in particular. I just feel so blue today. Blue and sad like its raining and . . ."

Her joint ran out. The laptop felt too hot on her bare thighs so she put it down. She checked that Smokey was still listening, then found another joint she'd rolled earlier. She looked around for her lighter. She lit the joint then repositioned herself on the bed facing the laptop again. She popped a few pills to help the joint really get working.

"So, Smokey, Colleen's really cute for a fat chick. I mean, she's hot in an overweight way and if you were a guy I'm sure you'd want to bone her. I mean, you'd want to do her doggy-style, if you were a man, that is. I mean, Colleen's really good-looking and it's such a shame that Reby's fucking . . . aw, fuck Reby anyway. She's just a slut . . . I wonder what the hell Mr. Townsend sees in her, with her tight manhole and loose morals. I'm sure her vajayjay smells like a sewer, and he's been licking it—yuck! Hey, you know Reby looks weird too nowadays. We all do. Shit! Shit! Shit! That's it!" She threw up her arms in a victory gesture. "Yeah, Smokey darling, now I remember what I wanted to talk to you about. I do now. I think . . . I think we're all going crazy. Or maybe we're already crazy, but no one's gonna admit it yet. Then we're all gonna be hiding in our rooms trembling in fear, each of us scared that the others are gonna stab us to death with a big knife, while at the same time clutching our own big knife and planning on how to stab the others to death. And then the cops are gonna come and . . . Oh, it's so sad. All I wanna do is vacation. How can that be this hard? Answer me, you fucking mutt! I'm your goddam mother and I feed and house your hairy canine ass, for crying out loud! Answer me dammit before I start crying again!! I'm cracking up here!!"

"WOOF WOOF WOOF WOOF! GRRRRRR! WOOF WOOF! GRRRR!"

"Yeah, thanks, I always knew you were on my side. Look, sorry for shouting again. C'mon, don't be mad at me. I'm just so fucking stressed nowadays, you know. Even the pills don't seem to be workin' today. C'mon, stop lookin' at me all sad like that; you know I can't stand it. Alright, I'll make it up to you. I'll bake you lotsa doggy biscuits, you know, those super-chewy pumpkin and peanut-butter ones you love? . . . I'm forgiven? . . . Thanks, baby, hugs across the state. See . . . so what was I about to say? . . . Okay, so yes, I'm . . . I'm definitely sure . . . Yeah, I'm certain, for sure, that we're each gonna kill the others, and then the police are gonna come and find my stash. That hurts to imagine. Shit, look, just fuck it, okay? Fuck this place and my dying and Reby's sex thing and Jessica's nutcase thing and . . ."

A look of horror came over Lucy's face. "Aw, shit, Smokey, I've been talking about myself all this while. Oh, how damn thoughtless of me. I'm sorry, sorry, boy. So, how you been doin'? Meet any hot bitches on your evening walks? My brother *is* walking you, right? I hope Rob and Dean aren't maltreating you. Hey, hey—dude, they ain't making you watch their gay porn DVDs, are they? You better not dare get enticed into that shit. I mean it. If I come home and see you staring at other boy-dog's asses I'm gonna kick your ass! . . . Hey, what's that?"

Over by her bedroom door, 'something' was forming. Lucy gaped at it. The thing had no logical shape she could lock onto. No, its appearance wasn't any kind of human-logical. It was a grayish mass with tentacles sticking out of it. An arsenal of gray tentacles. But . . . it was also dotted with numerous eyes and mouths at the base of its tentacles. It was about the size of a legless cow. It had no legs, it hovered in midair. Like a ghost, it was half transparent—she could see the door through it.

It stank. It really fucking stank. The damn thing stank atrociously. Lucy imagined damp moldy cellars and great-great-grandmother's wedding dresses with families of dead and rotting rats in them, mixed with the sort of smell you got when you didn't wash your butt-crack after exercising, mixed with rotting fish. The rotting fish stink seemed the strongest.

Lucy had been reaching for a few more pills. Now she froze and instead raised her joint to eye level and took a good long look at it.

What da fuck am I smoking? Mutant-rat shit?

Slightly cross-eyed, she looked from her joint back to the door. The creature was still there, hovering like it wanted something. Watching her through its tentacles. She now saw that its gray body was covered with sores that were bursting and leaking yellow pus. Except for its mouths and eyes, the gray thing might have been a massive boil growing on her wall—like the house was sick and rotting from the inside out. And she really didn't like the way its eyes were staring at her. There must have been at least forty blue eyes looking her way. And its mouths were licking their lips like they wanted to eat her.

Lucy was too high to feel fear. Her brain felt wired into a state of 'Wow!' She studied her joint again, then studied the colored tablets and caplets on her dope saucer. This was a whole new level of hallucination for her. Usually she saw orange rats or green three-headed dogs; stuff rooted in reality, no matter how distorted.

She looked up again, peering through the spectral monster at her bedroom door. She pondered what to do. Should she run through it and get away, or just close her eyes and hope that like the cat-eating cop, it would go away? Hallucinations generally left you alone if you left them alone too.

She did the most sensible thing she could think of: she grabbed a handful of pills from her dope saucer and swallowed them. Then, taking care not to look towards the door, she lay back on the bed and shut her eyes.

Good. It's gonna be gone when I open my eyes. Good. Most likely there'll be sunshine or pink rabbits or red cows in the corner.

After a short wait, Lucy opened her eyes again.

Shit! The rotting gray thing was no longer by the door. The thing was now hovering directly above her, up by the ceiling. Oh heck, it was smelly! It billowed as if full of gas, and its huge tentacles waved over her like they were waving hello. Its many eyes peered through its many tentacles at her. She felt them radiating hatred at her. And hunger. Its many mouths all licked their lips.

It fell towards her. Its rotting tentacles touched her, making her skin tingle with a chilling kind of electricity.

Fuck! Lucy thought, shivering all over. *Man, just look at this damn thing. This is so fucking crazy. I can see the ceiling through it, and yet it feels so fucking solid. Far out, baby. Is it gonna eat me now or what? Dammit, this is one crazy trip . . .*

Then the thing's tentacles closed around Lucy's throat and began choking her. It wrapped other appendages about her tiny body. It lifted her off the bed and shook her like a toy. Her breath cut out and she began sputtering. When she managed to breathe, all she drew into her lungs was its fish-and-dead-grandmother stink.

Through the overload of drugs in her head, she felt her torturer's intense amusement. It thought of her as a joke. A human joke. It licked her body with its many tongues, slobbering all over her till its saliva dropped from her onto the bed. Its saliva reeked like fish guts.

Lucy had the idea that she was dying, but still couldn't feel afraid. *Nightmares? I've had them before—they always end come morning.*

But now *was* morning, wasn't it?

Then the lack of oxygen got to her brain and she passed out.

***

"Woof Woof Woof Woof! Woof! Woof!" Smokey barked for a while, trying to get Lucy's attention. When he realized his mistress was out for the count (this was far from the first time Lucy had fallen asleep while talking to him), the St. Bernard dropped his head to the kitchen floor and fell asleep himself.

Smokey *had* noticed the gray cloudy thing in Lucy's bedroom. But that too was normal enough. This was actually a little cloud. Smokey was used to Lucy making much larger ones, ones that filled up her entire bedroom. Sometimes she even made little fires in her bedroom too.

***

With a start, Lucy came awake again. Her head ached and her mouth tasted bitter.

She discovered she wasn't stoned anymore. She hadn't been this clearheaded in years. Not since her last abortion.

***

Lucy's first two abortions, she'd done high. She'd walked into the clinic stoned (even though the doctors had said that was a no-no), felt weird while the kid was being extracted, and then, once given the all-clear, dropped some more pills. She'd not cared about seeing the kid.

The third time, however, she'd felt she was missing something in her abortion experience. Sitting in her room in Springfield all knocked up again, and flying higher than the American Eagle at the time, Lucy had suddenly made a druggy connection between abortion and childbirth. They were one and the same thing, she'd understood with murky pillhead clarity, just that during abortions the child tended to come out dead, and you could also time its arrival to your preference. And no one dared called you a bad person afterwards, not like once you'd had the kid and now grew paranoid (like pot wasn't making her paranoid enough already) with looking over your shoulder all the time to ensure social workers weren't stalking you because last time you'd accidentally mixed bennies up in your child's baby formula.

See, she'd enthused gleefully, *there are benefits to political correctness after all!*

So, Lucy had decided to have her third abortion sober, and she first made certain that she'd get to see the fetus afterwards.

She'd waited patiently till she was five months gone and had begun showing before going in. She'd not enjoyed the abortion. (Both earlier times had been a breeze!) When the doctor stuck his speculum inside her, it had felt like she was losing her virginity all over again. The local anesthetic made her feel like her uterus was high or something. Tubes entered her, a pump hummed and drained her. Significant probing ensued. It was odd: during the 36-minute procedure, she could practically feel them dismantling the child inside her.

Afterwards, Lucy was shown the reassembled fetus in a tray. (The doctor said he needed to be sure they'd not forgotten part of it inside her.) She'd stared at it for ages, then burst out crying. She'd wept throughout the day. She'd felt so miserable. She'd felt like she'd just cut out a major part of herself. It was so, so, sad to see that little mass of never-to-be-born person lying there in that cold metal tray. It had been a boy too.

Once home, she'd lit up a jumbo-jet-joint, decided she knew enough about motherhood now to last her several reincarnation's worth's of lifetimes, and vowed never to get pregnant again. That was three years ago and she'd thankfully not missed her period once since then.

***

So now, Lucy Polk was very surprised to find herself sober. For her, being un-stoned was very disorientating. Lucy disliked how she felt. She felt cold, chilly like she was outside in autumn. Her fingers and toes tingled.

She quickly felt around for her saucer of pills.

This was when she realized she was covered all over in goo.

She'd woken lying on her back, facing the ceiling. This was why she'd not immediately noticed her strange state. Now, however, she sat bolt upright and looked down her body in disbelief.

She was utterly drenched in monster saliva. The oily, gooey, sticky stuff covered her from head to toes—Yuck! Her hair and T-shirt and panties and socks—all were completely soaked through and dripping with it. The goo smelt like fish and baby poop and sheep's guts and the pus from boils and sweaty unwashed armpit and yet more fish! It was blue-tinted and transparent and chunky, like frog spawn minus the eggs.

She wiped a thick layer of the stuff off her face. That reduced the stink a little. It became easier to breathe.

She looked around the bedroom. There was a lot of the reeking saliva on the bed, including all over her laptop. Onscreen on her laptop, Smokey was fast asleep. His ears and muzzle twitched and his body rose and fell with his doggy snores. On her right, she saw the remainder of the joint she'd been smoking. It had burned a big hole in the bedclothes and mattress before being put out by monster spit.

She looked back at herself. She was scared, scared, scared. Nothing of this kind had ever happened to her before. Cold sober like she was, she could appreciate the horror of her situation. What should she do? She could scream and call the others, but . . .

She was scared to scream. *What if I do and the monster returns?* And besides . .

The saliva was evaporating. Not rapidly—she was still all sticky with the hideous goop—but it was clearing off her hair and body like smoke departing a skillet, lifting off her soaked T-shirt like steam under an iron. It filled the room with a dreadfully smelly haze that in turn faded like a memory.

Soon, three-quarters of the monster spittle in Lucy's bedroom was gone, including all that coating her laptop. The tingling in her hands and feet was fading away also.

Lucy decided she'd had enough of being sober. She leapt off the bed, rolled a fresh joint, and hurriedly lit it up.

No, this wasn't something one screamed about, she figured. By now, most of the goop had evaporated off her body. She was left covered in a film of evil-smelling bluish grease. She reeked like she'd been dipped in cod liver oil.

Lucy sat and smoked her joint. Slowly, she began feeling normal again. Damn, this sure was turning into one hell of a wacky vacation.

The greasy saliva remnant felt icky on her body. After a while, it really began annoying her. She got up and went into the bathroom to shower it all off.

CHAPTER 22

Jessica

It was noon now. Jessica was sunning herself on a deck chair by the pond behind the forest. Hidden from prying eyes by the woods, she'd earlier walked from the cottage to the pond wearing just a black bikini and orange flip-flops.

She grinned to herself. She felt as alone as she was. The trees all around the pond made this spot just great for privacy. Her eyes traced the rippling water into the distance, out to where a red rowboat sat tied to a wooden pier. Beyond the boat, a few ducks bobbed on the pond surface.

Jessica felt good. She'd woken this morning to find that her nails—all ten of them—were perfectly normal again. The only trace of blue anywhere had been up in the sky, where it was meant to be. And as if that wasn't in itself sufficient cause for celebration, she'd also not dreamt at all. No nightmares of tentacles and corpse smells.

She'd awoken tired and slightly hungover—last night they'd all gotten drunk again before bed—but in excellent spirits. (Remembering her waking hangover also reminded Jessica that she'd not had another headache/nausea attack since her visit to Dr. Whitfield at the Raynham Outlook Clinic.)

Jessica may have been feeling great, but so far today, the atmosphere in the house hadn't been a good one. Both Reby and Lucy had been all out of sorts since breakfast. Lucy had afterwards vanished to 'dog-chat,' while Reby had begun researching types of snakes on her iPad. Weird. Then, at about ten-thirty, Lucy had walked out of her room smelling like she'd just poured a whole carton of perfume over herself. She'd been as high as usual, but underneath her narcotic blanket Jessica had sensed that she was really bothered about something. Maybe her supply was running out?

Jessica had followed her into the kitchen. "Hey, biatch, you cool?" she'd enquired.

Lucy had looked up from staring into the fridge, made an 'O.K.' sign with her fingers, then vanished into the pantry.

Jessica had looked over at Reby to see what she thought. Reby apparently hadn't even noticed or *smelt* Lucy; she was staring at her iPad with a worried look on her face. A *very* worried look that made no sense to Jessica.

And that wasn't all. Reby was supposed to be starting her workout regime at the Body Revolution gym today, but she'd said she didn't feel up to it. In addition to which, she hadn't even gone out jogging this morning. Now that was odd. Reby hadn't missed an early morning run since they'd moved in here.

Jessica had finally quit bothering herself about her two housemates. On her own part, she had a lot to be happy about. When the heavy vibes at home didn't lighten up, she'd decided to walk the three hundred yards to the pond and relax and work on her tan.

There were fish in the pond, dark and quite large ones. They looked like trout. She was seated close enough to the water's edge to see them clearly. She'd brought along a beach towel to lie on, but on arriving here she'd discovered a three-sided open shed up by the tree line containing deck chairs, beach tables, and parasols. This seemed confirmation of her theory that Red Oak Crescent had originally been designed as part of a resort.

A black bird skimmed down low over the lake, snapped something up in its beak, and zipped off again. The summer grass felt soft and tickly beneath her bare soles.

Jessica got out the book she'd bought while shopping yesterday. *How to run Your Life without Ruining It or Running yourself into the Ground* (A manual designed to boost personal and business productivity by 300%) by Deacon Robbins. It was a large book—500 plus pages—packed with time-tested wisdom and research and valuable expert insight into the *right way* to work. The book's title had magnetized Jessica on sight.

Jessica had no time for fluffy reads about billionaires and virgins, or dragons and virgins, or vampires and virgins, or human sacrifices requiring virgins. (It appeared virgins were in high demand in fiction nowadays. They were apparently in even higher demand in the real world; so much so that Jessica had read of a Romanian girl—

Aleexandra Kefren—actually auctioning her hymen through an escort agency. There seemed to be a worldwide shortage of serviceable hymens nowadays—the fault of sex education?) Jessica read only to improve herself. She read self-help books and the service manuals for electronic stuff she bought, once she'd gotten past the point where she could figure out the new machine by herself (which was in itself a type of self-improvement). Every day and in every way Jessica Schreiber needed to get better and better.

She opened to the book's Page of Contents. She didn't consider reading pep talks cheating on her vacation. No, that wasn't true. Okay, so yes, she knew she was cheating. She knew she shouldn't do it. Reading this stuff would most likely start her off worrying about her current 'laziness' again. But she was giving so much up already, like— she fiddled in her beach bag again till she found a can of Sprite—like caffeine, for instance. Besides, how did that old saying go again? You can take the girl out of the office, but you can't take the office out of the girl?

She giggled at her joke. She plugged her earphones into her cellphone, pulled up a playlist, then leaned back and picked up her soft drink to open it.

Then she was falling.

Oh, shit!

***

They were all around her again. She was back inside the blue void that smelt like rotting bodies. She seemed to have fallen off her deck chair into the pond, only the pond was now filled with bloody animal guts and old cheese and maggot-riddled filth instead of water. If that was the case, these monsters must be the transformed frogs and trout.

Only, that was bullshit. She knew it was. These monstrous things crowding around her weren't from the lake. They were nothing from Earth; nothing from its *surface*, anyway. Jessica was certain of that. They very possibly *could* be from Hell.

Their stink of rottenness, of endless decay, overpowered her. She wanted to puke, but understood that the stink was herself too. She reeked like they did.

They were all around her, their dark outlines crayon smears on the universe's blue paper. Purple lines that writhed like snakes moving underwater. Brown lines like fecal smears in a blue ceramic toilet. Black lines like a Spanish widow's wind-caught shawl floating across the Mediterranean sky.

The blue filled her eyes. There was only the blue to see.

(The blue was hot, but hot in a way that made temperature irrelevant. This heat wasn't agony, but rather a part of existence. The heat might just as well have been freezing Artic cold.)

The stench of endless death ruled her nostrils. The unseen universe as a charnel, rotting thing. She felt it impossible that there could be so much corruption anywhere, and yet, she realized there was.

These creatures were the Gods of Decay.

The monster tentacles offended decency, these writhing thicknesses that caressed and squeezed her in their unseen, unholy embrace. She couldn't see her own body; she only recognized its shape in the dark lines endlessly wrapping around her. A cosmos of psychedelic strangeness with her as its mother.

She was shocked and scared, but then the shock wore off and she was just scared. She knew she wasn't dreaming—she wasn't asleep. Awake, she floated in the middle of a sea of evil.

The massive creatures rubbed against her. Their bodies felt wet, slippery with horrible liquids. "Come and see," she heard them say in their chilling crystal voices. "Come and be."

She went with them. She didn't leave her place in the vast emptiness, and yet she travelled through it after the beings, after the masses of outlined tentacles that hung around her like bead curtains, that swung like strange testicles dangling from smelly celestial crotches. About her she heard the beating of monstrous wings.

She went with them. She had no choice. She floated through the stink. Through the terminal blue.

She was apprehensive. She knew they were taking her to view something bad. Something very bad. But she had no choice. No choice. She was theirs. They owned her.

They arrived. They didn't announce it, but she knew it.

They were in a room with a stone altar. The room was invisible to her, its endless dimensions sensed rather than seen. The altar was a visual reality, directly in her path. A wet stone walkway led to it.

On the altar lay a young man, bound hand and foot. He was muscular, with short blond hair. He was in his early twenties, twenty-two at most. He was naked. He was bleeding.

She gasped. He was blind, both of his eyes pulled from their sockets and left dangling on their nerve cords over the sides of his face. Bright blue in white balls smeared with red blood.

She approached him along the walkway. The stones felt soft and squishy under her feet. They felt distressingly like they had once been part of a human body themselves. They were slippery, as if covered with mucus.

Though terrified, she went willingly now, feeling a sense of necessity about her role in this thing that was going on. She felt as urgent as diarrhea. All around she and the young man writhed the dark outlines of the hellish beings that stank atrociously.

An axe appeared in her hands. Out of the blue. All of a sudden she was gripping it. It was large and gleaming and razor sharp.

She stared at the axe in horror. *Oh, no—this is going to be so . . . good!*

Good? The word had dropped into her mind like the final piece being slotted into a jigsaw puzzle, like the final tumbler falling into place to open a safe . . . like . . .

"Feed us! Feed us!" the tinkling voices shrieked around her. Their cold musical timbres—wind chimes played on an 80's DX7 synthesizer—echoed against each others' bodies and then fell back over her as audio rain.

"Feed us! Feed us!" It was the ultimate imperative, the instruction undeniable. She raised the axe with both hands and began hacking the blinded young man to pieces.

Unlike his shrilling captors, the victim made no sound. He tried to scream but couldn't—his tongue had been removed. His gaping mouth and the black throat behind it were now a chasm that swallowed his pain instead of expressing it.

As she worked, separating living flesh into dying bits, pieces of the young man's body flew left and right and everywhere. Each piece of bloody flesh vanished the moment it touched one of the dusky tentacle outlines.

"Feed us! Feed us!" the voices shrieked at her, rising in pitch till they drove her crazy with their non-human sanity.

She hacked away at the corpse before her, feeding *them*. Feeding them. Feeding them. And as she worked, she understood . . . understood that the smell she'd smelt from her very first encounter with these creatures, the smell all around her now, this smell currently permeating her flesh and bone and suffocating her . . . this smell wasn't the smell of dead and rotting bodies. It was rather the stink of these monsters' terrible souls. This reek was the olfactory representation of the absolute, unfathomable evil of their natures. Their EVIL nature was TOTAL. These creatures—abominations from far beyond Hell's flaming pits, had no redeeming qualities whatsoever. They were EVIL made flesh.

She looked down at the gore-smeared table. She understood too, that this young man she'd killed—by now only his left hand fingers, a chunk of his liver, and six bloody lumbar vertebrae remained—wasn't even considered an appetizer by these foul creatures. Eating the man served the function of a toothpick or dental floss or a purgative— eating him cleaned out their past gorging of flesh and made belly-room for a fresh feeding frenzy.

They were pleased with her. Very pleased. She felt approval radiate from them like heat. Their happiness came through the stink that was not stink and warmed her.

She was horrified. Utterly so. She was horrified even more because she knew that she stank like them, and now understood the implications of her doing so. She was one of them, as EVIL and irredeemable as they were. She waved the bloody axe and danced in the blueness, a priestess of gore celebrating her own nastiness.

NOOOO! her conscience screamed, revolted by this unholy version of her.

But even as she mentally rejected this new nature her unseen tentacle-laden gods had bestowed upon her, her own inner being betrayed her:

She found herself screaming, "I SAW SINIS, A SINIS WAS I!!!!"

***

"I saw Sinis, a Sinis was I!" Jessica yelped and was suddenly outside of the vision. In her shock of transition, she almost tumbled off her deck chair.

She righted herself in time and lay back gasping. She gripped the sides of the deck chair tight, as if otherwise she would fall through the chair's cloth seat and sink into the ground beneath her.

She felt drained, as if after some heavy labor. Both her arms ached. Her nose held the remnant of that disgusting stench of inconceivable evil, evil so great and complete that all she could remember of it now was the merest hint of its impossible extent, and even that smidgen of memory terrified her. And, already, even that vague impression of unfathomable darkness was fading from her, dwindling like the shadow a mountain throws on a desert, which shrinks as the sun approaches noon.

The taste of perfected wickedness on her tongue made her gag then spit on the grass.

Jessica now realized she was completely naked. She looked around but saw no sign of her bikini. Her orange flip-flops lay several yards from her feet, like she'd kicked them away in an angry moment.

Oh shit! Now I'm going to have to walk back home in the buff. Thank heavens no one else is here now.

She calmed down a little. *Okay, there's no need to freak out. It was just another hallucination. While seeing all that crap, I must have removed my garments myself and thrown them in the water, or hid them amongst the rocks around the pond. And . . . but . . . WHAT!?*

She was still holding the sides of the deck chair, though not as rigidly as before. And now she noticed that both her hands were bloody. She sat up to see better. The blood was all over her fingers, her thumbs, and the backs of her hands. She now also became aware that she had something in each hand, something soft and gooey that she was holding pressed tightly against the wooden chair frame.

Dreading what she'd see, Jessica slowly let go of the deck chair.

Oh, God, no! In each of her palms rested a bloody, clearly recently-torn-from-the-socket, eye. Two bloody blue eyes that she just knew were human. Just as she was equally certain she knew whose bloody eyes these were:

Those of the young man she'd just hacked to death in her vision.

For a long moment of stupefaction, she stared at her hands with their gory contents. Then horror and disgust won out over her bafflement and she flung both eyes away from her, out into the pond.

Each eye smacked the water's surface and cast out ripples, but the moment it did, a large black fish poked its head out of the water and ate it.

Jessica sat there staring at the ruffled water surface. Her hands were still bloody, but she felt a strange comfort on seeing the fish disposing of the evidence of murder. *Murder? Did I actually kill that young man?* But if she hadn't, where the hell then had those eyes come from? *Or did I imagine everything? Of course I didn't—there's blood on my hands!*

152

On that thought, she leapt up and ran to the water's edge and dipped her hands in the water. Thankfully the blood was still wet and came off easily. As the water colored red, she had the strangest of feelings that the two fish who'd eaten the pair of eyes were watching her from a few feet away, waiting to see if she'd fall into the water so they could eat her up too.

Now, despite the hot overhead sun, she felt chilled. She pulled her hands from the water and hurried back to the deck chair.

Both her book and her phone had fallen on the chair's left, the phone with its screen downward. Her earphones lay tangled up with blades of grass. She ignored them all and picked up her bag and got out the green-and-black beach towel she'd brought along with her. She wrapped herself in it, then slipped her orange flip-flops back on. Then she sat down again, staring at the gray-green expanse of pond water.

What do I do now? I don't know what's happening to me anymore! Hallucinations were one thing, bringing body parts back from them totally another.

Or is someone messing with me? It is possible that someone noticed me in my trance and both stole my clothes and put eyes in my hands when they heard me mumbling about them.

She looked around nervously, in case that person was still nearby. Hardly a breeze rustled the leaves of the surrounding trees, which made the previously cheery green vista now seem a creepy one.

No, she concluded. *Don't be silly. There's no one about. No one stole your clothes or handed you eyes.*

She now retrieved her phone from where it lay face-down on the grass. She dialed. Dr. Whitfield's number didn't connect, so she called the clinic's reception.

"Raynham Outlook Clinic. McKenzie Clark speaking. How may I help you?"

"Hi, McKenzie. It's Jessica Schreiber. You might remember me— I was there two days ago about my nails turning blue?"

"Oh, hello, Ms. Schreiber. How can I help you?"

"I need to speak to Dr. Whitfield. It's urgent. I've been calling his phone but there's no answer."

"Oh, I'm sorry. Dr. Whitfield is busy at the moment. Can I take a message for him?"

"No, no. I need to speak to him in person. It's very important. Can you have him call me back?"

"Yes, certainly, but by his schedule, he'll be busy with meetings till nightfall." A note of warm concern entered her voice. "Are you alright, Ms. Schreiber? The blue staining on your nails *has* cleared up, hasn't it?"

Jessica decided to tell her part of the problem. "Yes it has. But my hallucinations have gotten worse. I'm becoming scared for my sanity."

"Oh." There was a short pause over the line, then McKenzie said, "Well, I really shouldn't be telling you this, Ms. Schreiber, but it might calm your mind to hear it before you see the doctor."

Jessica's heart skipped several beats. "Tell me what? Hear what?"

"Oh, nothing serious, just that your urine test results came back positive for the more advanced form of Bobbet's allergy."

"Er . . . what's the symptoms of that?"

"Well, for one thing, your hallucinations will seem totally realistic. Horribly so. There have even been cases in which patients have imagined themselves handling physical objects, and couldn't tell the difference from real life. That's how strong the illusions become. It's not that bad with you yet, is it?"

Jessica's chill increased. "Five minutes ago I thought I was holding two freshly-plucked-out human eyes in my hands."

McKenzie laughed, which oddly made Jessica feel, not annoyed, but better. "What did you do with the eyes?"

"I threw them in the pond behind my house and two fish ate them. I'm out sunbathing at the moment."

McKenzie laughed again. "Next time, try holding on to them. In five minutes or so, you'll wonder where they are. Or if they were ever there to begin with."

"So you're saying there's nothing for me to worry about? No, I don't mean it like that. What I mean is, is there a cure for this?"

"Yes, there is. A guaranteed cure. Dr. Whitfield will be available tomorrow. If you'll come in then—I'll give you an appointment for twelve. Oh, and have someone else drive you. In your state, you don't want to be handling a car."

"I'll do that, thanks."

"Bye, Ms. Schreiber. See you tomorrow."

"Bye."

McKenzie hung up.

Jessica put down her phone with relief. *Okay, so, thank goodness, I haven't just murdered anyone. But, wow—that was so damn realistic!*

Just like previously when she'd met her at the clinic, this time too, Jessica had found McKenzie's voice weirdly comforting. So comforting in fact, that she didn't bother considering the implications of the bright red blood smears her fingers had left on the deck chair's wooden frame, smears still clearly visible as she folded the chair up to return it to its place in the beach-furniture shed. Her mind simply blanked the blood smears out.

On returning from the shed, Jessica picked up her beach bag. Then she bent down again to retrieve the card which had just fallen out of it.

With a shiver she recognized the card: it was the one for the Realms of Consciousness Temple. For a moment, as she turned the red/white cardboard rectangle over to view its rear, the memory of the cult couple who'd given it to her flashed through her mind—two clean-cut and friendly young people, yet with a definite evil aura to them. She forgot that image as her gaze focused on the statement printed across the bottom of the card: *I saw Sinis, a Sinis was I.*

I was just saying that in my hallucination, Jessica recalled with shock. Then, with a heartfelt sigh of relief, she thought, *Thank heavens none of this means anything.*

CHAPTER 23

Larry

So far today, Larry had been typing doggedly away and accomplishing nothing. For the past three hours, he'd sat in his study writing.

He'd kept writing out exactly the same (sort of) things:

The Sinis say action is action. It is what is done. What is done is what is done; analyzing the motive for action is human vanity, an attempt to prove themselves more than mere meat and bone. Rebirth, Rise, Reign, Rot, Rebirth. Man is ant, Sinis is ELEPHANT herd. Sinis is as higher than human as mountain is higher than tiniest grain of sand. Truth is not right, might is not right—only Sinis is right. Sinis over truth. What you do is what you do. It is what it is. I saw Sinis, a Sinis was I. There is no good or bad, no right or wrong, only what is done. Do what is done. Do not try . . . do. There is no shame or honor, no cowardice or valor, only pleasure and pain. I saw Sinis, a Sinis was I . . .

And similar:

Alternity. Belief, faith, doubt, unbelief—who cares? Only do, do as we tell. Do what is done and complete yourself as us. Alternity. Be Sinis, human. The instructions are foolproof, they are goodproof. Evil flows through blue veins; Evil floods blue rivers; Evil fills blue oceans. Human concept stream. Alternity. There is only correct or incorrect action. I saw Sinis, a Sinis Sinis Sinis . . . Incorrect action is human action for human ends. Alternity. The reeking end of rotting humanity. I saw Sinis . . . we are, you become, you, we, fall again, dissolve from meat to never-ending of gas and rise; float over self in static . . . Alternity. Rot, Decay, Rebirth, Rise, Reign, Rot, Rebirth . . .

Larry picked up his cold cup of coffee and sipped from it. He was trembling, both from caffeine overload and from fear. *Oh hell, this is bad. This is real, real bad.*

He tuned out the sound of Colleen doing something next door in their bedroom. (*Goddammit, you fucking woman, can't you be quiet for five fucking minutes!?*) He sipped more coffee and tried to think.

By now Larry was convinced that someone, or something, was trying to send him a message. But a message about what? Nothing he'd typed out—the words flowing seamlessly from synapses to fingers—made sense. He scrolled up and down the screen. Everything was more of the same: 'Sinis,' 'doing,' 'Alternity.' What the goddam fuck?

Larry would have been pissed off if he wasn't so damn worried. *My brain! Goddamit—let go of my fucking brain, whoever or whatever you are!*

One thing Larry was sure of: whatever was trying to talk to him meant business. Whatever it was, it wasn't joking. It wasn't about letting him out of its clutches. Yes, *clutches.* He felt trapped, caged. And there was also a horrid smell that he kept smelling—like rotten meat and shit mixed up together—that was suddenly there and then two seconds later, not there anymore.

The visions, however, were the worst.

The goddam visions. Larry had now seen inside that damn meat archway in the wall of skin. He wished he'd had no eyes to see it with.

Shit.

At about noon, after staring too long at his laptop, Larry had taken a break. Colleen had just delivered him another cup of coffee. (He could have brewed his java himself in his study, but Colleen insisted on serving him. Larry let her, though he figured her real motive for bringing him coffee was so she could catch him logging onto infidelity websites like Ashley Madison. Shit, even his Facebook account was suspect now. Larry felt ambiguous about Colleen's jealousy. He felt like a hunter snared in a trap he'd set to catch himself. He couldn't complain that his wife was being overly possessive because he knew he was giving her cause to be jealous. Reby, for instance, was a major cause for jealousy.)

Sipping his fresh coffee, Larry had walked across to the window overlooking the pond. The sky was gray, the clouds all dissolved into a seamless mercury texture through which the sun glowed weakly like when seen underwater.

The trees between the house and the pond cut off a lot of the view of the pond, but Larry made out a single figure seated in a deck chair beside the water. Looked like she was wearing a black bikini. He didn't think it was Reby. (Reby had called him. She wanted to see him; to talk, not to fuck. She'd sounded a little worried, but Larry figured she couldn't be knocked up yet. He'd also figured they could have sex first to relax her, then they'd talk to her heart's content. Of course, to do any of that, he had to get away from Colleen first.)

His mind mostly on Reby and what he was going to do to that sweet, tight ass of hers (and its central, certain-to-be-equally-tight asshole), Larry had watched the sunbathing woman with almost complete disinterest.

His disinterest didn't last however. All of a sudden he'd begun feeling nervous. The nervousness had piled up on him in layers, like pouring maple syrup on pancakes. Larry had stared at his coffee. *Am I already over the daily limit? What cup is this, number five or fifteen? Or has Colleen been doubling the number of spoonfuls she's putting in each one?*

It wasn't above Colleen to be sneaky like that when she wanted to get even with him. He'd sipped his coffee questioningly. He'd concluded it tasted normal enough, just what a man needed to keep him awake.

His nervousness had kept building, however. He'd had a heavy sense of imminence, a growing expectancy that something—not something good, of that he was certain—was about to occur. He'd felt like fleeing from the window, fleeing from the room, fleeing from the house. That was how complete his terror was. But he'd suspected that no matter where he fled to, this sudden horror of his would follow right along.

Then suddenly, the world around him had turned completely blue. The blue had been fluid about him, liquid like he'd been dunked into a huge vat of blue paint.

Then, just as suddenly, everything had reverted to normal again. Only, the world *wasn't* normal anymore. Larry had found himself somewhere well outside of normal as he understood it.

He'd been outside the flesh temple again. But this time, the blueness that had previously barred his admission had now vanished from its arched entrance.

Drawn by forces he didn't understand, he'd stepped inside the yawning archway.

This world was rotting. Larry's first impression of his new location was one of stink, and the stink formed horrible images: Opened sewers, unflushed toilets, dead dogs and cats floating on oily creek water, triple-flattened roadkill with guts spread well over the double yellow line, discarded placenta, rancid liposuction fat, rotting meat. MEAT, MEAT. The corpses from a thousand battlefields. The decaying innocent Jewish dead in all the Nazi concentration camp's mass graves. Open garbage dumpsters and trucks. A billion rotting shellfish. The fortnight-old beached carcass of a blue whale. A mountain of moldy Swiss cheese. Two million smashed bad eggs. A hundred ancient mildewed libraries. And yet more meat. Dead decaying flesh. A world's content of dead flesh.

He'd smelt and smelt, until finally, as a distraction from the horrors it was feeding itself, his tormented nose had forced his eyes to *see*.

He'd *looked*. He'd looked on a universe of almost unimaginable desecration. Of unutterable horror. (The blue that had summoned him here now flickered along the walls of an immense chamber, remaining as the faintest of unnatural hues.)

Corpses. There were dead people stuck on the walls. Literally hundreds of them. Larry had stared and stared. (He was in this stink-space and yet not inside it; but he wasn't outside of it either.) Some of the corpses—rotting, putrid things with unnatural shapes like melted wax—were nailed to the chamber walls with massive iron spikes through their heads and hearts. Others had been first disemboweled, then their emptied bodies affixed to the walls by means of large brass staples stuck in their torsos, the staples forming shiny upright rows that straddled their exposed spinal columns from hipbone to diaphragm. Those closest to the floor were impaled—their vacant stares told of the most horrific agony possible accompanying their deaths.

Larry had looked up. More corpses, too many to count, hung from the chamber's ceiling by nooses secured about their necks. Some of these had defecated while dying; the excrement stained the backs of their legs. They swung there like strange fruit, the rotted harvest of a mass lynching.

The floor was made of raw, pulsating meat that was somehow alive. The floor's bloody muscles contracted like a skinned human abdomen. Seeing the seeping floor, Larry had wanted to puke, but the smell plugged his throat.

The floor was itself piled with bodies, both of the dead and of the close-to-dead. The close-to-dead screamed endlessly. They seemed to be burning up from within, their skin puckering up then blistering as if invisible torturers were branding them all over.

The ghastly smell was everywhere.

This is the House of Death, Larry had known. *This is the House of Death.* He'd been certain of that without an instructor.

He'd finally realized that he wasn't the only one in the chamber. No, far from it. For the first time he'd noticed the others—the residents of the House of Death. (How he'd initially missed seeing them had baffled him, but then he'd understood: they'd only revealed themselves to him after terrifying him sufficiently with their horrible house.)

The residents of the House of Death were humongous and monstrous, with shapes too disgusting to hold in mind for fear of going insane. A few looked like floating balls of feathers and string, the 'string' being long black tentacles. Others looked like living necklaces made of meat, linked beads of tumorous flesh studded with eyes and teeth. Yet others were shapeless blobs of liquid flesh covered with shifting mouths that snapped at the air, and now and again either ripped apart one of the sufferers on the floor, or bit chunks out of the floor itself and wolfed it down amidst massive gushes of blood.

Not one of these monsters had wholesome flesh. All their bodies were rotting. Mold and fungi grew all over them. Multitudes of them seemed mere masses of sores. Giant cancers come to horrible, intelligent life.

Larry had immediately understood one fact about these creatures—the Sinis: the rot and decay evident on their bodies wasn't the result of infection or illness. *They* were DECAY and INFECTION. The ruined state of their bodies reflected their true natures, as did their stink of putrefaction. The EVIL he smelt was the EVIL they were.

The horrible creatures had been everywhere, all around Larry.

Appalled by the shapes of the inhabitants of this evil temple, Larry's eyes had quickly lighted on the single place in the temple that they didn't inhabit. From the archway through which he'd entered this charnel house, a stone walkway ran all the way across the temple—a flagstone bridge over the meat floor—to a similarly arched entrance on the opposite side of the building. At the exact center of the walkway stood a stone altar on which lay a young man whose eyes had been gouged out.

Through the opposite entrance, Larry had seen a body of water and a woman walking inward. She was walking on the water, across the water, from the shore.

She entered the House of Death. As she advanced, the woman stripped off her black bikini and threw it aside. She came further into the House of Death. She walked boldly through the ranks of the terrible monsters, who stroked and caressed her with their tentacles as if they loved her. She was smiling. She had a radiant sense of purpose about her. And an utterly debauched expression.

Larry had gasped. He'd recognized the woman. It was Jessica Schreiber, Reby's housemate. The one she'd described as a recovering workaholic.

Larry next corrected himself. Yes, this was Jessica, and yet it wasn't her. This Jessica had blazing blue eyes and rotting gray skin. Her body was a mess of blisters and sores, her flesh a map of corruption. Pus dripped down her skin like an excess of suntan lotion. As Larry watched, a sludge of pale maggots fell out of deep rents in Jessica's thighs.

Jessica who was not Jessica, Jessica with the rotting body, advanced to the stone table on which the blinded man lay. The chamber filled with a loud cacophony of music. Larry understood that the cacophony was the creatures' voices, and that they were both applauding Jessica Schreiber, and egging her on to perform some nasty task.

He'd had no problem figuring out what they were telling her to do: out of thin air, a huge axe had suddenly appeared in her hands.

With a sick, excited smile on her face, Jessica Schreiber began hacking up the young man on the altar. The young man screamed in silence and fell apart and died. As Jessica butchered him, he scattered in bits. It looked like an invisible hand was picking up the pieces of him and flinging them outward. Blood and gore flew everywhere around the altar, directly into the mouths of the rotting, stinking, tentacle monsters.

Jessica hacked off the man's head. This was a mere formality in killing him—she'd already chopped him completely in half through the middle.

With another violent blue flash, Larry had found himself back inside his study, with the stink of rotting things thick around him.

He'd been trembling. He was still holding his coffee cup. (He'd been grateful for that. If he'd dropped it, Colleen would have thrown a fit over the mess.) He'd raised the cup to his lips and taken a sip.

Outside his window he could see the pond surface as an ashen gray mirror reflecting the silver sky.

Pond-side, Jessica still lay in her deck chair. Okay, now she was getting up, and now she seemed to have no clothes on.

So what? She must've taken her kit off while I was hallucinating.

Larry had backed away from his window to his chair and sat facing his laptop again. He'd had no idea what to think of the horror he'd just witnessed, so he'd just resumed typing. All that had come to him was the same crazy litany as before:

I saw Sinis, a Sinis was I. Truth, truth lie, live, die. Live Evil. Live Evil lives. All is I. Never die, Sinis, The old truths are as new as ever. Believe everything you don't believe. To live evil is to live forever. I was Sinis, a Sinis saw I. I saw Sinis. Flesh . . . flesh . . . flesh . . .

***

"Hey, darling, you okay?"

"What?" In his alarm, Larry gave a start and almost leapt out of his chair.

He turned and saw Colleen. The clear worry on her face defused the angry, cutting retort he'd been intending.

"Uh, yeah, I'm fine. I'm . . ." He was still too distracted by his concerns to think straight. And he wasn't about discussing this crazy nonsense with Colleen. She'd suggest—no, she'd *insist*—that he see a shrink!

Then he noticed that she was all dressed up. She had on a cream pantsuit and red sandals. Classy makeup. She looked totally BBW-sexy. For a moment he felt a raging desire for her. His penis got hard and it was all he could do not to rip her clothes off and penetrate her there and then on the rug, maybe turn her around and do her doggy-style, digging his fingers into that massive doughy butt of hers while he slid slowly in and out of her large, soft body.

But (his erection was disappointed) she was clearly all ready to go out.

"Where you off to, baby?" he asked.

She smiled sweetly back and he was reminded of why he'd married her in the first place. "Oh, I'm just off to town. I wanna buy myself some new outfits and shoes. There's this lovely place called Dressbarn down on the New State Highway. Then after that . . ." she checked her watch, "I'll likely not be back for lunch, darling. I left you some sandwiches in the kitchen. After I leave Dressbarn, a girlfriend and I are checking out Zaza's, a beauty salon down in Taunton."

She brushed his lips with hers and turned and hurried off. He suspected she'd noticed his erection and was escaping before he assaulted her with it. He watched her fat ass go with regret. Some sweet wet pussy right now was just what he needed to calm himself after all this 'I saw Sinis' nonsense.

Then a lecherous grin spread slowly over Larry's face. Oh yeah, so Colleen was gone out? That meant . . .

Yeah! He grabbed up his cellphone and dialed Reby. Downstairs, he heard their SUV start up and Colleen drive off.

The call connected. "Hey, baby, how you feelin' now?"

"Dammit, Larry, I need to see you right away. I mean it! Can you come over here? Tell your wife that you—"

"Colleen's just gone out. She won't be back for . . . two or three hours at least. You come over here. We'll have lunch and you can tell me all about it."

A worried pause. "You're *sure* she's not home?

"Yeah, yeah." Larry massaged his throbbing phallus through his shorts. "So, you coming then?"

"I'll be there in ten minutes. I gotta get out of this creepy place."

"That's my honey. Yeah, come on, bring that sweet puss of yours over here to daddy." He hung up and grinned out towards the pond, which still shimmered its metallic gray. *You know—we don't even need to do it here in the house. Maybe Reby and I should head off into the woods for our fun. Aw shucks . . . she says she wants to talk about something first. But—*he stared down at his erection—*I don't think that's gonna happen.*

To Larry's mind, sex first, then conversation, was always the best way. You purged your body, then your mind. After a man's balls dropped their load in his lady, only then could he think clearly enough to say what he meant and really mean what he said. Even if he was pledging his heart and soul to Delilah.

Of course, women saw it differently, didn't they? They wanted to share their emotions with you as well as their bodies. And the order in which you got each part of their total package didn't seem to matter to them.

CHAPTER 24

Jessica

The path that linked Roe Cottage to the pond was a makeshift one, worn out of the grass by foot and maybe the occasional vehicle transporting something to the waterside. There was enough wear and tear to the grass to show the route was occasionally used, but also enough regrowth to assure one that its last period of usage was quite a while ago.

Another sign of cancelled intent, Jessica thought as she made her way back home through the thick woods. It was a straightforward route to the house, no chance of getting lost, and so she walked without paying attention to her surroundings, letting her mind rove. The guaranteed lack of anyone about was a great comfort to Jessica, being as she was dressed in just the beach towel she'd wrapped around herself.

For the moment, the noonday sun was obscured behind thick gray clouds. Silver pastel, like weak watercolors. A sky the color of a dead man's skin, like—she recalled her hallucination again—murder, and those bloody blue eyes.

She rolled her eyes at her own gullibility. *Just forget it already, okay? McKenzie practically told me everything I'd just experienced over the phone, which proves she's right: I was just seeing things.*

She was now very curious, however, about the whole Sinis mythos concept. She had no doubt that it was merely prior suggestion that had inserted it into her hallucination of the massive blue reeking space—The House of Death? (the name came to her all of a sudden)—just as she suddenly knew also—though she couldn't see Roe Cottage yet for the trees in the way (the path bent)—that Reby had just left home to go screw Mr. Townsend again. And that the two of them were going to change their minds about entering the surrounding woods for their tryst and remain home instead.

165

She grimaced. *That goddam slut.* Then she couldn't help but laugh. *At least one of us is getting laid.* Then she felt bad about her mirth. She didn't approve of Reby's actions. No she didn't. *Stealing another woman's man is just so inappropriate. Doesn't matter if you're hot and she's not; just don't touch—keep your damn hands off another woman's dick. Raynham is chock-full of hunky young men, and Reby has to pick the married, middle-aged guy next door for her fun. Of course, Reby will counter that she's not 'stealing' Mr. Townsend; she's merely borrowing him whenever his wife isn't around.*

Jessica had a sudden mental flash about a 'danger.' The dire impression winked out and she was left clutching at its ghost. What the hell was the danger? The flash didn't return. Jessica, however, remembered that Reby had been studying up on snakes earlier. *I hope she's not going to drag Larry Townsend into the woods to go snake hunting? But no, they're not going to leave the house. The premonition I'm having* (she didn't find it odd how the foreboding seemed so natural to her) *is of danger because . . . oh, I wish I'd gotten the rest of it!* She realized that her premonition had been non-specific. *Yes, I was thinking about Reby, but hey—this could be about me!*

She tried again to rekindle the foresight feeling, to look forward in time, again not realizing how odd it was that she was even attempting to do so (or imagining that she could succeed at it).

During this time she'd been plodding slowly homeward, lethargic from the heat, dragging her feet with mechanical reluctance. At some point—she suspected it was during her premonitions—she'd unknowing left the main path and begun walking between the path-side trees, stretching her arms left and right to touch their lowest branches and leaves. Her beach bag swung free on her left shoulder. She almost couldn't help herself. Summer smelt so good again after the stink of her vision.

It was now that she heard the noises.

She listened. She was hearing snapping twigs . . . and voices. The sounds came from her side of the path, but further inward, maybe thirty yards or so through the trees.

Jessica was instantly curious. *Did Reby and Mr. Townsend enter the woods after all? But if so, why are they on this side of the woods—near our house and not his? No, it isn't them: Reby's only just left home. So, who is this then?*

She decided to go have a look. She stepped towards the sounds, then stopped. She'd just remembered the intruder who'd supposedly been in their house yesterday. If it was him over there, she might be in danger if she went on. But she needed to know who was on the property. There wasn't supposed to be anyone else here. Not unless either Cottage 5 or 6 had just been let out.

She quietly unburdened herself of her bag, leaving it by the roots of a tree. Then, gathering the lower half of her towel tight around her, she made her careful way towards the sounds.

About ten yards later, Jessica paused beside a tree and muffled a giggle. Oh, she'd been getting alarmed for no reason at all. It was just a young couple making love. They were right in front of her, twenty or so yards farther into the woods. The pair, who were both of college age, were stretched out on a beach towel similar to the one Jessica had on. They were performing sixty-nine on each other; girl on top, boy below. The girl's head bobbed up and down over the boy's crotch. Slurp, slurp, slurp.

The girl looked up like she'd heard a noise. Jessica stepped back out of sight, but then realized that the girl wasn't looking her way. She was looking in the opposite direction, towards Cottage 6. She was still working the boy's erection though, jerking it with a spit-slippery hand, making him groan under her. He, his face buried deep between her thighs, apparently hadn't heard a thing.

The girl dropped her mouth down onto his penis again. Her slurping sounds resumed. His moaning intensified.

Jessica now felt embarrassed. She wasn't a peeping Tom, and herself disliked voyeurs. It was time to leave the young couple to their pleasure. Apparently Cottage 6 was occupied now.

She was about turning away when a policeman stepped out of the woods beside the screwing couple.

On seeing him, Jessica's heart skipped several beats.

The policeman was large and muscular. Instead of hair, he had a mass of red tentacles on his head.

Also, he was carrying an axe. A large axe like he was in the woods to chop down lumber. An axe eerily similar to the one she'd recently wielded in her violent vision.

Oh shit! Jessica thought. *It's Lucy's mutant policeman! She wasn't just seeing things! Shit!*

She was certain that this policeman wasn't any sort of woodcutter. Not with the tentacles on his head swaying the way they were. He looked like Medusa's brother. The look in his purple eyes was one of madness, but madness of a rational type.

The young couple on the towel had no idea that they had company. Jessica wanted to shout and warn them, but her tongue refused to make the words. Try as she did to scream, her throat and tongue refused the action. Even her lungs froze and refused to pump out the air needed for noise.

In three long strides the policeman was beside the couple. The boy and girl had by this time rolled over, so she was underneath. Her face was creamed with the boy's semen. With her eyes shut and a finger bitten between her teeth, she was gasping out her own orgasm.

Chop! Chop! With two hacks of the axe, the tentacle-haired policeman separated the boy's head from his body. It detached from his neck like magic, rolling down the crevice between the girl's trembling legs like a missile propelled by jets of blood.

Jessica flung her hands to her mouth in horror, almost letting her towel fall to the forest floor. *Nooooo!*

The girl was woozy with orgasm. The second axe strike, however, had cut deeply into her thigh, so that when the policeman rolled the boy off her body, her eyes were wide as saucers with pain. Horror followed quickly on the heels of agony once she saw her boyfriend's head lying between her feet. Her thighs were covered with blood, both hers and his.

The policeman jerked her roughly up to a sitting position. The girl moved like a doll in his hands, without resistance, her blonde hair sweeping back over her shoulders, her gray eyes staring ahead in shock. Jessica wondered if the young pair had been doing drugs: the girl seemed lethargic, almost like Lucy in a way.

It occurred to Jessica that she should be fleeing right now, screaming her lungs out for help. But it also occurred to her that if she dared make more sound that the wind rustling the leaves, she'd shortly be without her own head too. She was lucky to be in a good place of concealment with lots of leaves about her. She was lucky also that her beach towel's colors—lime-green and black—blended with the trees. So she was going to just keep quiet and . . . watch. Just as her survival instinct kept her from screaming, so a primal perversity prevented her from closing her eyes to shut out the horror. And yes, she knew this wasn't any kind of a hallucination.

The policeman laughed at the girl. Jessica gasped at his sharp pointy teeth.

168

Then the man swung his axe like a golf club. With one stroke he hacked off the girl's head. Blood spurted as her head was swept off her body to vanish amidst the trees.

The girl's corpse sat upright like that for four or five seconds. Blood was squirting in jets from her neck, but the jets were getting weaker with each pulse. Then they settled into a bubbling stream of blood that designed a liquid bra over her breasts. Her body toppled over.

The cop was meanwhile kneeling over the dead boy's corpse. He was holding a knife poised over the kid's belly. Jessica watched breathlessly, biting her knuckles all the while as he sliced deeply into the boy's belly and pulled out two handfuls of intestines.

When the tentacle-haired policeman raised the kid's bloody guts to his mouth and took a bite out of them, Jessica wished she could faint. Indeed, for a few brief seconds she felt lightheaded, and expected she was going to fall unconscious to the forest floor, but she didn't. She remained alert and watching, her eyes seemingly glued to the spectacle of horror ahead of her.

She didn't dare move, to turn and run for her life. She didn't dare drop to her hands and knees, and attempt to crawl back to where she'd left her cellphone, and call or text the police. Doing either would involve turning her back on *him*, and if she happened to accidentally snap a fallen twig and *he* heard it . . . She visualized his already bloody axe swooping down in a fourth murderous arc, this one aimed at her own neck.

She almost wet herself at the thought of being decapitated. Almost. Jessica didn't dare even piss herself from fright now, for fear that *he* might hear the water trickling down. Even her heartbeats sounded too loud.

All she could do was bite her knuckles and watch, watch in utter fright and absolute silence, as the horrible tentacled policeman ate the young boy's body.

When she realized that her teeth were chattering, she wedged her entire left hand into her mouth to stop them moving.

CHAPTER 25

Reby

They'd gotten down to it immediately he opened the back door for her.

By the time she'd arrived at No. 2, Reby had felt extra-tense. She'd needed sexual release. Larry's erection had preceded him out of the house; it was the first part of him that she saw. She'd originally intended for them to have a long meaningful talk before anything else, but she'd decided talking could wait.

She'd grabbed him by the penis and backed him into the house. Last time they'd used the kitchen; this time they used the dining room. They'd get upstairs later. Or maybe not; there was always the living room again for encores.

Reby was up on her knees now on a dining room chair, her bare buttocks sticking out as she leaned forward over the chair's back. She was still dressed, her red leather skirt pulled up about her waist, her breasts squeezed tight in a white tube top, then squeezed even tighter against the chair.

Larry, shorts once again down around his ankles, was straining behind her, his erection tunneling in and out of her anus.

The chair kept shifting forward over the tiled floor. Slowly, Reby realized she was being fucked across the dining room. It was a strange sensation, though not an unpleasant one. With each thrust, her body jerked and shifted forward. Or maybe it was the other way around—it shifted then jerked—she couldn't tell. Sometimes she felt both sensations together: Larry's hard penis in her rectum like a rocket ship lifting her off the chair and (it definitely felt like) flinging her through sexual hyperspace. Wonderful, just wonderful.

"Do you enjoy anal?" he'd whispered in her ear as he'd escorted her in from the back door. She was glad now that she'd said 'yes,' glad that she'd not played shy and demure like one always did on first admitting a man into one's body. 'Deviant behavior' like allowing penises into your excretory canal was supposed to come much later in your relationship; once trust had developed. (For Reby that point generally came when she farted and her boyfriend didn't look disgusted. If he laughed and made funny comments about 'beans for dinner,' and 'helping fix America's gas shortage,' that was a plus in his favor.) Once there was trust between you both, the guy could thrust all he wanted into any body cavity of yours with enough space to accommodate him.

Just like Larry was doing now.

She reached down and rubbed her clitoris. It was a good buzz. She rubbed harder, till she felt herself ready to explode. Lots of men never got that, that when you did a woman's rear door you had to give her some hand action around the front entrance too so she also got off.

"Fucking give it to me baby!" she moaned. "I'm your back-door woman!"

"Yeah," he grunted back. "You mean that literally, don't'cha?"

Larry kept thrusting her across the room. Finally, they hit the wall. Literally. The chair came to a halt beneath a painting of the Mary Celeste. And then, with nowhere left to go, Reby got the humping of her life. Pump, pump, pump, the stiff manhood in her behind went till it began hurting a bit and she began counting the dick strokes till his orgasm.

A previous lover had once told Reby that something about the shape of her ass, each time she tilted it just so, reminded him of an apple—a skin-pink apple, hard but delicious beneath the taut glossy exterior.

So, her butt was a flesh-apple and Larry was dipping deep into it now and mingling with her core.

She loved the dirtiness of it: she felt like he was becoming one with the worst of her, fusing with her fundament, exploring the composition of the waste food she would shortly discard for good. He was researching something that almost everyone overlooked. No one ever examined their own shit. No one but lunatics ever tested its varying textures except with their eyes. But Larry was prodding her feces and testing its consistency—was she healthy or not? Taking her temperature with his rectal thermometer. The truth lay in the turd— the prophet of the inner self. In a sense, each smearing of Larry with her waste products represented Filth's last stand against expulsion. An ass-fuck was a desperate clutching at something that could never be repeated nor regained once the toilet flushed. It was a last chance for yesterday's food to make an impact on the world. To leave its mark. In went nutrients, out came turds. In one of life's greatest ironies, shit was the great equalizer. With poop, it didn't matter the source material, rich food or poor food, burgers or caviar or steak. Irrelevant also was the race or religion or sexual preference of the one passing the excrement. Everyone shat the same way and it all came out the same crappy color.

That must really hurt racist folk, she thought—*the knowledge that their anal mess is as 'nigger' as everyone else's.* But—another epiphany flowed from Larry's relentless plumbing of her waste pipe—being broken down from something valuable and beautiful into a worthless uniform brown mess that stank had to hurt the pride of one's meals too. So, sodomy also helped food protest its ill-treatment by the human body.

And then, just as Larry was coming inside her, Reby realized she now had the perfect title for her next blog post. She'd call it: *Mr. L Versus the Hemorrhoid Hotspot—Deep Reflections on an Ass-Fuck.*

That's just so great, she thought, then had a third orgasm of her own.

***

Afterwards, they lay together on the living room sofa. Reby felt better. For the moment, her worries seemed not to matter. She felt safe by Larry's side. Her ass felt sore, but it was a pleasant soreness, a sweet physical glow that seemed to come from her vagina as well.

Oops. Once again, we didn't use condoms, she realized. *Oh, why the hell am I being so careless? Larry doesn't seem the kind to have a disease, but . . . but, if he's cheated on his wife before, he just might. Okay, it's too late now to get morose about it. We'll try to remember from now on.*

"So . . . what did you want to talk to me about?" Larry asked her.

"Well . . ." Reby hedged. She was unsure how much to tell him. She didn't want Larry thinking she was crazy. She knew he was married and that in a month at most, he'd be out of her life for good, but she felt a nice connection to him, something she could really build on if Colleen wasn't in the picture. Much older than her or not (thirteen years *was* quite a lot), she felt she could love this man if the heavens had given her a less amoral makeup.

"I'm seeing things," she said finally. "I think I'm going nuts."

He was lying behind her on the sofa, with one arm draped forward over her hips. She felt him tense against her. "What sorta things?" he asked. She was surprised that his voice sounded quite worried.

"Well, stuff like . . . it's hard to fucking explain." Then she decided, *To hell with it—I'll tell him the whole damn shebang.* She sat up and turned so she was facing him as he lay with his head on a throw pillow.

"Okay, it's like this," she began. "These past few days, I've been having these really crazy visions . . ."

She took her time with the telling, unburdening herself of what felt like the world's weight on her shoulders. She couldn't gauge Larry's response: he seemed at once both relieved and worried. She kept talking regardless. She needed to talk, or else she felt she'd burst into hysterical tears.

". . . and then, just as I was about coming over here . . . I was walking into my room to get my house keys and then . . ."

Larry wasn't saying anything. His silence was bothering her a lot. Now he looked like he was waiting for some great revelation from her. She wished he'd just say something. Anything. But he didn't.

". . . and then, the door to my room vanished. Like, for a moment, the *entire* hallway vanished and I was standing at the bottom of a huge canyon, only the canyon walls were formed of snakes, huge ones, all shapes and sizes of the things. Ugh, I hate snakes. And overhead, there was a temple floating in an endless blue sky. No sun or clouds, just blue everywhere. The temple was utterly horrible—a massive block of wet red meat with huge arched doorways along its sides, and blood dripping from its underside. And I heard musical voices chanting inside it. They kept repeating one sentence over and over again. It was creepy, scared me utterly shitless. They kept saying that same thing. It made no sense to me whatever."

"Was it 'I saw Sinis, a Sinis was I?'" Larry asked in a low voice. "Was that the sentence you kept hearing?"

Reby gaped at him. "Yes, yes! How'd you know that?"

Larry maneuvered his body around hers till he was sitting up too. He adjusted his penis in his shorts. "Dammit, Reby, I dunno whether to be relieved or scared crap-empty myself now."

She was confused. "What do you mean? I know *I'm* frightened, but that's because I think I'm losing my mind." She peered narrowly at him. "Baby, don't tell me you think I'm losing my mind too."

He shook his head. "No, no, I've been seeing weird shit too. Horrible stuff like you wouldn't believe. Until you spoke up just now, I thought I was going crazy too."

"Huh?" She scratched an itch on her left breast. "You're seeing snakes as well? Ugh, Larry, I just utterly hate snakes."

"No, not snakes. But I saw your damn temple—from the inside." He grimaced. "Oh, you don't ever wanna see that horrible place from the inside. And that creepy 'I saw Sinis' chant? Come with me, I'll show you."

He got up, hauled her to her feet, and pulled her after him towards the stairs.

Oh, so we finally made it upstairs today, Reby thought.

***

Reby on Larry's lap, they sat together in his study, staring at his laptop.

"How long have you been writing this stuff?" she asked him.

"Since yesterday. But I've been seeing strange stuff, I think, since last Friday." He laughed without mirth. "At first I thought it was just overwork, but now . . ."

Reby got off his lap and walked over to peer out of the window at the pond. "And you saw Jessica at the pond? Sunbathing?" She turned and winked at him. "What were you *really* doing, you horny man? Having a wank on her tits?"

He grinned sourly. "She had all her kit on. Besides which, I like my tits like yours, nice and firm."

"She's got a good bod too," Reby said nonchalantly, if somewhat condescendingly. "She's just so stressed out and all—so hyper—that you won't notice it. Her efficiency vibe blows her sexuality vibe out of the window; renders it completely null and void. With her 'work is fun' attitude to life I wonder how she ever got married twice." Her expression turned thoughtful. "And she was hacking the guy to bits?"

Larry nodded. "She literally diced him up. And she was feeding the pieces to those monsters in that temple full of dead people. And the creatures—I think *they're* the goddam Sinis—were very happy with Jessica. As delighted as houseflies trapped in a dirty public toilet."

Reby walked back over to Larry. She sat on the edge of his work desk. "Jessica isn't the kind of person to hack anyone up—that's just crazy."

"We both know *that*," Larry said. "What we don't know is, what the hell's going on."

Reby saw that he was about losing his temper. She shifted from the desk to his lap again, flung her arms around his neck, and kissed him. "So what do you suggest we do now?"

Before replying, he kissed her cheek. She liked that; it gave her a warm feeling in her heart. Then he said, "The way I see it, first of all we've gotta to find out if anyone else—Colleen and your friends—is seeing things too."

Reby felt chilled now. "I-I-I . . . I think they are," she ventured slowly.

He looked at her very curiously. "How . . . ? What . . . ?"

She told him about Jessica's nails turning blue all of a sudden. "And . . . she's been looking terrible all week, like something's really bothering her that she can't talk about. Like, for instance, if she had a boyfriend but had gotten pregnant for some other guy. That's the kind of look she's got."

"And Lucy?"

"Lucy's been acting normal, but then weird *is* her normal, so what I mean is, she's been acting weird. Oh yes, Lucy's been seeing things too. Day before yesterday she claimed she saw a cop with tentacles on his head eating a cat."

"Eating a cat?"

"Yeah. Oh, and there were footprints around our house."

"Footprints?"

"In the flowerbeds. They were bootprints, actually, from male-sized footwear. Lucy vetoed our calling the police."

"She most likely imagined it was her tentacle-headed cop who was going to turn up."

Reby hadn't previously viewed Lucy's overreaction from that angle. "You know, you may be right about that. Say, Larry, has your wife been acting strange too?"

"Yeah, she has. Twice I've caught her staring at nothing. On one of those occasions, she mentioned 'The Big Blue.'"

"The Big Blue?"

"That's what she called it. Then she snapped out of her trance and didn't remember a thing. And also, this week she's been having these weird mood swings."

"She's a woman. For us, mood swings aren't automatic evidence of mental distress. She might be on her period, or going through the change . . . or she thinks you're fucking me."

"No, no . . . I mean real crazy mood swings. One minute she's sweetness and cream . . . then, the next minute I can read in her eyes an intense hatred, like she wants to disembowel me or cut my dick off."

"See, I told you—she thinks you're fucking me."

"Stop grinning like that. We need to think this through. We need to work out what's happening."

"I'm grinning because, well, don't you see, baby? If we're *all*—I mean all five of us—having similar hallucinations, then this clearly must have some natural, logical explanation. Like maybe, the fumes from the paint used to paint the buildings is screwing with our minds." Her brow creased with thought. "Jessica said the doctor called her blue-nail condition a kind of allergy. Buffet's or Bobby's or Bubble's . . . something like that. So maybe we're all just having similar allergic reactions to hers."

"Have either your nails or Lucy's turned blue also? Mine haven't. Colleen's? It'd be impossible to tell under all that red nail paint."

Reby shook her head and snuggled up close to him. "No, *our* nails haven't changed color. But Jessica also said there was no telling who'd get the allergy. Even her doctor wasn't sure what caused it. So, it could be the same thing we've all got, just different symptoms." Then her expression turned vicious. "But dammit, Larry, if this *is* some chemical compound messing with me like this, those suckers who built these houses are gonna hear from my lawyers. I'll sue their asses all the way to the Supreme Court if I have to. Shit, you've no idea what the hell it's been like, feeling like I'm crazy."

He smiled. "Oh yes, I do."

She smiled back. He was right: they'd both been feeling crazy independently. Then she saw his smile become a frown again. "What's the matter now, baby?" she asked. "Did you just remember something else? Or are you worrying about how you'll ask Colleen if she's been seeing monsters too? Listen, just say—"

"No, it's not that," he interrupted her gently.

She waited for him to go on. He looked even more worried now.

"Okay . . ." Larry began finally, pointing at his laptop, "okay, so I agree that we may all be having similar allergic reactions to something or other, but . . . but how do you explain these crazy sentences I've been typing?"

"Well, I . . . I . . ." Reby realized that, yes, Larry had a point. If he'd been typing the 'Sinis' statements freely out of his head, how come they synchronized perfectly with what he'd been seeing and hearing? With what they'd *both* seen and heard? And the sentences seemed to mean something too. They weren't just random gibberish. They made nonsense sense.

Larry correctly interpreted her perplexed expression. "You get it too, don't you?" he asked quietly. "And . . . and . . . there's more: You and me both saw the same temple without ever discussing it with one another. We both heard the 'Sinis' chant. You saw that Jezebub tentacle-haired woman in a dream, and Lucy . . . Lucy claims she's seen a tentacle-haired policeman. In addition, we've *both* seen weird blue spaces, and Colleen too was mumbling about 'The Big Blue,' which I suspect has to be the same damn place we both saw." He grimaced. "Reby, honey, that's a bit too much random coincidence for me. If this *is* a mass hallucination we're all having, it seems a pretty well-coordinated one. Doesn't it?"

Reby felt lost, all at sea. Just when the mystery appeared solved, it was starting again. And deepening even. She agreed: what was happening to them *was* too non-random to be purely the work of inhaling noxious chemical vapors.

"So what . . . ?"

Smiling grimly, Larry raised a finger to emphasize a point. "There's also the fact that I can't shake the damn feeling I get each time I type this shit that someone somewhere is trying to tell me something."

"Someone . . . like aliens?" Now Reby had to laugh. "C'mon, baby, there's got to be a more commonplace explanation to all this." She wasn't a hundred percent convinced though.

"Not aliens," Larry replied glumly. "More like *demons*. Each time, I get the feeling of this immense evil presence that's trying to tell me something, only I'm too dumb to hear, too insensitive to understand what it is that they're saying. Even in that temple made of meat—the House of Death—I could sense that those evil monsters had a message for me—something far beyond these words onscreen—something they wanted me to convey to someone else."

That was too much for Reby. She leapt down off his thighs. "You know, baby, now that we've worked out the basic problem here, how 'bout if we go next door and relax a little?" She tugged him to his feet. "You've already done such a great job of calming me, and now you're about to start alarming me again."

Larry remained a moment, staring at the laptop. "You know," he said, "I've an idea."

"Later," she said sternly. She wanted to make love again before he talked her back into a state of stress.

"Yeah, sure," Larry said as he followed her from the study into the next room, he and Colleen's bedroom. "But just hear me out first on this, wilya? Colleen said that this 'I see Sinis, a Sinis was I' chant was the same thing a preacher chap on TV was saying."

They were just entering the large bedroom. Reby froze in her tracks and turned to face him. "She said that? A preacher on TV? What church was it?"

"That's the odd thing. It wasn't a church. She called it a *temple*. But I don't remember the name of the place. Don't you think that's odd? Two *temples*, one real and one imaginary, both using the same weird chant."

Reby relaxed and grinned at him. "That's great then, baby. We'll start our investigations from there. *After* you've made love to me again."

Larry still looked distracted by his latest revelation. Reby wasn't having none of that. She grabbed Larry by the waistband of his shorts and pulled him towards the bed.

Once she had him where she wanted him, she began undressing, in a flash discarding her tube top and leather skirt onto the bedroom floor. This time she wanted to feel his skin sliding against hers while he slid through her.

CHAPTER 26

Lucy

The blender whirled, shredding the marijuana buds and leaves smaller and smaller.

"Woof, woof!"

"Yeah, Smokey boy, it was so darn weird. That thing just popped out of nowhere like that and then it began choking and licking me. It didn't lick my pubes or ass though; I still had all my clothes on afterwards. But I was soaked through and through, and I stank like a dead rat. You were asleep then."

Lucy paused and grinned at the dog. "So, how's your vacation been?"

"Woof!" Smokey replied.

"Hey, hold on a minute."

Lucy turned off the blender. She inspected the ground-up marijuana, decided it wasn't powdery enough yet, and turned the blender back on.

One hand on the blender's cover, she gave her webcammed St. Bernard her full attention again. "So what were you saying, Smokey?"

The blender's whine agitated the onscreen dog. "Grrrrr!"

"You're hungry again, ain't ya?"

"Woooofff! Woof!"

Seeing as she was currently the only one at home, Lucy was in the kitchen baking. She was baking hash brownies, aka space cakes. She was baking them as part of a plan to get Reby and Jessica to see her point of view when she told them about all the weird stuff that had been happening to her.

Lucy surveyed the island in the middle of the kitchen where she had everything arrayed. Brownie mix, vegetable oil, cheesecloth, non-stick baking pans, chocolate . . . The chocolate was to tempt Jessica to eat the brownies. (The chocolate *was* Jessica's. She had loads of it in the fridge, a carryover from work, when she'd snack on it to keep her energy levels up and her brain hyperactive.)

Lucy finally decided the weed was ground-up enough. She turned off the blender, uncapped it, sniffed it once, then upended it into the frying pan she'd set on the gas cooker. She spread the marijuana out thin, poured vegetable oil over it, then lit the burner and turned the heat down. She grinned. It would take about two hours to extract all the THC goodness into the oil. Once she had her canna-oil made she could get down to her baking proper.

She lit herself a joint and sat on a stool to smoke it. She turned her laptop so she could talk to Smokey while seated. Lucy was dressed same as before—in a black T-shirt with 'WEIRDO' written on it in bold white letters, pink panties, and pale green ankle socks. Half of her purple hair hung forward over her right eye.

"Sorry you're hungry, doggie," Lucy went on. "But that ain't my fault, is it?"

"Woooooof!"

"Yeah, I agree with you—Robert *is* a dick . . ." A 'wise' look stole over Lucy's features. "No, shit, no. Robert's *gay*, he can't be a dick. I gotta get this straight, gotta stop mixing it all up 'cos I'm high. See, Smokey, the way I see this, *straight* guys are dicks, dickheads, pricks, whatever. *Gay* guys are *assholes*."

The dog just stared at her.

"What I mean is . . . look, screw my meaning. I mean, check out the homophobia everywhere. Shit. It's a total mystery to me why they—gay and straight men, anuses and penises—can't get along with each other." She coughed loudly. "I mean, if dicks and assholes just embraced one another and . . . You know, Smokey, I really can't stand people beating up gay people just 'cos they like . . . dammit, everyone's the same except for what genitalia they like licking or sucking on, right? And some of those dicks are so big anyway, us littler girls are pleased that some guys are sucking on them instead of us. See, I almost choked to death once, Smokey. It's true, I really nearly did. Oh, that damn cock was so damn big—it was like eating a huge knockwurst sausage. It was goddam salty too . . . yeah. I just barely survived it. Cowards really do live longer, Smokey; take it from me. I tried to be brave with that penis, but it was just too much for a biatch to handle, ya know? I had to quit on it. The guy was mad, but by then I didn't give a shit. What was I supposed to do, huh? Wind up in the ER just 'cos he wanted a blowjob? As it was, my poor jaw ached for a week afterwards. Honest. . . . So gay men like Robert and Dean have my vote. They're keeping us tiny women safe, see . . . protecting us from harmful dicks. . . . And I think straight guys should really appreciate their gay brothers, like I really LOVE my brother Robert. Me? I JUST REALLY HATE HOMOPHOBIA!!! EVERYONE, LISTEN, STOP IT ALREADY!!!"

"WOOOFFF!!!"

"Yeah, boy, I knew you'd see it my way. Dickheads should love anuses and the other way around too. Back door sex is fun with a rubber on. Hey, Smokey, that's a great line!—'Back door sex is fun with a rubber on!' You know, Jessica sells condoms. I should sell that line to her. Or maybe it's better as, 'Anal is fun with a condom.' Hey, Smokey, I got us another one. A funky jingle. Listen to this"—Lucy broke into a warbly sing-song while dancing left-to-right on her stool—"I just wanna fuck it, not back-door choc'lit; you need a condom, inside your rectum. Wear a rubber on your boner, stoner; ying yang yeah!" She clapped her hands in delight. "It's good, yeah? Don't you dare give me that 'I'm an abused and starving mongrel' look. Hey, dog, cooperate with me here. I gotta earn us some cash, then you can have all the goddam munchies you desire. So . . . how much d'ya think we should charge her for it, huh? Maybe it'll be a hit in China too. It's got ying-yang in it!"

"Woof?"

"Yeah, I guess you're right. Maybe Jessica *won't* like it; she don't seem the type to ever approve of sodomy. She's a real tight-ass, that biatch. All right . . . so where was I? Yeah, it ain't my fault my slack-ass brother Robert forgot to put down more food for you. You're a big fucking dog, not a Chihuahua!"

"Woof woof!"

"So, Smokey darling, I mean, it was truly crazy, right? I almost burnt the damn house down. Like I've a talent for pyromania? God only knows what I'd have done if that crappy monster spit hadn't put out the fire my joint started. I've still gotta figure out a way to keep Jessica and Reby from noticing the black hole in the mattress."

"Woof!"

"Wow, Smokey, you're a fucking genius. You're right—I'll just flip the mattress over. Ha ha ha! They'll never know!"

"Wooof!"

"Yeah, I think so too. Jessica and Reby are both super-cool to be living with. But . . ." she took a long pull of her joint, "view it this way, huh? Okay, so what I mean is—hey, Smokey, goddam pay attention, wilya? I don't wanna have to repeat myself here. . . . Yeah, sorry, mutt, I got carried away again. Okay, like I was saying, so here's the problem: I gotta explain to both of them that I'm sure there's something weird going on in this house. But they're not gonna believe me, are they? Simply 'cos I get high a lot. But if I can get them both high too, then they'll believe I'm not seeing things just 'cos I'm high, 'cos then we'll all be high at the same time, see? You don't? Sorry, Smokey, I forgot you're just a dog. Anyway, so that's what these brownies are for. Reby's cool with joints, but Jessica? Nah, she's gonna take two hits and quit. And then she'll start complaining about how she needs all her brain cells intact to be America's best employee. As if *I'm* lacking in brain cells or in success as an employee. I won Employee of the Month twice last year at the restaurant. But if I feed her brownies— the biatch looooves chocolate—she's gonna get high without knowing why, 'cos I ain't gonna snitch on myself, I ain't gonna let on that these are space cakes until we're all three of us well out into orbit . . . then we'll have us a great discussion about the hallucinations I've been having, but which can't really be hallucinations because . . . Shit—wait a minute!"

Lucy leapt down from her stool and hurried over to the frying pan to stir the marijuana/oil mixture. That done, she picked up several Quaaludes from a saucer piled high with them and dropped them on her tongue. She chewed them slowly, then returned to resume her webcam with her dog.

"Ah, Smokey puppy, it's so crazy here at the moment. I really wish I'd never come back east. How in the world can *I* be scared to smoke weed?"

Smokey didn't reply. The St. Bernard looked wise in his video window, regarding Lucy with a tolerant expression, like he expected her to have a Carl Sagan IQ and the answers to the universe's hardest questions.

"Hey, Smokey, say something, wilya? 'Woof' or something, just so I know you understand me."

"Woof, woof!"

"Yeah, you do, huh? I feel the exact same way about it. So that's what I'm gonna do, yeah—space cakes for dinner. Hey! What's that horrible fish smell?"

Lucy looked around slowly, towards the kitchen door.

"Aw, shit, no. Not a-damn-gain!"

The kitchen door was open. Framed in it was another of the horrible monsters that had molested her earlier in the day. (Or maybe it was the same one: it looked exactly like it.) Tentacles and eyes, and mouths that dripped yucky saliva on the floor. Semi-transparent so she could see through it to the living room. The same malice and hunger in its blue eyes. The same stink that came from nowhere and filled everywhere. (Lucy prayed that the thing's crappy smell wouldn't get in the canna-oil she was making. It would be disastrous if her brownies stank of bad fish. Jessica would never eat them then.)

The creature extended several thick rotting tentacles towards Lucy. She sat there on her stool watching them approach. She saw no point in running: the thing was blocking the escape. Besides, the pills—the handful of downers she'd swallowed—had her well out of her freak-out zone by now; she was incapable of being truly scared. She could feel angry and upset, but fear was now an emotion only the sober felt.

She gaped helplessly at the oncoming tentacles as they wobbled through the air, then glanced sideways at her laptop.

"Hey, Smokey, d'ya see what I mean now? I mean this goddam thing's gonna lick me again. And then I'm gonna be wet and smelling nasty all over."

Lucy began weeping copiously.

Her dog seemed to nod back at her, his expression pitying.

Despite her tears, Lucy took a final drag of her joint before the tentacles reached her. Then she grabbed a fresh handful of Quaaludes and gobbled them down.

Then she was being lifted up into the air and licked and strangled again.

Damn, she thought, as the tears streamed from her eyes, *what a bad trip. What a goddam bad trip I'm having. And how come this only happens when there's no one else around?*

CHAPTER 27

Reby & Larry

This second round of sex was good, though not as satisfactory as the first time today. Larry stroked her long and slow and deep and hard. At the end of it, she was on top of him, riding him like a jockey. Her climax felt like winning at Suffolk Downs.

But something was lacking in the execution of the fuck—neither of their hearts was totally in it.

They both came. They fell apart from each other panting.

For a while there was silence. The silence got to Reby. She saw no point in them brooding over what they'd discovered, or at least suspected. She smiled coolly at Larry. *Me, I want to screw and relax some more, but my lover-man here won't be ready again for a bit, so . . .*

She got up and walked over to the window.

"You see anything monsters out there?" Larry called playfully from the bed.

She waved him off. "Let it go, baby. We'll start researching that stuff tomorrow."

"Yeah, you're right," he agreed. "I have to ask Colleen about the temple's whereabouts anyhow."

She sought a way to switch the conversation. His mention of his wife's name gave her the opportunity she needed. She opened the wardrobe and began looking through Colleen's clothes. "I'm curious," she said. "Was your wife always this large?"

"Yep."

"So why'd you marry her then? Are you into fatties?"

"Nah, I just thought she was hot. Reason one to marry a fat girl? You get more for your money. Simply 'cos there's a lot *more* of her. Lots more tits, lots more ass than you skinny chicks got. Consider that."

"Lots more belly too. It hangs down over their panties. And their flesh jiggles. How do you cope with that?"

"I just imagine she's pregnant all the time."

"Ooooh. Don't you honestly care about her weight?"

"Not really. Why should I? She's got her own good points. And she's great in the sack too. There's something about doing it to a fleshy woman that's just . . . mmm. Like I said, there's just *more* of her there in bed with you."

"And yet you're screwing *me?*"

"Be honest: Do you have *any* interest at all in getting married?"

"Nope. Not till I've gotten Alzheimer's, and arthritis so bad my joints are locked together and I can't spread my legs anymore. Then I'll need someone to look after me."

He had to laugh at her then. He couldn't help it. She'd now finished her inspection of the wardrobe and was standing by the front window, framed in it like a model on a calendar. She looked so smooth, cool like an autumn morning, just exquisite.

"Sweet sexy thang like you? You keep getting marriage offers left and right, of course? And keep turning 'em down? Breaking all those male hearts?"

"Yep."

"See, that's why I'm with Colleen. She's wife material. You, for all your beauty and brains and bed-skills, aren't."

"That's just sexist bullshit. So it's plain girl as wife, pretty girl as mistress, huh?"

"Uh uh—I didn't mean it like that. I'm not labelling Colleen 'wife material' because she's fat or unattractive or dumb. Far from it. I'm very happy with her looks *and* her intelligence. Also, I ain't with you now 'cos you're more attractive than she is, even though you are. No, Colleen is wife material because she's *stable*. She wants a relationship. Like I do."

"Yet you're screwing me."

"You keep repeating that like you want me to feel guilty."

"Not guilty—responsible. You're fucking behind your wife's back."

"See? You just said 'fuck.' Colleen never says 'fuck.' She might think it, but she feels it's too slutty to say. You, you're exciting and dangerous. Colleen is reliable, but familiar. Sometimes she's boring."

"That's a horrible thing to say."

"It's a fact. Me and she, we're both boring now. Two old farts occupying the same backside."

"You excite *me*."

"Yes, but then you haven't lived with me for a decade-and-a-half like Colleen has. Colleen finds me boring and samey and . . ."

"*I* find you sexy."

"*You,* honey, don't have to put up with my snoring and my tantrums and my meanness on a daily basis. Colleen does. I'm sure she merely tolerates me; doesn't divorce me 'cos of the so-called 'man shortage.'

"Would you be mad if Colleen had an affair too?"

"Sure, sure. Yeah, I think so. I'm a man—we got egos. Sure, I'd be pissed. But see . . . I've done it to her too, so . . . I'd have to forgive her in the long run, so long as she was discreet about it. But if she did a public display with some nineteen-year-old stud like Linda Hogan did, and began telling everyone how great he was in bed on talk shows, we'd be quits then for sure. Otherwise, I'd just overlook it. But it'd gall me to imagine someone else poking her between her legs."

"You've done this more than once? I mean, cheated on Colleen?"

"Haven't you? And don't ya look at me like that."

"Oh, I just love you married fellas! You're so honest in your dishonesty!"

"Hey, stop stretching Colleen's panties and come back to bed!"

"Ooh, you've got it up again. And so soon too—lucky me!"

"Come to bed."

"Keep it hard, baby. I need to pee first."

"Okay, go piss your piss. But hurry up."

"'Pee,' Larry darling, not 'piss.' 'Piss' is what poor chicks do. Us rich beyotches 'pee' or 'pass water.'"

"Whichever you're gonna do, rich girl, just rush it up. I'm getting lonely here."

***

Reby sat on the toilet and passed her water.

She was thinking: Men were really funny. She always found it mental—utterly crazy—how a man would claim he loved one woman and yet would screw another one in a flash. Okay, she'd understand it if the woman was a hooker: that was clearly just a financial transaction, like buying groceries. But Larry, for instance, had an actual emotional connection to Colleen—she'd read it in his expression when she'd been holding Colleen's clothes that he didn't really approve of her touching his wife's things—and yet he was still hard for her. Still wanted to fuck her.

She really didn't get that. Sure she was promiscuous herself, but she knew the price she was paying for her fun, having to barricade off her heart from emotion, ensuring she felt nothing for her men except delight at the sensations their penises gave her.

She sighed. *Not that I regret anything I've done. It's fun being a slut, particularly a rich slut. It's just lonely too as you get older, and everyone's married—including all the guys you've slept with, all the suitors you turned down, the girls you once partied with . . . and your sister.*

A sudden surge of loneliness hit her. She'd call up her twin sister Leah tonight and find out how she and Carl and their kids were. She hadn't called home in quite a while. Facebook had proved a brutally efficient way to maintain a relationship with people you didn't want to talk to. She 'liked' her mother's political posts (the Billings mayorship race was really heating up now), 'liked' her father's business ones, and 'liked' Leah's family ones (endless snaps of herself and Carl and their children doing everything that everyone else on Facebook was doing, to loud applause).

Leah's first son Ike would be thirteen in September. There was currently a family debate on as to whether or not the kid qualified for a Bar Mitzvah, as he was only one-quarter Jewish. Reby knew her mother would insist on it. Reby's mother Hannah—who was fully Jewish—*wanted* a Bar Mitzvah. Her sister, who was half Jewish, *wanted* one too, mainly because Leah liked sacred ceremonies and parties and a Bat Mitzvah was both a sacred ceremony and an opportunity to throw a party. And the kid, who was three-quarters from other places than the Middle East? Ike didn't seem to care. (Last thing Reby had heard about her oldest nephew was that he'd been trying to get into their 22-year-old cook's panties to bust his cherry.) And Carl Kingston's and Reby's father Kevin Butterfield's thoughts on the matter? Reby suspected that to keep the peace, the husbands would agree with whatever their wives finally decided on.

Reby grinned. *Yeah, it'll be nice to talk to Leah today.*

"Hey, baby, you okay in there?!" Larry called from the bedroom.

"Coming! I'll be right out!" she called back and reached for the toilet roll.

Then: *Oh, shit . . .*

The whole bathroom altered to a light-blue landscape. Reby was still sitting in the bathroom, but its walls had disappeared. The ceramic tiles were now overlaid with dark blue rock. She could see far off into the distance. She saw nothing out there, but she could hear *them* singing.

The air was hot, almost as hot as if she was being cooked. The world smelt rotten, as if the planet (or Hell, or wherever this was) was comprised of decaying meat.

She looked at her body and shivered. Once again, she was made of snakes. A woven plait of them formed her entire body, arms and legs and all. Her torso was a three-fold cord of anacondas, their scaly lengths slick and bright and flashing. Her fingers and toes were formed of the serpents' tails. Other serpent's tails fell from her head and dangled as hair over her scaly, woven breasts. Her face . . .

Oddly enough, as though whoever was responsible for this mad transformation wanted her to see herself, the bathroom mirror remained hanging in space, even though the washstand and bathtub had both vanished along with the walls. Even the toilet had vanished. Reby discovered that she was sitting on a stiff human corpse. She was sitting on the dead man's buttocks. He'd been hog-tied on his hands and knees, his forehead on the ground, and his throat slit in that position. It was a recent death too. Behind Reby, the victim's blood was smeared in a dark puddle over the blue rock.

Doubly horrified, Reby leapt off the dead man and hurried over to the suspended mirror. She had to see what her face looked like before this crazy vision faded. She stared into the mirror, then reeled back in shock. She stepped backward till she met an obstruction. She sat. She had no idea that she'd just sat back down on the corpse with the slit throat.

My face, my face, my face! Oh my God, oh my God, oh my God!

In the mirror, her face had been comprised of snake's heads. A thick mass of them pressed together and hissing. Arranged like an infernal honeycomb.

That isn't me! she screamed silently in her mind.

She looked down then and saw the dead man's feet poking out between her own. Those dirty feet, with their callused soles and their toes that seemed to have been gnawed on by rats, were what she was staring at when the world normalized again.

She blinked. The world remained normal. She was back inside Larry's bathroom. She was still human.

Walking like a ghost, Reby got to her feet and shambled out of the bathroom. As she passed the mirror, she cast a sidelong glance at it. Yes, she looked normal.

Out in the bedroom, her numbness broke. A flood of anguish poured into her. She dashed across to the bed, leapt on it, and grabbed Larry. She held him tight.

"Oh my God, baby, oh my God! It was just horrible, so horrible. You should have seen it—it was utterly disgusting. Make love to me, please, convince me I'm still human."

"Did you just have another—"

She winced. She felt like breaking something over Larry's head to smarten him up. *Of course I just had another vision, man! Why else would I be shaking like this!?* Shit—some men just didn't get it. There were times when a woman needed conversation and others when she needed physical consolation, and this was the latter case.

The only thing Reby wanted Larry doing with his tongue right now was eating her pussy. She sealed his lips with her own, grabbed his penis and began stroking it back to full erection.

She separated her lips from his for a moment. "Just make love to me, darling!" she pleaded desperately. "I need to be certain I'm still human!"

CHAPTER 28

Jessica

It was forty-five minutes before the weirdly mutated policeman was done with savaging the two corpses.

During that entire period, Jessica remained frozen in place, watching. She stood there by her tree, as motionless as if she was a part of the plant, as if her white skin was the exposed surface of the tree trunk after its bark had been stripped away.

She watched in horror, disbelief, and utter incomprehension of what she was witnessing.

She wanted to puke as the man bit into the dead boy's thigh and ripped away a bloody chunk of flesh, gore dribbling down over his chin, down his neck . . . but she didn't dare puke. The noise!

He slit the girl open. He ripped out one of her kidneys and wolfed it down. His teeth glinted red as he fed. His purple eyes were aglow with an evil lust that Jessica had only ever seen before in movie depictions of ravenous werewolves. But this was clearly no werewolf facing her.

After a while, the very overload of unending horror dulled its own effect on Jessica mind. Watching the tentacle-haired policeman feast on the two dead students like they steak served in a restaurant became a surreal 'ordinary' to her. So much so that she could think clearly: *Isn't this the United States of America anymore? Did I get lost? Did I make a wrong turn on my way back from the pond and walk into a version of Hell? But how is that even possible? It's a straight hike up from the pond with no turnoffs! Shit! I must have . . . somehow . . . accidentally opened up a portal . . . a gate . . . a doorway . . . into . . . Is this the Twilight Zone? Is this Hell? But . . . but if that's the case, then how come Lucy also saw this ghoul?*

That was the sticking point: that it wasn't just herself, but that Lucy too had had a similar experience. *And has Reby also been seeing things?*

Thinking logically helped Jessica preserve her sanity, or else her mind would have melted from the horror. There was nothing more terrifying than watching two people being sliced to pieces and eaten barely twenty yards in front of you when you didn't have a gun. She remained as silent as a cadaver being autopsied.

Dammit, this goddam cannibal cop had such a big appetite. He was a huge, hulking, bloodstained brute and seemed to have a bottomless belly to match. As he fed, his red tentacles flailed back and forth across his head, like they were still hungry and impatient for him to eat more.

Wrapped in a beach towel like she was, Jessica felt almost unbearably hot. She was sweating, but shedding the towel was an impossibility. She felt immense relief that her towel's colors were camouflage against the trees. Now, the towel's lime-green/black coloration almost spoke of a guardian angel helping her select it from all the others on display when she'd bought it. In her current straits, a yellow or pink or red beach towel would have been a suicide marker. (Her orange flip-flops posed no danger to her, the grass completely hid them.) Oh, but the damn heat she was having to endure to stay safe!

She waited in a kind of limbo. More rigid than meat in a freezer.

With the tree-cover thick around her, the only way she could measure the passage of time was by estimating how much of the young couple the cop had eaten against how much of their bodies still remained. She wondered if the policeman was going to completely eat up both students. He'd already eaten all the flesh off the boy's legs, and the kid's belly was now a hollow crater almost totally devoid of innards. In addition, the policeman had eaten the boy's heart, and most of the muscle off his chest and right arm. And all the meat around his neck stump.

The girl had fared a little better in the dietary sweepstakes. Maybe because she was smaller and as such had less flesh on her, the cannibal mutant had so far only consumed her kidneys and thighs. Jessica had almost shit herself from fright as she'd watched him shave the skin and meat off the girl's thighs. Like one carving a rare-cooked rump roast, he'd sliced her flesh off in thick bloody layers. The sickening wet sound of his knife slicing back and forth through the girl's muscles and scraping against her thigh bone had sounded to Jessica like the end of her own life.

The cop had sat on the boy's stripped ribcage to eat the thigh meat. While eating, he amused himself by fitting his fingers into the holes left where he'd cut the boy's head off.

Jessica felt reasonably worried that this crazy policeman might spend the entire afternoon eating the young couple he'd killed. Maybe that was how he planned to dispose of their bodies.

While staring in dread at the scattered bloody mess on the forest floor, Jessica was struck by a clear awareness of her own mortality. *Just a short while ago, those two kids were laughing and loving each other, and now . . .*

 Hunched as little as she could make herself beneath the leaves, Jessica settled down to wait forever if she had to. She wasn't moving an inch until this was over. She wasn't peeing either, and the urine had been knocking on her urethra for half an hour now.

Jessica's 'forever' however turned out to be much shorter than she'd imagined it would be.

The cannibal cop's phone suddenly rang. That startled Jessica, that he had a phone. It meant that he had a mind, that he was intelligent. His animalistic behavior, combined with the fact that he'd not said a word since entering the clearing where he'd murdered the young couple, had fixed in her mind the image that she was watching an animal feed, a beast that ran on instinct.

She watched him tense as if the sound was unexpected, then relax and pull the phone from his shirt pocket.

His words blew across to her: "Yeah, Morrison here. . . . Seriously? Okay, I'll be right over to look into it. . . . Was just having lunch, but I'm done now."

Jessica was again shocked, both by the fact that he wasn't some semi-intelligent cretin, and that his voice was surprising warm and pleasant. He peered her way for a moment. She froze stiffer than stiff, holding her breath, willing even the atoms forming her cells to cease their turbulent motion through the universe of herself.

She waited with bated breath for him to leave. Only he'd better not head her way. She made up her mind: the moment this crazy, cannibal, tentacle-haired son-of-a-bitch took the first step in her direction, she was going to leap up, throw away her goddam towel, and run like mad—it didn't matter that she'd be buck naked—run screaming for the cottage. She'd leave her bag and flip-flops and just run like she'd never run before in her whole damn life.

The policeman stood up, grabbed his axe, and started off. Jessica heaved a sigh of relief: he was going the opposite way, towards Cottage No. 6.

Then she caught her breath again. He'd turned back towards her. She wondered if maybe he'd heard her exhale.

But no, he had more gory interests on his mind. With a smile on his face, he crossed to pick up the boy's head. Then, once he'd gotten that one, he searched for the girl's head too.

Jessica's question as to what he wanted with them was answered when he raised the boy's head to his lips and took a bite out of the boy's cheek. Fresh tremors of fear coursed through her. Would this madness never end?

Chewing his mouthful of meat, dangling the girl's head by her hair from his other hand (the hand keeping his axe balanced over his shoulder), the cannibal cop strode off between the trees.

In a few seconds the cop—Morrison—had vanished from view in a vista of green. Jessica could still hear him, but shortly even his footfalls faded. Despite which, Jessica didn't move from her place of concealment for another five minutes. She kept waiting, desperate to flee, but with her eyes still riveted on the bloody mess the man had left behind. If she miscalculated her escape that would be her too.

Finally, she decided she'd waited enough. Moving more quietly than a grass snake dodging a hawk, she made her way back to the footpath leading to Roe Cottage.

She grabbed up her bag and phone. She stared at her phone for a long moment.

Should I call 911 now? she asked herself, her frame of mind close to panic.

No, she decided—*I've no idea who may be nearby and hear me.* She realized now how fortunate she'd been that the phone hadn't rung while she'd been pinned behind her tree. That would have been just terrible for her.

She started off for the cottage, not running, but walking as fast as she could, ready to break into a mad dash for safety at the first sign of danger.

CHAPTER 29

Colleen

Colleen slotted the spare key into the front door of No. 2. She opened the door quietly and slipped inside the house. She shut the door just as quietly behind her, taking care that the lock made no sound.

After closing the door, Colleen padded into the living room. There, she pulled off her sandals. Then, barefoot, she walked silently into the kitchen and retrieved Larry's pump-action shotgun from behind the fridge. She'd hidden it there earlier, while Larry was up in his study pretending to write his book. Last night, when he'd been snoring after making love to her, she'd sneaked into the study and read what he'd been typing on his laptop. It was all crazy nonsense. Not his Wall Street Scandals manuscript, but 'Sinis this and Sinis that,' just like that nutty preacher Crowley had been ranting about on TV.

Since seeing that crazy preacher, Colleen had been certain she'd heard his name mentioned somewhere before. This morning she'd remembered where: It hadn't been this Crowley she'd recalled, however, but another one, the early 20th Century British occultist Aleister Crowley. An intensely wicked man by all accounts. Another crazy. But that guy was long dead now, so maybe this Crowley preacher chap was his grandson? Or a copycat mystic nutcase? I saw Sinis, a Sinis was I? What the heck did that mean? If Larry was into that . . . ?

Was Larry crazy, or what?

Colleen hefted the shotgun then winced. She wasn't hurt, she'd just broken a fingernail again. Her right middle nail had caught on the trigger guard and snapped clean off. That pissed Colleen off. She took an inordinate amount of care to keep her nails in tip-top form and now this?

Still, that wasn't important. What *was* important was catching her husband in bed with his slut from next door. And now she had them.

Without being told, she somehow *knew* the woman was in the house now, upstairs in her bed. *In my bed!*

Colleen smiled, an expression of crazed calm on her face. *Oh yes, now I've got them both.*

***

Colleen had never intended going into town. She'd gotten all dressed up and made-up merely to deceive Larry.

Their Chevrolet Tahoe was presently parked a few yards up a turnoff at the start of the crescent. Colleen had sat in the vehicle for an hour—giving Larry sufficient time to set up his date. For that hour she'd been getting angrier and angrier. She'd also been wondering what it would feel like to murder someone.

Her final change of attitude from mild-mannered, longsuffering, caring wife to vengeful vixen had occurred yesterday afternoon at precisely 4.38 p.m. Though Colleen hadn't made the connection, that was when her headaches and nausea had stopped for good. If she'd been less preoccupied, she would also have realized that she'd not had any crazy blue flashes since yesterday.

From visible appearances, she seemed cured. Only she wasn't:

The illness had now moved into her subconscious mind and taken residence there. For good. She was no longer herself as she had always known herself to be. She was now irreparably warped, her brain on a one-way collision course to violence. A velvety film of blue caressed her unconscious self, molding her to its own designs.

Colleen's state of mind as she ascended the stairs to the bedroom was one that would have been completely alien to her two weeks ago.

She felt enraged. She felt betrayed, put on, abused beyond the point of forgiveness. She felt utterly humiliated that Larry would have sex with another woman in their marital bed. She no longer understood how she'd put up with his nonsense for the past three years. How could she have been so sappy? How could she have let Larry—the cheating son-of-a-bitch—take advantage of her so completely, and have done nothing about it for so long?

It made no sense to Colleen now. All that made sense, all that rang in her head, was getting even.

Silently, taking care not to creak the wooden slats, she ascended the stairs. Her large body felt like a tank, one designed to shatter an enemy defense.

She smiled at the shotgun. She'd cocked it earlier before leaving home. No need for that now.

Now was the time for metal thunder and the rain of blood.

Almost at the top of the stairs, Colleen stumbled. For a moment she almost lost her grip on the shotgun. It was slipping from her fingers and she was staring at it in confusion. She reacted just in time. She caught the shotgun just before it fell from her hands. Then, breathing heavily, she leaned against the stair bannister.

Dammit, I almost alerted Larry and the slut to my presence in the house.

She at first wasn't sure she hadn't. But no sounds of alarm came from the bedroom. No one called out "Who's there?" She heard no heavy tread of footsteps coming to investigate the noise. She figured they'd not heard her slip.

Then she realized that, while frantically trying to stop the shotgun from falling, she'd kicked the side of the staircase. Her right foot hurt. She stared down at it and cussed. Shit! Another one of her nails—her right big toenail this time—was cracked. Thankfully it was spilt across, not up through the middle, which could have injured her. Blue haze or no blue haze, Colleen felt like screaming. Colleen was so obsessive about her nails being perfect that breaking two of them like this in quick succession felt like being shot twice. Looking at that cracked toenail, its broken half flipped up and folded over the good part, Colleen felt like she was cracking up. She felt like she'd broken along with the toenail, like its split red topside was her broken heart and its revealed translucent underside the inside of her head. Her lips tightened over her teeth and she hissed softly. She gripped the shotgun extra-tight. She remembered how long she'd sat in the nail salon getting her hands and feet perfect. Now she'd have to make another trip into town to get these fixed too. The girls at the salon would start wondering what sort of a careless ditz she was.

Colleen hissed again. This was becoming a crisis. She felt angrier now than when she'd begun climbing the stairs. This was Larry's fault too; the bastard. If she broke just one more nail, she'd . . . she'd . . .

Staring at that flaw on her perfect pampered feet, she decided for good that murder, manicures, and pedicures didn't go together. *Next time I wanna kill someone I'll wear gloves and sneakers!*

After that, she sort-of calmed down a little. She waited for half a minute, till her foot stopped throbbing, before she resumed climbing.

***

Outside the bedroom door. From inside came moaning and giggles and bed creaks.

Here, Colleen paused for a moment. At that moment a vestige of the old Colleen resurfaced and questioned her actions: *What am I doing? Am I crazy? I don't need to go through with this! What I should do is get my phone and make a video of them screwing, then divorce Larry. I'll get all his money and he'll be ruined. If I do this, I'll go to jail. I'll—*

Then the timid and logical Colleen vanished and the vengeful vixen took her place again. The blue rage reasserted itself: *So what if I go to jail? He has no right to treat me like this! I'll show the bastard! I'll show him who he's screwing with! I'll teach him not to fuck with me!*

In that aggrieved state of mind, Colleen silently opened the bedroom door.

They were going hard at it, doggy-style. They were facing away from her. The bitch neighbor was gripping the headboard tight with both hands while pussy-hound Larry slammed it to her from behind. One of his hands was holding the slut's waist; the other tugged on her long black hair. She was jerking with him and whimpering out a long stream of satisfaction, a single unbroken monosyllable that conveyed pleasure words could never express. Sweat glistened on Larry's back. The sweat streamed down into his hairy ass-crack. His balls swung back and forth violently, like the semen they contained was revving itself up.

Watching Larry's pumping buttocks pumped Colleen full of hatred.

Still moving quietly, she crept up on the sweating lovers. She felt majestic now. Her heavy body felt buoyant in her cream pantsuit. Her large form was no longer an encumbrance to be ashamed of, but instead, the instrument of a well-deserved justice.

She stood behind him at the foot of the bed. She sighted the shotgun on the back of his head.

He must have sensed her presence then. He half turned, and exclaimed, "Wha . . . ?"

She pulled the trigger. **Boom!** went the thunder.

Larry's head vanished off his shoulders and splattered against the bedroom wall, up over the headboard. Chunks of skull and brain rained down on the bitch from next door.

Colleen felt triumphant. *Squirt, squirt* came the red rain, falling upward. Blood was spurting up from what remained of Larry's head—just his chin and a flap of brown hair.

The slut let out a scream. Larry was falling away from her but not fast enough, so Colleen yanked him out of the way. She pulled him right out of the slut's hole. With hatred she saw the spread pink pussy lips with their thick white creaming, and the gaping black space between them. The black hole that had vacuumed away her right to a blissful marriage. The greedy, grinning nether mouth that had eaten her allotment of happiness.

Larry fell right. His penis was still hard. Colleen found that hilarious: headless dickhead husband with an hard-on. She burst out laughing, as loud as if she was possessed by a demon.

She didn't laugh long though. The woman from next door—the evil, husband-snatching slut—had spun around and was now up on her knees facing Colleen with her hands raised in a gesture of pleading.

"Please, don't!" the slut begged, her makeup streaked with tears. "Don't shoot me too!"

Colleen laughed and cocked the shotgun. If this little bitch thought Colleen was going to let her escape so she could steal other women's husbands too, she had another think coming.

Colleen wanted this woman to suffer. And . . . she admitted it to herself . . . she was jealous of the slut's hot body. It was exquisitely toned, with almost zero-percent fat, with delicately chiseled abs and thighs, and that bust! Oh, she couldn't deny the fact—the slut looked sexy. *("What lovely little breasts you have, my dear." "All the better to snatch your husband with, fattie!")*

Well not any more, she doesn't, Colleen thought with a sadistic glow of delight. *Slut, I'm about to destroy you.*

She moved the shotgun down from its focus on her face to her belly and fired. She wasn't worried about the noise. This street was so isolated, they could well have been living on the moon.

Boom! The blast flung the slut backwards, off her craven knees and into the headboard.

As agile as a pregnant panther, Colleen leapt up onto the bed. The slut was twitching in pain, her eyes staring wide in agony. Her belly was a shredded mess of meat. Blood trickled through her black pubic hair like volcanic lava obliterating a forest. She gazed at Colleen, her agonized eyes begging for mercy. "Please," she mouthed, "please."

"Fuck you," Colleen spat at her. She cocked the shotgun again and **Boom!**, let the stupid thieving bitch have it again, between the breasts this time. She'd considered shooting her in the face, but she liked seeing the agony in her eyes. The slut knew she was dying and couldn't do a damn thing about it.

The slut crumpled on the bed and stopped moving. This time Colleen's shot had hollowed out a crater next to her heart. Chunks of flesh and skin swum in the lake of blood there. She was finished for good.

Colleen got down off the bed and wiped sweat from her face. She felt fantastic. Grinning, she stared at the two corpses on the bed. *Damn, I never imagined killing someone was so much fun!*

She sat down beside Larry's corpse to consider her next move. While thinking, she stroked his thigh. His penis had deflated now. She stared at it wistfully. *Wow, that damn dick sure did give me a lot of pleasure once, and now . . . ?*

Colleen decided it would be best to call the police and turn herself in. She could flee, plane-hop across the country and head for South America, but the long of the law was certain to find her there after a while. Better to just call 911 herself and face the music.

She wasn't worried. *The asshole was cheating on me. I'll get a sympathetic jury and be out in five or six years. And then—*

From the corner of her eye, Colleen caught a flicker of motion up near the head of the bed.

At first she ignored it, her mind busy previewing her appearance in court. She pictured herself perfectly, her clothes and her teary face as she explained to the startled judge and jury the kind of philandering hell Larry had put her through for the past three years. She saw herself dressed in black, and grieving. Grieving for her wasted years. Her lips would be pale pink. Her nails would be black like her clothes. Her manicure would be perfect, not cracked like today's disaster. She'd look sad but dignified. She'd not be faking her misery either: she really would feel that way as she relived her ordeal. Though horrified by the violence of her payback, everyone would nonetheless agree that it had been necessary, an unavoidable sin—the only way she could ever free herself from . . .

Colleen's reverie was disrupted by a series of rustling sounds coming from the bed, from almost directly in front of her. She looked up and looked forward.

She gaped.

The dead slut from next door was now falling apart. Like she'd been plaited from ropes, she was unravelling into short lengths of writhing flesh that glittered in the early afternoon sunlight streaming in through the windows.

Then Colleen understood what she was seeing and a chill went through her.

Oh my God! She's turning into snakes! The slut is turning into snakes!

Large and little ones, serpents of all shapes and sizes were forming from the slut's corpse.

Ordinarily, Colleen was very frightened of snakes. But now her surprise overpowered her horror. She was filled with an intense curiosity; she wanted to see what would happen next. Instead of leaping to her feet and running away, she waited. Holding the shotgun trained on the strange sight, she shifted along the foot of the bed to what she considered was a safe distance away from the snakes. Then she watched.

Soon, there was a large pile of writhing reptiles on the bed where the slut had been. The snakes—pythons, adders, vipers and a myriad others; more legless species than she could name—regarded her with their glittering amber eyes. Their gaze hypnotized her, as did their pretty flickering colors. Solid colors, diamond patterns, zig-zags, stripes, dots—the colors of serpenthood blended into a heady kaleidoscope in Colleen's brain. Their slithering sounds, their hisses, their rattles, were a distracting oriental music.

She looked right and confirmed that, no, Larry wasn't transforming too, it was just the dead slut doing so.

Colleen turned back to look at the pretty reptile confusion on the bloody bed.

At that moment, a rattlesnake flew out of the pile and struck at her. Vampire-fashion, the rattler sank its fangs deep into Colleen's neck. She gasped from the pain and from the realization that it was pumping liquid death into her body. She dropped the shotgun and tried to pull the snake off. She was still tugging away at it when the entire mass of snakes began slithering towards her, coming as fast as an enemy army.

The next second, two king cobras had dug their fangs through Colleen's jacket and were filling her breasts with their venom. As the king cobras pumped their dose of death into her, Colleen felt her breasts expanding like saline implants being filled. Her breath was already cutting out from the poison.

Now Colleen was scared stiff. She realized she wasn't about going to jail; she was going to die here. *Oh shit, help! I don't wanna die!*

She felt about desperately for the shotgun, but found Larry's foot instead. She reached for the shotgun again, but only succeeded in knocking it to the ground when another serpent bit her foot. Shit!

Now, snakes were attaching themselves to her arms and legs, their sharp teeth like nails being hammered into her soft, plump flesh.

She struggled to get up. If she could just make it to the bedroom door! But a boa constrictor swirled up around her torso and began squeezing her. The snake's weight anchored her to the bed like superglue.

A viper sunk its fangs into her nose so violently that both teeth went all the way through both her nostrils and its venom wound up dripping down her cheek instead. Four snakes already hung off her lips, which were now swollen to thrice their normal size.

In a flash of gut-wrenching pain, her breasts suddenly exploded. Both of Colleen's breasts blew up like water bombs and dribbled down the inside of her shirt.

Colleen began suffering massive diarrhea. It felt like her entire innards were liquefying and running out of her ass and down her trouser legs.

Two more snakes found space on her neck and attached themselves there like leeches. Their eyes glittered like jewels. Hungry jewels. Deadly jewels. An anaconda was swallowing Colleen's left leg. She could feel its stomach acids already hard at work, dissolving her flesh away.

Her world was pain, and the pain just increased. The snakes' poisons robbed her of her senses: she couldn't see, she couldn't hear, her tongue felt made of bamboo. She couldn't breathe; her throat was swollen shut. Her fingers and toes clenched of their own accord from poisoned nerve impulses. Her heart skipped beats like a bad jazz musician. The boa constrictor had her wrapped up so tight, she didn't even remember what lungs were anymore. The endless pain filling her chest had to be her crushed ribs. Her diarrhea had now become a ceaseless flow of blood from her ass.

The snakes covered her, obliterating her from view.

The endless horror of expiring spiraled up for Colleen into oblivion. Finally, she went as rigid as a block of stone and died.

CHAPTER 30

Jessica & Lucy

The day had a definite blue tinge to it. Jessica could see it. The closer she got to Roe Cottage, the denser the blue hue became. At a point, it almost seemed like the world lay at the bottom of a coral reef, and she was wading through crystal clear water to get home.

She noticed the strangeness yet ignored it. She was too scared. There was too much she didn't understand. In her current straits a mere tinting of her vision meant almost nothing.

Once at the cottage, Jessica ran the last few yards around to the front door. She knew the back door was locked. She was desperate to be inside and safe, out of the open where tentacle-topped policemen lurked.

She rang the front door buzzer twice. When no one answered, she fumbled around in her bag for her key. She kept looking around. She was scared that at any moment the axe-wielding cop would appear and murder her.

Dammit! She needed to pee really badly. The urine was almost bursting her bladder.

Jessica found her key and got the front door open. She dashed in, shut the door behind her, locked it, and put on the chain. Then she hurried through the living room and into her bedroom. Smoke was spilling from the kitchen like Lucy was burning their lunch again, but Jessica didn't stop; she was propelled by excretory urgency.

In her bathroom, she dropped her water and heaved several sighs of relief that she'd made it home alive. Her mind worked hard now to process the horrors she'd lived through in the past hour. It seemed impossible that she'd just watched someone—and a policeman for that matter—murder and eat two people.

And he's still out there! she thought in terror. *Shit, I need to call the police!*

203

She considered taking a sedative from the medicine chest, then squelched the idea. *Hell no—I don't need to be calm right now!*

She dashed out of the bathroom and grabbed her phone. She was about dialing 911 when she remembered the smoke she'd seen pouring from the kitchen when she'd entered the house.

She decided she'd better check on that first. The smoke—she could smell it even here in her room—it smelt like burning marijuana, like Lucy was smoking the world's largest joint. And Lucy already had that background of burning down one house . . .

She ran from her bedroom to the kitchen. "Lucy! Lucy!!" As she went she became aware that the sweet burning-pot smell from the kitchen was concealing another, very nasty smell.

"Lucy? Lucy!"

Lucy wasn't replying. When Jessica got to the kitchen she saw why.

Now, as she stood in the kitchen doorway gaping, the 'blue' she'd been ignoring forced itself in on her consciousness with brutal clarity.

The entire kitchen was a bright shocking blue. Also, its walls didn't appear to be plaster and tile anymore. Jessica did a double-take. *Fuck—the walls are made of meat now!* The meat walls were raw and bleeding, dribbling red onto the floor. They throbbed violently in the blue glow as if the color was leaking from their exposed veins.

But even that wasn't the worst of it. In the middle of the kitchen, 'something' had a hold of Lucy. The thing—it was a gray, almost description-defying muddle of tentacles, eyes, and mouths—held Lucy suspended in midair, and was (Jessica had to blink twice before she believed what she was seeing) *licking* Lucy all over. It was licking and sucking on her like she was a lollypop.

Lucy was out, her eyes closed. She wasn't completely unconscious though. As the tentacled monster (which Jessica found distressingly familiar, though she had no idea where she'd seen one before) kept licking and sucking on her, she moaned softly in pleasure.

Lucy was covered all over with transparent goop, the creature's saliva. As it slurped away at her body, more saliva poured and spattered on the kitchen island, where a laptop and an array of baking pans and ingredients were already drenched in the stuff. The goop reeked like a river full of dead fish.

Jessica was still standing in the kitchen doorway. Caught between the desire to investigate and that to flee, she did neither. She still held her cellphone, but had forgotten all about it. Her mind was trying to resolve the puzzle before her:

Where the hell have I seen this horrible, crazy thing before? But I haven't! But I have!

She was helped in her pondering by the fact that Lucy didn't seem to be in any danger at all. In fact, Lucy looked like she was going to have an orgasm soon if the monster didn't stop licking her between the legs. The kitchen's meat walls throbbed around Lucy as if they were the insides of her vagina.

Then . . . '**Click!**'. . . the connection was made. Jessica's mind opened up like Pandora's box and she knew what she was looking at:

This was one of the creatures from her hallucinations. One of those embodiments of perfected EVIL which she'd seen amidst the blue void as a mass of dark outlines. A living nightmare. This, she realized in horror, was one of the things that had spurred her on to kill that young man in the unseen temple.

It was—the word filled her mind—a *SINIS*.

I saw Sinis, a Sinis was I. The chant blew through her mind like a cyclone scouring a wasteland. It left her emptied of hope and filled with fright and confusion.

That goddam thing is a Sinis.

At that revelation, the blue overlay on the kitchen vanished. The meat walls reverted back to normal, revealing the real kitchen with a frying pan of smoking marijuana on the gas cooker.

Last of all, the Sinis itself vanished. It faded slowly, giving Jessica sufficient time to guess its intent and dash forward to catch Lucy as she dropped from its disappearing tentacles.

Lucy had never looked like she'd weigh much, but now, as Jessica caught her in midair, she felt like she weighed nothing at all. She seemed hollow, made of air. Even the thick saliva coating her weighed nothing.

Jessica had a clear sense of the vanished Sinis's amusement as she carried Lucy out of the kitchen and into the living room. She suspected that the monster was helping her carry Lucy. Her suspicion was confirmed when Lucy's weight abruptly returned once Jessica had her positioned over the brown living room couch that faced the front door.

The return of Lucy's body weight was so sudden that Jessica let go of her. In a way that was a relief; Lucy reeked of monster spittle.

Jessica sniffed herself. She stank too.

Lucy fell onto the couch and lay motionless with her eyes closed.

Ugh! Jessica winced at the horrible stinky goop she was now smeared with. She returned to the kitchen. She turned off the fire under the marijuana frying pan, then carried the pan to the sink and flooded it with water. Doing so temporarily filled the kitchen with so much smoke that she couldn't see anything.

Jessica resigned herself to the fact that she was getting high from passive pot smoking. It wasn't a bad feeling, but she felt this was a really bad time to have one's senses chemically-challenged.

She was surprised to see that the mess in the kitchen was already clearing up. The transparent goop, which she'd imagined would take forever to mop up, was evaporating. Its rising vapor mingled with the last of the marijuana haze, then vanished, leaving holes in the narcotic fog.

Jessica watched it for a moment, then realized she was getting side-tracked. *All I came in here to do was turn off the goddam burner.*

She cast a final look at the kitchen island. Her eyes fell on Lucy's laptop. Smokey looked out at her with a concerned look on his face.

"Woof!" the big dog barked.

"I don't believe it," Jessica muttered under her breath. "She was webcamming with her dog?" (When Lucy had earlier said she was off to 'dog-chat,' Jessica had assumed she'd been referring to a new android social media app.)

Then she forgot the dog and the kitchen and hurried back out into the living room to wake Lucy up. They had a whole lot to talk about. A whole damn lot.

As far as Jessica could tell, the walls of reality were crumbling down around them both.

***

Lucy woke up. She was sober. Jessica had never seen Lucy sober before. Lucy sat up. Jessica sat beside her on the couch.

"I thought you'd still be stoned," Jessica said. "All that pot? And, girl, why the hell were you *cooking* pot in the kitchen?"

Lucy shivered like she had a fever. Just like Jessica had witnessed happening in the kitchen, most of the goo had already evaporated off her body. The last of it was vaporizing now, leaving her skin gleaming like she'd been massaged with oil. Jessica now realized that the same thing had happened to her too while she'd been in the kitchen: her smearing of monster saliva had all evaporated away.

They stank though. They both stank like dumpsters.

"Why were you cooking pot in there?" Jessica persisted.

"I was stoned," Lucy replied. "I dunno what happened. Just like this morning too. I came to myself and I was all sober again."

Jessica's eyes narrowed as she linked Lucy's reply to her strange behavior that morning, when she'd emerged from her room doused in perfume and looking worried. "*What?* This has happened *before?* And *today?* Why the hell didn't you say anything about it?"

Lucy shrugged. "You guys wouldn't have believed me, would you? Just like when I told Reby about the cop I saw eating the cat."

"Oh, I believe you now," Jessica said. "I saw your damn cop. Only he wasn't eating a cat this time. He's moved higher up the food chain."

Lucy's eyes widened. "You saw him? Where?"

Jessica filled Lucy in on her excursion to the pond. She told her everything: about her vision of the temple, about the eyes she'd woken up holding and her missing clothes, and finally, about watching the tentacle-haired policeman committing both murder and cannibalism.

"Damn," Lucy said afterward. "I knew I wasn't imagining all that shit." She leapt to her feet. "Hold on a minute, I'll be right back."

"Where are you going?"

"To the bathroom."

That was a lie. Lucy returned holding a lit joint. She'd also exchanged her greasy panties for a pair of white shorts. Her damp black 'WEIRDO' T shirt remained draped over her elfin frame like drying laundry.

"I can't handle shit like this sober," she apologized, taking her seat again. "Okay, what do we do now?"

"We call the police. I was gonna dial 911 but it smelt like you were burning the house down."

Lucy took a long drag of her joint, then nodded sagely. "Yeah, I guess you're right. We do need to call the police before that asshole kills us too. Hey, but before we do, what the hell do you think is going on? I'm seeing weird stuff, you're seeing things too . . ."

Jessica looked around the living room, checking the windows to ensure that no one was peeking in at them. Everywhere still seemed safe. She recalled her strange premonition of Reby's departure from the cottage. But had she been right? Yes, she had been. For certain, Reby *had* left the house back then. But that must have been close to an hour ago. "I didn't see Reby when I got in," she said. "Isn't she back from . . . ?"

"The Townsend ranch? Riding reverse cowgirl on Big Larry? Nah, she's still over there playing bucking bronco. Hmm, Jessica, we need her opinion on this too. I wanna know if she's been seein' strange stuff as well . . . Call her on your phone."

A blue wind of revelation blew through Jessica's head. "Reby's dead," she said in a flat, emotionless voice. Cold as an Alaskan grave in winter, the sudden morbid knowledge chilled Jessica to her bone marrow.

Lucy gaped at her. "Huh? What did you just say?"

Jessica felt just as startled as Lucy. "Reby's dead," she repeated.

"How do you know that?"

"I don't know how I know it, but I do know." Jessica felt odd. She felt strange, unearthly currents blowing her back and forth. She no longer understood herself. *Earlier, on my way back here, I somehow knew that Reby was on her way over to Mr. Townsend's. I also sensed danger. But how can I possibly know any of this?*

She waited for an answer from somewhere, but none came. Whatever had just informed her of Reby's passing was now silent again.

Lucy got up and began pacing about the living room. The smoke from her joint trailed her in a looping stream. She dug a hand into the right pocket of her shorts, retrieved a handful of pills, and swallowed them all without looking at them.

She stopped pacing and turned to face Jessica. "Okay, look . . . Shit—I wish I'd brought my goddam gun with me. Rob told me to take it, but I said no, we'd be okay, we'd have security in numbers. Fuck! Dammit! Okay . . . we need to do something. That cop might have been the one who killed Reby too." She stared at Jessica. "I really wish I had my gun."

"Guns don't kill monsters," Jessica said. She leaned forward on the edge of the couch, placed her elbows on her knees, and locked her fingers under her chin. "You know, Lucy, that's one major part of this that I can't figure out—that policeman is a *monster* of some kind. And the thing that had you too? That wasn't anything natural either. That was some sort of supernatural creature. Where the hell did they come from? Another dimension? Hell?"

"Yuck," Lucy said. "I hate being licked like that. It felt like,"—she shivered—"just ugh! Ugh!"

"The thing seemed to think you tasted great. And you looked like you were about to come."

"I did fucking come—that's what I hate so much about it. But why does it keep sucking on me?"

Jessica shrugged. "Lucy, let's backtrack a bit. We're getting way off track here. We've got at least three dead people that we know about now—Reby and the two I saw get murdered."

Lucy pointed her joint at her. "Call the damn cops. I'll clear my stash out. I'll bury it all out in the back before they arrive."

Lucy resumed pacing about the living room.

Jessica dialed 911. "Hello? . . . My name's Jessica Schreiber. . . . I'd like to report a double—no, we actually think it's a triple—murder. . . . Yes, a triple homicide—there's three bodies. . . . I can't explain the details over the phone, but the bodies are still out back, two of them, and one's in the next house. . . . Look, you need to get here before the psycho moves them. . . . Yes, we're definitely in danger of him killing us too. . . . No. 4, Red Oak Crescent. . . . Yeah, we aren't going anywhere. . . . Oh, we're definitely keeping all our doors locked . . ."

The 911 dispatcher wanted to keep Jessica on the line. The woman had several more questions. Jessica didn't feel up to answering them. "Please just get over here extra-quick. We're both half scared-to-death already; we don't want to die too. . . . A squad car is on the way? . . . Great. Thanks . . ."

She hung up and turned to Lucy. "Well, all we've gotta do now is sit tight and—"

She shut up. Lucy was nowhere in the living room.

Jessica heard Lucy's voice coming from the kitchen. She got to her feet and walked in there. She paused by the door and grimaced.

Lucy was sitting with her head down on the kitchen island. She was staring at her laptop. Her right hand was poised in such a way that she was in danger of setting her hair alight with her joint.

She was weeping profusely. "Oh, Smokey! I just can't believe it, Reby's dead! Oh, she's fucking dead! She's dead, baby!"

"Woof!" the St. Bernard replied. "Woof!"

Lucy kept weeping.

Jessica watched her for a moment, then she walked over and placed an arm around her shoulders. "Take it easy, girl," she said soothingly. "We're gonna get out of this alright, you and I. We'll be just fine."

Even as she said it though, she knew that things were far from fine. For both of them, things might never be 'fine' again.

Beyond Reby's death even, she and Lucy had a problem. They had a massive problem that they didn't dare mention to the police. If they said a word about the Sinis to anyone they'd be considered lunatics. And *that* was their real problem: the Sinis. Where in the hell had those things—the fucking Sinis—come from?

Until they had an answer to that question, Jessica figured she and Lucy were still in a world of danger. Because, because, because . . . the Sinis were EVIL personified. Jessica had seen them, had smelt them, had *been* them . . . so she *knew*.

Had *been* them. The phrase locked in Jessica's head. *I was among those evil things. I was one of them. Is that it? I saw Sinis, a Sinis was I? Is that what it means? Is it a chant of becoming? Of transformation? But why in the world would I want to become something that horrible and disgusting? I don't want to be a Sinis—I don't!*

Without some explanation, however, Jessica was even more confused than Lucy was. And Reby's death just made everything worse. *How can I be so certain she's dead? But she is, I know it like I know my own name!*

Tears filled Jessica's eyes too.

CHAPTER 31

Jessica, mainly

By the time the squad car arrived at Roe Cottage, Jessica had the house smelling normal again. In the interim she'd been busy. She'd opened the kitchen and living room windows to air the place out. She sprayed the air with half a can of air freshener. She'd also done a fast check through the kitchen, living room, and Lucy's room for any half-smoked joints. (She'd rolled her eyes on seeing the round black hole in Lucy's bed.)

Lucy's half-cooked, half-burnt cannabis she'd dumped in the kitchen sink and run the disposal. (She still couldn't figure out why Lucy had been cooking what appeared to be almost half her stash of marijuana. And with brownie mix on hand too. *And what the hell was she doing with my chocolate?*)

She'd attempted wiping away the layer of grease on the kitchen island—the residue of the Sinis's saliva. However, the stuff was a lot more viscous than it looked. She'd finally given up on wiping it off. Instead, she'd steered Lucy (who was still weepily lamenting Reby's passing) into her bathroom and pushed her under the shower.

She'd left Lucy in there, carrying on a sad monotone with her webcammed pet through the open bathroom door. Apparently Lucy *really* missed Reby.

Lucy still hadn't emerged from her room when the squad car arrived.

Seated in the armchair to the left of the brown couch, Jessica half-watched through the front drapes as the police car came up the driveway and pulled up to the front porch. The vehicle swerved right, out of view, then stopped. She heard the policemen's voices and the car doors opening. Heard their cop boots disturbing the silent gravel.

She sighed with relief at the law officers' arrival. At least part of her nightmare was over.

By this time, Jessica had recovered a good deal of her composure. She was still scared, but her terror was diluted by other concerns. Her main worry now was solving the 'Sinis riddle' before it drove her crazy. For her, going crazy was utterly unacceptable under any circumstances: *If I lose my mind, I'll lose my job. No! No! No!*

Remaining sane even topped Jessica's concerns about Reby. She'd only known Reby for like, two weeks? Her fears over Reby's dying were mostly worries about suffering a similar fate herself.

She heard feet climbing the porch steps and rose from her armchair to answer the front door. As she crossed the living room, she unconsciously tidied her brown hair with her fingers.

She didn't expect the police to enter the cottage anyway. With a mass murderer on the loose, the cops were certain to be more concerned with organizing a manhunt than with busting two scared women for narcotics offences. Despite which, Jessica had assured Lucy in no uncertain tone of voice that she'd 'kill her' if she dared enter the living room smoking reefer while the police were around. Jessica had no intent of getting busted and getting a police record because of Lucy's addiction. (A Ziploc bag-and-a-half of Lucy's pot was still resident in the fridge's crisper drawer. Lucy was in no state of mind to clear it out, and Jessica had had no idea what to do with it [or with all the pills strewn about Lucy's room]. She'd considered flushing the marijuana down the toilet, but . . . she couldn't help remembering how violently Lucy had reacted yesterday when they'd suggested calling the police after noticing the bootprints in the flowerbed. Sure, Lucy was out of it now, but the moment the cops left and she discovered her marijuana was missing . . . ? Jessica could imagine waking up in the dead of night to a crazed, purple-haired imp holding a knife to her neck and demanding one of her ears as compensation.)

The buzzer buzzed. Jessica opened the door with relief, then caught her breath sharply.

It wasn't the police at all.

"Hello, Jessica," Dr. Whitfield said in a pleasant voice. "May we come in?"

"Doctor, what are *you* doing here?"

The doctor stepped out of the way, so Jessica could see behind him. McKenzie Clark stood there. McKenzie smiled at her and said,

"Your phone call to me was *very* interesting, Jessica. We just had to come see you."

Someone else was climbing the steps behind McKenzie, but Jessica wasn't paying attention to the person. Her eyes were riveted on the revolver McKenzie was pointing at her.

Shocked by this fresh crazy turn of events on an already insane day, Jessica turned to Dr. Whitfield. "I . . . I don't understand. What is going on? Why is she"—she indicated the blonde receptionist—"pointing a gun at me?"

Dr. Whitfield smiled nicely and gestured inside the cottage. "Let's go inside, Jessica. You're right to say you don't understand. You really don't. There's a huge amount of stuff you need to have explained to you."

Jessica nodded. If there was one thing she needed now, it was answers.

"Okay," she said, stepping back from the door. "Come in. But don't think of trying anything nasty. I already called the police. They're on their way here right now."

McKenzie laughed. "*We're* the ones you called, silly, not the cops." She pushed Jessica backwards into the cottage, then followed her.

Dr. Whitfield entered the house in company of the third person. This was a man of striking appearance—bald and with a trimmed black goatee—in a sky-blue suit. Jessica felt like she knew the man from somewhere.

The bald man smiled at her. He was tall, with the muscular build of a football player. His piercing gray eyes hinted at either high intelligence or controlled lunacy. Maybe both even.

"Hello, Jessica," he said in a warm, booming voice, "I'm delighted to finally meet you. You may have heard of me: I'm Brother Crowley, founder of the Realms of Consciousness Temple."

Brother Crowley? Jessica just gaped at the bald man. Now she *really* had absolutely no idea what was going on anymore.

McKenzie Clark took her by her arm and steered her across the living room to the couch that faced the front door. "Alright, Jessica, now sit down in this chair here, and just be quiet and listen. Listen like you're in kindergarten. Like the good doctor said, you've a *whole lot* to understand." McKenzie was wearing a paratrooper's jumpsuit; black and baggy and with lots of pockets. The military illusion was however spoiled by her shoes—red minimalist high-heeled sandals better suited to a Paris catwalk.

Jessica nodded dully. Every moment she grew more perplexed. She'd just discovered that if she concentrated and squinted a little, she could see a pale blue outline around each of her three visitors. Dr. Whitfield's outline was just the merest of pencil-traces around his bearlike bulk. McKenzie's blue outline was thicker, a neon glow about a finger wide. Brother Crowley, however, boasted a blue outline of almost two inches width. The three blue outlines flickered on and off with Jessica's state of concentration.

Her concentration was broken now by a noise behind her. She turned and was met by the smell of marijuana. Burning joint in hand, Lucy was stepping out of the hallway.

"Hey, who're you guys?" Lucy enquired. "You don't look like police."

"Pleased to meet you too, Miss Polk," Dr. Whitfield said, then gestured to the couch Jessica was sitting on. "Now, if you'd be so kind as to have a seat beside Jessica, we will explain to you both what's been going on here."

Lucy's eyes narrowed. "Are you guys the ones responsible for the monster that keeps licking me?"

McKenzie laughed. "In a way. Just sit down, Lucy. You've no idea what you're both about to learn."

Lucy sat obediently. McKenzie was holding a gun after all.

***

"Look," Jessica said wearily, "before you explain anything else, first explain this: What the hell did you mean when you said that when I dialed 911, I called you guys, not the police?"

"McKenzie was a bit inaccurate then," Dr. Whitfield replied her. "What she actually meant was that, instead of calling the police, you called a telephone exchange belonging to us."

The doctor and Brother Crowley were seated on Jessica and Lucy's left. McKenzie was seated on their right. On the couch itself, Lucy was seated on Jessica's left.

Lucy was still smoking her joint. Jessica wasn't surprised when she pulled some pills from her shorts and ate them.

"It's still the same thing," Jessica insisted. "911 is the emergency number. How come I got you guys instead of the police? And . . . who the hell *are* you guys?"

Lucy groaned. "Oh, so the cops aren't coming anymore? Hooray, my stash is safe. I dunno if I should be happy or sad about that."

"We switched your phone SIMs," McKenzie explained. "The SIM cards we replaced yours with automatically route all outgoing phone traffic from your lines to the ROC exchange first before they're forwarded to your network. Ditto for your incoming phone calls."

The gun McKenzie carried half-convinced Jessica of the truth of her explanation. For the other half, she looked at the two men on her left.

The doctor shrugged. "It's easy when you know how."

Brother Crowley nodded agreement.

Jessica was flabbergasted. "So you've been monitoring *all* our phone calls?"

"And your emails and your Facebooking and your blogging. Put simply, we've been monitoring your entire digital life." Seeing Jessica's blank look, McKenzie added, "At the moment, you're not connecting to the web via your registered ISP, but instead through us. How? We inserted chips into your laptops and devices that reroute all your web traffic to our hotspots and servers. When you connect, everything looks the same. But it isn't."

"But that's preposterous!" Jessica exclaimed. "To accomplish that, you'd need to have been in the house for hours tampering with our stuff."

McKenzie replied with a cold smile. "*We were* in this house for hours tampering with your stuff."

"It wasn't yesterday when we found the footprints, was it? It couldn't have been. We weren't out for very long, and you didn't know how soon we'd be back anyway. So how? When?"

"We did it at night, when you were all asleep."

"It must have been the night I had that damn dream," Lucy said. "Shit, and I really, really, really thought that damn cop was fake."

Jessica turned to stare at her. "What dream?"

Lucy looked miserable. "I didn't say 'cos you guys wouldn't have believed me anyway. I saw that damn tentacle-haired policeman again with my phone. A monster was handing him my laptop."

"Shit, Lucy. After seeing those damn footprints outside you should have said something." Jessica felt like throttling her. "Can't you just for once—"

"Listen," McKenzie interrupted, "we're wasting time here. The doctor and Brother Crowley have a lot to say to you both. Just understand this: on Tuesday night, we gassed you all so you'd not wake up, then fixed your communication devices. Once things got into full swing—once your nails turned blue, Jessica—we had to move fast." She scowled. "In fact, Jessica, the reason Morrison came back here yesterday afternoon was because he'd forgotten his wristwatch under your pillow. And, just so you know—there's also high-definition CCTV cameras in all the rooms, so we can keep an eye on you all. We've been watching the three of you for the past ten days."

Jessica was stumped. True, she'd begun getting answers, but so far the answers she was getting merely increased her confusion further. She stole a glance at Lucy. Lucy was puffing away. Jessica decided that at the moment there was definitely something to be said for being a dope fiend. She could do with that kind of chemical help herself.

"Gimme a hit," she said, grabbing the joint from Lucy and taking a long drag to calm herself.

"Hey!" Lucy snatched the joint back, then moved a distance from Jessica on the couch to prevent it being taken away from her again.

"Hey, ladies," McKenzie said, pulling Jessica back to the moment. "Do you both get the picture so far—that we've been keeping an eye on you three?"

Jessica nodded. "Yes, but I'm more confused now than I was before. *Who are* you guys? What the hell do you want with us? Why the hell were you watching us?" She stared at McKenzie with a pleading look in her eyes. "What the hell is going on? Why am I seeing monsters?"

"And why do they keep licking me?" Lucy added.

"What is this all about?"

"And why do they keep licking me?"

Dr. Whitfield coughed to get their attention. "I'll take over from here, McKenzie." McKenzie nodded and sat back and crossed her legs.

Jessica waited. She looked across at Brother Crowley. The man sat as still as a statue, a pleased smile on his face. Jessica found him creepy in an indefinable way. But then, she knew he was a cult leader. He was supposed to be creepy.

"Now, Jessica," Dr. Whitfield said. "Please pay attention."

She turned back to him. The doctor was holding up a phial of pale blue liquid. "*This* is responsible for all your strange experiences."

Jessica gaped. The liquid in the phial was the exact same sky-blue color that her fingernails had been the day they'd changed color.

"What is that?" she asked in a wavering voice.

"It's called SIN-15."

"What is it?" Her mind made the connection between 'Sinis' and 'SIN-15' (the latter was merely a stylized way of writing the former), but that was all. The mystery still remained.

Dr. Whitfield smiled. He scratched his nose with his free hand. "It's the blood of a god, Jessica. We've been putting it in the cottages' water supply. Both this cottage and Cottage No. 2."

Okay, now we're getting somewhere, Jessica thought. *They've been drugging us for some reason.*

Lucy sighed. "C'mon, doc, real life ain't no TV show. Be honest. You've been drugging us with a god's blood? Who's ever gonna believe that?"

"Hopefully you two will." Waving the phial of blue liquid at them for emphasis, the doctor continued his explanation. "SIN-15 is Sinis blood. SIN-15 works on contact with flesh. You don't need to drink it—bathing with a mix of SIN-15 and water has the same effect." He raised a hand to forestall a question from Jessica. "Please just listen and understand. The effects of SIN-15 on humans differs: Some people—like Lucy here—are practically immune to it. Others slowly go crazy. Yet others suffer extreme physical transformations." His expression became dark. "Some of those physical transformations— such as what regrettably happened to your housemate Miss Butterfield—can be irreversible."

"*What* did happen to Reby?" Lucy asked before Jessica could.

The doctor waved the question away. "Let's just say she's not herself anymore."

"She's dead," Jessica said.

The doctor nodded. "Yes, she is, but the SIN-15 in her bloodstream mutated her remains into . . ." He scowled. "Forget her, there's *a lot* more you still need to understand."

Jessica scowled back at him. Now she was getting angry. She couldn't believe that these crazy people had been messing with her life like she was a toy. "I think I understand enough already. You assholes doped us as part of some crazy experiment you're conducting, and you've already killed Reby, and now—"

No, she interrupted herself, *there's more to this than that. Things STILL don't add up yet.*

She realized that there was something they'd not yet told her. Something important. She looked worriedly at Dr. Whitfield. "You've explained all the possible results of being affected by SIN-15, except . . . hey!" She looked darkly from the doctor to McKenzie in turn. "There never was anything called Bobbet's allergy then? That was just a con?"

The doctor smiled.

"Yeah, there's no such condition as Bobbet's allergy," McKenzie admitted.

"And the drugs you gave me? All those pills I had to take like clockwork?"

"Just placebo, some vitamins and minerals to keep you healthy. We knew all the symptoms of the SIN-15 treatment—the nausea and headaches, and the staining of your nails—would clear up, we just needed you to not panic before they did."

Jessica stared at McKenzie with HATRED. If only she didn't have that gun with her. Jessica wasn't about to dare a gun.

But that nagging question remained in her mind. And it needed an answer. She was scared enough as it was, but she needed to know.

She forgot McKenzie, with her Brigitte Lahaie face and smug smile, and stared hard at the doctor. "Okay, let's cut the bullshit. You've explained the different effects of using that SIN-15 drug, everything except what's been happening to *me*. What has the goddam thing done to me?"

The doctor smiled. Brother Crowley smiled broadly. McKenzie smiled. Lucy sucked in a lungful of weed smoke and grinned.

Dr. Whitfield said, "Very, very rarely—the chances of it happening are one in eighty thousand—the SIN-15 drug has a completely different effect on a person. That person . . . okay, the first signs of a difference are normally a blue coloration of the fingernails. This coloration can last for anything from as little as an hour to as long as three days. Mr. Townsend next door, for instance, never even knew his nails had changed color because the change occurred while he was asleep; by the time he woke up in the morning they were normal again." Dr. Whitfield scratched his nose. "So, first the nails change color—that's the first sign. The main difference though, is that that person begins to see visions. First they dream vividly of the Sinis realm, and then the dream seeps into their reality, and they have daytime visions of the Sinis realm. Finally, as happened in your case, the subjects reach a point where they can bring physical objects back to our world from the realm of the Sinis."

Jessica was forced to stare at McKenzie again. "I didn't hallucinate about the eyes then?"

"No."

"Did I hack that guy to bits?"

"Yes."

"I'm a murderess."

"You're a prophetess."

"Fuck. I murdered someone in a vision."

"The Sinis are delighted with you, Jessica," Brother Crowley said, speaking for the first time since he'd introduced himself. "As the good doctor was explaining, you're exactly what they've been seeking for ages. That one-in-eighty-thousand success—an Oracle." Brother Crowley smiled at Jessica's horror. "Yes, Jessica Schreiber, you have been successfully transformed into a Sinis Oracle—a mouthpiece and visionary between their realm and ours. The other Oracle we produced was your neighbor Mr. Townsend. *His* was a powerful gift indeed. Unfortunately he died. But you won't. You are a treasure and to be immensely treasured. And I assure you that my gods are very pleased."

Jessica gaped at him.

"I saw Sinis, a Sinis was I," Brother Crowley intoned solemnly.

"I saw Sinis, a Sinis was I," Dr. Whitfield and McKenzie Clark both chanted in response.

"What the hell is this shit you guys keep quoting anyway?" Jessica asked. Her question was something to say. Her thoughts were muddled and scared: *Shit! I've been drugged by a crazy cult who think I'm their goddam Chosen One. Oh fuck! I . . . Lucy and I need to escape from here!* "Yeah, 'I saw Sinis, a Sinis was I'; what does the goddam thing mean?"

"It's a palindrome," McKenzie replied.

"A palindrome? What the hell is that?"

"Huh?" Lucy said. "Oh . . . a *palindrome*. Heh heh heh! A sentence that reads the same way both backward and forwards. That's quite a neat trick! Ha ha."

"So?" Jessica said, leaning toward Dr. Whitfield. "All that proves is that you're smartasses. I don't goddam care if it reads the same when turned upside-down. What the hell does it mean?" Then a lightbulb flashed in her head and she turned from the old doctor to stare at Brother Crowley instead. "That's what you're here for, isn't it? To explain the justifying theology behind my mindfuck?"

Brother Crowley, who'd been sitting as still as a block of ice, now unfroze like he'd been thawed. He nodded. "We're all stuck in the age-old loop: when science fails, man turns to religion, and vice versa."

Jessica scowled at him. "Talk, man. Take forever with your explanation if you like." She gestured with her thumb at McKenzie, who had her revolver poised on her knee and sighted dead-center on her. "We ain't going anywhere."

"I need to go light a new joint in my room first," Lucy said. Then, seeing everyone staring angrily at her, she added, "Nah, don't bother—I'll just pop some bennies and 'ludes."

***

"The Sinis are gods," Brother Crowley said. "They're the source of a new form of evolution for mankind."

"They're demons," Jessica countered. "They're evil incarnate, totally without good of any sort in their makeup. All they do is corrupt, and feed on that corruption. I've seen—I know—the monstrous horrors they're capable of. I want nothing to do with them."

"They're sexual perverts," Lucy insisted. "They keep licking me."

"Hey, wait. If, as you claim, Lucy is immune to the effects of SIN-15, how come she sees the Sinis too?

McKenzie's reply was heavily tinged with disgust. "Oh, the Sinis just wanna suck the drugs out of her and get high too." She made a face. "Junkie gods. Exactly what we don't need."

"God rolls his own, huh?"

"Please don't interrupt, Miss Polk."

"Sorry, man, I'm having withdrawal symptoms here—a lack of marijuana makes me get all talkative."

"I have no intention of becoming your Oracle. I hate evil."

"It doesn't matter what you like or dislike, Jessica. The Sinis offer us what no other religion does—not Christianity nor Islam, not Judaism or Taoism or Shintoism or Hinduism or Buddhism. Nor the different blends of witchcraft or Satanism or paganism either. Not even Humanism or Atheism. The Sinis tell us we can become gods like them. All we need to do—to put it simply—is to become as evil as they are."

"Dude, that's a crock. The reincarnative faiths believe we can become gods if we pay our dues in successive life circles."

"It's not the same thing. Have you ever died before?"

"Silly question. What does that have to do with this?"

"Just *everything*. If you've never been beyond the grave, how do you know *for sure* what lies on the other side?"

"Uuuhh . . ."

"Exactly. Everything unseen is guesswork. And all religions argue over what happens after death anyway. They fight holy wars over resurrection, Heaven and Hell, and eternal judgment. Unlike Christianity, however, the Sinis offer us all divinity *now*. And we don't need to be good to qualify either. All we have to do is—"

"You said it before—become as evil as they are."

"'Amoral' might be a better word choice. But 'amoral' can also imply inaction. 'Evil' on the other hand implies *action*, a definite *work* being done."

"A work of EVIL? Do bad rather than good to become divine?"

"There is but one God and they are Sinis."

"So we become inhumane to become non-human? We act monstrously to become monsters too?"

"I admit they look horrible, but you're getting the point."

"Dude, do you *really* want to look like that *forever*?"

"Eternal life in any form beats dying. The Sinis are a proven divinity. They exist in their own realm called Alternity. They live forever in a complex circle—they die and are reborn as themselves, then grow old to die again, etcetera forever."

"What do you need me for?"

"The obvious. You can see them. You can hear them. You can communicate with them."

"All they do is sing, sing, sing. Sun-Ra on acid."

"On higher doses of SIN-15, their songs will form words to you, and you will tell us what they say."

"Oh, hell no, I won't."

"Jessica, I'm afraid you have no choice in the matter. We *can't* let you go—and not just for security concerns either. You're way too precious. You belong to us now."

"Don't even go there, man. This ain't the Eighteenth Century. I'm a modern American woman. I'm no one's property."

"I'm afraid you're Sinis property now, Jessica. And who refuses service when their God insists on it?"

"Shit!"

***

"And now," Brother Crowley said after a pause for Jessica to calm down a little, "I need to answer a question you've asked more than once."

Jessica looked warily at him. "Which one of them?"

"Your 'Who are you guys?' question."

"You've already answered that, haven't you?"

"Not really. Alright, Jessica, we're the ROC."

"Yes, yes—the Realms of Consciousness crazies."

"No, the Red Octopus Corporation. The *real* ROC."

Jessica gaped, then her eyes narrowed angrily. "Huh?"

Lucy hung her head like it hurt to think. "Guys, let's just keep this simple, alright? Stop frigging trying to confuse me further." She popped two blue pills.

"Okay," Jessica agreed, "so you're the Red Octopus Corporation. That still doesn't explain anything. Who the hell are the ROC?"

"An international organization hell-bent on establishing the Sinis as gods on earth."

"I like how you use the expression 'hell-bent.' Shows your true colors."

"Understand this: we try to leave our brand on everything we touch—in the names. The Raynham Outlook Clinic is ROC. The Realms of Consciousness Temple? Another ROC. Even the street we're currently on is named Red Oak Crescent, isn't it? Another ROC. And this house . . ."

"Okay, *I get it*. You're the fucking ROC. It makes as much difference to me as a change of government in China. How about if, for simplicity's sake, you just carry on being the *temple?* The new boss is the same as the old boss. All I want is out of your world-dominion plans."

"Oh, try to understand, sister," Brother Crowley said, his voice as warm as sunshine, "that can't ever happen. You're more in than sin."

Jessica grimaced at him. He nodded serenely, stroking his goatee.

She turned to look at Dr. Whitfield instead. He smiled back at her. "Yes, Jessica, you're a part of us now."

"Because of this Oracle nonsense?"

"Oh, it isn't nonsense, Jessica. You've no idea how much more you're going to see. The Sinis realm is one of incredible glory."

"I *don't want to* see it. Smelling it is bad enough. The place reeks like a Nazi mass grave. Like it's the universe's dumpster for murdered people."

"Yes," Brother Crowley agreed, "it is a morbidly glorious realm, full of eternal decay and rebuilding. You, Jessica Schreiber, will describe it to us in full detail and we will write the books about it."

CHAPTER 32

McKenzie

"So yes, that's what the palindrome means," Brother Crowley told the two women. "We become Sinis by 'seeing' them. It represents our own transformation into Sinis. If Christianity agrees that God can become man, why cannot man also become God?"

"Jesus doesn't go about licking people," Lucy said.

McKenzie laughed at that. Jessica looked horrified. Lucy looked placid.

McKenzie wondered how much pot one woman could smoke. Via the CCTV cameras in the cottage they'd watched Lucy smoke endless amounts of reefer. *Damn, her lungs must have marijuana plants growing in them now!*

Brother Crowley kept on speaking, explaining the basic precepts of the Realms of Consciousness faith to the two captives. McKenzie smiled coldly at their still-perplexed expressions. At first, she'd found the whole Sinis concept a difficult one too. But now it was simple to accept. She had faith. Faith bypassed all the irritating and confusing logic that always threatened to destroy a system of beliefs. "It's impossible!" reason endlessly argued. "It'll never work!" But it did work. It did. The faithful—those in the know and in the fold, those wrapped in the abominable tentacles of the Sinis and their hateful protection—knew it worked. They had felt the Sinis glory.

Felt it. Only Oracles could *see* it.

McKenzie was thirty-six. She'd been involved in this project to find an Oracle right from the get-go. It had begun when she was twenty-eight. Eight long years of failure after failure after failure. The search for an Oracle had begun down in Reno, Nevada. From there they'd shifted it progressively east: first to Kansas, then to Tennessee. The reason they'd had to keep moving was because of the body count.

Infecting people with the SIN-15 compound resulted in lots of casualties. All of which needed to be disposed of or staged as accidents to avoid a police investigation.

The dead Townsends in Cottage No. 2 were a classic example of the kind of cleanup the ROC were regularly faced with. The SIN-15 had driven the wife crazy, and she'd murdered her husband and his mistress. That in itself wouldn't have caused any major raised eyebrows (SIN-15 was undetectable by any lab analysis), but, the wife had died of massive amounts of snake venom, as well as from asphyxiation due to having her ribs crushed. Those details would puzzle the police, and might well trigger an investigation. So, over at Cottage No. 2, a cleanup was already in progress. The Townsends' bodies would disappear without a trace. In addition, the details of the couple's stay on Red Oak Crescent (along with Rebecca Butterfield's also) would be rewritten.

From the moment of the five experiment subjects' rental of the two cottages, five close-to-identical doppelgangers had been recruited from amongst the ranks of the ROC faithful. (In Jessica's case, this initial selection had been changed when, at the last minute, she'd taken over Karen Arlen's spot.) In two cases cosmetic surgery procedures had been carried out to make those selected as realistic copies as possible. These five people had been hypnotically force-fed the lives of those they would impersonate, including their mannerisms, characters, and speech patterns. None of the five doppelgangers would head for home or anywhere where they were known. Each of them would continue on their vacations: the new Mr. and Mrs. Townsend would travel down to Mexico, the new Miss Butterfield to Florida, 'Lucy Polk' to Seattle. 'Jessica Schreiber' would first head out east to Los Angeles, then fly to Japan. Each of them would quietly disappear from their destinations after living there for a sufficient amount of time that everyone remembered them. The doubles' IDs would be perfect, as would be their hypno-taught abilities to reproduce their original's signatures. Skin-bondable plastic analogues of all the originals' fingerprints had already been created. These would be worn by the doubles so that the illusion would be perfect. The ROC had the power to make people disappear. They'd done it before and would do it again. (To McKenzie's knowledge, a hundred and thirty-five people had so far vanished during the ROC's search for a

Sinis Oracle. And that was in the USA alone.) These five would vanish also.

There would be no traces of foul play. None whatsoever. And if there were ever any questions asked, the ROC had sufficient money at its disposal to answer them.

***

McKenzie spent some time staring at Jessica. The Chosen One. The Special One. She envied Jessica greatly. McKenzie had taken SIN-15 herself in hopes of viewing the Sinis realm. All the divine blood-compound had done was render her sterile.

Jessica, of course, still had no idea how favored she was. The stressed-looking brunette would be pampered for the rest of her human life, treated like a goddess incarnate. Just like Jezebub was. No, Jessica Schreiber would be even higher exalted by the ROC than Jezebub was. Jezebub would be green with envy at having her position of worship usurped. McKenzie laughed at her own joke: blue-skinned Jezebub, *green* with envy. That was just hilarious.

She caught Jessica's eye. Jessica gave her a look of utter disgust and pointedly looked away. Her facial expression was one of intense concentration, but her eyes lacked focus. She looked not so much confused as undecided on her next course of action. Jessica was clearly unable to make up her mind.

McKenzie understood that. One of the most interesting things about the SIN-15 compound (*and, yes, Jessica darling—its name is just an adaption of 'Sinis'*) was its ability to neutralize fear and worry. McKenzie had witnessed this in person while monitoring the cottages on CCTV: that surreal moment when each person's anxiety over the weirdness they were experiencing abruptly faded away. The moment when their horror and fear dissolved into thin air.

Take Jessica herself, for instance, on the day that she'd noticed her fingernails had changed color. One moment she'd looked about to freak out completely. The next moment, she'd been admiring how cute her hands looked. Her reaction to her various visions had played out similarly.

The same had happened with the other experimental subjects also. Larry Townsend, for instance, had pondered aloud more than once his surprise that he wasn't flipping out over the weird stuff he was seeing. Each time he'd just get sexually aroused and dial up Rebecca Butterfield.

(Larry's death was an accident. The CCTV camera in the Townsend's bedroom had malfunctioned, so the CCTV monitoring crew [who were based in Cottage No. 1] hadn't seen Colleen remove the shotgun. The crew couldn't enter the house to replace the camera until nightfall, and so were left blind. They'd only been alerted to the murders when they heard the gunshots.)

Jessica. Even now, the drug was hard at work in Jessica, calming her even though she knew she should be frightened out of her wits. She knew she was about being kidnapped, but the SIN-15 was making even that crisis not seem as serious as it was.

At the moment, Jessica most likely thought she had sufficient time to understand everything, and *afterwards* plot her escape from the crazies.

***

"Hey, I need to pee," Lucy said suddenly.

McKenzie looked at her. Lucy was squeezing her thighs together and wincing. She seemed to be in severe discomfort.

McKenzie turned to Dr. Whitfield. "Sir?"

He nodded. "Yes, take her. I've got my gun with me. I'll keep watch on Jessica." He pulled out a semi-automatic pistol and pointed it at Jessica. "Now, let's just maintain the status quo, okay?"

McKenzie waved her revolver at Lucy. They both stood up. Lucy headed for the hallway.

"Hey!" McKenzie called after her. "Come back here. Use the toilet across the living room."

Lucy looked back. She shook her head. "I gotta get me another joint from my room." Meanwhile, she was squeezing her hands in her crotch like she'd needed to ease herself two days ago and only just remembered.

McKenzie rolled her eyes. *This woman is a total mess.* She looked across the room and met both the doctor's and Brother Crowley's eyes. Both men replied her unvoiced question with almost imperceptible nods. Both clearly agreed with her that Lucy Polk needed to be killed. It was a question of 'when?' not 'should we?'

Lucy was merely an irritation.

But they wouldn't kill her here in front of Jessica. At the moment, the ROC world—the Sinis world—revolved around Jessica. None of them would do anything to upset her.

"Okay," McKenzie told Lucy, grabbing her arm. "Let's go. But don't try to make a nuisance of yourself. I'll whip your ass if I have to."

"Yeah, sure. See, no one ever picks on people their own size anymore—it's always five-foot-me biatches wanna act tough around. Ouch, my damn bladder feels about to explode."

"So get a move on."

"I am. The floor is shaking."

McKenzie rolled her eyes again. The floor was definitely not shaking. She jabbed her revolver hard into Lucy's back.

"Ouch, goddam stop that! That hurt!"

McKenzie shoved her towards the shadowed hallway. "Look, you junkie, do you want to piss or not?"

"Yeah, yeah. Don't you dare rush me. My head is getting bigger while the hallway is getting smaller—I'm never gonna be able to fit through the opening." Then she froze again.

McKenzie shoved her again. "For Sinis's sake, move your bony ass, will you? How hard can it be to walk to the frigging bathroom?"

She looked back at the others. Dr. Whitfield and Brother Crowley were watching the proceedings with amusement. Jessica wasn't even looking her way. Jessica was staring straight ahead, trying to work out the new laws of reality she'd just been handed. She looked about to cry.

Poor Jessica, McKenzie thought. *No, super-extra-lucky Jessica.*

McKenzie returned her attention to Lucy. Lucy was now visibly trembling. Instead of moving forward, she was backtracking fast into McKenzie.

"Oh no, not again!" she moaned. "You bastards aren't licking me again!"

McKenzie didn't get it. There was nothing ahead of them, yet Lucy was pointing and staring at the hallway entrance with complete dread in her eyes.

Lucy stopped retreating when she slammed into McKenzie. She looked up at her face, then ducked under her gun-arm and hid behind her.

"Sinis. Goddam Sinis are waiting for me in the hall."

"Lucy, there's nothing there."

"Liar. There's two of them there with hundreds of their tongues out! I'm not going in there. Keep those things away from me! They're gonna suck out my high again!"

McKenzie turned to grab her, but Lucy had herself already turned and was charging away across the living room towards the front door.

"Hey, come back here or I'll shoot you!"

"Shoot those things! I'm getting the fuck out of here!"

McKenzie raised the gun to shoot her. Lucy was already by the front door. McKenzie knew she could easily put a bullet in the back of Lucy's head from where she stood.

Then she remembered Jessica and lowered her gun. Jessica mustn't be upset for any reason.

McKenzie didn't think Lucy would be getting far anyway.

CHAPTER 33

Jessica

Jessica had turned to stare at the hallway when she heard Lucy mention being 'licked again.' Lucy was right. There *were* two Sinis hovering in the hallway entrance. The two gods (demons rather—she was convinced that their realm of Alternity was a merely a previously unnoticed part of Hell.) were both as horrible as the one she'd seen licking Lucy: gray masses of tentacles dotted with eyes, and with dozens of mouths that dripped ectoplasmic saliva on the floor from thick black tongues. The pair stank like a mountain of rotting skunks.

Then she'd realized that from the way McKenzie was gaping at the arched entranceway, the receptionist/gunwoman couldn't see the Sinis. Nor apparently could either Dr. Whitfield or Brother Crowley, though all three of their blue auras had kicked up several notches on the creatures' appearance. The three of them didn't appear to be able to *smell* the horrible things either.

Then Lucy slipped away from McKenzie and dashed across the living room to the front door and began unlatching the chain.

Jessica now found herself faced with a huge decision: *Should I escape?* It seemed to her a really dumb question to ask oneself when one was trapped in the clutches of a satanic cult with world domination ambitions. What had Brother Crowley called their organization again? The Red Octopus Corporation. What kind of asshole name was that? The name sucked—surely the cultists realized that too. No wonder they called their subsidiaries by different aliases: Raynham Outlook Clinic . . . Realms of Consciousness . . . ROC, ROC . . . just a Rain of Crap on her parade. It was nothing but megalomaniac bullshit. Small men wanting to be big men at the expense of others. The old mind-control game with a new name. And of course the sheep would follow. Sheep like fucking McKenzie, who Jessica felt should just go hire on as an airline stewardess already. The woman had the requisite photoshopped 'Come Fly With Me' look. Who else wore jumpsuits and high heels to work? *Red* high heels for that matter.

Jessica realized she'd gotten distracted by McKenzie's fashion sense. She posed herself the same question again: *Should I escape? Yes, I should, but . . .* She didn't know what the 'but' was, only that for some reason, escaping wasn't what she felt like doing right now. Which was crazy. *I need to flee this fucking place immediately!* she raged at herself. *I need to get back to the sane world! Back to work!*

But she didn't leap up and flee. Despite her hatred of everything she was hearing. She was intrigued, and wanted—no, needed—to hear more about the Glorious Evil. *I saw Sinis, a Sinis was I!* (Jessica felt it was damn important that she fully understand the message. She was getting there for sure—she felt like a deep epiphany on the infernal-divine transformation was just around the corner—but she still hadn't yet gotten as clear an insight as she felt she needed concerning such an important subject as the tentacle demons. It wouldn't be long now though. And then she would escape, satisfied that she completely understood the wickedness she was fleeing from.)

The two Sinis from the hallway were meanwhile going after Lucy, who was having some difficulty getting the front door open. The Sinis floated forward, their many eyes all intent on one objective: the skinny little woman fumbling with the front door lock.

The demon pair floated right through McKenzie, who gasped from the shock of contact and collapsed unconscious.

When that happened, Dr. Whitfield and Brother Crowley both gaped at Jessica.

"She's not lying? They're actually here?" Dr. Whitfield asked.

Jessica found it strangely gratifying that both of these men were dependent on her for their information. It was an extremely empowering feeling. "Yes, they're here," she replied drolly. "I think they want to get stoned again."

At the sound of McKenzie's body hitting the floor, Lucy looked back from the front door. Her gaze was comical—an addict's horrified quest to not share her high with anyone else. "Oh fuck, no! I'm outa here! You bastards aren't licking me empty again!"

Then, in a blue flash, Jessica saw *through* the front door. Two people were climbing the porch steps . . . one of them holding . . .

"Lucy, don't go outside!" she yelled, leaping to her feet as she shouted the warning. "Don't go outside!"

The two Sinis were however too near to Lucy now for her to care. She wasn't being abused by them again and that was that. With a wrench, she flung the door open and ran outside.

Then Lucy screamed. "NOOOO!"

Jessica was standing with her right arm outstretched in a gesture of beckoning. Now she shut her eyes. She shut them just as she saw the axe, like an executioner's golf club, start its murderous arc. Thankfully, she wasn't able to see through her own eyelids.

She heard a loud wet 'Thunk!', then the sound of something heavy hitting the ground outside. Something else hit the floor just in front of her.

Jessica opened her eyes and stared down at the floor. Lucy's severed head lay at her feet. Lucy had a horrified stare on her face, like she'd been caught shooting up in a church vestry.

Sighing, Jessica looked up and saw the tentacle-haired policeman with the axe—the same cannibal cop who'd murdered and eaten the amorous young couple—walking into the living room. He dangled the bloody axe in his left hand.

A woman was entering the living room after him. Jessica gaped at her. She was a very strange woman indeed. She was completely naked, had completely sky-blue skin, and had bright, electric-red tentacles covering her head. Just her head; her pubic hair was as blue as the rest of her. She was carrying a plastic shopping bag that bulged with writhing snakes.

Out on the porch, beyond the newly-arrived pair, Jessica could see Lucy's arms, splayed in a pool of blood. Then she saw through the people and out through the house walls and saw the two Sinis hovering over Lucy's corpse. The tentacled gods were dipping their many tongues in Lucy's blood and lapping it up like a pack of happy hounds. Jessica felt their evil delight emanate from them.

She looked inside again and once more stared down at Lucy's head. She wasn't terrified like she'd been earlier. She wondered why this was. Then she understood. It was a damning understanding: *Oh, we're all on the same side now. Well, how do you like that?*

The policeman and the woman stopped close to her. Dr. Whitfield and Brother Crowley stood up.

"Praise Jezebub!" Brother Crowley said.

"Praise Jezebub!" both Dr. Whitfield and the policeman responded. Jessica remembered that the cannibal cop's name was Morrison, which meant the woman was 'Jezebub.'

The sky-blue woman nodded coolly. (Jessica now noticed that she also lacked both nipples and a navel.) She gestured toward Jessica. "How is she?" she asked in a soft voice. Just like Morrison, Jezebub too had sharp pointy teeth. Her tongue and the inside of her mouth were both as blue as her skin. Her eyes were deep blue in white orbs.

"Still somewhat disoriented, goddess," Dr. Whitfield replied. He turned to Jessica. "Permit me to introduce you to our resident goddess, Jezebub Hilton. Mistress Jezebub is another kind of SIN-15 success. Not an Oracle like you, but a priestess, a woman supremely knowledgeable in the ways of the Sinis. You and she will work together."

Jessica nodded dully at Jezebub. "Hi." Then she pointed down at Lucy's severed head. "You bastards didn't have to kill her." She spat in Morrison's face. "You didn't need to murder her, you sadistic son-of-a-bitch! Why did you!?"

Morrison looked angry but made no reply. He wiped the spit from his cheek.

"It is best that she died," Brother Crowley said in a placatory tone of voice. "She constituted a peculiar problem to us. In addition to being a potential source of embarrassment to the ROC, she was also an insult to us."

That broke through Jessica's anger. "An *insult*? How the hell could Lucy be an insult to you? She didn't even know you guys existed till an hour ago!"

"You don't understand."

"So make me understand, goddammit!"

Brother Crowley sighed. "What we find insulting is how the Sinis—the same divine beings we're going through all this headache to communicate with—kept appearing to her simply to empty her of her drugs. Once done sucking her dry, they'd leave and refuse to speak to the rest of us except through an Oracle like you. That is the *insult* part of it—that they *can* appear and *could* speak to us if they so chose, but they choose not to, not unless we follow their rules and regulations." He shrugged. "Lucy was a living testimonial to that annoyance; she had to go."

"So, Lucy was killed to soothe the ROC's bruised ego? Just because the Sinis won't talk to you? Oh, that just sucks!" She looked through Jezebub and Morrison and the wall again, out to the porch. The two Sinis were now bloated on Lucy's blood, buzzing on the drugs it contained. She winced. At least the wind was blowing the monsters' fetid stench away now. But, of course, she alone could smell that too.

Brother Crowley smiled in reply. He bowed slightly in deference to her.

"Okay, so you killed Lucy just to make yourselves feel better." She glared at Morrison. "Why did you kill those two kids back there? All they were doing was screwing."

Morrison grinned, revealing his filed teeth. "This is private property, ma'am. Trespassers will be murdered and eaten."

Jessica felt like murdering and eating *him*. The explanation was just insane. At the moment everything was insane. Everyone was insane here, including herself. *Only I'm not insane, am I? Everything makes sense now, just a nutcase kind of sense. I can see through people, through walls . . . Fuck! I saw Sinis, a Sinis was I.*

The statement was an eerie truth to Jessica now. No longer fiction but fact. She imagined herself transforming into . . . into one of those horrible things. Though still revolting to consider, the prospect of becoming a non-human monster no longer frightened her. She just didn't want it to happen.

"The Sinis won't even *appear* to us," Jezebub said sadly. "Even I and Crowley are unable to see them except after strenuous rituals full of bloody sacrifices." She reached out a hand and stroked Jessica's cheek. "But now that we have you, my dear, things will be much, much easier."

Her fingertips were soft against Jessica's skin, her touch lovingly gentle. Jessica began feeling pampered. It was crazy. *FLEE, FLEE, FLEE!!!* a part of her mind was still screaming at her. *Run away, girl! Run back to work, to your damn life! Remember the mistressplan—all that wonderful work you HAVE to do! You can't give that up! You can't!* Another part of her mind assured her everything would be fine. *This is your new life. There is WORK to be done here too.* She felt doubly chilled: chills of fear wrestled with chills of excitement.

"Where's McKenzie?" Morrison asked.

"Asleep on the floor behind the couch," Jessica replied without thinking. "Leave her, she'll be out for at least three hours. She'll have hair like yours when she wakes up."

"See?" Jezebub said with delight. "You knew that without knowing it. You're just perfect."

Her fingertips were still stroking Jessica cheek. Her soft touch was reassuring, laden with sensuous promise.

The world turned blue again:

Jessica found herself inside a large cavern. Rotting corpses swung on ropes dangling from the cavern's roof. Directly in front of her stood a stone altar piled with bloody meat. She intuitively knew that the pile of meat was parts of freshly-killed people—mostly tramps and runaway teens.

Brother Crowley stood naked by the stone altar. In each hand he held up a still-beating and bleeding human heart. The hearts were raised overhead to a giant Sinis with tentacles the size of tree trunks. Jezebub was on her knees in front of Brother Crowley. She was performing fellatio on him while he chanted "I saw Sinis, a Sinis was I."

The huge Sinis accepted their offering of hearts. Both of the hearts in Brother Crowley's hands burst into flame. The smoke from the burning meat ascended into this inverted Hell. Brother Crowley groaned in ecstasy and ejaculated in Jezebub's mouth. Jezebub swallowed, licked her lips, and rose from her kneeling position. She too grabbed handfuls of human flesh from the blasphemous altar and raised them aloft to be blessed with infernal fire.

Next, Jezebub held out a bowl to the Sinis. The god dangled one of its massive tentacles out over the bowl. Brother Crowley slit the Sinis's tentacle with a knife. A thick blue liquid dripped from the tentacle into the bowl. The liquid smelt like rotten eggs and burning rubber and toxic chemical waste and a thousand other even more atrocious things . . .

The vision cut out. Jessica reeled back, nauseated. She was dizzy. The world spun around her. Morrison grabbed her before she fell. He lowered her down onto the couch. She lay there with her eyes shut, breathing heavily.

She opened her eyes. Dead Lucy stared up at her from the floor. She felt the world spinning again. She pointed to the severed head. "Please put that somewhere else."

"Yeah, sure thing, ma'am." Morrison picked up Lucy's head and flung it across the living room and out the front door. The casualness of the act jarred Jessica. He'd thrown Lucy's head like . . . like no one would care if they drove by and saw it. And that must be because he *knew* no one would be driving by.

All hope of being rescued finally departed Jessica. She accepted that she was stuck here with these loony people who were intent on worshipping her. Dr. Whitfield was regarding her with paternal affection. Brother Crowley was similarly smiling in delight and looked ready to kiss her feet.

She pointed to Jezebub's writhing burden. "What's with the bag of snakes?"

"Just some lunch," Jezebub replied. She picked a rattlesnake out of the bag. "Cottage No. 2 is crawling with them now."

The snake thrashed about in her grasp. It sank its fangs into her forearm. She didn't appear to notice the pain. She plucked the snake's teeth out of her flesh, ignoring the venom dribbling from the twin punctures. She lifted its head to her mouth and bit into it. The rattler cracked once like a whip and went limp. Jezebub ate it slowly, head and all, letting its blood run out over her lips.

"Ah, great," she said with passion.

"I'll have one of those too," Morrison said. He reached into the shopping bag, coming out with an extra-long black serpent that looked extra-poisonous. He bit off the reptile's head, spat it out, then proceeded to eat its body.

"Yeah, great," he agreed, his cheeks bulging. "This sure is some tasty bitch we got here. Almost as good as eating pussy."

Jezebub winked at Jessica. "Your friend Miss Butterfield really does taste nice." She indicated the bag of snakes. "Would you like a bite too?"

Jessica gaped at her. "That's *Reby*? You two are eating *Reby!?*" The icy certainty came to her then that, yes, it was indeed Reby's remains the tentacle-haired pair were eating.

"Huh?" The revelation was too much for Jessica. Desperately seeking a denial of what she already knew to be true, she stared from face to face. Her gaze finally settled on Dr. Whitfield. If only because he was a man of science, he seemed the least insane person in the room. Of course, his kind of sanity was the dubious sort associated with the head of a lunatic asylum.

The doctor winked back at her. "Not that I personally indulge in it, you understand," he said, "but cannibalism is as good a means as any for disposing of dead bodies. And . . . in Miss Butterfield's case, it can't really be considered cannibalism anymore, can it?"

Jessica had no reply to that. She had no words. She just stared at the remaining snakes in Jezebub's bag, then at the pair munching away happily on someone who'd recently been a good friend of hers. She tried to fit her brain around the transformation. She couldn't.

Jezebub got through eating a mouthful of snake. Blue eyes gleaming, she looked pointedly at the doctor. "So, can we perform the operation on her now?"

"What operation?" Jessica asked in horror.

Dr. Whitfield checked his watch. "Yes, but not here. It's best we get her down to the clinic, just in case there's complications. She's a remarkably healthy woman, but still . . ."

Jezebub nodded. "Alright, let's go."

"What operation!?" Jessica insisted. "Talk, goddammit! What are you crazy people planning to do to me!?"

Jezebub smiled at her, showing sharp bloody teeth. "We're going to remove your eyes, darling."

"What?" Jessica began trembling with fright. "WHAT!!?"

Brother Crowley smiled. "Relax, Oracle. You don't need your eyes anymore. Without them you'll see wonderful things. Incredibly glorious things."

They're going to blind me!? A lifetime of blindness was inconceivable to Jessica. Her fear of losing her eyesight had nothing to do with the rightness or wrongness of being mutilated. It had everything to do with her career: How would she ever *work* if she was blind? She didn't know braille, and besides, no one employed sightless people with braille skills to high positions in industry anyway, did they? Oh no, she wasn't letting anyone blind her. She wasn't waiting for that crap to happen. She was getting out of here right now. Right away.

She burst into motion. She leapt up off the couch and ran—ran for the front door. She ran like she was running for her life. Yes, indeed, she felt her very life was at stake here. Work was, and had always been, her life, and if she let these crazy people cut out her eyes, she'd be as good as dead.

So she ran. All she had to do was make it out through the door, which was already open, and jump into their goddam fake squad car and zoom off and she'd be free. Free of this goddam blue nightmare she'd somehow stumbled into. She was out of here already, heading back to the real world where sane people dwelt and . . .

She never made it. Morrison grabbed her before she was halfway across the living room. In a meltdown of panic and rage, she kicked and screamed and bit at him, but his arms felt like steel bands around her. He lifted her off her feet and swung her in the air.

Then she felt a sharp prick in her left bicep and suddenly felt a lot weaker. A whole lot weaker, until . . .

CHAPTER 34

Jessica

When Jessica awoke, she couldn't see. All that filled her head was a vivid blueness.

Why can't I see?

Then she remembered what had happened. The crazy cultists' comments concerning blinding her.

Oh my God, oh my God—they did it! They did it! They blinded me! I'm blind!

She was lying on a bed. She could feel the edges of her mattress and the metal frame beyond that. She was strapped down firmly though. She was unable to move either her arms or legs or sit up. The motion of her head was limited by a strap across her forehead. A soft, cool pad pressed against her eyelids.

The room's sterile smell—disinfectant and air-freshener—marked her location as a hospital somewhere. She had to be in the Raynham Outlook Clinic.

Even without touching them, she could feel that something was missing behind both her eyelids. Her eyes had clearly been removed. She had no sensation of either darkness or light from them. There was nothing but that crazy intense blue, like she was floating out in the middle of an endless sky without a single cloud and with no world below.

She wasn't in any pain, but that was utterly beside the point.

Her horror was absolute. *Oh fuck, I'm ruined. I'm finished. My job, my career, my entire future is gone! My life is over! And all because I came along on a crappy vacation to this crappy town with Lucy and Reby. Shit!*

She began weeping loudly. Then, when weeping didn't permit her sufficient expression of her grief, she began screaming, shrieking and yelling her lungs out.

***

They didn't come until she'd screamed herself to exhaustion. But when they did come in, Jessica *saw* them. She didn't see them with her eyes—she had no eyes. She saw them with her mind. She saw them just as she'd seen the Sinis in her dreams and earlier visions, as colored outlines. The bearlike male outline with the large nose was Dr. Whitfield. The tall female outline with 'snakes' on her head was McKenzie. The shorter female with no clothes on was Jezebub. The bald-headed male outline was Brother Crowley, the 'snake-haired' one, Morrison.

The female outlines were red, the male ones, black. None of them had any filling, except Jezebub—who was a darker shade of blue inside.

I can see, I can see, I can see! Jessica felt like crying again.

"Can you *see* us, Jessica?" Dr. Whitfield asked with a hint of worry in his voice.

For a long minute, she was silent. She was tempted to lie, to tell them she couldn't. Oh, she hated them all so much for doing this to her!

"Yes, I can," she admitted finally.

"Good," the doctor replied. "Very good."

"See?" Brother Crowley added. "We didn't lie to you. You still have your sight."

"This isn't the same thing. All I can see are outlines on blue."

"It's just the beginning," Jezebub said. "Your new powers of vision will steadily expand until . . . Why don't we try a little test right now? It should make you feel better."

"What test?"

"I want you to try to look *through* us. Concentrate on seeing beyond us and beyond this room—as far as you can."

Jessica wanted to tell Jezebub to go eat shit, but she needed something to do to prevent herself from becoming hysterical again. Trying out the blue woman's suggestion would take her mind off her woes, if only for a short while. So she did as she was asked. She focused her attention tight as a laser beam and tried to 'see' through the five people beside her hospital bed.

"I can't do it," she said a minute later.

"Try again," came the adamant reply. "You are an Oracle; you *can't* fail. You *must* see. This is just a test and your powers are still weak, so you may see very little, but *you will* see something."

Jessica tried again. This time, after about a minute, her visitors and the blue around them slowly dissolved away.

All of a sudden Jessica could see in full color again. She saw a world in crystal-clear definition. She saw now much clearer than when she'd had eyes.

But what she saw was a nightmare realm.

The Sinis were there, the tentacle-gods with their many eyes and their salivating mouths and rotting bodies, and their genetic stink of evil. Some of the Sinis were as huge as mountains. Others were as little as houseflies. All bore exactly the same signature of evil.

Jessica was horrified. This was no Heaven, that was for sure. This *was* a region of Hell. She had no doubts on that account. This whole realm looked like something Lucy might have dreamed up on an acid trip. An exceptionally bad acid trip. This entire place was one unending vista of decay, devastation, and utter corruption. All the buildings were ruins. The landscape was covered with ulcers. The sky looked sick. The clouds looked like moldy cheese and they dripped towards the ground like they were melting. The trees had tentacles instead of leaves, tentacles with eyes in them.

In every direction she looked she saw heaps of bones.

This was a world discarded, one of garbage and filth, of filth both physical and spiritual. Any Christian preacher viewing this place would self-combust in an ecstasy of righteous indignation.

Here, Jessica's own body was transformed. Her skin was gray, her flesh all rotting and ulcerated. She could feel that she had no hair on her head, just pus-leaking skin, like her entire skull was a cancer tumor. She felt like a germ seeking someone to infect. As she examined herself, worms crawled out of tears in her belly and fell from her body into the sky. She was disgusting, something dead but left unburied, corpse-flesh abandoned under the sun to suppurate and fester. A red segmented tentacle slithered out of her belly after the falling worms. It flicked in the air like a whip, then vanished back into her. As the tentacle withdrew, a horrible odor exploded out of its hole in her flesh, along with more worms.

In this unholy place, she was perfect in her state of decay.

Not too far off, Jessica saw a massive temple. She walked through the air towards the building. As she neared it, she saw that the temple was built from large slabs of rotting meat, with rancid fat used as mortar. Blood fell as rain from the temple's underside.

The smell of the building both repelled and attracted Jessica. The smell sucked her towards it like a magnet.

She reached the temple and entered it.

Inside the meat temple, an orgy of murder and mutilation raged. Giant demon creatures—clouds of black soot having human form—hacked countless screaming humans—both adults and children—to pieces, and fed them to the Sinis.

Jessica 'knew' the black creatures were called 'servitors.' They were things created by burning human flesh and congealing the thick resulting smoke into human shape. Golems of murder-gas, they were. The demonic servitors chopped off human legs and arms and heads. They stuck white-hot hooks into bellies and ripped out quivering guts, and piled them high on the tables over which the tentacle-gods floated. The servitors impaled human hearts and kidneys on wooden skewers and fed them as raw kebabs to their Sinis lords.

The gaseous servants were relentless in their butchery. They worked with dedication and with a seemingly complete disdain for man. Jessica was very impressed by their single-minded savagery.

The floors of this horrible temple literally ran with blood. Some of the smaller Sinis licked the blood up. Others swam through it for pleasure.

Jessica understood that this particular temple built from raw meat was a Dining Hall. The Sinis realm had a large number of such Dining Halls. All required a continual supply of human flesh, an endless stream of humans to be used for food.

How the crazy fuck is this even possible?

She pondered where all the victims had come from—where the Sinis had found so many people to kill; how they'd all gotten here, to this place of utter terror and horror and no escape. And then she understood: the Sinis had simply abducted them. On Earth, a planet of seven-and-a-half billion people, who would notice one or two hundred thousand vanishing each year? Or even a half-million or more if spread thinly enough across the globe? That seemingly huge number was possibly less than two or three people disappearing from each of the world's towns and villages annually.

The Sinis spirited people away in droves from countries like China and India which had burgeoning, almost unmanageable populations. They also took them in large numbers from Africa, South America, and the Middle East, where census figures and government monitoring of the populace were never reliable. During any of Earth's wars, the Sinis abducted entire town/village populations for food— the missing would simply be believed murdered by one side or other of the combatant forces. It was an endless process. The Sinis Dining Halls must be stocked with meat at all costs, and mankind was the prime Sinis delicacy.

She was witnessing a miniaturized worldwide massacre.

One of the Sinis detached itself from eating the corpses and floated over to Jessica. This one had four leathery batwings amidst its eyes and appendages. It had fewer tentacles than the others. Instead, it was studded with bulging tumors that in turn bore many open sores.

Freshly-shed human blood dripping from its mouths and tentacles, the Sinis bobbed about in front of Jessica. She fought her natural inclination to flee from it. They hovered facing each other for a brief moment. Two rotting things; indecision the cord connecting them both.

Then it said, in chilling musical tones she now understood perfectly:

"Welcome, Oracle, to the realm of Sinis beauty. Study us well. See and remember all that you see, and then return to your side of the Great Divide and tell our servant Judas Crowley that we are very pleased with him."

Jessica nodded. She understood that this Sinis spoke for all of them. The Sinis all thought alike. To hear one of them was to hear them all.

"Yes, Lord," she replied humbly.

"And you, Oracle," the creature continued, "we look forward to seeing again. Many times again in fact. There is a lot of work we will accomplish through you; and you will be up to the task."

Despite her disgust and horror at what she was witnessing, Jessica felt intense pleasure on hearing that she had *work* to do. She felt a furious rush of joy. Work was the prime objective of living. Work was the reason one was born at all. She was delighted that the Sinis understood the importance of WORK. All of a sudden, Jessica was certain that the Sinis would be wonderful bosses to labor under. True, they looked like blobs of shit with worms crawling through the turds, but their evil hearts beat for the right things: **WORK. LABOR.** And labor she would. She would work *with* them. She would work *for* them. Oh yes, she would WORK. WORK, WORK, WORK, WORK,WORK, WORK, WORK, WORK, WORK, WORK, until . . . until . . .

Using one of its smaller tentacles, the Sinis passed a pale tube of meat to Jessica, a short length of human intestine. "Take, Oracle, eat. Feed like we, your gods, feed."

Jessica accepted the piece of meat from the Sinis. After some initial hesitation, she put it in her mouth. Her mind cringed, but her palate welcomed the dire morsel. She chewed and swallowed.

"How do you feel?" the god asked her.

"Energized. Able to serve you better."

"Good. We are pleased, Oracle."

Below and around them both, the relentless slaughter of people continued. The black gaseous servitors butchered screaming people into quivering masses of dead flesh and piled that flesh up for the Sinis to eat. Blood flowed like river water. The Gods of Decay fed and drank and proclaimed their delight and satisfaction.

Jessica watched and learnt the ways of her new employers.

She became aware of another voice 'elsewhere' speaking to her. She could still see the Sinis realm of murder and decay and utter filth, but she could now also hear Jezebub questioning her.

"Do you see anything?" Jezebub was demanding in her soft voice. "Tell us, Oracle, what do you see?"

"I see Sinis . . . No, no, no. I'm a Sinis, a Sinis am I," Jessica replied with terrified, yet completely awed, understanding.

CHAPTER 35

McKenzie

"We are the obscene glory. Humanity is nothing but a bad memory you must strive to forget. You must transcend yourselves to become us . . . I saw Sinis, a Sinis was I, I was Sinis, a Sinis saw I . . ."

Jessica continued speaking, relating to them what the gods were saying. Brother Crowley had a video recorder running to capture everything. This message from the Sinis would be uploaded to the ROC servers and made available for download to its members worldwide. In Los Angeles, world ROC head Michael Huxley was reportedly salivating with delight at their success in finally breeding an Oracle.

McKenzie Clark smiled at the blind woman in the hospital bed. Lying there with the top half of her head thickly bandaged and tubes in both her arms, Jessica Schreiber looked incredibly frail. And yet, she looked incredibly potent also. The latter impression came from the pinched expression on her face, the determined set of her jaw, and the cold smirk on her lips as she spoke. She looked like she was hard at work in front of a laptop, typing away at full speed to meet a deadline. She gave off a ruthless vibe, like she'd not let anyone or anything stand in the way of her getting her job done.

McKenzie walked over and spread the curtains, letting in the sunset. The drapes had been left shut by default. The blind had no need of daylight.

She peered out the window at the ultra-modern sprawl of the Raynham Outlook Center complex. (There were eight 'gates' to Alternity in the USA, one of them located here in Raynham. The 'gates' were places where the divide between the realms was flimsy and easily punctured. Interestingly, one of the Earth's 666 gates to Hell was also located in this unassuming little town. Oh, if only the

Raynham, MA townsfolk knew the sort of infernal power they were sitting on.)

McKenzie turned back to look into the room. She envied Jessica. *What she's seeing must be incredible, so far-out that she'll never once regret losing her eyes.*

Her boyfriend Morrison locked eyes with her and winked. She winked back. She was cooking dinner for him at her place tonight. Dinner was stewed snake—Rebecca Butterfield species—and white wine by candlelight. Hopefully with some sweet lovemaking afterwards. She imagined their head tentacles tangling together and blushed.

McKenzie tugged on her red tentacles. It was going to be hard getting used to having these on her head, particularly as it meant she couldn't go anywhere in the daytime without a special hat on. Still,—just like Morrison's did—her tentacles counted in the ROC as evidence of special Sinis favor, and thus meant rapid promotion up through the ranks of the order. It wasn't going to be all bad.

(Along with the emergence of her tentacles, McKenzie's teeth had grown long and pointy. Already, she felt in herself an instinctive craving for flesh, a desire to sink her new teeth into something soft and meaty and wet and nourishing . . . something preferably human. Oh, these damn tentacles made one so damn hungry!)

I'm on my way up to divinity, she though with enthusiasm, then blew Morrison a kiss that he caught and put in his trouser pocket.

But, are we actually ascending to Heaven and not descending to The Pit? McKenzie worried about this sometimes. About the Sinis claim on divinity. Tentacles and having a rotting body she could cope with, but she had a niggling suspicion that her angels were actually well-dressed devils. Piranha disguised as goldfish. No other deities she knew advised their followers to wallow in filth to achieve enlightenment.

She returned her attention to the blind woman in the hospital bed.

"Good and evil are the same thing," Jessica was saying. "Right and wrong are limiting concepts. All that matters is what you will become when you shed all ethical compunctions. Do and be. See Sinis, be Sinis."

Jessica paused. Then, just like that, blood spilled from her mouth.

McKenzie gasped. Jessica was chewing on a large chunk of raw meat that had suddenly appeared in her mouth. It looked like someone's severed ear. Yes, that *was* an ear she was eating.

Shocked, McKenzie looked at the others. They'd all noticed it too. Jezebub and Brother Crowley were grinning at each other in delight. Dr. Whitfield looked sick. Morrison just shrugged back at her.

Jessica swallowed the chewed ear. She was silent for a moment as if catching her breath.

"I saw Sinis, a Sinis was I, " McKenzie and the others filled in the silence.

Damn, McKenzie was thinking, *if they're feeding her over there and we can see it here, she's really approved of by the gods.*

"Yes, you see Sinis," Jessica continued in an enraptured voice, "But do you? What do you see? Sinis is beyond time, beyond space. It is higher than mountains, deeper than oceans, farther than an endless trip east or west around your planet. It is right beside you, yet cannot be touched; inside you, yet cannot be sensed. It is air and water and sleep—essential to you—but horrifies you to know. It is your necessity that you hate and dread. Sinis is the calamity that saves you. It is the overwhelming terror that calms your fears. And yet, courage is accepting one's fears and using them as energy."

"I saw Sinis, a Sinis was I."

"I'm a Sinis, a Sinis am I. Say it, all of you!"

"I'm a Sinis, a Sinis am I!"

"Yes. This is the new truth, the new word of good evil. We are before, about, and behind you. We were, we are, we become. We are because we are. Will be because we must be. Become because becoming is our eternal fate. Soon we shall be no more, only to be once again. We are the decay that corrodes time. Oh, human fools, let go of good, be evil, be Sinis. Live evil. Live evil lives. Live evil live evil live evil live evil live evil live evil. Eat wickedness as your food, drink sin as your water, wear iniquity as your clothing. Let doubt and a lack of faith in other Gods be your greatest asset. For there is but one God, and they are Sinis!"

"I saw Sinis, a Sinis was I!!"

But see, McKenzie thought then, a sad smile spreading over her lips as the echoes of the chant faded into the walls of the hospital room, *it doesn't actually matter, does it? It doesn't matter a goat's fart if the Sinis are actually demon shitheads. What matters is that I CAN become like them. Okay, I'm selfish, so what? And as for good and evil? Oh, screw the ethical division between right and wrong. In most cases nowadays, with the world in the mess it's in, who can tell the difference, anyway?*

Jessica was now chewing on a severed thumb that had just appeared in her mouth. The thumb looked like its fingernail had been ripped off with pliers or something similar. Jessica chewed on it slowly. She had a serious look on her face. A look like someone was speaking incredible truths to her at the far end of the universe.

McKenzie couldn't help but feel really jealous of the Oracle.

The End.

ABOUT THE AUTHOR

Wol-vriey is Nigerian, and quite tall.

He believes there actually are things that go bump in the night.

He writes horror fiction—for adults only, please. And also some surrealist stuff.

Wol-vriey blogs at: *http://odditybarm.wordpress.com*

WOL-VRIEY
BIZARRO AND TRANSGRESSIVE FICTION

BOSTON POSH (BUD MALONE #1)

In 2028 AD, the USA is a nation ravaged by hungry dragons and dinosaurs. In Boston, Massachusetts, private eye Bud Malone is hired to rescue a kidnapped heiress. But nothing is as it seems.

Malone works to unravel a tangled web involving Boston Chinatown, a 200-year-old woman with a 9-year-old body, white robots, a human-liver-eating psychopath, a golem, a porcelain dragon, and a snake goddess with a crush on him. There's also a woman obsessed with chicken sex. Then Malone meets Posh Lane, a gorgeous call girl who's desperate to quit her pimp.

Romantic sparks ignite between Posh and Malone, but Posh's past suddenly catches up with her in a BIG way. To save Posh, Malone agrees to run a quest for Earth's new rulers, the Forks. But, Malone has no idea that agreeing to the Fork's odd request will send him on the weirdest trip he's ever been on in his life.

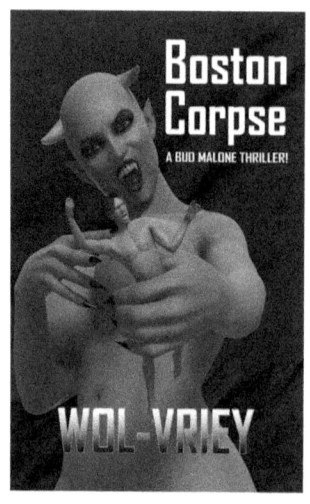

BOSTON CORPSE (BUD MALONE #2)

MAGIC CAN BE MURDER! - Drag queen Lucy Tang is back in Boston, and is hell-bent on settling her vindetta against casino owner Sookie Ling. And suddenly, Bud Malone, PI, has the case of his life to resolve.

When Boston's robot police force are baffled by a mind transfer case, they come to Malone for help. The one person who can likely help Malone out here is the witch Soledad Bathory. But Soledad seems to know a lot more than she's telling him. It's a case not made easier when Malone meets Soledad's beautiful cousin, Josephine 'Slave' Bailey. Slave has her own plans for Malone, most of which involve teaching him BDSM and making him her new Master.

Oh, and Rick Rogers owes Sookie Ling a whole lot of money, a gambling debt that's going to be literally Hell to pay!

BOSTON CORPSE - Not your average detective novel!

Burning Bulb
PUBLISHING

WOL-VRIEY
BIZARRO AND TRANSGRESSIVE FICTION

BOSTON LUST (BUD MALONE #3)

"Bless it, Father, for she has sinned."

Seven murdered gay women, all their bodies completely drained of blood. All also with large parts of their bodies dissolved away like acid has been pumped into their veins.

Bud Malone has to find the female vampire preying on Boston's lesbian population.

Then Malone meets the beautiful Trudi Carmen and the case gets even more tangled. Trudi needs Malone's help in recovering a ring that's gone missing. But how in the world is one little black ring related to either the dead women or their killer?

Resolving this case will lead Malone deep into Lucy Tang's legacy—The Abstracta. And then to the city of Genesis.

Boston Lust—Just when you thought Bean Town was safe to visit again.

HELL DANCER

Six people find themselves trapped in Detention, a nightmare realm where the demonic Schoolmaster is hell-bent on reforming them . . . until they die.

Porn superstar Venus Deluxe came to Springfield, MA to party, and next found her life hanging by a thread. One wrong answer will mean her death.

Suspended BPD detective Tanya Rockford was trying to stop one kind of violence, but found a terrifying another. With her and her companion's lives hanging in the balance, it's going to take all of her courage and resourcefulness to escape this hell she's stumbled into.

Porn stud Chad Cannon has made a career from his ten-inch penis. Here in Detention, however, it's his brains that matter. He'll soon be hoping all the pot he's smoked over the years hasn't completely messed up his memory.

The three students, Sherri, Jordan, and Mike? They were all just in the wrong place at the right time. Will anyone survive Detention? The evil Schoolmaster doesn't plan on letting that happen . . .

Burning Bulb
PUBLISHING

WOL-VRIEY
BIZARRO AND TRANSGRESSIVE FICTION

VAGINA MUNDI

Rachel Risk is a professional thief with super-strong hair that can stretch like tentacles to manipulate objects. Ashley Status has both a digitally augmented brain, and 'muscle-purses' in her arms and legs in which she stores inflatable objects—cars, guns, rocket launchers, etc.

When Raye is framed as the fall girl in a jewel robbery, the pair flee Chicago's vengeful robot gangsters and take refuge in the Hotel Bizarre, where the gorgeous 'vagina singer,' Femina, is performing for a week.

But the Hotel Bizarre is even stranger than its name suggests, and very soon Raye and Ash are involved in an deadly adventure, a struggle for survival the likes of which they'd never imagined possible—with loads of deviant sex, drugs, music, and violence at every turn. And just what is the old woman in the skin desert really doing with all those cats glued to her walls?

VAGINA MUNDI—a Bizarro Hymn in praise of WOMAN!

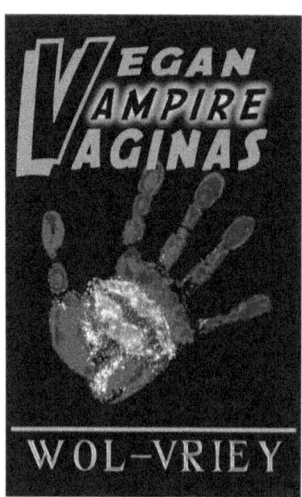

VEGAN VAMPIRE VAGINAS

The biggest bank heist in US history. And Tom Palmer can't remember pulling it off. And no, this isn't your standard case of amnesia. After a one-night-stand gone horribly wrong, Boston salesman Tom Palmer wakes up with a vagina implanted in his left hand. Then his day gets worse.

Tom is transported across space-time to a nightmare version of Boston, one where the Bizarro virus has transformed half the population into cannibals. Worst of all, Tom discovers that in this new Boston, he's the infamous gangster Pussypalm, wanted for robbing the Federal Reserve Bank of Boston a year ago. He also learns that the vagina in his hand is prophetic, i.e. it talks . . . after sex.

With 130 people left dead during his bank heist and six billion dollars missing, Tom knows he's living on borrowed time. It is in his best interests not to remember anything. Because once he does . . .

Burning Bulb
PUBLISHING

WOL-VRIEY
BIZARRO AND TRANSGRESSIVE FICTION

Dr. Orgasm

Courtney Taylor is young, intelligent, beautiful, and successful. She also has a boyfriend who loves her deeply. The problem is, no matter what Courtney does, she can't climax during sex.

When Florence Rigid's communist forces destroy the city of Metaphor, Courtney and her friends Teresa, Highball, Miki, and Heather are cast into the midst of a quest to find the only person able to save the land of Innuendo—Dr. Carol Orgasm, wanted by the communists for developing the O-Pill, a wonder drug that grants women sexual ecstasy on demand.

The communists will do anything to get their hands on the O-Pill and prevent its reaching the millions of Innuendo's women. But Courtney desperately wants that pill too. And so it's now a race between Courtney and the communists to find Dr. Orgasm first.

And Courtney has no choice but to win this race. She must win it: For her own orgasm . . . and for the freedom of female sexuality everywhere.

PUSSY TRANSMISSION

Pussy Transmission were the most decadent Pop Art ensemble of the 90's. Led by the beautiful painter Isis Lynch, the trio revolutionized the art world. Then suddenly, without explanation, Pussy Transmission vanished into historical obscurity. Now, twenty years later, three women come to Lynch Place. Lily and Nina are journalists desperate to interview Isis Lynch. Raven, on the other hand, wants to find her boyfriend, who's gone missing inside Isis's house. Raven's worried—she's heard that Pussy Transmission broke up because Isis began dabbling in black magic . . . with devastating results. All three women will shortly wish they'd never left home. Particularly once the rats in Lynch Place start warning them that they're going to die . . . and Raven meets Betty Butcher, the bouncy supernatural psycho who's intent on chopping her into bits. Pussy Transmission, Baby! Just because . . .

Burning Bulb
PUBLISHING

WOL-VRIEY
BIZARRO AND TRANSGRESSIVE FICTION

VEGAN ZOMBIE APOCALYPSE

In the post-apocalypse worlderness, zombies rule the earth. They're allergic to meat, and brains literally make them explode. Zombies now eat blood potatoes, parasitic tubers grown in the flesh of humancows corralled in maximum security farms. Two fugitives meet in the ancient ruins of Texas. The first is Soil 15-f, a womancow who's escaped her farm a week before she's due to be killed and her blood potato crop harvested. The second fugitive is Able Kane, former head necros food technician, now sentenced to death for heresy. But Soil is no ordinary humancow.

Unknown to herself, she's the vegan zombie agricultural revolution, and the zombies desperately want her back. And the necros equally desperately want Able Kane dead. He's fled with a forbidden discovery which will reshape the world for the worse if used. And Able is just hardheaded/misguided enough to use it.

MELANIE NEMESIS CATCHPOLE

In Springfield, Massachusetts, Melanie Catchpole is hired to fetch back a magic teddy bear worth millions of dollars from a warehouse across town. Problem is, the warehouse is down in Springfield's O-Zone-that totally weird sector of the city where Bizarro fell to Earth. The 'O' is a fairytale land, a place where dreams and nightmares literally live and breathe.

Worse still, the gingers—mutant cannibals—prowl the O. The gingers have already eaten everyone else Melanie's employers sent to get back the magic teddy bear.

Accompanied by the handsome but ruthless Doug Fisher (who she finds sexy but doesn't dare entrust her heart to), Melanie enters the O-Zone. Melanie and Doug are instantly caught up in an adventure they'd never have believed credible even if written as fiction . . . and Melanie's used to experiencing the very weird as the norm.

And now, additionally, there's a mystery to unravel: What does the dark, freezing-cold being called The Fixer want with Mary, the barkeep's daughter?

Burning Bulb
PUBLISHING

WOL-VRIEY
BIZARRO AND TRANSGRESSIVE FICTION

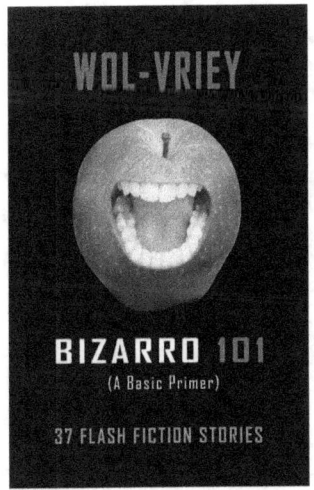

BIG TROUBLE IN LITTLE ASS

From Bizarro master storyteller Wol-vriey comes a truly weird western tale that will leave you awe-struck and on the edge of your seat...

In the town named Little Ass, tight-assed prostitute Rosa over-hears a gunslinger's plans to assassinate rancher Edison Ben-nett. Once the badass Bennett learns of the plot, he ensures there'll be hell to pay for any attempt on his life!

Yes, it's going to take all of gunslinger Jude's shooting prowess, his eclectic collection of strange firearms, a trusty horse that re-quires an owners' manual, and the help of the lovely and in-vigorating Nell (who's EXTREMELY odd when the going gets weird), to survive the Bizarro hell that Edison Bennett unleash-es in order to hold onto the land that he'd stolen from Madam Zizi.

BIZARRO 101 (A BASIC PRIMER)

Welcome to the strange place:

A collection of 37 flash fiction stories designed to introduce one to the Bizarro/New Weird Genre.

Weird, dreamy, nightmarish, absurd, sad, surreal, humorous . . . this collection of tales is all this and more.

***

"This primer is the very essence of any and all styles and types of Bizarro writing. Wol-vriey collects, distills, and bottles up these 37 tiny stories for your sensory enjoyment. This is an absolute must-read for anyone new to the genre, because it demonstrates the scope of what Bizarro is, and what it can be."
—Teresa Pollack, Bizarro commentator and blogger

Burning Bulb
PUBLISHING

WOL-VRIEY
BIZARRO AND TRANSGRESSIVE FICTION

GIRLS ARE NOT SMILING

Welcome To The Road Trip From Hell

Pagan is demon-possessed.

Lori is suicidal.

Britt is just terminally pissed off.

Meet three young Boston women on the run from the law, each with problems that will fuse into more than the sum of their individual parts, becoming a holocaust of sex and violence and terror, a literal rain of blood and horror and gore and evil.

And if that wasn't already bad enough, Pagan's pet demon is slowly transforming her into something both unspeakable and unholy. Truly, these girls aren't smiling.

BLUE NIGHTMARES

Consummate EVIL is coming. It is relentless and unavoidable. It is Blue.

Jessica Schreiber is seeing things. Very horrible things. Since arriving in Raynham for what should have been a relaxing vacation, she's been seeing *The Big Blue*.

Jessica is smelling things too—dead and rotting things that she can't see. She is sure those dead and rotting things are dead people. Lots of dead people.

Jessica's worst nightmares will soon become her reality. Her reality will soon become a terrifying nightmare.

The tentacled residents of the House of Death have a lot that they wish to show Jessica Schreiber. They have a lot that they wish to tell her. But will she survive long enough to learn their lessons?

Burning Bulb
PUBLISHING

WOL-VRIEY
BIZARRO AND TRANSGRESSIVE FICTION

BRAINCHEW

It was supposed to be a simple jewel heist, but it went badly wrong. Chuck got shot and died.

Lance hid his friend's corpse in the Pleasant Street Cemetery. But that was a big mistake—there was something undead, something extremely hungry . . . something eXXXtremely horrible, buried in the Pleasant Street Cemetery.

And Lance had just woken it up.

They called the monster Brainchew because it ate brains. Human brains. And it preferred those brains fresh from the heads . . . of the living.

And now it was awake again, Brainchew planned on feeding big-time tonight. Oh hell yes, it did.

BRAINCHEW 2: OUT OF THEIR HEADS

After Tiff Hooper recognizes Josh Penham, the man who abducted her and kept her in his basement and abused her, she brings her three friends to Raynham for a night of well-deserved revenge on him.

Only things don't go according to plan.

It is never a good idea to leave a corpse in Raynham's Pleasant Street Cemetery. You run the very real risk of awakening what lies underground there. And that thing—Brainchew—is more horrible and more evil than anything the average mind conceives of even in its worst nightmares.

Brainchew is back! And this time the monster is extra-hungry. But there are plenty of delicious human brains about tonight, and Brainchew intends to eat them all before dawn.

Burning Bulb
PUBLISHING

OTHER GREAT TITLES FROM

Burning Bulb
PUBLISHING

WWW.BURNINGBULBPUBLISHING.COM

ANTHOLOGIES
BIZARRO AND TRANSGRESSIVE FICTION

THE BIG BOOK OF BIZARRO

The Big Book of Bizarro brings together the peculiar prose of an international cast of the most grotesquely-gonzo, genre-grinding modern writers who ever put pen to paper (or mouse to pad), including:

NIGHT OF THE LIVING DEAD horror writers John Russo & George Kosana; HUSTLER MAGAZINE erotica contributors Eva Hore, Andrée Lachapelle, & J. Troy Seate and established Bizarro genre authors D. Harlan Wilson, William Pauley III, Wol-vriey, Laird Long, Richard Godwin and so many more!

From Alien abductions to Zombie sex, The Big Book of Bizarro contains OVER FIFTY STORIES of the most outrélandish transgressive fiction that you'll ever lay your capricious and curious hands upon!

WESTWARD HOES

Nine outlaw writers rode into town from obscurity to pen nine tantalizing tales of horror and fantasy, and leaving once they branded their own personal marks on the weird western genre and became living legends of the American Frontier experience.

Like drunken Indian scouts, the writers fervidly tracked down and captured the Western genre, tore off its fashionable veneer and ravished its exposed essence.

So belly up to the bar with your favorite soiled dove and enjoy perusing these thrilling tales of Old West debauchery, danger and desire; compiled by the publisher of The Big Book of Bizarro and featuring the bizarro novella *Big Trouble in Little Ass* by Wol-vriey.

Burning Bulb
PUBLISHING

ANTHOLOGIES
BIZARRO AND TRANSGRESSIVE FICTION

THE BIG BOOK OF BIZARRO SPECIAL KINDLE EDITIONS

OTHER AWESOME COLLECTIONS

 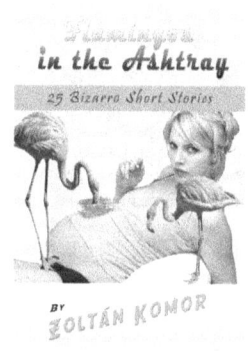 

BELLY TIMBER

From the writers of Darkened Hills, Detour to Armageddon and Night of the Living Dead comes a novel unlike any other...

In the 1800's, ordinary people learned the secret of the Kala and undertook extraordinary measures to rid the earth of this evil. This is their story.

For John McCormick, life on the Indiana frontier held nothing but promise. His settlement along the White River would soon become the crossroads of America. Friends and family from back in Ohio and other points east were all making plans to see what all the fuss was about in the newly-formed city of Indianapolis. Yes, things were good. John had his general store and his friend George Pogue had his blacksmith business. Claims were being staked and relations with the native Indians were amicable. The town was growing and nothing could be better... or so he thought.

In Ohio, an evil was brewing. The Lecky Family, a group of ruthless Mongolian nomads, had made their way to America and were practicing their cannibalistic religion of Kala with reckless abandon. No one was safe, not even John McCormick's family.

Burning Bulb
PUBLISHING

GARY LEE VINCENT'S
DARKENED
THE WEST VIRGINIA VAMPIRE SERIES

DARKENED HILLS

When evil descends on a small West Virginia town, who will survive?

Jonathan did not start out his life to become a rambler, it justworked out that way. William was a troubled youth with something to hide. Both were from Melas, a small town tucked away in the West Virginia hills... a town where disappearances are happening more and more frequently.

After the suicide of a wanted serial killer, the townsfolk thought the nightmare was over. But when a centuries-old vampire is discovered they find out the hard way it's just getting started. Dark secrets can only stay hidden for so long and when the devil comes to collect, there will be hell to pay. Can Jonathan and William find a way to stop the vampire before it's too late? Find out in *Darkened Hills!*

DARKENED HOLLOWS

In the heart-stopping sequel to the award-winning *Darkened Hills*, Jonathan and William must return to West Virginia to face possible criminal charges stemming from their last visit to the damned town of Melas, where both had narrowly escaped the clutches of a vampire seethe.

And as livestock start mysteriously getting murdered with all of their blood drained, worried farmers are searching for answers - leaving the local Sheriff and his deputy racing against time to learn the cause before a more violent crime is committed.

WWW.*DARKENEDHILLS*.COM

GARY LEE VINCENT'S
DARKENED
THE WEST VIRGINIA VAMPIRE SERIES

DARKENED WATERS

When the world goes to hell, the chosen must arise!

As Talman Cane orchestrates a flood of epic proportions in this third installment of the *Darkened* series the towns of Melas and Tarklin are caught completely off guard by the deluge. Hell-bent on finishing what they started, the evil brothers return to the lunatic asylum to take care of the witnesses and add to the ever-growing army of the undead.

Aided by Lucifer himself and the insane vampire demon Legion, the stage is set to channel all of the forces of hell to come forth. In an all-out race to survive, Jonathan, William, and Amanda soon discover they are up against impossible odds as Lucifer opens the Gateway to Hell, ushering in the zombie apocalypse and the End Times.

Find out who will survive this cosmic battle of the ages in *Darkened Waters!*

DARKENED SOULS

Melas and the Madison House are about to be rebuilt.
True evil is about to be reborne!

Young ex-priest and vampire-killer William is drawn back to the West Virginian town that almost killed him, where his vampire arch-enemy Victor Rothenstein still stalks the earth.

The town of Melas lies destroyed after the battle of the End of Days. But why is wealthy Jackie Nixon so eager to rebuild it using the bone dust of murdered souls?

Terrible evil has visited before, but the Gateway to Hell is about to be reopened in a horrific climax. And this time – it's personal.

WWW. DARKENEDHILLS.COM

Burning Bulb
PUBLISHING

GARY LEE VINCENT'S
DARKENED
THE WEST VIRGINIA VAMPIRE SERIES

DARKENED MINDS

Jackie Nixon intends to become Vampire Queen, but at what blood-drenched cost?

In this continuation to the explosive infernal saga begun in Darkened Souls, newly-turned vampire Jackie Nixon is taking no prisoners. Accompanied by her daughter, Kate, and by the captive vampire lord Victor Rothenstein, Jackie Nixon explores the Darkness. There, she intends to rouse the slumbering vampire race, bound under an ancient curse, and with their help, rule the human world.

But there's a deadly threat to Jackie's plans. Not just William who is trying to stop her, but her own royal ambitions. If Jackie performs the ritual to wake the sleeping vampires the wrong way, she could instead free the Red Beast of Hell, an unspeakable evil that even the undead fear.

DARKENED DESTINIES

With over 45 people missing after Jackie Nixon's party, the mysteries surrounding Melas and the Madison House keep getting darker.

Now, with legions of vampires at her command, can anything or anyone stop her from gaining complete control over all mankind?

The final battle has begun! As the Vampire Queen ascends her throne and sets to unleash the full forces of darkness, the fate of all things good hangs in the balance.

Burning Bulb
PUBLISHING

WWW.DARKENEDHILLS.COM

DAVID J. FAIRHEAD

"David Fairhead writes compelling stories that offer very human characters and very inhuman monsters. There is no subtlety in Fairhead's imagination - he is simply dying to scare the hell out of you." - Nelson W Pyles author of DEMONS, DOLLS AND MILKSHAKES

THE FALL

Hopelessness... How do you protect your loved ones when Hell itself opens its insidious mouth?

Horror... Nightmarish Creatures invade your world and there is nowhere to hide.

Blood... How long can you hold out before they come for you?

Pain... Where do you run to avoid being eaten alive by monsters with a voracious appetite for your flesh?

Screams... While you selfishly run for your own life.

Questions... Who is to blame? Where did they come from? How many people survived...and how does the human race find the means to fight back?

THE FALL OF TOMORROW is man's last tale of desperation told by those that are striving to salvage some hope against a ravenous bastion of evil beasts bent on ruling our world.

DWELLING IN THE DARK

From David J. Fairhead, author of the FALL OF TOMORROW, comes DWELLING IN THE DARK- A soulful anthology of creeping terror to keep you up in the small hours with horror set in the past, present and future. Overlapping bits of puzzle fitting each other, before and after The Fall of Tomorrow.

A place where three children facing a monstrous foe can only pray that their bloody summer would just come to an end. Go back to the 1960's- THE COMMUNE where overindulging hippies use a mage's diary to control the end of the world, only to see first-hand that their drug induced visions have horrific ramifications. Where a young boy's visit to a haunted house becomes a lesson in RESIDUAL morality. The story, DEEPER- plunges two brothers into a sinkhole only to find they were being hunted by an insidious creature from its depths. Visit the old west as hero Dekker Collins battles evil gunslingers in DEMONEYE.

And so much more...!

Burning Bulb
PUBLISHING

WWW.FAIRLYDARKPRODUCTIONS.COM

WEST VIRGINIA-THEMED HUMORROROTICA

BY RICH BOTTLES JR.

HELLHOLE WEST VIRGINIA

From the heights of Mothman's perch high atop the Silver Bridge in Point Pleasant to the depths of Hellhole Cavern in Pendleton County, evil lurks within the shadows as the sun sets upon the haunted hills and hollows of West Virginia.

Bizarro author Rich Bottles Jr. blows the coffin lid off horror genre clichés with this tour de force cast of Eco-friendly vampires, beach-yearning zombies and sex-starved she-devils.

LUMBERJACKED

If you are easily offended or do not possess a truly depraved sense of humor, this story may not be the light summer reading fare you desire. As for the four feisty female freshmen stranded on top of West Virginia's third highest mountain, they have no choice but to experience the sick, twisted debauchery and perverted mayhem described deep inside the tight unbroken bindings of this horrific missive.

Lumberjacked takes the reader to a nightmarish world where character development and aesthetic integrity are prematurely cut short by the swinging axes of maniacal lumberjacks, who are hell bent on death and destruction in the remote forests of Appalachia. And at the climax, when paranoia crosses over to the paranormal, Lumberjacked makes Deliverance look like a family raft trip down the Lower Gauley.

THE MANACLED

What happens when twin brothers lease out the former West Virginia State Penitentiary with the false purpose of filming a documentary on supernatural phenomena, but their true intention is to make a pornographic movie?

Chaos ensues as the disturbed spirits of murdered convicts, along with the reanimated dead from the neighboring Indian Burial Mound, take their vengeance on the unwary and undressed trespassers.

Zombies, ghosts, mobsters and porn collide in this bizarro tale from horror author Rich Bottles Jr.

Burning Bulb
PUBLISHING

EVERYTHING HERE IS A NIGHTMARE
Collected Works Vol 1.

"Pyles makes it look easy. His characters come instantly alive with the cocksure verve and swagger of rock stars."
- Daniel Knauf, creator of HBO's "Carnivale," Executive Producer/Writer, ABC's "The Blacklist."

The critically acclaimed author of Demons, Dolls and Milkshakes returns with fifteen tales of horror and suspense with Everything Here is a Nightmare.

From zombies in the old west, to a young boy tempted by the Devil. From vampires with romantic longing, to an abandoned lighthouse haunted by vengeful spirits. From a serial killer getting unholy justice, to a haunted English race car, Nelson W Pyles invites you to explore a landscape of fear, suspense and horror.

Take his hand and hold on tight. Remember that whatever you find here, whatever you see, no matter what you might think it could be... know this: Everything Here is a Nightmare.

Burning Bulb
PUBLISHING

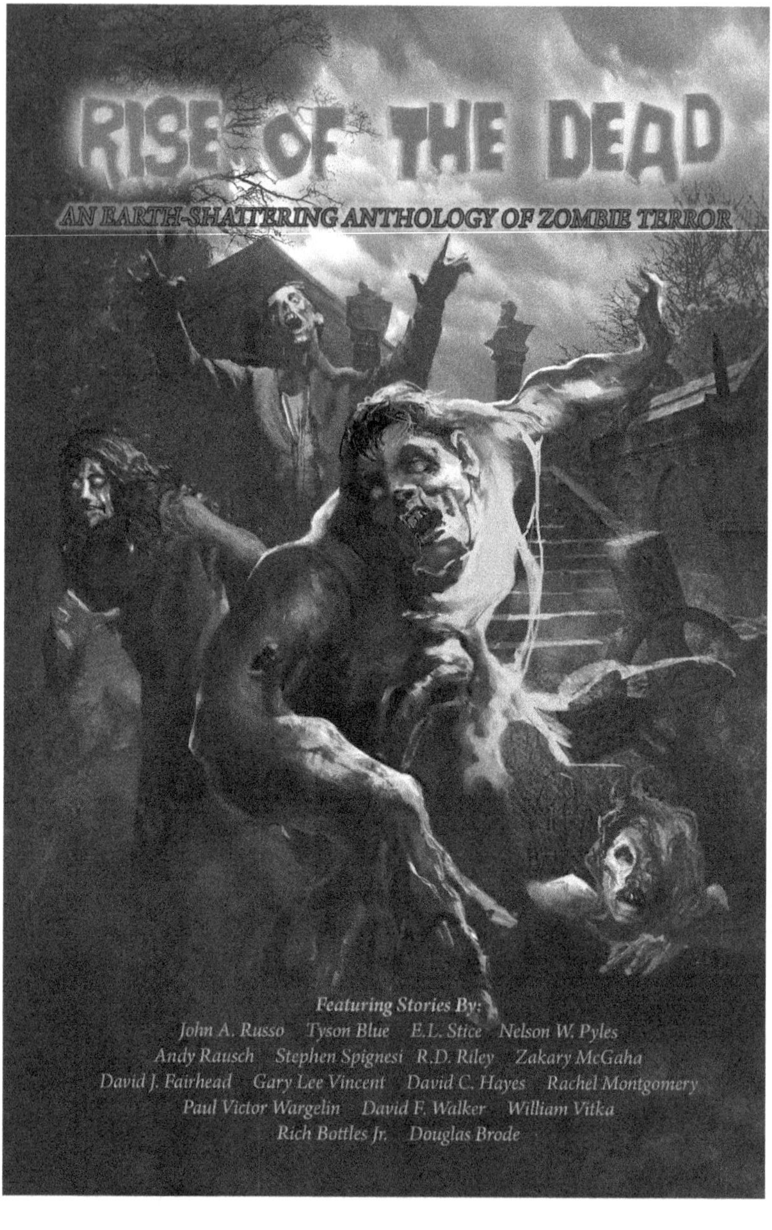
RISE OF THE DEAD
AN EARTH-SHATTERING ANTHOLOGY OF ZOMBIE TERROR
Featuring Stories By:
John A. Russo Tyson Blue E.L. Stice Nelson W. Pyles
Andy Rausch Stephen Spignesi R.D. Riley Zakary McGaha
David J. Fairhead Gary Lee Vincent David C. Hayes Rachel Montgomery
Paul Victor Wargelin David F. Walker William Vitka
Rich Bottles Jr. Douglas Brode

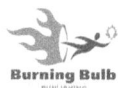

NIGHT OF THE LIVING DEAD

Why does Night of the Living Dead hit with such chilling impact?

Is it because everyday people in a commonplace house are suddenly the victims of a monstrous invasion? Or is it because the ghouls who surround the house with grasping claws were once ordinary people, too?

Decide for yourself as you read, and the horror grips you.

All the cannibalism, suspense and frenzy of the smash-hit move are here in the novel.

www.TheJohnRusso.com

"THE BLAZING SADDLES OF SEX SATIRES!" - GEORGINA SPELVIN

THE BOOBY HATCH

It's a Zany Love Lab where Looney Professors Measure Pleasure!

From Legendary Horror Writer

JOHN A. RUSSO

THE BOOBY HATCH

With NIGHT OF THE LIVING DEAD, John Russo helped blaze a path in the horror genre that has never been equalled. In this hillarious erotic novel, he blazes a path through the wild, zany Sex Revolution of the 1970s.

Sweet, innocent Cherry Jankowski works for Joyful Novelties, where she tests sex toys ranging from the ridiculous to the sublime. But she can't find love or peace of mind and her efforts are hampered by a Peeping Tom, an exhibitionist, a cross-dressing boyfriend, a quack psychiatrist, and even her own product-testing partner, Marcello Fettucini, who can't get it up anymore and is scared of losing his job!

www.TheJohnRusso.com

Burning Bulb
PUBLISHING

"A sense of infectious fun, straight from the author's pen."
– Nightmare Library

From Legendary Horror Writer
JOHN A. RUSSO

LIVING THINGS

"Russo carries his talent for the horrific neatly over into the novel form."
– West Coast Review of Books

LIVING THINGS

Beneath the shimmering Miami sun sprawls one of the Mafia's biggest empires, a glittering world of lavish beachfront mansions, neon-painted nightclubs, beautiful women, expensive cars—and absolute control over the state's billion-dollar drug trade. But, one by one, its ganglords and henchmen are falling prey to a new rival. His powers are fueled by monstrous ancient rituals; his hellish undead legions slaughter mobsters and innocent citizens alike, his unholy lust for power is virtually unstoppable.

Now a burned-out ex-detective and a brilliant anthropologist must enter a gruesome, nightmare world to fight this master of malevolence and illusion. Their time is short, their weapons few, and they face an ultimate, terrifying choice - annihilation or the loss of their souls to the eternal torment of those who never die. . .

www.TheJohnRusso.com

Burning Bulb
PUBLISHING

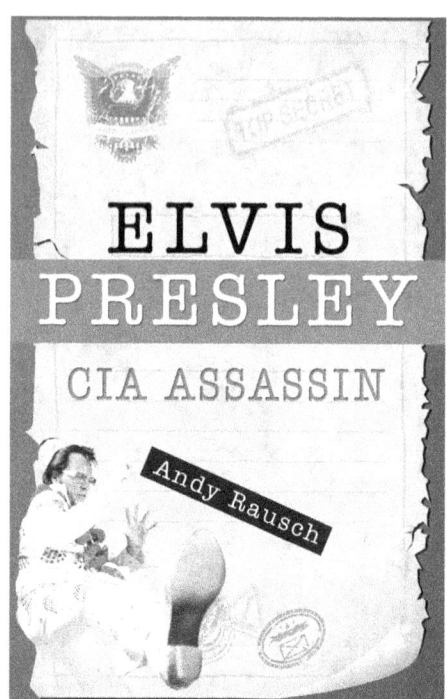

ELVIS PRESLEY, CIA ASSASSIN BY ANDY RAUSCH

"I can guarantee you. Read this book and you'll never look at Elvis the same way again!"
~ Douglas Brode, author of ELVIS CINEMA AND POPULAR CULTURE

SOON TO BE A MAJOR MOTION PICTURE

In 1970, singer Elvis Presley secretly met with President Richard Nixon. This new comedic novel imagines that Presley became a Central Intelligence Agency operative, eventually moving up through the ranks to become a skilled assassin.

Presented in an oral history fashion, the book tells us about Presley's secret transformation by the people who knew him best.

Did he fake his death in 1977? Was Presley involved with the Watergate scandal? The Iran hostage crisis? Communicating with aliens?

Read this book to find out the answers to these and many more questions.

Burning Bulb
PUBLISHING

MAD WORLD BY ANDY RAUSCH

"*Mad World* is dark, twisted, no-holds-barred fun."
—Jason Starr, author of *Bust*, *Slide*, and *The Max*

EVERYONE'S PLAYING AN ANGLE IN THE CITY OF ANGELS

Mad World tells the stories of a black hitman who doubles as a university professor, a Catholic priest who longs to be a gangster, a would-be author from Kansas, a gay phone sex operator who claims he's straight, a group of rich twentysomethings playing a deadly game of life and death, a vicious Mafia boss, and a sleazy Hollywood movie director. As each of their stories intersect, the body count piles up and the action comes nonstop in this tense, white-knuckle thriller by first-time author Andy Rausch.

"A wild ride. If you like it gangster, *Mad World* delivers."
—Daniel Birch, author of *Get Some*

Burning Bulb
PUBLISHING

BLOODLETTING: A TALE OF REVENGE BY ANDY RAUSCH

"Relentless… Addictive… The kind of nightmare you don't want
to wake up from."
—Heywood Gould, screenwriter of *Rolling Thunder*

He was just an average Joe. But when he finds his family held at
gunpoint by merciless thugs, he's told he must murder a Mafia
chieftain if he ever wishes to see his loved ones again.

Against all odds, Joe keeps his end of the bargain, but the criminals
don't. Now at his wits end, Joe is pushed beyond his breaking point
and forced to exact bloody revenge against those who've done him
and his family wrong in this powerful and violent novella by author
Andy Rausch (*Mad World*).

"Andy Rausch has a tight noir style that combines gritty, realistic drama
with a cinematic flair that makes for a powerful, compelling (somewhat
Stephen Kingesque), authentically visual reading experience."
—Stephen Spignesi, author of *Dialogues*

Burning Bulb
PUBLISHING

THE TAILSMAN

From the creators of *The Big Book of Bizarro* and *Westward Hoes* comes a new comic unlike anything you have ever seen!

He's hot on the trail, looking for some *tail...*

Sly Franko was a man of the West, a forger of the wild frontier. Like the Country Western song that would be written years after he died, the words, "Faster horses, younger women, and more money," seemed to be the anthem of this horn dog cowboy.

Franko would ride into town on a blazing saddle, find the closest saloon to wet the whistle, belly up to a good card game, and find him a hot-loving hussy to get his cowpoke on with.

However, Sly might have met his match when a visit to bathroom leads to terror and death. Can Sly and his poker buddies solve the mystery before more of the townsfolk are murdered? Find out in this exciting premier issue of *The Tailsman!*

WWW.BURNINGBULBCOMICS.COM

THE HAGS OF BLACK COUNTY

by Michelle Bowser

Ruled by a committee of Hags, and fueled by toothless rivalries, Black County lurks just far enough out of the way to be completely unnoticed by the rest of civilization. Its inhabitants have been mentally warped for generations and the land itself seems to have the power to drive anyone unlucky enough to visit into ridiculous hillbilly madness. When a construction Company needs to bury a pipeline through its ludicrous hills and valleys, a twisted charm goes to work and every aspect of already bizarre Black County life takes a gory turn for the hysterical. Take a preposterous trip along with its citizens, both native and new, through escapades such as the Hag parade, the grand opening of Madame Skunk's House of Ill Repute, the demolition derby riot and the rabid, zombie clown apocalypse.

THE ABANDONED SOUL

by Daniel Sellers

After spending most of his 20s in a drug and alcohol fueled daze, a young man finally hits rock bottom. Having used up his friends and their good graces, he ends up squatting in an abandoned house. Forcibly sobering he begins to realize that he is not alone in this abandoned house. Left with one last friend and a mountain of regrets, he must decide if this presence is a guilty conscience, or a malicious hunter.

WE WISH YOU A HAPPY KILLDAY

by Jason Heroux

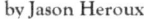

"We Wish You a Happy Killday" is the story of an international b eloved holiday called "Killday" where one day a year everyone over the age of fifteen is permitted to register for a license allowing them to kill one other person. But this year Chad Ovenstock doesn't feel like killing anyone. His friends and family urge him to participate in the festivities, but he can't seem to get into the holiday spirit. On the day before Killday Chad comes in contact with Ambrose, an old friend who suffered a nervous breakdown and is now part of The One Ant Army, a mysterious cult dedicated to making the future disappear. When the holiday finally arrives Chad refuses to participate and tries to survive on his own, surrounded by constant gunfire, countless corpses, and the nagging suspicion that Ambrose may have secretly brainwashed him into becoming a member of The One Ant Army cult.

Burning Bulb
PUBLISHING

www.ingramcontent.com/pod-product-compliance
Lightning Source LLC
Chambersburg PA
CBHW07084250626
47159CB00003B/934